MORE PRAISE FOR

INTERNMENT

A *New York Times* bestseller

"*Internment* is **a scathing indictment of our current political times**. Ahmed has gifted us with Layla, a courageous young revolutionary who fights against all boundaries of hate and ignorance. A must read for activists who continue to push back against the big What-Ifs." **–Ibi Zoboi**, National Book Award finalist and author of *American Street* and *Pride*

"A **riveting and cautionary tale**. *Internment* urges us to speak up and speak out, to ask questions and demand answers, and when those answers prove unsatisfactory, to resist." **–Stacey Lee**, award-winning author of *Outrun the Moon*

"**A testament to what girls are capable of** when they are overlooked, *Internment* is **a masterwork of dignity and grit**." **–E. K. Johnston**, #1 *New York Times* bestselling author of *Exit, Pursued by a Bear* and *Star Wars: Ahsoka*

"**A powerful and poignant exploration of a nightmare made real.** It's a testament to Ahmed's writing, then, that the heart of the story is one of hope. Read *Internment*. Raise a fist." **–David Arnold**, *New York Times* bestselling author of *Mosquitoland* and *Kids of Appetite*

"*Internment* sets itself apart....**Terrifying, thrilling and urgent.**" *–Entertainment Weekly*

"[A] raw portrait of a young activist coming into her own.... **A potent and impassioned reminder** of what American nationalism led to in our not-so-distant past." *–The New York Times Book Review*

"**[Gives] understanding [to] the extreme dynamics of race** in America from a Muslim perspective." –*PBS NewsHour*

"Samira Ahmed's *Internment* is **timely in the most harrowing way**....Will stay with you long after it ends." –Popsugar

"This is a **bold, powerful, and reflective** read that doesn't hold back any punches." –BuzzFeed

"This heart-thumping book **horrifies and inspires**; Layla's struggle reminds readers to speak up and that only the persistent and resistant can make a change." –*Teen Vogue*

"An action-packed thriller that **will make your teen sit up and think**." –*Family Circle*

"Ahmed continues to fight against the current political climate by ultimately bringing us **a story of hope and resistance** when we need it the most." –Book Riot

★ "Taking on Islamophobia and racism in a Trump-like America, **Ahmed's magnetic, gripping narrative, written in a deeply humane and authentic tone**, is attentive to the richness and complexity of the social ills at the heart of the book." –*Kirkus Reviews*, starred review

★ "**A poignant, necessary story** that paints a very real, very frank picture of hatred and ignorance, while also giving readers and marginalized individuals hope." –*Booklist*, starred review

★ "An **unsettling and important** book for our times." –*Publishers Weekly*, starred review

★ "By the end of the first two pages of this title **the reader will be breathless with the anticipation** and excitement of what's to come." –*School Library Connection*, starred review

★ "**Sensitive and stirring.** For all collections." –*SLJ*, starred review

INTERNMENT

INTERNMENT

SAMIRA AHMED

LITTLE, BROWN AND COMPANY
New York Boston

Little, Brown and Company
Hachette Book Group
1290 Avenue of the Americas, New York, NY 10104
Visit us at LBYR.com

Originally published in hardcover and ebook by
Little, Brown and Company in March 2019
First Trade Paperback Edition: March 2020

Little, Brown and Company is a division of Hachette Book Group, Inc.
The Little, Brown name and logo are trademarks of Hachette Book Group, Inc.

The publisher is not responsible for websites (or their content) that are not owned by the publisher.

The Library of Congress has cataloged the hardcover edition as follows:
Names: Ahmed, Samira (Fiction writer), author.
Title: Internment / Samira Ahmed.
Description: First edition. | New York ; Boston : Little, Brown and Company, 2019. | Summary: "A terrifying, futuristic United Sates where Muslim Americans are forced into internment camps, and seventeen-year-old Layla Amin must lead a revolution against complicit silence." —Provided by publisher.
Identifiers: LCCN 2018017615| ISBN 9780316522694 (hardcover) | ISBN 9780316522663 (ebook) | ISBN 9780316522830 (library edition ebook)
Subjects: | CYAC: Prejudices—Fiction. | Muslims—United States—Fiction. | Concentration camps—Fiction. | Revolutionaries—Fiction. | Science fiction.
Classification: LCC PZ7.1.A345 Int 2019 | DDC [Fic]—dc23
LC record available at https://lccn.loc.gov/2018017615

ISBNs: 978-0-316-52270-0 (pbk.), 978-0-316-52266-3 (ebook)

Printed in the United States of America

LSC-C

10 9 8 7 6 5 4 3 2 1

For Thomas, Lena, and Noah.
Hearts of my heart, the reasons for
everything.

And for everyone fighting for liberty
and justice for *all* so that this nation,
of the people, by the people, and for the
people, shall not perish from this earth.

Though you muffle my voice, I speak.

Though you clip my wings and cage me, I fly.

And though you batter my body,
commanding me to kneel before you,

I resist.

—Ali Amin

CHAPTER 1

I strain to listen for boots on the pavement. Stomping. Marching.

But there's nothing. Only the familiar chirp of the crickets, and the occasional fading rumble of a car in the distance, and a rustle so faint I can't tell if it's the wind or the anxious huff of my breath. But everywhere it's the same as it's always been: the perfectly manicured lawn of Center Square, the gazebo's twinkling fairy lights, the yellow beams from the porch lamps at every door.

In the distance, I see a funnel of smoke rising into the air.

Most of the town is at the book burning, so I should be safe.

Or, at least, safer.

I don't measure time by the old calendar anymore; I don't look at the date. There is only Then and Now. There is only what we once were and what we have become.

Two and half years since the election.

Two years since the Nazis marched on DC.

Eighteen months since the Muslim ban.

One year since our answers on the census landed us on the registry.

Nine months since the first book burning.

Six months since the Exclusion Laws were enacted.

Five months since the attorney general argued that *Korematsu v. United States* established precedent for relocation of citizens during times of war.

Three months since they started firing Muslims from public-sector jobs.

Two months since a virulent Islamophobe was sworn in as secretary of war—a cabinet position that hasn't existed since World War II.

One month since the president of the United States gave a televised speech to Congress declaring that "Muslims are a threat to America."

I thought our little liberal college town would fight it longer, hold out. Some did. But you'd be surprised how quickly armed military personnel and pepper spray shut down the well-meaning protests of liberals in small, leafy towns. They're still happening, the protests-turned-riots, even though the mainstream media won't cover them. The Resistance is alive, some say, but not in my town, and not on the nightly news.

Curfew starts in thirty minutes, and this is a stupid risk. My parents will absolutely freak out if they find that I'm not in my room reading. But I need to see David.

I force myself to walk calmly, head forward, like I have nothing to hide, even though every muscle in my body shrieks at me to run, to turn back. Technically, I'm not doing anything wrong, not yet, but if the police stop me—well, let's just say they have an uncanny ability to make technicalities disappear.

Breathe.

Slow down.

If I rush from shadow to shadow, I will attract attention, especially from the new motion-sensitive security cameras mounted to the streetlamps. Curfew hasn't started yet, and I'm allowed outside right now, but it's already dark. Even here, where almost everyone knows me and my parents— maybe *because* of that fact—my heart races each time I step out of the house. I cross at the light, waiting for the walk signal, even though there are no cars.

I spy a flyer for the burning taped around the lamppost at the corner: JOIN YOUR NEIGHBORS. The words are superimposed on a cascade of banned books, dangerous books. A hard knot forms in my stomach, but I keep walking, eyes still on the poster, and bump headlong into a woman rushing in the opposite direction. She stumbles and drops her bag. Books and flyers fall to the ground.

I bend down to help her pick up her things. "Sorry, I wasn't looking where I was going." I try to be polite, deferential. Stay calm, I say to myself. It's not past curfew yet. Don't act guilty. You're not guilty of anything. But these days, actual guilt is an afterthought.

The woman keeps her head turned away from me, refusing to meet my gaze, shoveling the books and papers back into her bag. I reach for two books and glance at the titles before she grabs them from my fingers. *Palace Walk* by Naguib Mahfouz. *Nameless Saints* by Ali Amin—my father.

For a split second, she looks me in the eye. I suck in my breath. "Mrs. Brown, I—I'm sorry—" My voice fades away.

Mrs. Brown owns the Sweet Spot on Jefferson Street. She made my favorite birthday cake ever, a green-frosted Tinkerbell confection for my fifth birthday.

She narrows her eyes at me, opens her mouth to speak, and then clamps it shut. She looks down and pushes past me. She won't even say my name. Her flyer for the book burning somersaults away in the breeze. I shrink into myself. I'm afraid all the time now. Afraid of being reported by strangers or people I know, of being stopped by police and asked questions to which there are no answers.

I pick up the pace to cross the town square, staring straight ahead, wiping the fear off my face, fighting the tears that edge into the corners of my eyes. I can't suffer looking at the university's gleaming glass administration building—all clean lines and razor-sharp edges that cut to the bone. David's mother teaches chemistry at the university. My dad teaches poetry and writing. *Did* teach, I should say. Until he was fired—mysteriously deemed unqualified for the tenured professorship he'd had for over a decade. That's another "Before": two months since my dad lost his job.

My mind lingers on Mrs. Brown. She knows me. She's seen me. And in minutes I'll be in violation of curfew. I'm obviously not going to the burning; I should be home. The hard knot in my stomach grows.

I remember a lesson from my psychology class about an experiment in which volunteers were asked to torture people who were in another room by pressing a button that supposedly delivered an electric shock. It didn't really, but the volunteers didn't know that; all they heard were screams. Some resisted at first. But most of them pressed the button eventually, even when the screams got louder.

David is waiting for me at the pool house in his neighbors' yard. They're on vacation in Hawaii. Vacation. I can't even imagine what it would be like to be able to go on vacation right now and not worry about being stopped by the TSA for a secondary search that could lead to being handcuffed to a wall for hours. Or worse.

David is taking a risk, too, though we both know it's not the same for him. He may be brown, almost browner than me, and Jewish, but right now, it's my religion in the crosshairs.

We were suspended for two days from school for kissing in the hall, in the open, where everyone could see. We weren't breaking any laws. Not technically. But I guess the principal didn't want to look like he was encouraging relationships between *us* and *them*. Apparently, PDA is against school rules, but I've never heard of anyone pulling suspension for it. Even worse, although David got booted, too, only my parents and I were called in for a lecture about how I should know my place at school, keep my head down, and be grateful for the privilege of attending classes there. I was gobsmacked. My dad nodded, took it in stride. My mom did, too, even though she wore a scowl the entire time we were in the office. Then, when I started to open my mouth to say something, my mom shook her head at me. Like I'm supposed to be thankful to go to the public school where I've always gone, in the town where I've always lived.

Why were they so quiet? Especially Mom? She's almost never quiet.

I left school that afternoon, and my parents were too scared to let me go back.

The pool house door is ajar. I catch my breath for a second before stepping inside.

"Layla," David whispers, touching my cheek with his fingers. David has his dad's gray-blue eyes and his mom's deep-golden-brown skin. And a heart bursting with kindness.

A single candle glows at the center of the coffee table. He's drawn the curtains in the small studio space—a white sofa piled high with navy-blue pillows, some with appliquéd anchors on them; a couple of overstuffed arm chairs; lots of faded pink and ivory seashells in mason jars; and, on the wall, a framed poster declaring LIFE'S A BEACH against white sand and cerulean sky and sea.

We're alone. I imagine that this is what it must've been like decades ago, before the cold lights of computer screens and tablets and phones permanently eliminated the peace of darkness from our lives. Without saying a word, I walk into David's arms and kiss him. I pretend the world beyond the curtains doesn't exist. Being in his arms is the only thing that feels real right now. It's the only place where I can pretend, for a moment, that we're still living in the Before, in the way things used to be. I pretend that David and I are making plans for summer, that we'll play tennis some mornings, that we'll go to movies. I pretend that I'll be graduating in a few months and going to college, like my friends. I pretend that David and I will exchange school hoodies. I pretend that high school relationships last into college. Most of all, I pretend that this magic hour is the beginning of something, not the end.

We sink to the sofa. While we kiss, he runs his fingertips along my collarbone. A whisper-light touch that makes me shiver. I nuzzle my face into his neck. David always smells like a nose-tickling combination of the floral laundry detergent his mom buys and the minty soap he uses. I know his mom still does his laundry. She babies him. I tease him about it—about how in college all his white clothes will come out pink because

7

he won't remember to separate his wash. I sigh. I brush my cheek against his, feeling the odd patch or two of uneven boy-stubble. We hold each other. And hold each other.

It would be a perfect moment to freeze in time and make into a little diorama that I could inhabit for an eternity. But I can't.

I rest my chin on David's chest. "I wish I could stay here forever. Is there a magic portal that will transport us to some other dimension? A Time Lord, maybe?"

"Should've stolen the TARDIS when I had the chance."

My dad badgered us into watching *Doctor Who*, starting with the old-school episodes, and we got hooked. Since then we've had on-and-off binge-watching sprees. Despite the sometimes ridiculous production values, the monsters can be terrifying. It's one of our things.

I give David a small smile. He could always make me laugh, but humor stabs now. I miss dumb banter. I miss laughter that doesn't make me feel guilty. I miss laughter that is simple joy.

Everything about being with David feels natural, like the crooked, happy smile he's wearing right now. Like the comfortable moments we can pass in silence. Like our ability to just *be* with each other. We've known each other since grade school, but it was last year at the homecoming bonfire that we had our first kiss. David sat next to me and took my hand, intertwining his fingers with mine. It felt like waking up to a perfect sunrise. Around us, everyone was drinking and rowdily mock singing the school fight song and making out, but all we did was sit there, holding hands. And as the crowd started to thin in the shadows of the dying embers, I turned to look at David. And when I wiped a bit of white ash from his forehead, he brought my hand to his lips and kissed my fingertips. I reached up and kissed him, my heart pulsing in every cell of my body.

Looking back now, I think I gravitated toward David because, like me, he was different. His dad's family is Ashkenazi, and on his mom's side are Jewish refugees from Yemen. Maybe politics and borders were supposed to keep us apart, but David and I built a safe space, a nest where our differences brought us together.

I look into David's eyes and squeeze his hand. We both know that I have to go, that this evening can't last. Without a word, we stand up from the couch. I zip my hoodie. David wraps his arms around my waist and peppers my face with gentle kisses. My heart thrums in my ears. I could live in this moment forever, let time fade away until we wake on the other side of this madness.

"I wish we had more time," David says.

I know he means he wants us to have more time together *tonight*. I can't help but take his words as meaning something more. Time has a weight to it now. A mood. And it's usually an ominous one. "'The world is too much with us; late and soon,'" I say, and kiss David on the cheek.

He knits his eyebrows together, a little confused.

"It's from a million-year-old poem by Wordsworth that my dad made me read, about how consumerism is killing us and we don't have time for anything really important, but I sometimes read it as, the world is out of whack—"

Our phones beep at the same time. I check my screen, and a Wireless Emergency Alert flashes:

One People, One Nation. Tune in at 9:00 p.m. for the president's National Security Address, to be broadcast on all channels.

It's a reminder about the weekly speech tonight. Two weeks ago, the president's speeches became required viewing. All other programming on television and radio stops. The internet doesn't work. The text of the speech scrolls across phones. Technically, I suppose, you could turn your television off, but my parents keep it on, with the volume low. My parents are too afraid now of making mistakes.

"Can you believe this crap? The alerts are supposed to be for, like, missing kids, not speeches from bigots." David shakes his head and squeezes my hand tighter.

"I really have to get back," I say. "The bonfire will be over soon. People will be walking home." I think of bumping into Mrs. Brown, her squinting eyes. "My mom will die if they catch me."

David takes a step back; his jaw clenches before he speaks.

"Bonfire? Let's not use euphemisms. They're burning books in the school parking lot. They're fucking burning books. My mom's a damn professor, and she's going along with this. And my dad, both of them, really—"

"I know," I whisper. "It's my dad's books. His poems." My voice cracks, and tears fall down my cheeks. I brush them away with the back of my hand. "They're burning his poems. He pretends it's not happening. But those words *are* him. He's trying to hide it, but I know it's killing him. Both of my parents. All of us. Is this how the end begins?"

"It's not the end of anything," he says. "Especially not of you and me."

"Sure. Right. As if your parents haven't forbidden you to see me."

"It's my dad. He's being a total asshole. And my mom, she's going along with him. I think she's too terrified to speak up."

Part of me thinks I should say something, tell David that his parents aren't *so* terrible. But I can't. I won't. They stay quiet, using their silence and privilege as a shield to protect themselves.

"We'll fight this. People will fight this—*are* fighting," David says, trying to reassure me. I know he thinks he needs to be strong, to make it seem like he believes his own words, but I don't think he buys it; I can tell from the way his smile curves down at the edges. I can tell because his left hand is balled into a fist even as his right arm envelops me. I nod and give him a grin that doesn't reach my eyes. We accept the lies we tell each other and ourselves, I suppose. It's one of the ways we are surviving the day-to-day without going mad.

At least *this* isn't pretend. I nestle into David's chest, and he kisses the top of my head.

When we first got together, I thought it might be weird to date a friend, someone who'd known me so long. The first time we walked through the school doors and down the hall holding hands, my palm was so sweaty it kept slipping away from David's. He held on tighter, knitting his fingers through mine. Kissing my forehead when he dropped me off at my locker. Easy. Natural. Kind. Like we were something he always knew we would be.

There's rustling outside the window. Our heads snap up. A bright LED beam dips back and forth across the lawn. David raises a finger to his lips. I don't move. I can't move. My heart pounds in my chest.

After an eternity, the light goes out.

"You've got to get home," David whispers to me. "I'll walk you."

"No. It's too dangerous."

"It's more dangerous for you."

I look at my watch. Seventeen minutes past curfew. What was I thinking?

We clasp hands and tiptoe to the door, slowly opening it. David sticks his head out first, then whispers back, "It's okay. No one's out here."

I take a deep breath and step out. That was close. Too close. This was foolish. Perfect, but stupid.

We race across the lawn, an acrid burning smell heavy in the night air. Over the tops of the roofs a column of smoke still rises, higher now than before. Blackish-gray wisps of words and ideas and spirits, a burnt *qurbani* ascending to heaven for acceptance. I can't tell if the tears in my eyes are on account of smoke or grief.

"Stop!" a voice like sandpaper yells from behind us, flooding the darkness with a cruel light. We keep running, faster now.

"Go!" David shouts to me as he slows to swivel around, pulling his hand away from mine.

I stop, almost stumbling over myself. "I can't leave you."

David pushes me into the darkness. "It's not me they want. Run!"

CHAPTER 2

Tears blind me while I race home. As I approach my yard, it dawns on me that I might be able to outrun the person who was chasing us, but no matter how fast I sprint, I can't escape this new reality of curfews and clandestine meetings and cinders rising in the air.

I push through the front door and slip inside, quickly shutting it behind me. I'm panting, my heart racing, wiping the tears from my face with my sleeve, terrified out of my mind that David might've been caught by whoever was waving around that flashlight in the darkness. I'm smacked with the smell of frying onions and *adrak lehsan*. The smell of home juxtaposed with the sweaty, breathless odor of desperation and the taste of rust in my mouth.

My parents rush out of the kitchen. My mom's mouth falls

open. The blood drains from her face, and she rubs her eyes with her hands, clearly wanting to erase this moment. She steadies herself against the whorled bird's-eye maple console table in our foyer, my parents' first flea market find as a couple, years before they had me.

My dad is every inch the professor. Thin but not muscular, with wavy hair that always looks a bit messy, grays sprouting up here and there among the dark chestnut brown, and black-plastic-framed glasses that he prefers to contacts. He takes his glasses off and rubs the little reddish indentations along the sides of his nose. He always does this when he's contemplating something deep or worrying.

"Layla," he says, "explain yourself. Were you outside? Now? At night?" His voice is firm, but he doesn't yell. My dad is not a yeller. He barely raises his voice at me, even when I deserve it. This is clearly one of those moments.

My mom's voice, however, is less restrained than my dad's, as always. She doesn't wait for me to answer him. "You were supposed to be in your room. It's after curfew. What were you thinking? I can't believe you would do something this foolish. Do you know what could've happened?"

She shakes her head, clenching her jaw, fury and fear flashing in her eyes. They're lighter brown than mine, with specks of hazel and green, what she claims is the assertion of her distant Pashtun blood.

My mom's voice trails off because we all know what could've happened. There are whispers of Muslims who have disappeared. Muslims like us, who answered the census truthfully when asked about our religion. Muslims who refused to hide.

I stare at my worn gray Converse All-Stars and try to scrape off the dirt from one scuffed toe with the other.

"Layla. Answer your mother," my dad says. Mother. He might not yell, but he uses formal titles when he's really mad.

I answer, my voice barely a whisper, "I was with David."

"David? You broke curfew to see David? Are you crazy?" My mom turns her back to me, pauses, then walks into the large main room of our house, a living room that flows into a sunroom in the back. She falls into a cream love seat tufted with multicolored cloth buttons and stares into the fireplace. She's like me; I know that her synapses must be on rapid fire, but my mom's practiced meditation for years. She says it's the only way she's found to calm her mind. Wordlessly, she reaches up to the nape of her neck and undoes the loose bun she wears when cooking. Her dark hair, accented with the occasional gray strand, falls around her face, shielding it from me. I see her fingering her rosewood tasbih bracelet. I don't need to see her mouth to know she's uttering a prayer.

"*Beta*," my dad says, using the Urdu word for "child." If "mother" and "father" are signals of his anger, "*beta*" is the clearest sign of his love. "I know this is hard for you, but understand that David won't face the consequences you will. You can't take these risks. Your mom and I, we're afraid for you."

"I know. I'm afraid, too. But David is the only bit of normal I have left. Please don't make me give that up."

My dad winces a little, like my words have struck him. He glances down at the tan leather Indian *khussa* slippers he wears inside the house, like he's measuring them up, as if he's wearing them for the first, and not the millionth, time. Even though he's not going to work anymore, he's still in his teaching uniform: navy V-neck sweater and jeans.

"*Beta*, you can't leave again so close to curfew. It's too dangerous. We know it feels like prison. But it's for your safety. It's not up for discussion." Dad prides himself on being even-keeled, even when he's angry. Now, as he stares at me, it's like looking into my own wide, dark brown eyes.

I nod like I agree, which I don't, but I need this conversation to end because I'm desperate to text David to find out if he's okay. I'm not sure Dad believes me, but he accepts my nod as acquiescence. More pretending. More lies we tell ourselves because reality is too much to hold all at once. He gives me a mirthless smile and walks toward my mom.

I make my way to the foot of the stairs and take a seat. I dig my phone out of my pocket. I need to tell David that I'm home, I'm safe. He's probably out-of-his-mind worried, too, like I am about him.

One thing that isn't pretend? Surveillance. I may do stupid things, I may risk getting busted after curfew to see my boyfriend, but I'm not dumb enough to send a regular text. We use the Signal app so our texts are encrypted.

ME: I'm home. Are you okay?

DAVID: Yeah. It was Jim.

ME: From down the street? What the hell?

DAVID: He's Patriot's Alliance.

ME: WTF is that?

DAVID: I guess some new initiative to keep us "safe."

ME: Right. "Safe" from people like me. Wait. They're the ones using PatriotAPP to snitch on their neighbors, right? Assholes.

DAVID: He didn't see that it was you. I told him it was Ashley. That we ran because the flashlight freaked us out, we thought he was a serial killer or something. I think he believed me. He gave me this bro pat on the back. It was gross.

ME: Will she back you up?

DAVID: She better. She's my lab partner now, so I'll sabotage every damn experiment if she doesn't.

A fireball grows inside my chest. Of course he was going to get a new lab partner when I left school. Of course his life was going to continue. I'm so filled with jealousy that Ashley—mild-mannered, sweet-since-forever Ashley—gets to sit next to David for an entire hour at school without having to risk anything. I want to throw my phone to the ground, stomp on it, and crush it into tiny bits of glass and metal. But what's the use in complaining about how unfair life is? It's always been unfair to someone, somewhere. Now, I guess, it's my turn.

DAVID: Layla?

ME: Here.

DAVID: I love you.

ME: I know. 🖤

DAVID: I'll come by after school tomorrow if I can. Okay? Sweet dreams. 😘 😴 😘

ME: 😍 🖤 🖤

What I want to text: 💔
When I look up from my phone, I see that my parents have slipped into the kitchen. I can hear them pulling dishes out

of the cupboard and setting the table. I run upstairs to put my phone away. No phones at the dinner table in the Amin household.

I hurry back down and find my parents already seated in the dining room. I take my usual chair, the gray tweed perfectly molded to the shape of my body. No one says a word. My dad catches my eye for a moment, but my mom doesn't look up. She has the shorter fuse, and the flames of her anger take longer to put out than my dad's. They have their differences, but they almost always present a united front. I learned that when I was a kid and would try to play one off the other to get my way. Never worked.

"Spinach?" my mom asks me. I can still hear a little edge in her voice, but I can also tell she's trying to soften it.

"No, thanks," I say.

She offers some to my dad.

"As long as it's not too garlicky," he replies.

"After twenty years of marriage, I think I know how you like your spinach." My mom smiles at him and hands him a steaming bowl of *palak gosht*.

I look at them, across the table from me. I grab the edges of my hoodie and twist the fabric in my hands. Minutes ago I raced in the front door, scared I was being chased by some government agent who turned out to be the middle-aged dentist who lives down the street from David, and my parents greeted me with looks of horror on their faces, and now they're married-flirting about spinach.

"I don't understand how you guys are acting all normal," I say. "A little bit ago you were freaking out at me for being late for curfew, and now we're talking about garlic? They're burning books—Dad's books."

"What do you expect us to do, Layla?" my father asks in a soft voice. "How do you propose I stop a mob?" My dad has this calm-down-Layla voice that he turns on when he wants to reassure me, make me feel safe. But hearing it in my ears right now, it feels weak.

"I know you've both been too afraid to say anything, to do anything, but your silence isn't shielding us from hatred."

My mom walks over to me and puts her arm around my shoulders. Part of me feels like leaning into her embrace, but there's a part of me that's angry, too, so I stiffen at her touch. She pulls away and takes a deep breath. "Of course we want to say something, do something. But if we speak out, we'll be jailed. Then who will take care of you?"

For a moment, I feel ashamed for guilt-tripping them. But I push that feeling away because the more I think, the more anger rushes through my veins.

"We can't ignore what the government is doing—what they're making everyone do. Dad got fired. We have curfews." I shake my head. "You're too busy talking about spinach and garlic to *say* something. *Do* something. *Anything.*"

"*Beta*," my dad says, "we're not ignoring the reality of our lives. We're not hiding. We didn't deny who we are when we had the chance, did we? If I recall, when I wavered, when I questioned if maybe we should lie, you and your mother held steadfast. And you were right. We answered the census truthfully. We are Muslims. We are Americans. And we will continue to live our lives knowing that those two identities aren't mutually exclusive."

"Well, maybe we should've lied on that stupid census. Maybe it's dumb to hold on to principles when your beliefs can get you in trouble," I tell them. "Other people lied. Sara and Aidan? They're in London now, avoiding this whole mess because they checked 'no religion' instead of 'Muslim.' Easy."

My parents look at each other. My mom puts her hand on mine. "I know we argued about it before, but your father and I believe this now more than ever. We will not deny who we are. We won't lie about being Muslim. Muslims have been in America since the first slaves were brought here. Can you even imagine what they went through to hold on to Islam? What they endured?" Tears come to my mom's eyes.

I turn to my dad. "Remember what you said before? About *taqiyya*? What about living to worship another day? Maybe you were right."

My dad sighs and shakes his head. "*Beta*, I spoke out of fear, out of an instinct to protect you and your mom. And I do want to protect you, but I'm ashamed that I allowed myself to think, even for a minute, that hiding who we are would have been the right answer. *Taqiyya*, concealing our religion, is forgivable, but only under extreme duress—only to save lives. And the census was hardly a life-threatening situation.

Look at Hazrat Summayah. If she didn't conceal her faith, it hardly seems acceptable for us to do so."

"She was tortured and impaled! That's kind of a high bar for duress, don't you think?" I pause, waiting for my parents to disagree with me, but they only exchange sad glances. I sigh and continue. "I understand what you're saying. We can't erase ourselves. But look at what happened to Nabra, and those Muslim students at Chapel Hill, and that seventy-year-old New Yorker who was almost beaten to death after two guys asked if he was Muslim. And those mosques that were burned down in Texas and Seattle? Remember those 'Punish a Muslim Day' flyers that mysteriously started showing up around Chicago and Detroit? Don't you think we should've protected ourselves then? Now look at us. I feel like we can't even breathe."

I can see my words like knives, wounding my parents. My dad's face falls. My mom walks back to her chair, her hands clenched in fists at her sides. "Layla. We made a choice. And it was the right one. What do you think you're going to accomplish by rehashing it now? The past is the past."

"*Beta*, we will do everything in our power to protect you," my dad says, gently taking my mom's hand in his. She unclenches her fist to accept his gesture. "But we can't live a lie. It's not only that every person in this town and campus knows who we are—we host the interfaith *iftar* every year, after all—"

"Hosted," I say, cutting my dad off. "As in past tense. That all ended after the election, didn't it?"

He continues, not missing a beat. "We have a moral and ethical obligation to tell the truth."

So much of my dad's poetry is about finding truth in small things. Of course he believes this. And my mom—her whole chiropractic practice is based on a holistic health approach to life. Sure, my dad calls her a spitfire, and she is tough. But her love is fierce, too, and lies and deception don't enter her worldview. They both, in their own ways, so desperately want to see the good in people and the world.

During the election, with paranoia and Islamophobia and isolationism as the prevailing themes, my parents held on to this hope. During the primary debates, when the now-president said on national television that there was justification and precedent for a Muslim registry, my parents, along with so many others, dismissed it as fearmongering, red meat to rile up the base. They clung to their belief in the American ideals of equality and freedom of religion even when they heard our leaders say that men gathering around Confederate statues with hands raised in Nazi salute were "very fine people." When politicians seized on an attack at a French nightclub to warn about creeping Sharia and sleeper cells on US soil and polls began to favor the Muslim ban and the registry, so many of us said, "It can't happen here."

The thing is, it's not like half this country suddenly became Islamophobes because of any single event. But the lies, the rhetoric calling refugees rapists and criminals, the fake news, the false statistics, all gave those well-meaning people who say they're not bigots cover to vote for a man who openly tweeted his hatred of us on a nearly daily basis. Through the political dog whistles and hijabis having their headscarves ripped off and mosques vandalized with swastikas and the Muslims who went missing—through all of it, my parents prayed and believed that things would get better. They seem to have this eternal flame of hope.

But that's not me.

I stand up and take my plate to the kitchen. I'm not hungry anymore. I leave my parents to their hopes and prayers.

CHAPTER 3

The president's grating tone wafts up to my room. It's not loud enough for me to hear, but every National Security Address hits the same notes. America First. Lots of euphemisms and misplaced superlatives. And fearmongering and the need to close borders and chain migration and illegals. And how he will make it all great again.

My parents keep the television on in the living room even though they're in the basement, watching *Pretty in Pink* on an ancient portable DVD player. It's one of my mom's nostalgic high school faves. I've seen it dozens of times. I honestly can't believe the disc hasn't cracked in half yet. If I were a little bummed out, I'd probably welcome the distraction that is Ducky's charm and the ridiculousness of Steff as a high school senior in an oxford unbuttoned to his midriff. But I'm not merely bummed out. I'm sick to my stomach. I feel like my skin doesn't fit right. Saccharine sentimentality isn't going to stop me from feeling helpless and terrified.

I lie across my bed, mindlessly flipping through pages of a poetry anthology my dad assigned me. My *nanni* made my bedspread as a gift for my mom when I was born. I guess it was really a gift for me, though. She quilted it together from her old cotton saris, and even some that had been worn by my great-grandmother. Much of the multicolored fabric is faded now, the color worn away by time and sunlight, but it's the softest, most comfortable thing in the world. She passed away two years ago, but when I'm wrapped in this quilt, it's like her arms are reaching out to hug me when she knows I need it most.

I'm reading *Macbeth* for AP English—a class I am no longer taking. My father is homeschooling me, and he insists we follow the curriculum. He also likes to add his own flourishes, hence all the poetry—right now it's Wordsworth and Emily Dickinson and Faiz Ahmed Faiz. My parents pulled me from school because they were too scared of what might happen to me, terrified that my suspension could lead to much worse. I put up a giant fight, but a part of me was scared, too.

Homeschooling doesn't mean slacking off, though. Not to my parents. I still have the syllabi from all my classes, and David's been bringing me assignments. And since my dad lost his job, he's been taking his commitment to my learning seriously. I think it gives him something to do besides worrying about finding employment. He can't. At least not as a professor at any school that receives public funding.

My parents haven't said anything to me about money, but I know they're worried. My mom is still treating patients in her chiropractic office—she's known some for years—but in the past couple of weeks, I've noticed her coming home early. Last Friday, she didn't go into work at all.

I grab the poetry anthology and flip to an Emily Dickinson poem and read the title out loud: "Hope is the thing with feathers." The wind kicks up and whirls, and the leaves of the old oak outside my window brush up against the pane, stealing my attention. I put the book down. An eighties teen movie might not be what I need right now, but I'm also too agitated to read a poem about hope being a bird. I can't concentrate. All my feelings are churned up, and I'm not in the mood to be inspired.

A car pulls up outside the house. A door slams, then another. I roll off my bed onto the worn blue dhurrie rug that feels almost slick under my feet and step to the window to see who could be coming to our house this late.

Below my window, two men in dark suits are walking toward our front door. My throat gets thick and my pulse quickens. Are they here for me? This can't be for me. Dudes in suits seem excessive for a girl breaking curfew. If anyone were to come to arrest me, wouldn't it be the police? But nothing is what it should be anymore.

A dark van with a black-and-white logo emblazoned on the door parks behind my mom's sedan. I squint to make out the van's logo, lit only by streetlamps: EXCLUSION AUTHORITY. A door of the van slides open, and four white men in sandstone-colored uniforms step out and flank the sidewalk leading to our house. Behind their van, the police chief pulls up in his squad car and steps out.

Run, I say to myself. But I can't move. I try to scream to warn my parents, but no sound comes out of my mouth. Run. You have to move, to run. The doorbell rings, immediately followed by a loud pounding at the door. I hear my parents; they're already in the foyer.

Run.

Hide.

Scream.

There is no running or hiding or screaming. I'm frozen. One of the Army guys (are they the Army?) turns and sees me at the window. I drop to the floor. My breathing is loud. Short, quick breaths. I crawl across the floor of my bedroom, the wood boards under my rug creaking ever so slightly. I open my door a crack. Then more. Not that I need to. Suit #1's voice bellows through the house.

"Identify yourselves," the voice says. "Are you Ali and Sophia Amin?"

What the fuck? Mrs. Brown. It had to have been her who reported me. Or maybe Jim from Patriot's Alliance didn't buy David's lie about Ashley. God. I did this. What have I done? I stand up, and my body moves forward in a jerk, then another, and then I'm flying down the stairs. Both men are in our foyer, facing my parents. These men—the Suits—they're both white and broad-shouldered and expressionless. One of them has his hand near his hip. I narrow my eyes. It's a gun. His hand hovers near a gun.

"Stop!" I yell. "It's my fault. My parents had nothing to do with it."

My mom turns toward the staircase, eyes wide. Suit #2 draws a gun, and suddenly time slows down, like it's viscous, and my entire body is drenched in sweat. I can't feel my limbs, and the edges of my vision begin to blur. The only thing in focus is the gun. Pointed at me. My mom screams, and my dad yells my name, but the sound is muffled, like they are far away. So far away. And I can't get to them.

My dad moves forward to try to reach me, but Suit #1 grabs him and throws him to the ground, twisting his arm behind his back. My dad's glasses fall off and slide across the floor. There is more screaming. Earsplitting, unnatural animal sounds, and I realize they're coming from me.

Then there's only silence and the weight of the air in the room pressing on our bodies. And my short, shallow breaths, forcing my chest to rise and fall too fast, making me light-headed.

Suit #1 nods at Suit #2, who points his gun away from me and reholsters it under his suit coat.

Suit #1 releases my father's arm and pulls him up.

I've never seen this look on my father's face before. It's terror or fear or confusion. No. None of those are the right words. We're all small, scared, helpless animals, our legs caught in the teeth of a steel trap. I understand; this has nothing to do with me. How stupid am I? This isn't about breaking curfew. It's about something far, far worse.

Suit #1, obviously the one in charge, pushes my dad toward my mom, whose face is wet with tears. She reaches out for my dad, her arms, her entire body, shaking. Suit #1 speaks, his voice a taut wire. "Under order of the Exclusion Authority and by the powers vested in the secretary of war under Presidential Order 1455, we are here to serve notice and carry out your relocation."

Relocation. What does that mean? I turn from the Suits to my parents; my mom is sobbing into her hands, and my dad looks like the house is burning down around him.

"Relocation?" I repeat. "For us? To where? Why?"

Suit #1 turns toward the stairs, narrowing his eyes at me. "Near Manzanar. And you would do best to keep quiet."

I clamp my mouth shut and bite my lip. The looks on my parents' faces. I clutch my stomach; I'm afraid I might throw up.

Suit #1 addresses my dad. "You are the author of this book, *Nameless Saints*, correct?" he says in a gravelly voice, gesturing to the book in his hand. Suit #2 has barely uttered a word since the pair marched into our house.

"Yes," my dad answers slowly, uncertainly.

His poems. They're coming after us because of poetry? I rack my brain to try to think what could be in these poems that would get us in trouble. His last book was published a couple of months before the election. But my dad—his poems—they're not fire-and-brimstone political. His poems are about people and moments and polishing tiny nuggets of truth.

"And this poem? 'Revolution'?" Suit #1 asks, showing my dad a page in the book.

"Yes," my dad says, his voice low. It's probably my dad's best-known poem. When it was published in the *New Yorker*, my mom and I had Mrs. Brown make him one of those picture cakes, with the cover of the issue his poem was printed in. Mrs. Brown, the woman who was off to burn my dad's books. Dad once came to school to do a writer's workshop with us in English class. I memorized his poem so I could recite it that day.

Revolution
By Ali Amin

Speak to me with your tongue while it is still
  free,
while your body is still yours.

Let your words travel through the air,
uncontrolled
spontaneous
necessary
tumbling through clouds of dust that dim
    the sun.

Until they reach my ear
and so many ears, spilled onto the table,
waiting.

Speak the truth while it is still alive, while
    lips, cracked and bleeding, can still move.

Time is beholden to neither lover nor tyrant.

Say what you must.
I will listen.

CHAPTER 4

Ten minutes.

That's how long we've been given to pack up our lives, to leave our home. To prepare for relocation. How do we even begin? That's not even time enough to say good-bye.

Suit #1's voice blasts at us as we begin to walk upstairs to collect our things. "Only the necessities. One bag per person." He turns away, stops, and yells back, "Guards are posted in the front and back."

My parents and I continue up the stairs quietly. There are no more words. I feel like a fish that's been caught on a line and slapped onto a stone. My tail flaps; my body lurches. I'm about to be gutted, and all I can do is watch the knife coming for me.

My dad silently ushers all of us into my room. My eyes

scan this space that suddenly feels like it's not my own, not the place I've spent every night for over a decade. The book left open on my bed, the disheveled *kantha* quilt, the long black cotton scarf with red roses embroidered on it, my phone plugged into the nightstand. My phone. David. I need to tell him. I stutter-step toward my phone.

Boots stomp up the stairs.

"No," my mom whispers, snatching the phone from my hands. There's no time to protest, let alone tap out a text. I can only watch, wide-eyed, as my phone falls to the ground, hitting the carpet with a soft thud and a bounce that lands it on the bare wood floor under my bed. I drop to my knees to reach for it amid the dust and detritus.

"I'll take your phones now." I look up. It's the Boots. A man in a khaki Army uniform steps into my room, hand extended. His jaw juts out, showcasing a prominent underbite.

My dad reaches into his pocket and turns over his phone. He doesn't make eye contact with the guard, or with me or my mom.

"My . . . my phone—" Mom stumbles over her words, then clears her throat. "It's on the small table in the foyer." She takes my dad's hand, and they step a little closer to me. My mom reaches for me. I take her hand and let her pull me to standing. She nods at me. I look down at my phone, the bejeweled rubber case, the scratches on the glass surface, the screensaver of David and me—a selfie of us on a hike not far from here. His arm is around my shoulders, I'm flashing a peace sign, and we both have these goofy grins on our faces. There's a tightness in my chest. There's a deep coldness in my bones, and my blood is like ice.

My mom turns to me and carefully unwraps each of the fingers that clutch my phone. My knuckles are white. Without another word, she gives my phone to the guard.

"Ten minutes," the guard barks at us, and then turns and walks out my door.

My dad pauses, then quietly shuts the door. We're alone, the three of us, in my room. I burst into tears. My parents surround me, wrapping their arms around each other and me. One of them kisses the top of my head; I'm not sure who. The other kisses my forehead.

I don't know anything anymore. I don't even know if this is real. I can't feel my body. It's like I'm watching all of this from outside myself. And it seems like it should be science fiction.

"We only have a few minutes," my dad says, his voice cracking as he releases us from his embrace.

"Take what you think you'll need, *beta*," my mom says, stepping back.

A vise grips my heart. What I need? I need all the things I can't have.

My dad takes my mother's free hand. They look at me, ashen-faced, red-eyed. They are about to walk out, but my mom returns to me, grabs my hand, and motions for my dad to take the other. In this small circle of our family, my mom turns first to me, then my dad, silently, her eyes glistening with tears. She starts to whisper a prayer.

My Arabic isn't so good, besides memorizing *duas* for daily prayers. But this one I know because it was always on Nanni's lips. She even carried a copy of this verse in her purse, on a little laminated card. The Verse of the Throne. The protection prayer. My *nanni* used to tell me that this was one of the most powerful verses of the Quran. That whoever recited this verse would be under God's protection. My dad once told me about the poetic symmetry of the verse. You should imagine yourself walking through the verse, he said, stopping at the chiasmus, the middle line: *He knows that which is in front of them and that which is behind them.* When you read the four lines before and the four lines after, you'll see how, thematically, they are concentric circles that loop around that middle line.

I may not be the most stalwart of Muslims, and my practice may waver, but this *dua*—maybe because of how I remember Nanni reciting it as she would blow the prayer over me—this one always gives me a sense of calm, but something more, too. Like my *nanni*'s voice endowed each of the words with the strength of her belief, like the words were tangible. I reach out for that peace right now, that strength, but it feels like grasping at air.

"We have to hurry," my dad says when my mom finishes the short verse.

"Can you do this?" my mom asks. "Do you need me to help you?"

No, I want to say. I can't do this. I won't. My heart is breaking, but underneath there's this flickering flame of fury, too. How can we do this? How can you go along with this? I want to yell at my parents.

But I whisper, "I don't understand how this is happening." My voice is barely a scratch. "How can we be dangerous to the state? A poet, a chiropractor, and a high school senior?"

"It's not about danger. It's about fear. People are willing to trade their freedom, even for a false sense of protection." My dad shakes his head. "'There never was a democracy yet that did not commit suicide.'"

"What does that even mean?" Behind the terror, I can feel the flames of anger, burning, rising. How can we resign ourselves to this?

"It's John Adams. He meant democracy is fragile. All we can do right now is go along." My dad turns to the window and raises his eyebrows. "They've stationed police outside the door. If we don't cooperate, it will be much, much worse for all of us."

"Hurry, *beta*," my mom says as she and my dad rush out to pack up their lives in suitcases.

My head spins. My chest rises and falls, which is the only way I know I'm still breathing and standing here in the middle of my room. The bed's not made. I can't leave without making the bed. Who cares about the fucking bed? Why didn't I text David? Does he know? How am I supposed to leave here without telling him? Will he think I've disappeared?

Suit #1 told us where we are going. A relocation center. Near Manzanar.

He used Manzanar like a landmark. Like the word was so everyday. Like "sun" and "grass" and "sky." Words you use a million times without thinking. Like the irony wasn't lost on him, because our world has no more irony in it.

Only minutes are left, and I have to figure out what to take. But for how long? A couple of days? A month? The Japanese Americans were interned until World War II ended. Years. Shit. Could it be years?

I grab the biggest duffel I have and start filling it with jeans, T-shirts, socks, underwear, pajamas. My black hoodie. A zip-up fleece. How cold does it get? Shoes. What shoes? A hat. Gloves. What do I need? How am I supposed to do this? Books. We can have books, right? I grab a couple of books from my nightstand, knocking over a digital frame currently displaying a picture of David and me at homecoming. I pick it up and hold it to my chest. I feel giant sobs coming on again, but I can't. I don't have time. I put the frame back on my nightstand, not sure if they allow pictures at...at wherever they're taking us. What if they confiscate it? I'd rather have it here, at home, safe. Intact. From my desk, I snatch a handful of pens and a blank notebook.

There's a knock on my door. My mom.

"Dad's downstairs. We have to go."

I'm not ready. This is mad. I can't go. "Mom." My voice breaks. She moves toward me, but I hold up my palm, and she stops.

"Make sure you remember socks and underwear." She gives me a small, wan smile.

Socks and underwear. I wonder if all moms do this—try to make the terrifying seem mundane. She steps away. She knows that I need a moment.

I look around the room. There's a little bit of space left in my duffel, so I take some rolls of washi tape and a blank journal I got in Paris last summer. The cover has a drawing of a girl and her dog curled up on a giant pot of red jam. The label says CONFITURE DE MOTS. I glance at my bookshelf— the yearbooks, my shoebox of notes and cards from David. I saved every note David ever passed to me in school. He laughed and called me a romantic when I asked him to write me notes instead of texting. But I love the notes. Each one is a little gift. A tangible surprise that doesn't eat up gigs on my phone. And now I'm leaving them forever? For someone else to look at? What happens to our house? Will it be searched? Is it still ours?

Too many questions and no answers. And I desperately want to take that box with me, but there is no room and no time.

A door shuts downstairs, and my mom calls up for me.

I pick up my duffel and turn off the light. But before I shut the door, I go back and straighten the *kantha* quilt on my bed. I see Fluffy—a brown stuffed dog with one ear almost falling off who joined me on my first day of nursery school. It was the only way I'd allow my parents to leave; he made me feel secure. My impulse is to take him. But I leave Fluffy on my pillow, where he has spent thousands of nights, in a place that was once safe.

I stomp down the stairs. I reach into my pocket, an instinct to grab the phone that isn't there. I clench my empty hand into a fist, and a tear plops onto my knuckle. What would I text to David if I even had a chance? Good-bye? I love you? Find me?

I meet my parents in the foyer.

There are a million shards in my heart, but the one that really stabs is having my damn phone taken away. Maybe it's dumb to think of it this way, but it's not only my phone. It's all my pictures, every memory of school and tennis team and David. I stifle my sobs. Dread clutches me, but so does anger. They didn't merely take my phone; they took my voice, my choice.

An invisible hand pushes us outside the door. The nights are so quiet here. That's one thing I always liked about our little town. The crickets in summer, the trees whispering on the breeze. You can actually see stars. But not tonight. *Tonight*, there is only dark sky.

I take a last look inside. A guard has his hand on our door-knob. On our door. He's going to pull it closed. But...the dishes. Are there still dishes in the sink? I can't remember if we loaded the dinner plates into the dishwasher. Will someone do the dishes? My mom hates leaving dishes overnight.

The door slams behind us. My parents don't even look.

I swing my head around. There are cars at the curb, the van we saw earlier, and more Exclusion Guards. The Suits. The Suits are conferring with the chief of police. There is talking around me, I hear words, but the words don't make sense. Like everyone is speaking in tongues. My parents shuffle me into the backseat of the chief of police's car and shut the door. There's no air. I try to open the door, but apparently you can't open the backseat doors from the inside of a police car. So I watch as my parents exchange words with Suit #1, who hands them some papers. Then they turn to the chief, who also has something to say, but seems to be having a hard time looking my parents in the eye. We know the chief. We've known him since his daughter, Ivy, and I were in kindergarten together. My dad nods. My mom stares at him blankly. Then the chief opens the back door for them, and they slide in next to me. I move over to make space for them. We don't look at one another. We don't say anything. It's like we're all in mourning, but for different things, in our own way.

The chief starts up the car. I see something, someone running toward us. I squint into the darkness. I can't see.

David? Could it be David? Does he know? Did he see me?

The chief pulls the car away from the curb.

I yell David's name, but the chief doesn't respond. It's like no one can hear me. I strain to see, but the chief has the light on inside the car, and all I can see is the reflection of a girl who doesn't really look like me. I try to roll the window down, but it won't roll down. I look at the girl in the window; her face is puffy and red, and her watery reflection looks like a ghost. I look at my parents; they're ghosts, too. The world has shattered, and all that's left is this alternate universe full of broken people with nothing to hold on to.

CHAPTER 5

We are silent for a long time as we pass through the town center to head onto the highway to Los Angeles. Car lights whiz by us. Even in the middle of the night, there's traffic in LA. The chief is in the right lane, driving impossibly slow, like he's trying to prolong the ride to scare us more. But he doesn't really need to bother. There's so much anxiety in this car that it feels like the backseat is shrinking, crushing us into a small cube of vinyl and sweat and fear.

The chief clears his throat. "Now, you all know I'm sorry about this, um, formality. Doing my job, following orders that come from above my pay grade. I'm sure you folks will be cleared in no time. The bigwigs need to see you're not a threat."

He's trying to fill the silence because he's uncomfortable, but all he's done is make it worse. My dad continues to stare at his own feet. My mom takes his hand. Say something, I want to tell them. Call him out. He knows us. Ask him how he can do this. I watch my parents, but they don't say a word.

I look at my palms, tracing the remnants of the tiny crescent marks that I pressed into my own skin. Words rise from my gut to my throat, and they taste bitter.

"How's Ivy?" I ask the chief.

My parents both swing their heads in my direction. My mom grabs my hand and squeezes it, an indication I should stop talking—but fear and anger are waging a war inside me right now, and I can't stop myself. If I can't leave this car, if I have to hear the chief's "following orders" excuse, the least I can do, the one thing I can do, is remind him that he knows us. He's "escorting" us away from our whole life, and I don't think it's my job to make him feel comfortable about that, even if my mom is giving me the death stare to silence me.

"Did she decide on a college yet?" I don't have the energy or acting skills to make my voice sound chirpy, like I want to, so my delivery is totally deadpan, which I suppose fits with how I feel.

I see the chief glance into his rearview mirror, and I make eye contact with him for a second before he looks away. "She's fine. Thanks for asking. Not quite settled on a school, though."

"Yeah," I say. "I know the feeling."

Maybe my mom is right when she says I'm sometimes stubborn for no reason. I imagine they aren't saying anything because they're afraid something worse could happen.

I'm not sure what else we can lose, but if I'm being honest, I'm terrified that we'll find out.

Union Station in Los Angeles is an art deco–mission revival mash-up wonder of inlaid marble tile, vaulted wood ceilings, and light fixtures that would make Frank Lloyd Wright proud. We've been here before. Normally, I'd close my eyes, ignoring the gum wrappers and wadded-up tissues that litter the sticky floor, to wonder at this echo of a time when people dressed up for dinner on trains with names like the *Sunset Limited* and the *Pacific Sunrise*, when train travel was romantic and featured in black-and-white movies. But now, as I stand outside in the broken quiet of the night, my synapses are firing with a million questions at once. I wrap my arms around my body, literally trying to hold myself still because my fight-or-flight adrenaline is in overdrive and I don't know which way it's going to lead me. Both, I think.

There are guards here, too. Same as the ones who were at my house, but more. Dozens more. This time, under the glare of extra lights that have been set up outside, I focus so I see them more clearly. There's been increased security in public places—airports, train stations, even shopping malls. Somehow, seeing soldiers with giant guns strapped across their chests always makes me feel more scared and less safe. Maybe scaring people is part of the plan. But the soldiers here, the Exclusion Guards—their sandstone-colored uniforms look crisp, new. Jacket, pants, cap, boots, and bulletproof vest,

46

like the kind the police have, but more heavy-duty and with shiny black plates across the front, like something Batman might wear. Our military is diverse, but not this shiny, new branch. They're all white, it seems. A victory for nostalgic racists longing for the "good old days" of segregated units and separate bathrooms.

A gauntlet of guards lines the sidewalks to the entrance, some at the curb, others with their backs to the stone building. Their eyes alert. Their fingers aren't on the triggers, but the air is so charged, it feels that way. I notice an American flag patch on each soldier's sleeve, and below that a black rectangle with EXCLUSION AUTHORITY embroidered in white.

Outside the main entrance of the train station is the first checkpoint—a series of desks. That's what the chief calls it. There are a couple dozen other people lined up, each with a bag in hand. Some other desis, an African American family, a few people who look like they might be from the Middle East. It's after midnight, and everyone looks exhausted, almost jet-lagged. And it's quiet—so quiet you can hear the buzz of the makeshift lighting that has been set up outside.

"This is where I leave you," the chief says, as if he's dropping us off for vacation instead of pointing us toward a sign that shows people where to line up according to last name. Which is next to a sign with enumerated instructions of what to do. This is Los Angeles; I'm used to seeing signs in public places with instructions in multiple languages. But not here. English only. And the chief gestures us toward a damn desk, so casually. As if men with giant guns meant to keep us quiet and herded in is normal. It's not normal. So why are people acting like it is?

The chief extends his hand toward my dad, who takes it in his own—but when I see my dad's face, he seems almost as surprised as I am that's he's acquiesced to this handshake. Maybe it's a reflex he couldn't help.

"Good luck, Ali," the chief says, then quickly darts away, as if *he's* the one who is afraid of *us*. The irony is not lost on me.

"Thanks for your service, Chief." I don't hide my sarcasm. My mom shushes me even though the chief is probably no longer in earshot.

"Layla, you really need to watch your tone," she whispers. "You're far too sarcastic for your own good. There might be a time for it, but it's certainly not right now."

I shake my head. "Mom, I think tone policing is the least of our problems."

"Maybe," my dad adds. "But your mom is right. Don't draw attention to yourself. We need to blend in if we're going to get through this."

This? I don't suppose any of us know what to call the experience yet. Like World War I wasn't called that when people were fighting it. How could it have been, when they didn't know what would come after? Anyway, probably no one is thinking about an appropriately weighty yet catchy phrase to call our quagmire right now. We're all too busy looking away and trying to believe it's a collective nightmare we will eventually wake up from. I guess it's pretty bad when a nightmare feels like a privilege.

We approach the station for *A–E*. It's essentially a small desk with a Black Suit behind it.

"Reassignment documents," he demands.

An Exclusion Guard at his side looks up and away, not making eye contact. Like everyone else. I wonder if it's in their regulations: no eye contact with the Muslims.

My dad hands him the documents we were given back at home. Home. It's disconcerting to even think about what's happening there. Are the Suits ransacking it? Destroying our things?

The Black Suit takes our cards from my dad and places each one over a reader—the kind the TSA uses to scan your passport when you come back from a trip abroad. He hands them back to us. "Go inside. Report to Window Three for your IDs. It will be on your right as you enter the building."

We shuffle inside Union Station along with nameless others. There are at least a hundred people in line at the old ticket windows, struggling to find a place to look that isn't a painful reminder of what our collective reality is. All of them with a bag in hand and a stunned look on their faces. Someone cries out, breaking the silence; then there's sobbing from one group, and then another. The clacking of computer keys continues, neither machine nor operator moved by tears. A couple of little kids—toddlers—run around, ignorant of what is happening. A baby screams. My mom once told me that she always knew what my cries meant, each one a little different: hungry, a wet diaper, tired, wanting attention. But a scream? My throat swells, and tears reach my eyes. Those kids, that baby—they have no idea what they are about to lose. I guess I don't, either. Who even knows what's happening, exactly, except that we were taken from our homes, and now we're about to board a train to…somewhere. I tap my heel hard against the marble mosaic floor. Then harder. I shiver. This place is a tomb.

The Authority Suit at Window 3 reels us in with a beckoning finger. My dad hands over our cards with the QR codes. The Suit grabs my left hand and tries to pull it forward, but I snatch it back, a natural reaction to his unwelcome touch. The man raises his eyes to meet mine, his jaw set. He turns to my dad and then looks like he's going to call a guard over. My dad grabs my hand and offers it to the Suit.

"She'll comply." That's what he says. My jaw drops. Those words. She'll comply. We will do what we're told. We'll go along. We won't cause trouble. Don't hurt us. That's what my dad means.

The man clears his throat and nods. "We need to stamp the inside of your wrist with your ID number."

I snap my mouth shut. I turn my hand over, palm facing up. What else am I supposed to do? He grabs it and places it in a black machine that looks like it could make espresso.

"Hold still," he says as a two-inch rectangular metal bar

descends and presses into the soft flesh on the inside of my wrist for a few seconds. When the bar rises up, I see nothing on my skin. It's UV. Ultraviolet. Invisible ink. Permanent, the man explains, like an automaton.

He doesn't look me in the eye, either. No one does. He stamps my parents' wrists and then gives us seat assignments on the train and warns us not to sit elsewhere. As we head to the platform, I grip my wrist like someone has cut me with a knife. I hold it close to my face, then farther away, squinting, holding my wrist up to the fluorescent slants of light that pass through the hall. I can't feel the mark; I can't see it. But it's there. Forever. I rub at the thin skin on the underside of my wrist until it turns red.

The platform is full, but there's no jostling. The Authority has frightened all the fidgeting out of us. A loud monotone voice over the intercom instructs us: "Go directly to the train car you have been assigned. Present your left wrist for scanning as you enter the car. Sit in your assigned seat. The Exclusion Authority thanks you for your cooperation."

My mother takes my hand as we enter our train car. I try to pull it away, but she only squeezes it tighter. Looking around, I shake my head, like I need a double take. The car is a normal train car. I don't know what I was expecting. I look down the aisle: A rubber mat runs along the center, with rows of three navy-blue cloth-covered seats on either side. Foggy, scuffed-up windows offer limited views onto the dim platform. A chemically vanilla smell wafts around the car—the kind you spray to mask pet or unpleasant cooking odors. A regular, nondescript conventional train that has probably been decommissioned, since California rail has gone high-speed. There are seats on these trains; they're not cattle cars—like the kind I've seen in my history textbooks—carrying people to their deaths. But we're being forced onto them with no real idea of where we're going or what to expect at the end of the line. I feel pressed. Like when we read *The Crucible* last year. I couldn't wrap my mind around Giles Corey being pressed to death—stones being laid upon his chest, one after another, to make him admit to witchcraft, and he refused to speak except to say "More weight" when they urged him to confess. That's what the air feels like in this car, why it feels hard to breathe. We're being pressed by fear and hatred and the law.

The dozen or so people in this car are all like me, going through the motions, stepping forward, trying not to run screaming from the train into the arms of Exclusion Guards with large guns. No one speaks. My tongue is wood.

We find our seats: 18A, B, and C. I slide toward the window, my mother in the middle, and my father in the aisle seat. My parents put their bags on the luggage rack, and mine fits under the seat in front of me.

Remembering a poem, I lean over to my dad: " 'There was a man with tongue of wood / Who essayed to sing—' " I pause, waiting for my dad to finish the Stephen Crane verse, but he pats me on the arm and turns away. This is our little game—one of us quotes a line of a poem, and the other quotes a line in response. It's a variation of an Urdu game, *bait bazi*, where one person quotes a line from a poem and the other has to quote another line of poetry that begins with the last letter of the verse used by the previous player. That seemed impossible to me, so Dad eased the rules. But he doesn't feel like playing, and I don't know what I was thinking—that a line of poetry could make any of this better? But I whisper the lines to myself anyway:

> *There was a man with tongue of wood*
> *Who essayed to sing,*
> *And in truth it was lamentable.*
> *But there was one who heard*
> *The clip-clapper of this tongue of wood*
> *And knew what the man*
> *Wished to sing*
> *And with that the singer was content.*

Perhaps my dad was right to brush this poem off. I always think of David as the person who knows what I wish to sing, and now all I imagine is him showing up at my house, ringing the doorbell over and over and hearing it echo in the empty rooms. I wrap my arms around my middle and stare out the train window, into the dark. My own reflection stares back at me, but I barely recognize myself.

The train jerks forward as we pull away from the station. My mom puts her face in her hands, and muffled sobs rise from seats around the car. My dad envelops my mother in his arms, kisses the top of her head, and whispers "I'm sorry" over and over.

I put my hand on the dirty glass and watch the city disappear in a haze. As we move past Santa Monica, I catch a last tiny glimpse of the ocean while a thread of dawn inches its way into the darkness before we track inland, north and east and north again. The last overly watered lush golf course gives way to rock and scrub and desert brush. We race by Vasquez Rocks, and my heart seizes for a moment as I think of David and our many hikes there amid the ancient stones, the slabs jutting into the air, sweeping into sharp peaks against azure sky. Once we took a lesser-traveled path off the Pacific Coast Trail and followed it to the top of a ridge, where we discovered a golden plateau of desert sunflowers. We passed the afternoon in delicious solitude and hiked back down in the fading light, a withering crown of yellow blooms encircling my black hair. It was perfect. I didn't know then how the memory would be a gift.

The train jolts and slows, recapturing my attention, before gaining speed again. My mom's head rests on my dad's shoulder. I watch as his heavy eyelids droop and then close. We haven't slept since yesterday. Probably no one on this train has. It's only been hours since we were taken from our homes, but each excruciating moment since has felt stretched, elongated beyond what it should be. It's like all of us on this train are part of an Einstein relativity experiment—every

American has been hurtling through space at the speed of light except us. We've been left behind to age, harnessed by earth's unyielding gravity.

I should close my eyes, rest up for the unknown world that lies ahead, but I'm antsy. I need to move. I slip by my snoozing parents and walk down the aisle, toward the next car and the bathroom. Some of the heads turn to look at me; others don't bother, but everyone who can't sleep has similar glazed-over, red-rimmed eyes.

I press the large black rectangular button that opens the inner door and step into the wide metal vestibule between train cars, then into the next car, which looks empty except for a couple of people who seem to be dozing in the front.

I take a few more steps forward. One of the sleeping men moves, and I see him.

Shit. A guard.

There's barely time to panic. Quickly, I turn on my heel, hoping that maybe he hasn't seen me or that he thinks it was a dream. I open the door and step back into the vestibule. It jostles and I feel dizzy, like I need to sit down right now. But I also feel rage, because why do I have this sick, panicky feeling when all I wanted was to stand up and stretch my legs and maybe pee?

The door swooshes behind me. I turn to face a stocky guard. He's so aggressively tanned, he's almost orange. We're alone in the small metal vestibule, desert passing by through the small window.

"What are you doing out of your seat?" he demands. Instinctively, I take a step back, stumble, but regain my balance.

"I, um, I was looking for the bathroom," I manage to say.

He scrunches his light-brown eyes at me and clenches his jaw. But he seems to look through me, like I'm not there. "You were told to stay in your seat." He speaks slowly, enunciating each word, bursting with restrained resentment.

"I'm sorry. I thought—"

"You thought what?" He takes another step toward me.

I inch back farther, closer to the door at the other end of the vestibule, which will take me to my car, where I'll be safe. Safe? I catch myself. Because there is no safe for me. Suddenly I'm acutely aware of how small this space is and how loud the train wheels sound against the tracks, and I wonder if people will hear me if I scream.

The door behind the guard slides open again. A tall, broad-shouldered Exclusion Guard steps into the vestibule. God, now there are two of them and I have literally nowhere to run. My hands shake. I can't call for any help because the people who are enforcing the law on this train are the ones I'm afraid of. Every fiber in my body wants to scream and cry, and I want to pound my fists into the metal walls.

"What's going on here?" the tall guard asks. His dirty-blond hair is cropped short. He twists his sandstone infantry cap in his hands. His sleeves are rolled up, exposing a small tattoo on the inside of his right forearm. Two arrows crossed, an *N* between the arrowheads. I turn my eyes away so he doesn't see me looking.

The stocky guard straightens up and salutes. I guess the Exclusion Guards have ranks, too. "Sir, this internee was out of her seat, sir."

That word slaps me across the face. Internee. Is that what we are now?

Speak. I need to force myself to speak up. If I don't speak for myself, no one will. "I'm sorry. I was trying to find a bathroom."

Compass Tattoo studies me, narrowing his eyes a bit. I bite my lip and glance down at my shoes. Am I shaking? It feels like I'm shaking.

He clears his throat. "Private, I think we can let this slide."

"Sir, the internees were given clear orders, and so were we."

"There are bathrooms on this car for a reason. We can't expect all of them to stop having bodily functions, can we?"

The stocky guard glares at me, shifting his weight from one foot to the other, then squares himself to the other guard. "No, sir."

Normally any conversation that includes the phrase "bodily functions" and me in the same sentence would have me burning with embarrassment. But not now. Now I'm enraged because my bathroom use has to be regulated and is up for debate.

"You can go back to your seat, Private."

"Sir. Yes, sir," the guard says and steps back into his car. I watch the door slide shut.

"I still have to use the bathroom," I blurt out. I don't know why I say this. I should go back to my car. I don't even really need to use the bathroom. But I feel like somehow I should assert my right to do so. Which is maybe a stupid hill to die on.

Compass Tattoo nods. "Fine. Then hurry up and get back to your seat. And stay there." I can't tell if his words are a caution or a threat.

I've mostly been trying to avoid looking at the guards directly, but as I turn to leave, I raise my eyes to meet his. He holds my gaze.

A caution? Or a threat?

CHAPTER 6

Independence, California. The town where we disembark for internment is called Independence. I balk at the irony of the name. And at how sunny the day is. There should be dark clouds and storms. Permanent night. But the earth, the sun, and the moon keep on their course, utterly oblivious.

A loud voice barks from the PA: "Stay with your families. You will board buses for Camp Mobius by identification number. Show the underside of your left wrist as you exit the station. Stay calm and exit in an orderly fashion."

Camp Mobius? I guess that's what they're calling it. They give it a name, like it's a summer sleepaway camp, and not a prison.

"We're in the first group. Let's get in line." My dad walks numbly forward.

"How can you be so calm about this?" I hiss at my parents. I know it's not their fault, but I'm tired, and nothing makes sense, and I desperately want an explanation for something, for anything.

My mom takes my elbow. "Layla, enough." My mom's voice is low but not soft. "We're not calm like we're meditating. We're keeping our cool so we don't get shot. Understand?"

"They're not going to shoot us. We're American citizens. They can't."

"Our government is jailing us because of our faith," a voice from behind me says. I spin around to face a girl who looks about my age. "They can do whatever they want. They already are. It's a brave new world."

"We haven't gotten to that book on the syllabus yet," I say. "What happens?"

"Spoilers." The girl grins. I like her already.

"I appreciate your commitment to protect the secrets of nearly century-old literature."

"I pride myself on my anti-spoiler crusade."

I laugh a little. "So you wouldn't tell me the focus of the next Star Wars anthology film, even if you knew?"

"Never. But obviously it should be Lando."

"Duh. I'm Layla, by the way."

"Ayesha. First of My Name, Protector of Stories, Mother of Dragons, and Soon-to-Be Interned Muslim."

"If you're Indian, that's two things we have in common. Not so much that dragon thing, though."

"It's Game of Thrones. You never read it? Watched it?"

I shake my head no.

"Your loss. And I'm Pakistani, but, you know, a desi is a desi."

"Show your wrist," an Exclusion Guard officer calls out. I move forward in the line and show the inside of my left wrist. I feel naked. The guard passes a UV light over my arm and a small fluorescent barcode appears at the base of my hand, a number unique to me, 0000105. It doesn't hurt when he scans me, but I still feel like I've been branded. The guard nods, and I board a bus with my parents. We crowd onto a single bench seat in the middle of the school bus. Ayesha, her younger brother, and her parents file past. She nods at me. "See you when we get there."

The two-lane highway from Independence to the camp is quiet except for the small caravan of buses heading into the desert. The landscape is bleak but undeniably beautiful. A liquid blue sky stands out against the snow-tipped peaks of the Sierra Nevada. And the sun gleams. Too bright, almost. Can nature be ironic? Destructive, yes. But nature's overwhelming power is amoral. If people die in a storm, they're collateral damage, like any other object in the storm's path— a lamppost, a car, a house. The unintentional side effects of wind or wave or current. Unlike people, nature carries out no vendettas. Yet the simple loveliness of the sky and sun and mountains makes me feel like nature is complicit in my country's betrayal.

After ten short minutes the buses pass Manzanar, the old Japanese American internment camp. It's desolate. I shudder when I see the weathered wooden sign that declares MANZANAR WAR RELOCATION CENTER. Every head in our bus turns to stare as we drive by, and I'm taken by how huge the space is. It's the desert, and nothing is out here but empty land and what looks like thousands of acres enclosed by a simple wooden fence. There are a few barracks and a sign pointing to the Visitor Center. Manzanar was a historic site, run by the National Park Service, my mom told me, but a couple of months ago, the Park Service lost its funding and this place was shut down. I glance back as we drive on. A tattered American flag still flies atop a pole in the center of the camp. Everything looks sepia-toned except the flag, with its faded red stripes and blue field of stars.

We drive on. Those abandoned flimsy barracks at Manzanar occupy my brain. Is that how we're going to live now? There's a damp patch of sweat on my jeans in the shape of my right palm. I feel the panic and anxiety coming off everyone in silent waves. I don't think any of us really believe this is happening.

The buses slow down as we approach a perimeter of chainlink fence that must be, I don't know, at least fifteen feet high. All around, as far as I can see, the fence is topped with curling razor wire. Watchtowers rise into the sky, guards with guns looming above us. It's prison. I close my eyes and feel my mom squeeze my hand. I hear her muttering a prayer to herself. I join her.

I wonder if others felt this way—the Japanese Americans who were imprisoned during World War II. Did they also feel this surreal separation from the experience, like they were detached from their bodies, watching themselves enter this camp, like ghosts, shades of who they were? Did they wonder how long they would be here? Could they have imagined it would be years? Did some try to block it all out, compartmentalize, imagine that it was only one more day? Because we aren't even through this giant electronic gate yet and I feel like my real life is already a million miles away.

Exclusion Guards at the gate entrance clear the drivers after a visual inspection of the inside, outside, and underside of the buses. The gate opens and the buses enter the camp, kicking up so much dust I can barely see out.

"Everybody off," the driver snaps at us after coming to an abrupt stop inside the gate. "Single file. Report to the Hub." He points at the light-gray behemoth of a building that squats in the center of camp. "Register by last names and get your quarters assigned."

Like leashed zombies, a few hundred of us stagger toward the largest building on the site. Families walk in tight huddles, arms around one another. Lots of brown and black faces—like you'd see at any mosque. There are also Muslims here who could pass as white—probably of Arab or Persian descent; white, but without all the privilege.

One detail that's impossible to miss? Just like in the train station, every person with a gun is white, and not white like maybe they're Bosnian—the kind of white that thinks internment camps are going to make America great again.

The Hub is marked by an American flag fluttering fifty feet up in the air, and large black plastic letters above the door: MOBIUS. Exclusion Authority bureaucrats mill around on their phones amid a heavy presence of armed Exclusion Guards. Some Authority guys step in and out of a gray modular building attached to the Hub. An office of some sort? As we proceed to the Hub, I start to understand the extent of the camp and how the razor-wired, sky-high security fence pens us in for miles, cameras trained on us. And there are rows and rows of FEMA trailers. I've seen them on TV before, the trailers the government puts up for people who've lost their homes in natural disasters. But now the natural disaster is being Muslim.

My vision clouds. I blink against the dust, and my knees buckle a little. I grab onto my dad's arm. Every muscle in his arm is taut. He straightens his backpack. He and my mom are holding hands, and I catch them looking at each other. They're run-down. The few wrinkles they have are highlighted by this dust that's blowing everywhere. They look so small, so human. When you're a kid, you think your parents are invincible and all-knowing, and then you start to grow up and realize that they're simply flawed human beings trying to make their way in the world the best they can.

We all look like ants marching in this dust straight into a giant trap where we'll be stuck or where we'll be fed poison that we inadvertently spread to the rest of the group. I bite my lip, but I don't even feel it. What's that thing people always say about history? Unless we know our history, we're doomed to repeat it? Never forget? Isn't that the lesson? But we always forget. Forgetting is in the American grain.

Someone yells out ahead of us. There's some kind of tussle.

"NO! NO! NO!" I hear a boy scream and then see him run away from his mom—I suppose it's his mom—a middle-aged woman wearing a bright-blue turban-style hijab. The boy, with curly chestnut-brown hair, is maybe eight or nine years old. She runs after him and grabs him, speaking to him in Arabic. The crowd parts around them. Then her son hits her in the face. There's a collective gasp from the crowd. When the woman reaches up to her cheek, the boy breaks free, pushes against anyone standing in his way, and starts running back toward the main gate, where the buses entered. He doesn't get far. Three Exclusion Guards draw guns and aim them at him. A kid. They're pointing their weapons at a kid. A fourth guard grabs him and pins him to the ground. I'm frozen. I literally can't move. The action slows down. I hear the muffled scream of the boy's mother as she runs through the crowd, shoving past people, some of whom stumble and fall and curse, adding to the chaos.

"Please! Don't hurt him! He doesn't understand," the mother cries. She claws at the guard who holds her son down. He shoves her off, and she falls backward. One of the other guards directs his gun away from the boy and toward the mom. The little boy is crying. The mom's piercing wails seem to echo through the camp and into the mountains far in the distance. Then another man—Compass Tattoo from the train—appears. He says something I can't hear, then puts his hand on the shoulder of the guard who has the boy pinned down. The guard nods and releases him. Compass Tattoo helps the little boy up. The mother scurries to her son on her knees and tenderly wraps him in her arms, trying to protect him, shifting her body away from Compass Tattoo. But he doesn't touch his gun or hit her. He whispers something in her ear and then takes her by the elbow, helping her up. The woman wipes her face and keeps her arm around her son's shoulders. The boy's face is blank, expressionless. Quietly, the woman leads him back to their place in line, the murmuring crowd parting to let them through.

The guards put away their guns, and one of them shouts, "Show's over." And we continue, herded like animals, toward the Hub.

Show's over. My God, a show. Like our pain is entertainment.

I look at the guard with the tattoo and then to the gun at his side. He catches my eye, nods, and takes long strides to a black-suited man who has been watching the scene unfold from a short distance. The man's face is red and blotchy, but not like he's sunburned—more like his tie is too tight and he can't get enough air. Who wears a suit and tie in the desert?

When I turn to my parents, I see tears running down both

their faces. We join the crowd and continue our walk. No one talks. Silent as the grave. I take a shaky breath, and then another. I say Nanni's favorite prayer to myself. I'm so glad she's not here to see this. I try to find solace in her memory. But as I'm saying the words, my muscles tense and my breathing grows loud. I say the prayer again. But it doesn't feel meditative, as it usually does. It doesn't calm me or quell my anger.

Thoughts and prayers. God, all the times I've heard politicians utter those words.

Aurora.

Orlando.

Las Vegas.

Sandy Hook.

Umpqua.

Virginia Tech.

San Bernardino.

Sutherland Springs.

Parkland.

Santa Fe.

I don't have a measure for how I should feel or what I should think. But thoughts and prayers weren't enough to save any of those people in any of those places from getting shot. And they're not going to be enough for us now. Prayers can only go so far. I remember something else my *nanni* used to tell me: Praying is important. But you can't simply pray for what you want. You have to act.

We line up outside the Hub by last name and proceed through the security check—full-body scanners and luggage imaging like at the airport, but with a ticket to nowhere. After the scan, we walk inside the main hall of the Hub, where dozens of registration tables are set up. I soak in this bizarre nightmare, scanning the camp and what appears to be the only entrance gate—heavily guarded—and the watch-towers and the razor-wire fence as far as I can see. And the people. Everywhere, all of them, dazed like me. It's like a United Nations of internees. Old and young. Black and brown. Some in hijab and kufis and the traditional dress of their ancestral countries, many in T-shirts and jeans and shorts. But we're all citizens of the United States, forced on a dead-end journey into the desert. The Muslims who aren't citizens are going on a much longer trip—deportation. Green cards and visas instantly invalidated with a stroke of the presidential pen. Maybe they're the lucky ones, if they have other homes to go back to, take their chances in. For those of us who were born here, America is literally the only home we've ever known. And all those angry mobs on television chanting "Go home," they don't get that this *is* our home.

Our turn comes to check in and get our room assignments. An auburn-haired woman with a tight bun and pursed red lips peruses the laptop on the desk in front of her, reading the data from our barcodes.

"Ali, Sophia, Layla Amin." She says it like a fact but apparently wants an answer, because she gives us a hard stare when we stand there in silence.

"Yes. I'm Ali. My wife, Sophia. And this is our daughter, Layla." My dad places his hand, in turn, on our shoulders, like he's introducing us at a social event.

"You've been assigned to Mercury Home Number Seventeen, Block Two," the woman says, and hands us three key cards. "Report to the Hub auditorium at seventeen hundred hours for orientation."

"Is Mercury Home the new euphemism for 'trailer'?" I ask. The woman raises an eyebrow at me. My dad pulls me back by my elbow.

"Where's Block Two?" my mom asks.

"Here's a map. There's a file titled 'Regulations' on the home screen of your media unit in your dwelling. Familiarize yourself with it."

I trace my infinity charm with my finger, thinking of my phone in the hands of a stranger, or maybe even destroyed. All my pictures with David, the tennis team selfies—lost. Everywhere around us are uniformed men with guns. It's terrifying, but I feel a rage rising in me, too.

"Do we have phones in our trailers? Even prisoners are allowed phone calls," I say.

"Layla." I hear the fear in my dad's voice when he chastises me.

"You're allowed preapproved calls. There are phones in the recreation area of the Hub." The woman points down a hall at the end of the large open room we're in. "You can request to make a phone call from the Hub, subject to approval. They'll explain at the orientation."

"Are we also allowed to eat?" I ask. My stomach has been grumbling since we got off the bus, and I feel my hangriness coming on.

The woman blows out a puff of air. I can tell I'm trying her patience. "There are box lunches waiting for you near the exit."

"What about news? How will we find out what's happening outside, um—"

"MO-BE-US." The woman reminds us of the name of the camp like we can't speak English and somehow her speaking slowly and very loudly will suddenly make us fluent.

"We do actually speak English." I say. "Just FYI."

"Layla," my mom says sternly, and takes my hand.

The woman gives me a sour look but ignores me, continuing where she left off without missing a beat. "The Director decides what news you get at Mobius and grants you access via the media units in your dwelling. All the answers you need will be given to you at the orientation." The woman, clearly irritated, looks straight past me. "Next," she says.

We stand there for a moment, unsure of what to do. The confusion and anger of hundreds of people fill the hall and make the air heavy and hard to breathe.

"Next!" The woman raises her voice, on the edge of yelling.

We walk out of the Hub and into the bright daylight. I look up, shielding my eyes from the sun; a small drone hovers in the air above us. It pauses, like it's looking at me, and then flies toward the red-faced man in the suit, who wipes a handkerchief across his brow. The drone is shiny red metal, smooth, an ellipsoid, but as it approaches the man, three black legs unfold from its belly and allow it to land vertically, like a mechanical spider leaping from air to ground. It follows behind the man like a pet. Drones are everywhere, but I've never seen one like that, like it's almost alive.

The Mercury Homes are arranged by blocks, eight identical mobile homes on each side of the block, tan with white trim around the windows and three aluminum steps leading to a white door with the house number on it. A small metal nameplate on the door spells out MERCURY HOME. I laugh, imagining that FEMA purchased these trailers from some company trying to appeal to the retro, rich-hipster crowd. They're not shiny like Airstreams, or as cool, but I could totally see someone trying to retrofit one of these and renting it on Airbnb, appealing to people who don't really want to rough it but want to pretend like they are. The trailer sales must've been a bust, because they've been downgraded to prison glamping. My mom waves the key card in front of the round electronic lock pad, and we enter.

I glance around. Bile rises in my throat. I guess Mercury Homes are better than the shanties we saw when we passed

Manzanar. It's a mobile home, but it's still prison. The front door opens into the common area—a combo kitchen-dining-living-room. The unit is spare, narrow. Square footage–wise, it feels smaller than our kitchen and dining area at home, so I'm guessing cabin fever is going to come on fast and strong.

My mom places our camp-issued lunches on the compact table, sniffs the air, and rubs her nose. The entire space smells like the inside of a bottle of bleach. I wonder what they were trying to scrub away.

My dad clears his throat and goes to open one of the rectangular windows above the built-in sofa, which is covered in tannish-brown vinyl. He jimmies it up a few inches but then immediately shuts it when he gets dust in his eye. My mom walks over and tells him to sit down so she can get a better look. The vinyl squeaks as he takes a seat.

I grab a sandwich from our box lunches. Peanut butter and jelly on white bread. Of course. I scarf it down in a few bites.

Then I walk a few strides through the narrow kitchen to two side-by-side doors and throw them open.

"Found the bedrooms," I shout at my parents. But there's really no reason to raise my voice. Even though they are at the opposite end of the trailer, they're still basically within spitting distance.

My mom nods at me. Looks like my dad's eyes are clear of dust, but they're still glassy and wet. My mom's are, too.

It hurts to see them this way. They look old. And tired. Like they've walked here from home. Our real home. Our only home. I remember reading about people who, well, aren't in our situation—not exactly—but who are displaced, uprooted, and how some of them try to make the best of it, keeping home as a feeling in their hearts, not an actual physical place. But I don't want to do that. I can't. It would feel like a betrayal to my old life, to myself. I have one home, and it's not going to be this place. The government might be able to steal our lives from us, but they can't steal our thoughts.

I close my eyes for a second and take a halting breath.

I peer into the rooms. The bedroom on the left has a double bed, and the one on the right has bunks. "I think this one is yours." I point to the room on the left. "Unless you two want the bunks?" My parents look up at me with forced smiles. They've barely said a word since sitting down. I imagine they want to say something, I don't know, parental, but they must feel like I do, like their bodies are full of holes.

I enter the room on the right.

The low metal bunks are pushed up against the wall. The mattresses and pillows have plastic on them. On the opposite wall is a square window that looks onto the mountains in the distance. Below the window are a blue plastic chair and a small desk that drops down from the wall like an airplane tray table. Next to the desk is a tiny round metal sink; in the corner is a closet full of shelves with a clear plastic curtain serving as a door. I swivel around and take a deep breath. The room is about the size of my old bathroom.

I have no idea what to do next. I know I need to busy myself, because if I continue standing here, I'll slowly fade away until I cease to exist. I wonder if that's how they did it, the Japanese Americans who were sent to camps in World War II. Maybe they survived by going through the motions. Day by day. Waking. Counting the hours. Eating dust. Sleeping. That's my immediate plan for now: Get through it. Survive the madness. Keep my eyes open.

I unzip my bag. I neatly refold all my clothes and place them on the shelves. I save some shelf space for toiletries, since the sink barely has room for a small cup and my toothbrush. I also find a spot for my paperbacks *Great American Poetry* and *Macbeth*. Neither is exactly in my top five desert-island books, but I guess I wasn't discerning when shoving stuff into my duffel. Next, I tear open the bedding package and make up the bottom bunk, saving the other set of sheets. I'm not sure how we do laundry, which might kill me because I love the feel of fresh sheets, but the touch of this internment-chic bedding doesn't exactly scream high thread count. An oval Mylar mirror hangs above the sink, and when I wash my hands, I notice my grimy face. It's the dust. I rinse my eyes with cold water and scrub my face until the white washcloth is gray-brown. I wash it with hand soap, then hang it to dry on the towel rack screwed into the wall.

I walk back into the main room. "Where's the toilet and shower?"

My mom leaves the couch and takes maybe ten short steps into the kitchen and opens two small doors that I thought were cabinets. One is a shower; the other, a toilet.

"I see they spared no expense to incarcerate us," I say.

My mom hugs me. Tight. "I'm so sorry, sweetheart. We had no idea it would come to this."

I let my mother hold me. When she steps back, her eyes shine with tears. I want to say something to calm her, make her feel a little less horrible, but a tiny black fish-eye camera attached to the ceiling distracts me.

"They're watching us in here, too? Are we allowed to use the bathroom privately, or are they surveilling our bodily functions as well?" I burn at the violation. I have to get out. The walls of this trailer feel like they're closing in on me. I can't breathe. "I'm going to go look around. Maybe I'll find the laundry room."

"I'm not sure you should be roaming the grounds. I don't know if it's safe."

"Mom, please. There are tons of people outside. Besides, there are so many armed Exclusion Guards around, it's not like I can get mugged."

"The men with guns are the ones I'm worried about," my mom replies. She turns to look at my dad, who gives me a small smile that looks like it takes some effort. "Fine, but be back in an hour. We don't want to be late to the orientation."

I grab a key card and tuck it into my back pocket. "Don't worry." Possibly the most ridiculous two words I could ever say to my parents.

I step outside, blinking against the blazing sun.

I walk past row after row of identical Mercury Homes. Little kids play outside, kicking up dust while their parents mill around, faces drawn and blank, fear in their eyes. Not sure what to do or how to be. I can see some of them trying to make the little ones feel comfortable by sporting uneasy smiles whenever a child looks at them. I think about my dad's smile before I left. It's impossible for me to understand what it must feel like to be a parent—to know that one of your sacred duties is to protect your child, and then to feel that you're failing and completely helpless to change that.

"Layla?" I hear my name from behind me.

I turn, raising my hand above my eyes. "Ayesha?" The girl I met at the train station. She runs her hand through her bobbed hair and smiles at me.

"Couldn't stand it inside anymore, either?"

"It's like a—"

"Tomb," she says. She pauses a beat, glancing at a guard as he passes by us. "We're in the same block, three trailer homes down from you."

I gesture down the row of Mercury Homes, and she joins me in a slow walk. There are armed guards posted every two blocks. Their fingers aren't on the triggers of their guns, but it feels that way.

"How do you know where our trailer is?" I ask.

"There's a directory in the media unit of the trailer," Ayesha says, then widens her eyes in mock horror. "You mean you haven't gone through the regulations file yet?"

I smirk. "I was saving the regs file for pre-bedtime viewing. I hear it's riveting."

"Total clickbait."

"Are we allowed to walk anywhere in the camp?"

"I guess. Just don't walk into the fences or you'll be shocked. They're electrified."

I smirk. "I'm going to put this out there, to be transparent: I can't have a friendship based solely on puns."

"What about witty barbs?"

"Add the occasional bon mot and I'm in." I want to laugh a little, but I don't have a laugh to give. Light, easy laughter feels lost. Like a phantom emotion. Still, I'm grateful for even the passing sensation.

Two guards on patrol pass by, turning their heads toward us. Without thinking about it, we both walk in the opposite direction.

"Do you know there's a camera in the Mercury Homes?" I don't whisper, not exactly, but seeing the guards everywhere makes me feel on edge, so I speak softly. "I mean, how are we supposed to shower?"

"The cameras are only in the common area, not in the bathrooms or bedrooms. And supposedly they don't record sound. But we probably should assume they actually *do*. Safer that way. So I guess you really didn't check out the regs, did you?"

"No. I was busy exploring our internment lodgings. And unpacking."

"Unpacking? You mean the ten articles of clothing we were allowed to bring?"

"I brought twelve—I'm an amazing packer."

"Rebel. You should totally have your own reality show: *Packing for Uncertainty*."

It's a joke. It feels both natural and totally inappropriate to joke. Like this whole conversation, really. Every syllable is awkward, and every reaction feels wrong. It doesn't seem like there's any right way to simply *be* in here. Like we're on a journey with no map, no compass, and no destination.

"Let's go over there. I think I saw a little garden." Ayesha directs me down a wide main road that divides the camp into halves. On the map we all received, it's called the Midway.

"A garden?"

"I think it's more like a small outcropping of rocks and shrubs."

We walk down the Midway. I'd call it a road, but there are no cars in the camp—at least none that we're allowed to drive. There's a small parking lot to the left of the main entrance, but like everything else, our cars are back home. It's not until I walk down the Midway, toward what is essentially the back of the camp—the side that faces the mountains, not the road outside the camp—that I realize how large Mobius is. Yet its size is dwarfed by the vastness of the desert around us. There's noise, but not city noise. No planes overhead that I've seen yet. No sirens. And besides the little kids trying to occupy themselves, there's a lot of eerie silence. Many pairs of eyes that dart about and then are quickly cast downward when guards pass. Tearstained faces. Dusty hems and cuffs. People walking around aimlessly, like Ayesha and I are. Searching. Looking. Wondering if there's a way out. But all we see are guards and guns and a fence whose sole purpose is to keep us locked in here—that, or kill us.

The back of the camp appears less heavily watched. There are still armed guards walking around, and watchtowers, but it's a little quieter. And there are evenly spaced orange plastic crowd-control barriers—you know, the kind you sometimes see along parade routes or at outdoor concerts—between the fence and us. Ostensibly, they're to prevent us from walking right up to the fence and getting electrocuted, but there's space between them to slip by, and they're only hip-high. And what about the little kids? I suppose no parent will let their child out of their sight in this place. I pray that none slip away from their parents or think this is a good spot for hide-and-seek. Hopefully, the DANGER—ELECTRIC FENCE signs that show a lightning bolt zapping through a body and that are posted every ten feet will keep both kids and adults away.

The government—the Exclusion Authority—built all of

this, this whole camp, under the cover of darkness. I wonder what else they've built. What else can they do to us when America isn't looking?

We are nearly at the end of the camp: nothing but the fence and, beyond that, the desert. Off to the side is the garden—a bit of an overblown name for it, since it's mostly large, uneven rocks surrounded by pale-green shrubs, the color of eucalyptus. Here and there are dry stalks of yellow flowers that look almost like mustard plants. If this corner were all you could see of the camp, it would be beautiful. Yellow petals, brown dirt, blue sky. If we weren't prisoners, this place would feel peaceful. If history had no ghosts, I wouldn't be terrified of what might come next. If. But "ifs" are always loaded, aren't they?

Ayesha bends low and plucks a small purple flower that's growing from underneath a rough-surfaced, arrowhead-shaped rock. She takes a seat and twirls the blossom between her thumb and index finger. I wander over to another boulder and kneel in front of it, brushing some loose dirt from its face.

"What are you doing?"

"I think there's something carved into the stone. Maybe a petroglyph?" I break off a twig and scrape at the dust in the outlines. I use my fingernail to flake off some dirt. I'm parched, and it dawns on me that I shouldn't stray far from the trailer without water. I give the outline a final brush with my palm and sit back on the hard ground. "Dammit. That doesn't look prehistoric."

Ayesha kneels down next to me and reads over my shoulder, "'S.A. plus T.J.' I mean, maybe they were, like, really advanced prehistoric peoples. Or maybe aliens?"

"Aliens who etch little hearts into stone in the middle of the California desert. Of course, Occam's razor. Go with the hypothesis with the fewest assumptions needed. Vandalizing aliens it is."

I look at Ayesha, who cracks a smile and then lets out a laugh. Then we both start laughing. It's not even really funny, but my sides hurt, and tears roll down my face. Ayesha leans back against a rock and belly laughs, then covers her face with her hands and begins sobbing. Her shoulders shake. Neither of us laughs anymore.

I don't know exactly what to do. I put my hand on her knee. "Hey, hey. It's going to be okay. We'll figure a way out of here."

She sniffles and wipes her nose with the back of her hand. "A way out? How? The only way out is through an electric fence."

"I know," I whisper. "Don't give up hope. Not yet. It's too soon."

"Don't worry." Ayesha sniffs. "I know being scared is a superpower."

"What?"

"It's something my dad told me once, when I was in the district spelling bee. He said that my fear made me more alert. That I could channel my fear into focus."

"Did you win?"

"Nah, second place. But, you know, I was up against another desi; he won state." Ayesha grins a little. "Desis kill at the spelling bee. And my dad was right: When I'm scared, I always feel like I can fight a little harder."

I nod at Ayesha and smile. I stand and reach out a hand to help her up. As we're dusting off our clothes, I notice a small depression past the orange barriers, at the fence line. I squint. It looks like something has burrowed underneath. A small animal, maybe, or—?

We hear a shout. Then more shouting. We step away from the garden and see a young man yelling at a guard. His friends are holding him back. We move closer to hear. Two other guards rush over.

"You Islamophobic asshole!" the young man yells. "We were in middle school together. What the fuck is wrong with you?" He's our age, maybe a little older, tall and wiry. Two friends pull at his arms. One is speaking to him, too low for us to hear.

"Back off, Soheil," the guard barks. "I could have you taken away. Trust me—you don't want that." He motions to the other guards to keep their guns away, moving his palms down, like he's pressing the air.

My chest tightens. The guards could do anything to Soheil in here, and who could we turn to? There's no police for us to call. No one to protect us. We should do something. They could hurt him. I start walking closer, but Ayesha grabs my arm and pulls me back, shaking her head.

"Don't be stupid," she says. "They have guns."

I want to bark at her. But I look into her wide, terrified eyes and take a breath. She's right. I glance down at my hands; they're trembling. I curl the right one into a fist and pound it against my thigh. I grit my teeth and nod at her.

Soheil puts his hands up, shaking his friends off him and retreating a few steps.

I can only glimpse part of the guard's face, but I see his shoulders relax. "It's going to be fine, Soheil. Chill. Everyone is doing their jobs here. You need to do yours."

"What the hell is my job?" Soheil asks, and then spits on the ground in front of his feet.

"To do what you're told," the guard says, then joins the other guards to help them disperse the small crowd that has gathered.

Soheil shakes his head and walks away. Toward the garden. Toward us. Every moment in the short time we've been behind this fence has been a revelation. And in this moment, I realize that Soheil was lucky that guard did nothing but brush him off.

"Are you okay?" Ayesha asks as Soheil nears. He looks up, startled. Clearly, he hadn't noticed us.

Soheil lets out a noise somewhere between a harrumph and a loud exhale. He looks over his shoulder. Neither the guards nor the small crowd are there anymore. No one wants to linger.

"I'm fine." He pauses. "Actually, no. I'm not fine. Not at all. This is some next-level fascist bullshit."

Ayesha and I simply nod. I kick a small stone, and we all watch it skitter away. We stare like it's the most riveting thing in the world, which, in the absence of our phones, it basically is. Then we all look at one another.

"I'm Soheil," he says, breaking the silence. "Soheil Saeed," he adds rather formally.

"We heard," I say. "I'm Layla."

"Ayesha." Ayesha grins at him. He smiles back, and it seems to release the tension he was holding in his shoulders.

"My *teita* would know the perfect ancient Egyptian curse to put on these assholes."

"Like the curse of King Tut?" Ayesha asks.

Soheil chuckles a little. "He wasn't the only pharaoh, you know. She, my grandmother, didn't really believe in curses, but I loved hearing about them, and about all the coincidental deaths that surrounded excavations. Teita was an archaeologist and a storyteller, and, believe me, ancient curses and mummies made the best ghost stories."

"Share," I urge. "One of the curses, at least."

Soheil runs his hand through his wavy dark hair. His light-brown eyes look off into the distance, then snap back to us. "The curse inscribed on a statue of a High Priest of Amun says any transgressor will 'die from hunger and thirst.'"

"It's a little on the nose for a desert, don't you think?" Ayesha says.

He gives her a little side-eye grin. "How about 'He shall be cooked together with the condemned.'"

"Succinct," I say. "I think I like that one. May our enemies be cooked with the condemned."

"Yeah, well, we're the ones most likely to die from hunger and thirst, not the guards or any of those fascist bureaucrats in the Hub. And definitely not the president," Soheil says.

"You think they're going to starve us?" Ayesha asks.

"This is a prison camp. Have you seen pictures of the concentration camps in World War Two?" Soheil asks.

I see Ayesha take a step back, like she's been hit in the chest.

Then it occurs to me that she hasn't imagined anything worse than this. Probably a lot of people haven't. Everyone is scared in a deep way—like, in our bones. And maybe thinking of what more they might do to us is too much to bear.

"This isn't a concentration camp," I say. Part of me feels like I need to shield Ayesha, because she's not ready to consider the nightmare scenarios. "And it's not going to help anyone if you talk like that. It's too scary."

"Good. I want to scare people. We should be scared. Then maybe people will rise up and do something."

"I get it. Some fear is good, but not if it makes you draw so much into yourself that you're petrified. That's not good for anyone. Take a look around. Don't be stupid."

Soheil's jaw tightens. He looks like he's about to say something but stops himself. Then he glances at Ayesha, and his face softens. "I...I'm sorry. I didn't mean to freak you out."

"It's okay. We're all on edge."

"Where's your block?" I ask, trying to ease the tension.

Soheil points across the Midway. "I'm on Block Six, with a hodgepodge of other Arab Americans."

It's only when Soheil phrases it that way that I realize we've been segregated by ethnic group.

Ayesha realizes it, too. "Damn. Our whole block is desi," Ayesha says, then looks at me. "I don't suppose it's a coincidence that they separated us?"

Soheil rubs the back of his neck and grimaces. "I don't think the Authority leaves anything to coincidence."

"Divide and conquer," I say. But I don't think either Soheil or Ayesha hears me; they're looking at each other with awkward half smiles.

"Oh my God," Ayesha says, glancing at her watch. "We're going to be late for the orientation. My mom is gonna freak."

"I'll catch up with you guys later, after we've been properly oriented, or whatever the hell they want to tell us about this fucking place," Soheil says.

Ayesha and I turn and walk toward our block as Soheil heads to his. With each step, another muscle in my body tenses. Ayesha clutches her stomach.

I see others walking back to their trailers, many already making their way to the Hub in small family groups. And it's so quiet. Too quiet. We're all different people, but each of us, to a person, has the same look: abject fear.

As we near our trailers, I turn to look back toward the mountains, the stunning granite peaks off in the distance. They're beautiful and stark against the sky, and I imagine how stunning the moonrise will be if we can see it this evening, a silver crescent hanging above the summit. But then I look again, and I see only fences and razor wire and guns.

I shiver as a desert chill sweeps through me.

CHAPTER 7

"Where were you?" my dad asks the moment I step back in the trailer. "The orientation is in fifteen minutes. Hurry. We can't be late."

"I'm sorry. I ran into Ayesha—the girl I met at the train station. We were walking around and didn't realize how big this place is, and we got a little lost."

"And you're covered in dirt!" My mom looks at me, wide-eyed. "What were you doing?"

"Nothing. It's the dust. I'll go clean up." I hurry to my room. I guess I'm calling it my room now. Funny how our minds cling to normalcy—desperately searching for the familiar in an environment that's totally foreign. No. That's wrong. It's not like being in another country, where you feel a weird sort of thrill when you find a piece of home, a person from your city, say, or even a vintage Coke sign. This place isn't foreign; it's forced. It's poison being shoved down our throats.

I quickly wash my face and scrub the dirt from my hands. I change into a gray Wilco T-shirt I got when David and I saw them in concert last summer. It seems like a million years ago now, and David a million miles away. I can't get all the dust out of my hair, so I opt for a ponytail and a green Wimbledon baseball cap. I think of the tennis team. A few of us agreed to help the coach run a clinic during the upcoming summer for the new varsity potentials to prep for the fall season. There will be drills and running lines and scrimmage matches and laughter and gossip. But not for me. My racket and tennis skirts are in my closet, awaiting cobwebs. Seems impossible that the entire world could lose all sense and decency in an instant.

And yet here we are.

We walk toward the Hub with hundreds of other families. An alarm blaring over the speakers silences everyone and signals the meeting. Again, I'm struck by the Americanness of the throngs of people. Every race, dozens of ethnicities, different ways of dressing, and, certainly, widely varying opinions about politics and life and Islam. But I guess that's the old America. Now we all have one thing in common—a religion that makes us enemies of the state. The state all of us are citizens of, the one most of us were born into. As we approach the Hub, I'm gutted by another realization: The armed guards, the ones looking down on us—they're all American, too. I scan the Midway for the face of the guard with the compass tattoo, the one who seemed— I stop that thought. It doesn't matter what I see in his face or in his eyes. To him, I'm the enemy. And to me, he is my jailer.

We walk into the vast Hub auditorium. UNITY. SECURITY. PROSPERITY. The words fill a giant screen at the back of the stage.

Even with the hundreds of people filing in, the space feels cavernous. I shudder when I think of the many internees who might be forced to join us here or be taken to the other camps, as yet unnamed and unpopulated. Muslims make up only about 1 percent of the total US population. But that's still almost three and a half million people. How can they imprison all of us? That would be like arresting 90 percent of Los Angeles. Besides the logistics, the very thought of it should be impossible to imagine here in America.

A large man wearing a black suit walks to the center of the stage—it's the same blotchy-faced man who watched the guards take down that kid. The loud echo of his footfalls quiets the buzz of voices in the hall. His face still looks like his tie cuts off the circulation to his head. He's flanked by what seems to be his own security detail. They don't wear military uniforms but suits, like the Secret Service, and with their fashy haircuts and vicious grins, they'd fit right in at a Unite the Right rally. The man stares at us as we enter, his eyes like daggers and his blubbery purple lips drawn into a plastic smile. If he were to add a polo shirt with a whistle around his neck, he'd look suspiciously like Mr. Connors, the thick-necked football coach at my high school. His voice thunders through the crowd. "Welcome to Mobius. I'm the Director of our camp, which takes its name from the Mobius Arch Loop Trail nearby."

"Welcome?" I whisper in Mom's ear. "He makes it seem like we had a choice to come here." My mom squeezes my hand and gives me her *be quiet* look—lips in shushing gesture, eyebrows drawn together.

"Now, we want to make life here as peaceful and enjoyable as possible. Take a little time to familiarize yourself with the camp and its layout. It's a big place, and there are a lot of opportunities here. There are recreation areas for the children as well as for adults. We're planning a vegetable garden. There's the warehouse where you can collect your rations and, of course, the Mess, where we'll take our dinners together as a community."

I stare at the Director, almost in awe of how he is able to twist the idea of imprisonment to make it seem like sleep-away camp. Community. Opportunity. Recreation. Garden. He speaks like he's the entertainment director on a cruise ship, not the warden of a prison camp. Looking around, I see people staring ahead, wide eyes brimming with fear, with tears, seething with anger. Some of them hush their babies, gently bouncing them so they don't cry out, trying to give them some comfort.

Watching this simple act of love destroys me. A prison camp isn't a place for children; it isn't a place for anyone. I lock eyes with a toddler. A little girl who can't be more than two or three. Her green eyes are bright, but dark circles under them betray her lack of sleep. Like the rest of us, she's tired. She stares at me, and in that heart-shaped face I see something familiar. Something I've seen before. I rack my brain.

Refugees.

Syrian refugees. That's who she reminds me of: a photo of a little girl, probably her age, staring through a chain-link fence into a photographer's lens. But that girl—the photographer caught her in the moment when the light in her eyes was extinguished. Stamped out not merely by fear but by being forgotten, by the complacency of the world around her. I first saw that picture in the daily digital news feed our history teacher made us subscribe to, and I think it might be the loneliest picture I've ever seen. This little girl, the one with the heart-shaped face—God, I don't want that light taken from her.

But I also see a few people nodding mechanically, probably thinking we should go along, maybe believing that will get them out of here sooner. I can't figure out if they're utterly clueless or genuinely hopeful that justice will prevail.

"You'll notice we've divided the blocks by your ethnic and cultural backgrounds. The Authority believes you'll be more comfortable among your own people."

My people are Americans. All of them.

The Director continues in his upbeat vocal swagger. "To help ease your transition, each block has its own minders. And the minders speak your language, for the most part. So they can understand everything." The Director pauses and then repeats himself. "Everything."

What an asshole. Each of his words bulges with threats. We're watching you. We're listening. We're everywhere.

He continues. "They're available night or day to assist you." He points to a row of a couple dozen people seated behind him. They are us: some in hijab, some in topis, some in jeans and T-shirts. Every race and ethnicity represented at the camp. Who needs your government to bring you down when your own people will do it for them?

The Director motions for the minders to rise. "These fine people share your background, understand your concerns. They come from your community, and they have kindly volunteered their time to help ease your transition into life at Mobius—"

"Traitors! Fascists!" A woman with her light-brown hair pulled back into a tight ponytail stands up in the middle of the auditorium and shouts at the minders onstage. A wave of murmurs pulses through the crowd, and some people at the back join her spontaneous protest. "Traitors!"

The Director's face reddens, but he keeps his voice calm. He motions to the guards to remove the woman who began the chants. "We won't have disruptions at Mobius. We are the first camp, and we will set the standard. And there will be consequences for anyone straying from the regulations."

As he speaks, two Exclusion Guards yank the woman from her seat and drag her to the aisle. The first guard pulls out handcuffs. The woman spits in the face of the second guard, who responds with a slap so hard that she falls to the floor. I feel sick to my stomach watching. The second guard moves to pull her up, but she flails at him and kicks him in the shin with the heel of her shoe. Then he tases her. A buzz fills the air, along with a piercing scream. He tases her again. The guards grab her arms, hoist her up, and drag her limp body out of the auditorium. All eyes in the room watch the door as it slams shut.

A silence descends. People are either too scared or too stunned to speak. No one seems sure where to look—at the floor, at one another. Some people cover their faces and mouths with their hands. I shake my head at my parents, tears stinging my eyes; I have no words. What use are my words in the face of this? My mom pulls me closer and grasps my hand tighter.

Eventually, our heads return to the stage and the Director, who has been standing there, unfazed, watching the scene unfold, not saying a word. It's a terrifying kind of quiet. The kind in a horror movie that tells you something unspeakable is about to happen and you're helpless to stop it.

The Director clears his throat. "Remember our motto." He points to the screen behind him. "Unity. Security. Prosperity. Now, dinner. Minders, call out your block number and walk them to the Mess."

When the minders call their blocks and march the short distance from the Hub to the Mess, hundreds of us follow in stunned silence. I think we're all shaken—not only at the cruelty of what we witnessed, but at the everydayness of it. How the Director didn't flinch; how the guards delivered those volts with such ease. I wonder where the woman was taken—if that display was merely the tip of the iceberg. A drone hums overhead, recording our silent procession.

The Mess is a giant characterless cafeteria, like you'd find in a public high school or a prison. Long tables with blue plastic chairs lining the sides. My Converse squeak against the gray-and-white checkerboard vinyl floor as I follow the masses inside. I guess it's vinyl? Some kind of epoxy coating, maybe? It actually feels a little squishy, soft underfoot. It's a large hall with a kitchen and a food line at one end, and stone-colored walls with colorful posters about handwashing and hygiene. Like I said, school or prison. There's a whiff of the bleach that is in our Mercury Home, but mixed with fried oil and what I used to call eau de cafeteria when I still ate lunch at school.

The Mess is also divided by blocks—small cardboard table tents are labeled with block numbers so we know where to go. The din rises as people find their tables and their voices, though I can't imagine anyone is actually saying what is on their mind.

My parents and I sort of hang out by our block tables, not sure what to do next. Then our minders pass by, introducing themselves. "I'm Saleem and this is my wife, Fauzia. Glad to meet you." They're young—I bet they're only in their twenties, and they don't seem to have any kids. I saw them on our block earlier. They're desi Americans, like us. But, you know, more backstabbing and collaborating. I wonder how they came to this, what the impetus would be to turn against your own.

I look around as people take seats in our segregated sections—South Asian, African American, Arab, Southeast Asian. East Asian and Latinx, too, though they seem to be fewer in number. Soheil was right. Everything is deliberate. Divide and conquer. We may all be Muslims, but we still have our prejudices and racism. It's simpler to play on our internalized "-isms" if you separate us and feed our fears—easier to make us "other" ourselves and do the Director's work for him. Today, we're all Muslims who've been forced here, but maybe it wouldn't be hard to tap into our bigotry to turn us against one another, to turn our gaze away from where our anger should really be directed. Classic colonial conquest strategy. Just ask the British.

Ayesha approaches us. She's holding hands with a younger boy and walking next to a middle-aged man and woman; I assume they're her family.

"Auntie, Uncle." Ayesha addresses my parents with the automatic honorific accorded all desis of parental age. Some of us may have lost our "mother tongue," as my *nanni* used to call it, but the custom of *tameez*—respect—for elders stays strong, despite decades of assimilation.

"These are my parents, Asfiya and Zaki, and my little brother, Zoubair," Ayesha says. Our parents shake hands.

"As-Salaam-Alaikum. Nice to meet you," my dad says. He pauses, then speaks again. "So much dust in this place."

"Yes, we can't even open the windows in our, um, Mercury Home," my mom says.

Ayesha's mom jumps in. "I don't know how we'll keep the clothes clean at all."

I look at Ayesha, and she shakes her head a little. I guess dust is going to be like the weather, the thing you talk about when you can't think of anything else to say.

We are allowed to get our food only when our block number is called. When it's our turn, Ayesha and I head toward the line, and our parents follow. We file past the cafeteria workers to collect our plates of rice and some unrecognizable vegetable stew. There are milk boxes, fruit cups, and Jell-O. "I feel nauseous," she says, looking at the food. "I don't know if I can eat."

"Same," I say.

"It's like junior high lunch all over again." Ayesha grimaces as we walk back to our table.

"Down to the hairnets and surly looks from the cafeteria workers." I scowl as I take my first bite. "And apparently, the only seasoning is salt. Is this supposed to be some kind of desi dish?"

"Serving this in a Pakistani home would be sufficient reason to be disowned." Ayesha scoots closer to me and whispers, "The Director—holy shit."

My upper body stiffens. I look around, worried that someone will hear her. But the clatter of lunch trays and cutlery is loud enough, so I let go of the tension in my shoulders. "I know. That was terrifying. It's like he's not even a real person. But the thing is, he *is* a person, which I guess makes it even more frightening. The scariest monsters are the ones who seem the most like you."

"Where do you think they'll take that woman?" Ayesha asks, lowering her voice to the barest whisper, even though I don't think anyone else can hear her.

Part of me doesn't want to think about it. "Jail, maybe? I mean, besides this open-air prison we're all in? I guess there's probably some kind of holding area here. I don't know. I kind of don't want to know what's happening to her," I admit. "I hope they don't hurt her. I mean, more than they already have."

I know I'm being naïve, but I want to hold on to some hope for the woman—for all of us. Even if it's a false one.

"It's not like we have civil liberties in here—or lawyers." Ayesha puts her hand over her mouth as this dawns on her.

"It's like Guantanamo, except in California. I'm scared of what will happen if we get stuck here. There's got to be something we can do...." My voice trails off.

Ayesha's eyes grow wide. She opens her mouth, then snaps it shut without a word. Maybe I've said too much.

We're quiet for a while. I don't think either of us can stomach any more discussion about the consequences the woman from the auditorium might be facing.

I push aside my plate of internment slop and tear open the fruit cup.

"So, which is your favorite?" Ayesha breaks the silence.

"Favorite what?"

"Star Wars film. Remember our conversation from earlier? At the train station? About Lando being the best?"

"Shit. That really was just earlier today, wasn't it?" Ayesha nods and looks down, then shovels a little bit of rice onto her fork and raises it to her mouth. She puts it back down. And sighs. My stomach twists a little. I know what Ayesha wants: a second of normalcy. I can give her that. I take a deep breath. "Well, I haven't seen anything before *The Force Awakens*, and I only went to that because my parents made me."

"You haven't seen the prequels or the original trilogy? The podrace? Young Luke? This is a travesty. We have to fix that."

I grin. "My mom had this girlhood crush on Luke Skywalker," I say. And it's true. "She talks about waiting in line to see *Star Wars* when she was kid, and I swear to God there's this reverence in her voice, like it was a religious experience. She joined Twitter to follow Mark Hamill."

Ayesha laughs. "I totally like your mom. But, hello, Riz Ahmed is in *Rogue One*. A desi in Star Wars. I still haven't recovered."

I laugh a little. It's nice to chuckle, to feel a moment of lightness. But I immediately silence myself because it also feels wrong. The moments of almost-normalcy hurt.

Saleem, our minder, stands. He's got a neatly trimmed brown beard, which I think he hopes makes him look older, but it doesn't hide his baby face. Fauzia stands up next to him and smiles at us. They're almost the same height and build, maybe five foot six, both kind of skinny, with shoulders like swimmers. Her smile feels almost genuine. Not Saleem's, though; apparently, he's not a good enough actor to make his slight smile look anything but forced.

"Block Two, we will walk back to our Mercury Homes together. Remember, we operate as a team." Saleem tries to make eye contact with as many people as possible while he speaks. He's so rigid and rehearsed, he sounds like a talking manual.

"There are lots of things to learn about, and I'm sure everyone would like to settle in," Fauzia adds. "A ten p.m. curfew is strictly enforced. We want our block to be perfect. The Director has promised extra privileges for the blocks that meet standards without any violations. Remember, if you have any questions, our door is always open." She pauses and then adds with a hesitant smile, "There are cameras, and drones will be monitoring. You'll be…safe. Unity. Security. Prosperity. *Khudafis*." Fauzia leaves us with the Urdu greeting "go with God." But I notice that Saleem grabs her hand and squeezes; she bites her lip and clears her throat. "I mean, have a good night."

Everyone in Block 2 begins to stand. A few hours, a creepy camp motto, one violent display of authority, and we do what we're told.

I do not like being told. Especially when what I'm being told is so clearly wrong.

Ayesha and I say good night. Her parents are in a hurry to get back to the block, so they speed-walk ahead. I don't blame them. The trailers might have cameras in them, but outside, in the open, it feels much more like we're animals in a pen, waiting to be slaughtered.

It's completely dark. The searchlights from the watch-towers sweep the grounds with swaths of light while guards patrol on foot, guns and Tasers at the ready. Their blank faces hide any feelings or fleeting doubts. As we turn the corner to Block 2, I stumble. The dirty-blond-haired guard with the tattoo is posted between Blocks 1 and 2. And like all the others, he has a Taser and a gun.

He turns and sees me looking at him. He tilts his chin and catches my eye, then spins his head back into its rigid, proper place.

CHAPTER 8

My body is wrecked, but I can't sleep. Every time my eyes close, I see that Suit in my house drawing a gun. Stop. Breathe. Sleep. Now I see the boy, the screaming mother. Stop. Breathe. Sleep. The woman getting tased. Over and over again in my mind.

I drag myself out of the lower bunk and splash cool water on my face.

We can't stay here. We can't be here.

But how the hell do we get out?

There has to be a way out. No wall is impenetrable.

I slip into my clothes and dusty sneakers and tiptoe out of my room. My parents' door is shut. I walk on cat feet through the tiny kitchen and living area, grabbing a key card off the table. I slink out of our trailer, making sure the lock clicks as quietly as possible. My parents will go ballistic if they catch me sneaking out after curfew.

There's a chill in the air, so I pull my hoodie up over my head. The same hoodie I wore when I snuck out to see David. I've been trying so hard not to let my mind rest on him. How I wish I'd been able to call him, see him, before I was taken away. How heart-shattering it is not to have said good-bye. I have to push him out of my mind, at least for now. If I actually allow myself to think about—to feel—how desperately I miss him, I won't be able to get out of bed.

There are fewer guards posted. The two closest ones are up a block, chatting. One smokes, the orange embers of his cigarette wafting to the dusty ground. Searchlights sweep the camp. I stay close to the trailers, hoping to hide in the shadows. I count the time between sweeps of the beams of light from the guard towers and sneak from trailer to trailer, trying to avoid detection and the consequences that come from breaking curfew. I flatten myself against the aluminum siding of a Mercury Home when a searchlight passes. Too close. My heart thuds in my ears. My breathing quickens.

I pause because I'm suddenly and stupidly aware that I don't exactly know where I'm going. And that I'm utterly alone out here in the dark. We're so far from anywhere that Mobius might as well be the moon. But I see the garden in the distance. And I remember that hole, or whatever it was, I saw at the fence before Soheil got in that scuffle with the guard. If an animal dug its way in, I wonder if maybe there's a way out.

The wind is still, and for that I'm thankful. I could do without another lungful of dust. The calm in the camp is eerie. In the distance, a high-pitched bark echoes in the foothills. It feels like the sound of loneliness. Goose bumps rise on my skin. There are no dogs at Mobius. Pets are forbidden. So maybe it's a coyote or a wolf or a fox. Honestly, I'm pretty sure I don't know the differences among any of those animals. What I do know is that for this one little moment, I'm glad an electrified fence exists between me and those sounds.

The mobile units are pretty close together, but a wide-open space stands between the last trailer and the garden. I hold my breath and wait for the searchlight to pass, then run across to the garden. I crouch down in the dirt against one of the big boulders as the light sweeps by again, but the edges of the bright beam fall short of me. I breathe.

I inch my way up to the boulder Ayesha and I came to earlier; that's where I was when I spied that burrow, that hole by the fence. I run my hand against the surface of the rock, feeling for the grooves of the initials we found before. When I find them, I rub my hand over the letters. They have a story. In some other time, two people came here willingly. They were probably young and in love. Who knows where they are now. Whether their love survived. So I'm pretending they are together somewhere, happy. It's make-believe, but it gives me a little hope. It reminds me that once there was a normal.

I flatten myself against the ground and creep forward so I'm facing the mountains, peering through openings between the orange plastic barriers. I squint into the darkness, searching for that hole. But it's impossible to see. I don't have a phone to illuminate my way. There is only the brilliance of the wandering searchlights, and I don't plan on getting caught in their beams. Still, I scan for that hole or, I don't know, some other way to get through the fence. An electrified fence. Maybe it's not really electrified. Maybe it's only a threat, a scare tactic. Maybe that's how an animal got through. That imaginary animal through that hole I can't see. And even if it wasn't totally stupid and risky, how could I possibly dig my way through? I look up at the razor wire. Even if the fence isn't electrified, even if I could scale it, how would I get over the top without being slashed to ribbons? And how would I even test it to find out if it *is* electrified?

What the hell am I even thinking?

I take a deep, shuddering breath and cry. I lay my cheek against the ground, and my tears mingle with the dirt. I feel jagged streaks of mud caking onto my face. I clench my hands into fists. Crying only makes me angry with myself. There's no use for tears here. But my rage—that I'll hold on to.

I hear the crunch of a footstep and then a small spray of pebbles hitting a rock. I gasp, then immediately cover my mouth with my hands.

A low male voice speaks from the other side of the rock: "You shouldn't be here."

My heart races. I turn and push myself off the ground. My

knees wobble, but I stand. My eyes dart around, then land on the face of the guard from the train. Compass Tattoo.

There's nowhere to run.

I take a deep breath. Then another.

Think.

Don't be stupid.

Smile.

The guard's eyes soften, but his jaw is tight. "What're you doing out here?"

"I…um, lost my necklace earlier, but I found it." I finger the silver infinity charm at my neck, my last link to David. "It was a gift from my boyfriend." I choke out the words. Don't cry. Not now. Not in front of him.

"You're breaking curfew. You realize that? You understand the consequences of breaking the rules here?"

"Are you going to report me?" My voice falters. I clear my throat. "To the Director?"

The guard takes a step closer to me. He blinks. I'm suddenly aware of the muddy trail of tears on my face. I brush away the dirt with the back of my hand. In the dark it's hard to read his face clearly, but he seems to grimace, like he's been hurt. Then he clenches his jaw. He takes me by the elbow, and I swear his fingers shake a little. He looks past me toward the mountains, then around us. We're alone.

"Please," I whisper. "I'm sorry."

He rubs his forehead with his free hand. "We need to get you back. Now."

He hurries me through the camp, dodging the searchlights, weaving in and out of the trailer homes to avoid unwanted attention.

The entire camp is asleep. I look up at the sky and see stars. Everywhere. I keep having the same sensation over and over: If this place weren't a prison, it would be beautiful. But as it is, I feel like the sky will light on fire any second now, and all the stars will crash into one another and burn away to ash. I slow down as we approach my Mercury Home. I probably shouldn't ask, but my curiosity too often gets the better of me. "Why aren't you turning me in?"

"Because I'm not—" He cuts himself off.

"Not an Exclusion Guard at an internment camp?"

He stops and looks me in the eyes. "Things aren't always as they seem, Layla."

He knows my name. I don't think it's good to be known in this place. We walk the last few steps in silence. But if he knows my name, it's only right that I know his. "What's your name?" I ask as we stop in front of my door.

He narrows his eyes at me, like he's trying to read something but the print is too small. He bends down and whispers, "I'm Corporal Reynolds. Don't do this again. There are snakes. And men who *will* shoot you."

CHAPTER 9

When I was walking out to the Mess the other night, I overheard two girls, probably from seventh or eighth grade, from Block 3—another desi block. One of them was talking about making a small curtain for the tiny window in her bedroom out of an extra pillowcase she'd decorated with markers. She seemed really happy to have something pretty to look at so her room "felt more homey," she said. My gut twisted when she said those words. That she was happy with something so small, so simple. People need to do what they can to manage the day-to-day in this place, but making Mobius feel like home is the last thing I want. To me it would feel like giving up. Still, I followed the girls back to their block after dinner and gave them the washi tape I'd brought along for some reason but hadn't bothered unpacking. Sometimes it's the small things that give us hope and make life bearable.

I'm sitting cross-legged on the floor of my little nondescript, white-walled prison room. Ayesha's on my bottom bunk. This room, this unit, it's claustrophobic, but Ayesha shares hers with her brother, so the small space of my room gives her a sibling-free refuge. Privacy. A tiny bubble where the cameras and guards and drones aren't looking at us.

I sigh. "We have no idea how long we're going to be in here, do we? We elected this guy who sees all of us as a threat. He doesn't have to let us out. We're like netted fish, struggling to find water, but we don't realize we're drowning on dry land. We have to get out."

Ayesha whispers, "What do you mean? How do you propose to get out?"

"I don't know. But we have to figure out something. There have to be others who feel the same way. I know there are. There's not just fear in the camp; there's anger, too."

"Anger can't turn off the electricity to the fence. And unless you're planning on getting out in a body bag—" Ayesha brings her hand to her mouth, stopping the words, but I was thinking them anyway.

"No. I'm planning on getting out alive. Think about it. There's never been a wall that people haven't been able to get by."

"You mean like the border wall?"

"Yeah. And the Berlin Wall. Did you learn about that in

history? Some people made it over in a hot-air balloon, or by digging a tunnel under the wall."

"We don't have shovels, and we don't have a hot-air balloon," Ayesha says. I shrug and let out a little groan. "Look," she continues, "I'm not saying that I'm not with you. I'm saying be realistic. Be smart. You're talking about the possibility of getting *killed*. My parents aren't going to go along with some escape plan. Would yours?" Ayesha's pitch rises as she speaks.

I shake my head. "They're too scared. But others aren't. Soheil. Us. I know we can't do something stupid, but I don't want to be buried and forgotten here."

I stand up and start pacing the tiny room, twisting the ends of my hair around my finger. I take a deep breath and puff out my cheeks, exhaling. When I turn to walk back in the other direction, I see Ayesha chewing on her bottom lip. She's worried.

"You're right," I say. "I didn't mean to sound flippant. Sorry. I don't know what's wrong with me. It's the dust. It's the isolation. It's the fence. It's David. I want to talk to David. To hear his voice, or maybe—"

"David?" Ayesha interrupts, and I realize I have been trying so hard not to think about him that I haven't told Ayesha about him, either. Saying his name out loud is a reminder of everything I've lost.

"My boyfriend. I guess he's still my boyfriend." I touch my infinity necklace. "I don't know when I'll see him again. And who's he going to take to prom?"

Ayesha's mouth drops open, and she tries to hold in a laugh. "I'm sorry. I'm so sorry. I didn't mean to laugh. I love how prom is on the list right after freedom and breathing."

"Oh my God. That's totally ridiculous, right? There are these moments when I still think this place isn't real—like it's a horrible dream. And for that minute, my mind feels free to think about, like, prom."

"I get it. We have to have those moments of remembering that we're human and thinking of regular stuff, or else the weight of this place would crush us. Like, have you seen *Footloose*?"

"The movie?" I ask.

"Yeah, it's, like, one of my mom's favorites from middle school. She made me watch it for mother-daughter bonding or something. Original only, not the remake. The entire premise is sort of ridiculous. Like, these kids stage a revolt because they're not allowed to dance in their town—some preacher says it's against the Bible or something."

"Like Sharia law for Christians." I roll my eyes, since every Muslim understands the hypocrisy of right-wing xenophobes. They're all terrified of a word they don't understand, scared that religious law is going to infiltrate the land, but meanwhile they support the death penalty, are anti-choice, and think creationism should be taught in schools because of... wait for it... religion.

Ayesha smirks at me. "Something like that. Anyway, they stage this dance outside the town limits to get around the law."

I grin at Ayesha, letting my mind float back to David, imagining prom with him. Thinking of the last real smile we shared and then our final terrible, helpless moments together when he was yelling at me to run.

"David," I say out loud. Ayesha looks at me. "David. He's on the outside. Maybe he could help us somehow. I mean, his dad used to work at the State Department. Though it's not like his dad has lifted a finger to help us so far. I doubt he's suddenly grown a conscience. I don't know. I might be grasping at straws, but that's all I've got right now."

"Can we even have visitors? You could try to put in a phone request to talk to David, but the Director's people totally listen in." She pauses. "Do your parents know you have a boyfriend?"

I nod, and Ayesha rises, knocking her head on the edge of the bunk as she stands up. "Dammit."

"Are you okay? I keep doing that, too. Everything in this place is against us, even the stupid too-low bunk."

Ayesha rubs her head. "I'm okay, but go on. I'm fascinated by this whole parental-knowledge-of-boyfriend situation."

I grin. "I don't give them all the details, but, yeah, they know. David comes over for dinner. He sometimes comes to the mosque with us. Last Ramadan, he even fasted a few days."

"Whoa. Is he going to convert?"

"What? No. We've never even discussed it. His family is Jewish, and that's really important to him. I mean, half his dad's family was killed in the Holocaust, and his mom's family are Yemenite Jews who were refugees—some of them just disappeared from camps." I pause, suck in my breath, listening to my words echo in my brain. History suddenly seems terrifyingly present. "They've gone through so much to hold on to their family and their faith. David feels that very deeply, a kind of gratitude that his family survived, an obligation to never forget and also to speak truth."

Ayesha looks at me with wide eyes. "Wait. So David is brown *and* Jewish?"

I nod. "Honestly, when we first met in grade school, I thought he was desi. I think I just wanted to not be the only one, you know?"

"A desi Muslim girl from an immigrant family and a brown Jewish son of a refugee—you're like a dream team for Model UN."

I grin. "David knows his dad has white privilege, but he's seen his mom get hit with anti-Semitism *and* racism, so he kind of gets it, you know? We try to be open to learning about each other's faiths—ask questions, talk things out."

Ayesha nods. "That's so great."

"And, oh my God, for Shabbat dinners his mom makes *marak temani*—an amazing Yemeni stew—and this flaky, fried bread called *malawach* that I love more than my mom's parathas. Don't tell her I said that!"

Ayesha laughs. "That would earn you a one-way ticket to a boarding school in India."

I give her a tiny smile and then clear my throat, pretending

I don't feel a lump welling in it. "Anyway...can you imagine anyone wanting to convert now? Publicly? It would be too dangerous."

"A woman converted at our mosque a couple of months ago. She knew the risks. And honestly, her Arabic pronunciation puts mine to shame."

"What? Seriously? Is she in here, too?"

"Nah. I don't think so. It was after the census. Also, she's white, and I don't see any white converts in here. White-looking Arabs, yes. White-white Americans? No. Maybe they'll be brought in here soon, too. But you've looked around. You know."

"There's, like, a hierarchy for bigots, isn't there? Like their hatred of Muslims isn't equal. They dispense it in degrees. They hate some of us more. Like, the darker your skin or the more foreign-sounding your name. And if you're black *and* wear hijab, you're getting the brunt of it."

"Honestly, I think some racists think Islam is a race or ethnicity and not a religion. Like we're all brown and from Muslimistan."

A knock interrupts us. My mom's muffled voice comes through the door. "Honey, we need to get Ayesha home. We don't want her parents to worry."

"Just a sec. We'll be right out."

Ayesha grins. "Your parents knock and don't immediately barge in? They're a dream. Maybe we can get them to talk to my parents."

I take my parents for granted sometimes. I know plenty of

kids, Muslim and not, who envy the trust my parents have in me. I've never really had to hide who I am in front of them. I know a couple of girls at the mosque who want to date openly and not sneak around. And others who are willing to be arranged. And there's a girl who is both hijabi and the homecoming queen. The thing is, my parents always told me never to judge another Muslim's religiosity. Each of us practices in our own way, and God alone judges. "'Let there be no compulsion in religion.'" Can't count the number of times my parents have quoted that *ayat* passage to me.

Ayesha and I exchange sad, knowing looks that don't need words. I open my door. My parents and I walk her the few steps back to her trailer. Ayesha's mother sits on the steps to their Mercury Home in anticipation. Who can blame her? The fever pitch of anxiety and fear is the everyday current mood at this place. We're all hyper alert, a constant rush of adrenaline coursing through our bodies. I wonder what the crash will be like when it comes.

While my parents exchange salaams with Ayesha's mom, I give my friend a quick hug and whisper, "I'm going to see if I can get to David. Maybe there is some way he can help us." I'm really not sure if David could do anything for us, even if I am able to reach him somehow, but I want to leave her with a little hope as we say good-bye and gaze on the melancholy, drawn faces of our parents. I swear all the parents here have only two looks anymore—terrified worry, and a mask with a fake smile trying to hide their terror so their kids don't notice.

When we leave Ayesha's trailer, there's still an hour before curfew, so I convince my parents to take a short walk with me. Every time I'm outside now, I'm always watching. Looking for a way out. Paying attention to the guards who seem a little bored. In the dark, the searchlights and watchtowers are a menacing reminder that we're locked away. And I know the drones hover somewhere above our heads; I can feel the hum in my bones. The three of us quietly find our way back to our Mercury Home. Corporal Reynolds is stationed at the top of our block. He catches my eye but then quickly turns away.

CHAPTER 10

"Honey, get up. Your dad and I are heading to the community-planning meeting at the Hub. Then we're going to prayers—a few people are gathering for namaz in a trailer in Block Eight. Eat something."

I roll over and try to rub the exhaustion from my eyes. I never seem to sleep deeply here. It's like I'm asleep, but always on the edge of waking up. On the edge, period. "Okay, Mom. Got it." I stick my hand out from under the blanket and give my mom a thumbs-up, since she's popped her head inside the door. Once she leaves, I get out of bed and stare into the mirror above the sink. Dark circles have taken up residence under my eyes.

My parents seem to be settling in. Everyone is. Meeting

people, organizing a school, scheduling regular prayers, divvying up work. My mom's actually seeing chiropractic patients at the clinic that some of the doctors have set up in a partitioned section of the Hub. Every day for the past couple of weeks, my parents have been dropping hints that I should make friends, find something useful to do, form a book club. But the so-called library here is pathetic—there are barely any books, and it seems like all the internment-approved titles are by long-dead white dudes. I don't want to settle in. I don't want to adjust to the constant surveillance and the threatening gaze of white guards with weapons, and the permanent smile of death from the Director's purple lips. I don't want anyone to get used to it.

And I need to see David. For no reason. For all the reasons.

I swing my legs over the side of the bottom bunk, making sure not to hit my head as I get up. It's a lesson I learned the hard way during the first few days here at Mobius. I brush my teeth and scrub my face, being careful not to use too much water. Everything is rationed. There is food and water for everyone, but no extra. The worst is the shower timer. I miss taking long showers and washing and conditioning my hair. We all get five minutes a day. There is no luxuriating. No luxury, period. You can't even cheat, because the shower turns off automatically. Another valuable first-week-of-internment lesson: Take a shower at night so you don't feel like you're sleeping in a sandstorm. The most important lesson I've learned, though? Don't count all the things that existed for you Then that you don't have Now. Don't make that list. It will drive you mad.

There's a knock at the door. I let Ayesha in. We've been hanging out, doing our best to escape the claustrophobia of living behind a guarded electric fence—gabbing, taking circuitous walks around the camp, meeting other kids who have nothing to do.

And plotting how the hell we can get out of this place. Trying to reach David and get him to help feels both childish and impossible. But there's no other solution we've come up with that doesn't involve death—or at least the chance of it. We're starting to realize that maybe it's a risk we have to be willing to accept if we really want to get out of here and aren't just pretending at escape. I haven't shared this with Ayesha yet, but I'm giving myself two more weeks to figure it out. I work best with a deadline.

"Is David swoon-worthy?" Her question totally comes out of left field.

"I'm sure he thinks he is." I laugh. "But I never tell him that, since I don't want him to get a big head. And is there anyone you find swoon-worthy? Someone in this camp, perhaps? Someone you've been talking to in the dinner line? Someone named Soheil?"

Ayesha grins. "Maybe. He seems to go out of his way to talk to me. And I am definitely encouraging him to do so. He's cute. He's smart. He's funny. But what can flirting be in this place besides an exercise in futility? I mean, it's not like we're going to go out on a date and then to prom."

I grab Ayesha's hand and squeeze. I'm glad she has a little distraction.

I take a long, deep breath while David's smiling face fixes itself in my mind. "I miss David. A lot. I know it's only been a couple of weeks since I last saw him, but it feels like I haven't seen him in years. It's this place. It messes with time."

"I know. And I swear if I hear the Director's word vomit of Unity, Security, Prosperity again, I'm going to scream. People are so scared of getting tased and disappearing that they're all keeping quiet. My parents are at the meeting, too, and my little brother is playing soccer with a bunch of kids from this block and a couple of others. Some of the minders are the coaches. It's fucked up."

The disappearances started last week. At first I didn't notice, but there's been talk. The whisper network, Soheil called it. Someone goes missing, taken in the night or ordered to report to the Hub for questioning for some reason, and that person never comes back. I guess they—the Director, his private security detail, the guards—try to keep their actions quiet. Except when they don't.

Three days ago, I heard that two guards caught a man leaving the Hub after curfew. Apparently, he'd snuck in and attempted to access a computer. They stopped him as he was trying to get back to his trailer undetected, and he slashed one of them in the arm with a knife he'd stolen from the Mess.

When his partner tried to find him, the guards said he was gone. Not taken to a hospital, not in the brig. Gone. That's all they told him. I saw that man, the partner of the one who'd gone missing. I was walking toward the Hub, and there was a crowd watching him run from guard to guard, frantic, asking questions about his boyfriend—where he was, when he'd return. The guards ignored him for a couple of minutes. Then one of them lost his patience with the man. The guard butted the man in the shoulder with his rifle. The man fell to the ground. The guards handcuffed him and took him away, too. The thing is, he didn't even fight back. And the rest of us who saw it happen just stood there. Doing nothing. Saying nothing. And then we dispersed. Two men, vanished.

That's why I have to figure some way to get out of here— to escape. When people lose hope, that's when the Authority knows they've broken you.

"Soheil is in, right?" I ask.

"What?"

"He'll help us?"

"I don't know. I think so, but I haven't asked him directly. We mostly talk about, like, our favorite fandoms and the crappy food here."

"I saw him arguing with his parents when they were walking out of the Mess last night. His mom tried to shut him down, but I heard him say he wasn't going to play dead when our rights were being trampled."

Ayesha whisper-sings, "'You say you want a revolution—'"

"What's up with you and the golden oldies? It's like an affliction."

"It's my parents. They skipped the lullabies and started us with the Beatles, and then worked their way up to Nirvana, which is where their extensive knowledge of music comes to a screeching halt."

I'm not paying full attention; I'm staring out my little window as an idea forms. Corporal Reynolds is talking to the guards posted at my block. This place inspires secrets. I have mine, but so do others.

"Follow me." I get up from the floor.

"Oooh, are we hitting the mall? Maybe a movie?"

"The shortest distance between two points is a straight line."

"Are we speaking in code now?"

I shake my head. "I keep thinking about how I can get to David. We're allowed phone calls, right? I'm going to ask."

"But they're totally listening in on the calls. And you have to submit a requisition."

"Yup. I know. But I'm going to roll the dice on a hunch." I walk out of my room. Ayesha follows. When we step out of my trailer, I turn to her and say, "Go along with it, okay? And then go back to your trailer. Now look concerned, like you're trying to console me. I'm going to start crying."

Ayesha knits her eyebrows together. "Well, that won't be hard, because I am concerned that you're about to do something stupid."

I stop and turn to Ayesha and take her hand. "Listen. You

don't have to go along with this. I know there are risks, but we've been talking for days. I'm tired of talking."

Ayesha nods. I wait for her to head toward her trailer, but she squeezes my hand and smiles.

We turn back toward the guards, toward Corporal Reynolds. Fake crying isn't hard. It's stopping yourself from crying that is more challenging in this place.

As we near the head of the block, I clear my throat loudly and wipe away my tears. Corporal Reynolds looks at me; so do the other guards. He takes a step toward us. I haven't spoken to him since he caught me outside after curfew. I wipe my clammy hands on my jeans. Ayesha puts her arm around my back and squeezes. She also steadies me, because my knees buckle a little.

"Ladies." Corporal Reynolds removes his mirrored-lens sunglasses as he steps closer. "Is there a problem?"

Here goes nothing. "I need to make a phone call."

Corporal Reynolds takes a deep breath. "There's a procedure for that."

"I...it's just that—"

"It's her one-year anniversary, and she wants to talk to her boyfriend. She hasn't gotten to talk to him since we've been in here." Ayesha tilts her head toward me. "Can't you help? Please." The tone in her voice is pitch-perfect—concern, pity, slight pleading for a rescue.

He looks at us. Pauses. Pausing is good. It means he's

thinking about it. My shoulders tense; I feel Ayesha's arm tighten around my back.

Corporal Reynolds nods. "Okay, come with me."

Ayesha and I exhale. I give her a little hug, and she whispers, "*Jazak Allah.*" Tears spring to my eyes, maybe because it's the first time it actually feels like I really need divine intervention in my life. May God reward us all.

Corporal Reynolds and I walk toward the Hub. The adrenaline surging through me makes my heart feel like it might explode out of my chest. I swallow and keep swallowing. I'm so parched. I try to focus outward. He keeps his eyes ahead as he strides forward. When he realizes I have to speed up to keep pace, he slows down. Even, regular steps. His broad shoulders round forward ever so slightly when he walks. He keeps his hair cropped short in the back. I can tell it's been recently cut because of the uneven tan on the skin visible between his shirt collar and the back of his fitted sandstone infantry cap. His sleeves are rolled all the way down today, so I don't see his compass tattoo.

I feel like I should say something. I'm not quite sure why, but this silence feels weighty, too inflated, and I want to let the air out. Maybe it will help me breathe. But my mind goes blank. I clear my throat. "Corporal Reynolds, um...sir? I was wondering if you binged the new season of *Jessica Jones*? We don't get it on the inside. And I'm dying to know what happens. But mainly what happens with Jessica Jones and Luke

Cage. I hate that Iron Fist is making a cameo. He's so whiny. I couldn't even watch his series; it was totally whitewashed."

Corporal Reynolds slows down and furrows his eyebrows at me for a second before his face relaxes a little. "It's on my watch list, but I haven't started this season. I'll let you know."

"Thanks," I say. Then I work up a little more courage to continue. "And thank you for letting me call David."

"We'll see how it goes. Don't say anything to anyone."

I nod. I glance at his holstered gun, and then I'm in my home and the Suit is drawing his handgun on me and the other Suit is throwing my dad to the ground and I hear my mom's scream. She would be screaming right now, too, if she saw me walking anywhere with a guard. I shake my head and mutter to myself to remember to breathe.

"Did you say something?"

"Me? Oh, I'm just—" I decide to tell the truth. "I'm reminding myself to breathe."

"Breathe?"

"My family was forced into a prison camp for basically being alive, and you have a gun that you can use to shoot me if I do anything I'm not supposed to. So, yeah, I'm trying to breathe." My jaw clenches. I can imagine the look of horror on my mom's face if she were listening to me. How frightened she and my dad would be. I'm terrified, too, but I'm so tired of doing what I'm told to do and going along with this bullshit.

The corporal slows his steps, then stops short and turns

to me. "I'm not going to shoot you." He speaks slowly, enunciating each syllable. He opens his mouth, hesitates. "Also, you're right. Lewis Tan should have played Iron Fist." The curve of a smile almost appears, but he seems to force it off his face. Then he continues walking, faster. I hurry to keep pace, allowing myself a small grin.

We get to the Hub, but he directs me to a trailer located beside the admin building, where the Director has an office. Corporal Reynolds looks around before he points me to a side door, which he quickly opens and then ushers me through.

It's a trailer like the one my family was assigned to, but without a kitchen or living area. The unit has been retooled into an office. There's a rectangular table—like the kind we set up for bake sales at school, but narrower—pushed against one side of the trailer. Three gray metal folding chairs are beside it. He motions to one of two phones on the table. I take a seat. He picks up the handset and enters some kind of code. He hands it to me.

"Two minutes," he says.

I hold the phone to my ear. I don't remember the last time I picked up a landline. I mock my parents for still having one. But there it is: a dial tone. A regular landline dial tone, reaching out from the past like a security blanket, a sign that the world beyond this fence still exists. The phone slips in my sweaty palm, and I quickly reposition it at my ear. With shaking fingers, I press the buttons that will lead me to David. Or at least to his voice. There are only three numbers besides my own that I've memorized: My parents' cells. And his.

I wonder if he'll sound different. I wonder what I should say to him to get him here somehow—to get his help—while the corporal and whoever else listens in. He's turned his back to me, at least. It's not much, but it's a gesture to give me a pretend kind of privacy.

Ring.

My heart thumps in my ears. It reverberates through my entire body. A sort of lightness swells in my chest, and I think it's something like hope. It hurts. Like a muscle I haven't used.

Ring.

Two minutes. Think, Layla. Get David here. Tell him you love him. But don't waste all your time on sentimental mushy stuff.

Ring.

Panic grips me. I look around, and my eyes fall on the microwave clock flashing the time in bright-green numbers. It's a school day. David's in school. Right now he's in English class.

No. No. No. No.

Ring.

Ring.

"Hey, it's David. You know what to do."

The phone beeps. And then there's only silence. "David," I whisper, choking on my words. But then fury surges through me and I slam the phone down. My mom's voice pops into my head: *Take a breath, Layla.* I push her voice out of my mind, shove it away, along with every ounce of reason I have. I'm angry. Rage burns my insides. I can't temper my feelings with logical thinking.

Corporal Reynolds whips around, startled by the loud clatter of the handset against the phone's base. "Is there a problem?"

"A problem? A problem?" I start to laugh but choke on it. "Where should I start? It's not one problem; it's a million. It's my life. It's the fact that I'm in this fucking camp because I had the gall to merely exist." My stomach twists in knots, and I can hear my voice getting louder and my breath faster. But I don't stop. I step closer to Corporal Reynolds. "And you and everyone in here, every guard, every politician, every neighbor who watched us get taken away and said nothing—this nightmare is on you. I can't even make a goddamn phone call to hear my boyfriend's voice without begging. And I'm so sick of it. I hate the president. And I hate you. I hate you so much right now because you can shoot me for no reason at all and no one will say a word. And I hate myself, too, because I'm so fucking stupid to yell at a guard, and now I have to bow down and count on your mercy to not throw me in the brig or disappear me like all those other people who just wanted to live." I suck in my breath. Hot tears splash across my face. I wipe them away with my sleeve, waiting. Waiting for Corporal Reynolds to say something, to do something. To handcuff me, to punch me, to take me away.

But he doesn't. He shifts his weight from one foot to the other while staring down at his boots. Then he lifts his head and meets my gaze. The air in this trailer is too thick to breathe. My cheeks are burning up. Still he says nothing, just stares at me with a sort of pained look in his eyes.

Finally, he takes a deep breath, clears his throat, and gives me a slight nod. He steps forward, opens the trailer door, and walks out.

I pause. I feel a little like throwing up. I can't take back anything I said. More important, I don't want to take it back. Maybe this was totally stupid, but a part of me feels good. Maybe even happy. Does that make me even stupider? I don't know. Maybe it just makes me human.

I open the door; the sun blinds me. I raise my hand to shade my eyes. Corporal Reynolds is waiting for me. He gives me a sad sort of smile. We walk back to Block 2 without another word.

CHAPTER 11

I pick up a little rock and throw it toward the mountains. That's exactly what I feel like: a little rock against a mountain. I sit leaning back on one of the boulders in the garden. David's message plays over and over in my head. I only choked out one word before succumbing to my anger and slamming down the phone. God, I'm a genius. He probably thinks I've lost my mind. Maybe I have. At least I got to hear his voice on his message. But it's a shitty consolation prize.

I'm at the farthest end of the rock garden, trying to give Ayesha and Soheil some semblance of privacy. Ayesha's worried about being caught alone with him, so I'm her cover for this quick visit with Soheil.

Out of the corner of my eye, I see Soheil inch closer to Ayesha—they're perched on one of the giant rocks. I quickly turn away, occupy myself again with throwing pebbles. I'm not looking, but they're only about ten feet away. I can hear everything, but I pretend not to.

"Do you think it's weird we met in here?" Ayesha asks Soheil.

"'Weird' is one way to say it. Another is 'fucked up,'" Soheil responds. "But I'm so glad we did."

Ayesha laughs. "Yeah, it's not exactly how I imagined a meet-cute."

"How did you picture it?"

"Well, I guess I saw myself entering this giant auditorium. It's packed, people jostling for a seat. Excitement crackles in the air. It's the Star Wars panel at Comic-Con. Then I see him, across the crowded room. This handsome guy—"

"You forgot dashing," Soheil interrupts.

"Oh, sorry. There's a handsome, dashing guy across the room. Our eyes lock. All we see is each other, and then the action slows around me, the faces blur. He walks up to me. And my heart is beating, like, super fast. And he extends his hand and says, 'Hi, I'm Riz Ahmed.'"

I try to stifle a snicker. I turn my head to catch Ayesha's eye, but she's only looking at Soheil, whose laugh is loud and warm.

The camp-wide siren sounds.

"Why don't you guys go ahead to dinner. I'll catch up," I say to Ayesha and Soheil.

"You okay?" Ayesha asks.

"Yeah, I'm good. Need a minute alone." I smile as the two of them set off.

Dinner in the Mess. Again. I don't think I can stand much more of this. More pretending. More fake smiles and meaningless exchanges with the minders, who always make sure to say hello to each of us during dinner. More sitting on edge but faking like everything is normal. More wanting to scream but holding it in because screaming gets you dragged away. In the Mess, we're all together in an enclosed space, minders and guards everywhere, and the air is so charged with fear and anxiety, but we can't acknowledge it; we're too scared to draw attention. In this place, the last thing you want is attention.

I close my eyes. As the sun sets, the evening cools. If I block everything out, for a minute—just for a minute—I can breathe without a weight on my chest. I let my mind float where it wants to go. It always settles on everyday things. Going to the movies. Air-conditioning. Ice cream. Kissing David in the stacks of the school library. School. For the barest second, I pray that I'll wake up from this nightmare and be home. Then I force myself to open my eyes and face the stark desert. There's no place for nostalgia here.

"Layla." The sound of his voice makes me jump up. Corporal Reynolds is alone. He hasn't turned me in for yelling at him. And for saying I hate the president, which used to be free speech but qualifies as treason now. Not clapping for the president at his damn State of the Union address is practically sedition. And some people still think this is a democracy.

I wipe the dust off my jeans. Pretend everything is okay. Well, as okay as it can be. I nod. "I know. I know. Mealtime. I'll hurry and get to my five-star dinner," I say, and begin walking toward the Mess. I usually meet my parents there. They'll panic if I don't show up on time.

Corporal Reynolds grabs my elbow.

I freeze. I look up at him, my mouth open. Waves of dread wash over me, and every internal alarm I have is blaring. Maybe I was stupid for thinking he wasn't going to turn me in. Maybe he was waiting to find me alone so I would be easier to take away. Oh God, how could I have been so careless?

"I...I'm sorry. I didn't realize I was late. I'll run to catch up with the others." I lick my lips. Suddenly I'm parched. I blink back tears.

"It's okay. You're fine. I'm not taking you anywhere. Sorry. I shouldn't have touched you." He lets go of my arm. "Layla," he starts again, but this time his voice is softer. "Hang back a second. I have something for you."

People make their way to the Mess. The guards stationed at the blocks usually follow us to dinner before switching shifts. Everyone's back is turned toward us. My instinct is to run. It's always to run. But where? I wonder if after a while your body starts to wear down when you don't listen to that fight-or-flight response. Does it start to give you the wrong signals because you've ignored all the earlier ones? Does that swooshing sound in your ears ever stop?

"I'm sorry you couldn't get through to your boyfriend yesterday."

That's what he came to tell me? I stare up at him in disbelief.

"Look," he says, and then carefully pulls what seems to be an ancient flip phone from his pocket and places it in my hand. "It's a burner."

My brain does not process what he's giving me.

"Put it in your pocket. I'm going to escort you back to your trailer, and you're going to walk into your bathroom clutching your stomach, and then call your boyfriend. You only have a few minutes. If anyone asks, you got sick by the garden, and I brought you here and then to the Mess. Do you understand?"

A million thoughts whir through my brain, but I can't speak. I only nod. We walk down the Midway. A couple of other stragglers ahead of me jog toward the Mess, but when we turn toward my block, it's empty. No one wants to be late to anything here. We're constantly reminded there will be consequences. No specifics. But that word lingers in the air here. Consequences.

When I get into my trailer, I head straight for the bathroom, bent over, arms wrapped around my middle, like Corporal Reynolds instructed me.

David picks up on the first ring. "Hello?"

"David," I whisper. "It's me."

"Oh my God, Layla."

"Shh," I say, not knowing where he is or if anyone might be listening on his end.

"I can't believe I'm hearing your voice. How are you calling me? Holy shit. Are you okay? What are they doing to you? Are you hurt? Did they say anything about when they might release you? Do you—"

His voice. David's voice. Home. But this isn't the time for nostalgia. Or sentimentality. Or even feelings, really.

"David," I cut him off. "I miss you so much. I love you. But I—"

"I love you, too. I miss you. I can't believe how fucked up everything is right now."

"David, I need your help. Can you come here? Can you visit me? I'm at—"

"I know where you are. My dad's old State Department contacts told him. My father's a jerk, but I told him if he didn't find out where you were, I'd never talk to him again. And of course I'll come there. But do they allow—"

There's a loud knock at the trailer door. Crap.

"David, I have to go. Please, I'll figure something out. I need you. Maybe we can come up with a way to sneak you in."

Another loud knock on the door, and then I hear it open.

"Good-bye, David. I love you."

"Layla. Wait. Listen, it's lunch; that's why I have my phone. But from now on I'll keep it on me all the time. Let it ring once, hang up and dial again. Then I'll know it's you. Also, I love—"

"Layla." Corporal Reynolds's voice fills the entire trailer. "We have to go. Now."

I hang up on David, slip the phone in my pocket, and step out of the bathroom.

Corporal Reynolds practically pulls me out the door. "The next shift of guards is arriving," he whispers. "Remember, you were sick so I escorted you to your Mercury Home." He quickly scans the vicinity, then gestures for me to give him the phone. He palms it and kneels in the dirt to adjust his laces, tucking the phone in the gap between his sock and boot.

He takes me by the elbow and walks me past the guards, who are taking their positions at the head of our block. The two salute him. He nods, and we continue to the Mess.

The other guards give him deference. I mean, they're required to, I guess. But for some of them, the look in their eyes makes it seem like more than a robotic gesture.

I look at Corporal Reynolds as we continue on. Not sure what to make of him, exactly. He's a guard with a gun. But he's also taking a risk to help me. Corporal Reynolds is a puzzle with lots of pieces, but half of them are missing. So I can't really see who he is.

"Why are you doing this? Helping me?"

"It's only a phone call," he says. Then adds, "I have my reasons." His tone is gruff. Like he's mad, but at himself.

"Thank you, Corporal Reynolds," I say as we approach the Mess. And I mean it. I don't exactly trust him; those missing puzzle pieces could be anything. They could be hiding a monster, but my gut tells me that what he's hiding isn't so nefarious.

Before we are in earshot of the guards outside the Mess, he bends down and says softly, "Call me Jake. And believe me when I tell you this: Whatever you're planning, whatever you think you might be able to do, think again. Don't do anything stupid. You can get yourself hurt or killed in here. More easily than you know."

CHAPTER 12

There is no news. Not inside the fence. I mean, we hear things. The whisper network is never silent: talk of protests on the outside, marches. The government trying to censor the outcry on social media. Word of a second camp being readied. But it's whispers mostly, bits of rumor from the staff here who aren't military, the ones who feel twinges of guilt that make them feign not a friendliness but a base level of civility. Maybe their neighbor is Muslim; maybe they had a Muslim classmate. Maybe they'd never met a Muslim until they came here, looked one of us in the eye, and realized we are human beings who laugh and cry, like they do. Who are flesh and bone. And who bleed. And that scant thread of civility, that nod or half smile, that extra pat of butter on a scoop of mashed potatoes, sometimes comes with tiny tidbits from the world beyond the fence before it makes its way around Mobius. Like the telephone game—when the final sentence is uttered, it doesn't quite sound like what it started out as. But you can imagine what it was. You can hope.

There's a knock on my door. My parents. Both of them. Standing there with their tea and an extra cup. Tea is their normal morning ritual, but having it in my bedroom is not. In some way, maintaining some rituals helps them. They pray, and my mom always has her tasbih bracelet with her. I know they also enjoyed the normalcy of the way they structured their lives back home. When Dad was fired, and when Mom's patients started dropping off, they were sometimes like ghosts of themselves. They never said anything like that to me; they always tried to shield me, to protect me even from the slightest troubles, but I could tell. And here it's so much worse. I mean, Mom is spending her days at the clinic cracking backs, and Dad is meeting with other teachers and professors to ready a makeshift school, beginning with the younger kids. They're trying to help other people, in their own way; because, knowing them, I can guess at how helpless they must feel inside. I feel the same way.

"*Beta*, have some tea with us?" my dad asks. "We thought it would be fun for you, like breakfast in bed."

I knit my eyebrows, unsure of what they're talking about. But I move aside and they step in and my mom closes the door behind them.

I pull out the chair at my little desk and gesture for my

mom to take a seat. She hands me my cup before sitting down. I take a sip. Sugar and milk, how I like it. My dad finds a comfortable spot to sit cross-legged on the floor, his back against my door. I position myself in the small floor space between the chair and my bed.

Then I look at them and shrug. "You guys have something you want to say to me?" I ask. There are no cameras in the bedrooms. So this definitely means something. There's no other reason they'd squeeze in here for tea, which they prefer to take leisurely—a reminder of what life was before.

My mom nods at my father, who clears his throat. "Some of the others were saying that they—"

She interrupts him. "A couple of the other parents were saying they saw you going somewhere with that guard, the tall one who never smiles."

I tense up but try not to show it on my face. "None of the guards ever smile, Mom. They're guards, not the fun squad on a Carnival cruise."

My mom raises an eyebrow at me. "No need to be so sarcastic. Are you saying it's not true? You weren't seen walking to the Hub with that guard?"

Shit. I guess I've been kind of careless. Can't let that happen again. "I...it was nothing. I asked him if I could call David."

"What?" My mom raises her voice. "Are you crazy? Asking a guard for a favor? Do you understand what he could do to you?"

"*Jaan.*" My dad uses his favorite term of endearment for my mom—my soul, my life—and pats the air with his palm down, a quieting gesture. "Let Layla explain." They both look at me.

"I'm sorry. It was nothing. I asked him if we really get a call allotment and if I could call David. I walked there with him but then remembered David was in English class, so I wouldn't be able to get through anyway. That's all." Mostly that's the truth. It's all I can give them now, without worrying them even more.

My mom's bottom jaw practically hits the floor. "Layla, do you have any idea how foolish you were? To even ask him? You put yourself in danger. We don't ever want you to be alone anywhere with one of these guards. You never know what they could—" She doesn't allow herself to complete that thought.

My dad picks up her thread. "Layla, the best thing we can do here is keep our heads down. Don't attract attention. Fade into the crowd. Stay as anonymous as possible. That's how we'll survive."

I had raised the cup to take a sip of tea, but I put it down on the floor next to me, harder than I mean to, and some of it spills over. I pull my hand back and wipe the hot liquid from my pants. "Survive? Is that all we want now? To survive? What about wanting to live? Have we all forgotten that? Have we all decided that our entire lives are going to be spent here? Did I miss the memo?"

"Layla." My mom usually tries hard to soften the edge in her voice when she feels it coming on, but not this time. "You're young. Too young and too foolish to understand what's happening here. We have no rights and no power, and no one in this family is going to take any risks. Do you understand me?"

"*Beta.*" My dad tries to temper my mom's voice by adding his calmer tones. He takes a breath. "Do you remember that line I wrote, 'Only when you open yourself to the heart's silence can you hear its roar'?"

"I thought you wrote that poem after I was born, about finding love in quiet places."

My dad smiles. He stands up, walks over, and squeezes next to me on the floor and strokes my hair like he used to when I was little. I look at my mom, and there are tears in her eyes. "It is about that. But it's also a reminder that being quiet doesn't always signify weakness. Sometimes it takes great strength to find that silence. Sometimes it takes incredible strength to survive."

My mom takes a deep, quivering breath. My heart hurts for her. For both of them. I worry about them, too, but I can't imagine how much more they worry about me. I mean, they built their entire life around my existence. I know they mean well. I don't share their worldview. But I'm not going to tell them that.

"I'm sorry. You're right. I should've been smarter, more careful. I…I just miss David so much." My voice cracks when I speak.

"We know, *beta*," my mom says. "I'm sorry I raised my voice. We're terrified of something happening to you. There are people who—"

"Mom, I know. You don't have to tiptoe around it. Some people disappear. And no one knows where. I was there with you at the orientation, remember? Don't worry. I'm not going to do something stupid. I'm mostly hanging out with Ayesha, listening to her talk about Star Wars."

"Obviously, Ayesha has refined cultural taste, and I totally approve of this friendship," my dad says, and chuckles a bit.

"Hah. I already told her you and Mom are total Star Wars nerds."

My mom gives me a wistful smile. "I'm telling you: Young Luke Skywalker, he was my first crush. And first love is one you never forget."

"I thought I made you forget all your past loves." My dad kisses my mom on the cheek.

"Of course, *jaan*. I only have eyes for you now. And young Luke."

We laugh.

First love is one you never forget.

I have to talk to David again. I know I said I wouldn't take any more risks, and I hate lying to my parents. But lies are a part of life in Mobius. It's how we survive.

CHAPTER 13

My parents head off to their "jobs." I clean up the dishes and wipe up the tea I spilled on my floor. Normally I'd go find Ayesha right now, and we'd hang by the rock garden. Soheil has been showing up a lot, too. And last night when we were in line for dinner at the Mess, Soheil whispered something to Ayesha. Later she asked if we could skip our normal meet-up. I guess she's getting bolder now; she's dropping me as her chaperone. I'm happy for her. We all need distractions in this place.

My mom's words still ring in my ears: *First love is one you never forget.* David said he'd get here, and I believe him. But I have to talk to him again because it's not like he can randomly show up at the front gate. I pull on the hem of the vintage *X-Files* tee I liberated from my mom's closet years ago.

I rub my sweaty palms against my well-worn jeans. There's only one way to get a phone.

I step outside. After talking to my parents, I know that the drones and the guards aren't the only eyes that are on me. I look around. Now that a lot of the adults have "jobs," most of them are occupied during the day. There's a kind of day care where the grandparents take care of little kids. The block is pretty quiet.

The guards patrol in shifts. Corporal Reynolds is on our block duty today. Carpe diem.

I don't run, or try to walk in a hurry. I don't do anything that might seem unusual. I casually stroll toward the guards like I'm going to pass them. There are no drones above. Now is as good a time as any to take a stupid chance. I trip. "Ow!" I yell out, louder than necessary. The guards turn to look at me. Corporal Reynolds says something to the other guard on duty with him and then walks to me. I'm on the ground, rubbing my ankle.

"Are you okay?" he asks, kneeling next to me.

"Yes. I wanted to get your attention but wasn't sure how."

He shakes his head. "You have to stop doing dumb, risky stuff like this."

I don't have time to take offense. "I need to talk to David. Can you get me a phone again, maybe?"

"Jesus." Corporal Reynolds rubs his forehead. He sighs. "Get up. And pretend it hurts to walk."

I slowly push myself up. He takes my elbow and escorts

me back to my Mercury Home. I do my best to feign a limp. And I think I'm pretty good at it because I've totally sprained my ankle before while playing tennis, so I know how it feels. Not that I'm winning any Oscars, but good enough. When we get to my door, he whispers, "Go inside. Stay there. For once, please listen. I'll be back." I nod and walk in.

I wait inside, like I was told. Minutes pass. I pace the room a little, remembering to limp for the camera. Then I sit down at the table, lifting my leg to let it rest on the chair next to me. I try to forget that any minute I could be talking to David. So I let my mind drift elsewhere. I wonder what Ayesha and Soheil are doing right now. Actually, no, I don't wonder. I hope she's maybe sneaking her first kiss. I hope she's smiling. Soheil is a good guy, I think; I pray my instinct about him isn't wrong.

The knock at the door makes me jump, even though I was expecting it. My startle reflex is a lot more sensitive these days.

I fake-hobble to the door and open it slowly, ever conscious of the camera in here.

Corporal Reynolds looks at me and allows a small smile to crack his normally serious veneer. He hands me multiple ice packs. "For your ankle," he says. "You should probably lie down with your leg propped on a pillow. That's what the nurse told me."

I take the ice packs, thank him, and shut the door. I want to run into my room, but I don't. I take my time, reminding myself to limp. Once I'm safely in my room, door shut, I pull the top ice pack off the bottom one. A black flip phone is in a small plastic bag, along with a note:

> IN THIRTY MINUTES, THERE WILL BE A SHIFT
> CHANGE. THE GUARD I'M WITH WILL TALK TO
> THE NEW GUYS. BRING THE PHONE BACK TO
> ME, BETWEEN THE ICE PACKS. SAY THANK YOU.
> WALK AWAY. DON'T BE LATE. RUN WATER ON
> THIS NOTE UNTIL THE INK RUNS. THEN RIP IT UP,
> PULP IT, AND FLUSH IT.

I dial David's number. Let the phone ring once, hang up, then dial again, like he told me. It rings three times before he picks up.

"Layla?" He whispers. "Sorry, I had to grab the bathroom pass to walk out of class."

Hearing his voice makes me feel like a boulder has been lifted from my chest, letting me breathe again. "David." I start crying softly but wipe away my tears. I quickly clear my throat. "David, can you get here? I need you to help me figure some way to get out of here."

"I'll be there tomorrow. It's not a far drive."

"What will you say to your parents?"

"Fuck them. I asked my dad if he could use his State Department contacts to help get your family out, and he said that's not how it works. That they'll only let people out who are useful to them. I hate him for going along with all of this.

And my mom…I don't know how she can stay silent about what's happening. I know they're scared, but it's like they've forgotten everything they taught me."

I barely register David's words. Hearing his voice is thrilling and heartbreaking at the same time. Then I'm slapped with the realization of what I've done—the ridiculous risk I've asked him to take by coming here. It's not worth it. I don't know what I was thinking. "David. I love you so much. But I was wrong to ask you. You can't come. It's dangerous. Impossible. We don't have visitors."

"Layla, we'll figure out a way. Remember when I said this wasn't going to be the end of you and me? I meant it. I'm with you. Always. Is there someplace we can meet without anyone knowing?"

"David, I don't know. There are guards and cameras everywhere. There are drones flying patterns above the camp. There's no place they can't see us."

"Is there anyone on your side who could help?"

I hesitate. "I'm not sure. Maybe I could ask Corporal Reynolds."

"Corporal Reynolds?"

"Don't freak out. He's a guard here. He's the one who got me the phones to call you. He's helping me."

"Layla, *that* seems dangerous. Are you sure he's not trying to trap you?"

"I don't think he'd go to all this trouble to turn me in. I mean, they don't need reasons to take you away in this place."

"Jesus. Fuck. I can't believe this is the world now."

"Tell me about it. I trust him, David. I mean, as much as it's possible to trust a stranger in the camp—a guard. I think my gut is right about him."

"If you trust him, I do, too. Please be careful. I love you, Layla."

I hear a bell ring in the background. I would do anything to be at school right now, back to the way things were. To the Before. Not now, in the endlessly painful After.

"I'll figure something out. I'll call you, or maybe I can ask him to. Either way, see you tomorrow? Maybe? I hope?"

"I love you forever. And I *will* see you tomorrow."

This might be the dumbest idea I've ever had; it's definitely the chanciest. But we've made the choice. The only direction now is forward.

CHAPTER 14

My hands shake as I pull on my black hoodie. I guess it's my official sneak-out uniform now. David is here. Close. So close. I pray that nothing goes wrong. Corporal Reynolds agreed to help me. To help us. I'm pretty sure he feels bad about all this. He should. And on the outside, I might care that I'm using his sympathy or guilt to get him to conspire with me, but what other choice do I have?

I tiptoe out of the trailer. It's a little past midnight. I have to get to the rock garden on my own. There are no guards outside, like Corporal Reynolds told me. I stick close to the Mercury Homes, avoiding the searchlights. They travel across the camp in a pattern. So I count the seconds and run from shadow to shadow. My heart races, pounding in my ears. And my skin is covered in goose bumps. The logical part of my brain is screaming at me to stop, to go back to the trailer. But I don't stop. I can't.

Corporal Reynolds is waiting for me at the garden. When he sees me, he puts his hand up, telling me to wait. A beam of light passes inches from where he is. Then he beckons to me to hurry.

"I sent the guards at this end away. And a buddy rerouted the drones, but you have five minutes. Tops. You hear me?" His voice is tight. Strained. And his face looks stricken, but I'm not sure by what. "The Director is off-site today. That's why I was able to redirect a few things. But don't think you're safe. Not even with me by your side. Not for a second. Do you understand?"

I nod. I hear the weight of his words—how serious he is about what he's saying. But I can't feel them. My only emotion right now is a giddy elation because David is here. Here. In this place. Where I thought everyone had forgotten us. But Corporal Reynolds is staring at me with expectant eyes. My halfhearted nod isn't enough. "I get it, Corporal Reynolds. I'm in danger all the time."

"Yes. You are. And like I said before, call me Jake. I think it's fair to say I've crossed the guard line, here."

"Jake? Thank you," I whisper. Before I realize what I'm doing, I put my hand on his arm, a tiny spontaneous gesture of thanks that startles both of us. I pull my hand away.

Jake points across the Midway to a red metal toolshed at

the back. There's a jeep parked next to it. We hurry toward it, not saying a word, but I'm utterly certain the drumming of my heart is echoing through the canyon.

Jake stops me at the door and hands me a flashlight. "Remember what I said: five minutes. Keep your ears open. If you hear my voice at all, don't move. Don't make a sound. Don't come out. I'll open the door when it's safe. Got it?"

I nod. And put my hand on the doorknob.

"Layla," Jake whispers, "there are no cameras in there. But speak softly."

I push open the door. It's so dark inside.

"Layla." It's him. It's his voice.

I turn on the flashlight, and David steps toward me and wraps me in his arms. I cry into his shirt, and he holds me tighter. It feels so good to be held by him. Is it possible to miss something even more while you're experiencing it? Then we kiss. It's slow and soft and lovely, and makes me want to cry and laugh at the same time. For one perfect moment, the entire world disappears.

David gently pulls me down to the ground. He turns so his back is against the door and draws me to him. He folds his right arm around my shoulders and knits my fingers through his.

I want to sit here and not say anything. All night. Me. David, with the floral notes of his clean clothes and the minty smell of his soap and the intimate, familiar ways our bodies fold into each other. It's what all humans want, isn't it? To be known? And David knows me. But we don't have world enough, or time. We have minutes. Seconds. Soon, we'll return to reality—barbed wire and electric fence.

"Layla, listen, they're not closing this place down. Another camp is opening in a few weeks. They've expanded the Muslim ban. Total immigration lockdown, and for tourists, too. Even if you're not Muslim but are from a Muslim-majority country. But I have an idea."

The news guts me. "An idea? For what?"

"Look, I don't know if this would work, but remember how I told you my dad said something about people making themselves useful?"

I nod, not sure where David is going. Not sure I want to know.

"It got me thinking. What if, like—" He pauses, takes a deep breath. He's never uncomfortable around me. But now I sense his muscles tense. His words are all stuck in him, and he's trying to force them out.

"David, you're making me nervous. What is it?"

"Do you think you could convince your parents to help the government with—"

My mouth drops open and I turn to David, grabbing the flashlight and directing its glare at his face. He puts up his hand to shield his eyes, so I lower the beam. "What? You want my parents to help the assholes who put us in here? What the fuck, David? Did your dad put you up to this?"

"No. He has no idea. I thought that maybe if I could go to him and tell him your parents would, like, cooperate somehow, then he'd try to help get you guys out of here. I wasn't thinking that they'd be holding guns to people's heads; they'd have to, I don't know, translate stuff, maybe? Keep the Authority informed."

Tears flow down my face. David has punched a hole through my center. I open my mouth. Stutter. I have so many words I want to scream right now, but they're all frozen inside me. And I can't scream. Not here. Not anywhere in this camp. "David, have you lost your mind? You're the one person I have. The one person I trust on the outside, and now you want to make my parents—what—collaborators? You want us to inform on other Muslims to save ourselves? They would never do that, and neither would I." I scoot away from him, then stand.

David reaches out to touch me. I pull away. He stands up and cups my cheek with his hand. For an instant, I relax into it, the warmth, the familiar curve of his palm touching my skin. I sigh. Then I step back, the rage building inside me. I turn my back to him, trying to figure out what to say. He comes around and draws me into his arms, but I shove him back. He bends down and whispers into my ear, "Layla. Listen to me. Please. I'm sorry. I didn't mean to insult you or hurt you. But what if this is the only way to get you out? To keep you safe?"

"Who are you right now? Your mom is brown. Her last name is Shabazi, and without your dad's protection, some ignorant fascists might've mistakenly forced her into this camp, too. And you want us to cooperate with them? Do you actually believe your dad would even go for your stupid idea? Did you even think this through?"

"I was thinking I love you. That's all. I'm terrified—scared that you'll get hurt, or worse. I want you out of here because I know what happens to people who get sent to camps. My whole family knows. Don't you understand? I'm going crazy every second you're away from me." His voice breaks. "I don't know how else to help you."

I clench my jaw, but David's words also pierce my heart. "If you even knew me at all, you would've realized how stupid it was to even ask." I look up at David, fury in my eyes. But there's also doubt in my heart. What I wouldn't give to be out of here. To be free. To know my parents are safe. To do regular, everyday things. To take a walk. To breathe. To sleep. But even if I begged my parents to do this, I can't imagine them giving in. If they wouldn't lie on the census—a small lie to hide us— they certainly aren't going to become traitors or spies. Even if they never saw who they were hurting, they would know that they were condemning people to internment—or worse. And living an ethical life, a moral life, is important to them. I can hear my dad's voice now, and I repeat the words that come to mind: "In the quiet of night, the heart knows the lies you told to survive."

"Who said that?" David asks.

"My dad," I whisper.

"Okay, then. Exactly. Sometimes you have to do what you need to do to survive. Live to fight another day."

"No, David. That's not what the poem means. It means that you can never escape your lies, even if you think you have. Even if it was to survive. The lies—your deception—are always with you."

David sinks into himself like he's been punched. I don't think I've ever seen his face look so pale. Only now do I notice the bruise-like circles under his eyes. He looks like he hasn't slept in weeks.

Tears well in his eyes. He clears his throat. His voice is barely a whisper. "I'm afraid for you. I'm afraid of what they could do to you. If something happens to you…"

"Don't you think I'm scared, too?" I take a few steps to the door.

"Layla, I'm sorry. Please. I'm staying in town. I'm not going home. I'll figure out another way. I'm not leaving here without you."

The door opens. Jake is standing there. I can't imagine what the two of us look like. What I look like. Face wet with tears, eyes swollen.

"David, stay here, like I instructed you. I'll drive you out under the tarp, same as the way we came in. Don't make a sound."

David nods at Jake's instructions, then looks at me and says, "I love you. I'm sorry." He steps back into the darkness, and Jake closes the door.

Jake and I hurry across the Midway. I let him guide me, pulling me away from the light beams and into the shadows. Tears run down my face, too fast for me to wipe them away. I thought David would be able to help me somehow, and instead he wants us to become informers? I swipe my sleeve across my nose. My entire world is upside down.

Jake produces a tissue from his pocket and hands it to me. "I don't think…" He pauses and rubs his hand across the back of his neck. "He's trying to help your family."

I ball my hands into fists. Anger wells inside me. "Don't you think I know that? And were you listening in on us?"

"I heard most of it. It was hard not to. It's a flimsy toolshed; it's not soundproof. He's desperate, that's all."

"I'm desperate, too. But what he's suggesting—that's not an option. We can't do that. If we do, we'll be as bad as—" I look up at Jake and then stop myself and turn away.

"Go ahead. Finish your sentence. You'll be as bad as me?" He winces as he says this.

My mouth goes dry. What I said might've been terribly stupid or dangerous. I can't speak.

Jake's eyes scan the area with each step. He's cautious, always observing and adjusting his behavior to the situation. He never speaks if anyone could possibly overhear. "Layla, listen to me. I told you before. It's not cut and dried. On the outside or in here. Things are happening. People are organizing. They're making their way down here. That little town, Independence? It's filling up with media and protestors—Occupy

Mobius, they're calling themselves. The secretary of war got doxed by Anonymous—you know, the hactivist group?"

I stop and look at Jake, my eyes wide, and nod. My stomach churns. We were getting dribs and drabs of news from the outside, but nothing like this. Inside here we're frozen in time. Stuck. But outside, the world is still moving. "Why are you telling me this?"

"Because what I think David wanted to tell you—what he might've told you if he weren't so terrified of losing you—is don't give up."

We arrive back at my trailer door. "So maybe there's still hope?" I whisper.

Jake takes a half step toward me. "Insha'Allah," he whispers.

CHAPTER 15

Insha'Allah.

Jake's voice rings in my ears. I'm not sure what it means that he said that. God willing. Everything and nothing? Like so much of life inside here, where you have to read into the tiniest gestures—whether they are dangerous, whether a wave means to hide or to say hello.

I slide my hand under my pillow and pull out the note Jake passed to me this morning when I was getting some of our food rations—a note from David, which I guess he scribbled and gave to Jake after he'd driven him out of here. The note is an apology. It's a promise to help me in whatever way I think is best. Before seeing David, I thought our getting out was the most important thing, but when David came up with this ridiculous collaborator scheme, I realized I couldn't leave everyone behind. There are too many people who could get hurt. Perhaps I'm stupid and too short-sighted to see what the real fallout could be. Maybe this pain in my stomach is remorse; maybe it's fear because I'm starting to understand what I have to do.

"You should consider it," Ayesha says when I tell her about David's proposition. We're at the rock garden. She doesn't say it, but she keeps glancing across the Midway, looking for Soheil, I'm assuming.

"How can you even suggest that?"

"It might be your only way out. We keep talking about escaping, but how? Even if we got ourselves and our families out, where would we go? Try to get to Mexico? With all the border security? If we didn't die trying to get through the fence or smuggling ourselves out in a supply truck, we'd get shot trying to climb the border wall, even though we were going *into* Mexico."

I grab Ayesha's hand. "I'm not leaving you behind. I didn't even tell my parents about it. I don't want them to be tempted. They might do it for me, but I can't imagine them being able to live with themselves if they made that choice."

"They're scared. Parents will do anything to protect their kids. If I had that offer, I don't know if I could say no." Ayesha's voice cracks.

"Remember what your dad said to you about fear when you were in the spelling bee? Soheil, too? About how we should be scared, about how we can use that?" Ayesha looks up at me, and it doesn't escape my notice that her eyes brighten every time Soheil's name comes up. Small blessings—I'm increasingly aware of and thankful for them. "We can't fight back in here—not by ourselves. Jake told me there's stuff happening on the outside. We need to make those people see what is happening on the inside."

"Jake?"

"The guard who helped me make the call to David."

"You're on a first-name basis with that guard? He can hurt us, for no reason. He has a gun to shoot us. Do you even know what you're doing right now?"

Shit. "I don't think it's like that with him." I explain what Jake said to me, but Ayesha isn't convinced.

"Anyone can say 'insha'Allah.' It doesn't make them Muslim, or even if they are, it doesn't mean they're on our side. He could be saying that to win your trust."

I get what Ayesha's saying. I spent half the night lying awake wondering about it. Some Muslims I know, like this one uncle, says it all the time, like it means "hopefully." One of the girls at the masjid complained that her mom basically used it as a nice way of saying no—"Mom, can I go to the movies tomorrow?" "Insha'Allah, *beta*." I know non-Muslims who say insha'Allah, God willing. But Jake's saying it doesn't feel flippant or like a trick. "I know how it seems. How it is. But I think he wants to help us. He used the word as a sign, or a—"

"A shibboleth. He used it as a shibboleth," she says.

I shrug.

"It's a word you can use to distinguish who's on your side and who isn't. I can't remember all the details, but it comes from a story in the Hebrew Bible. One group was able to detect their enemies by their inability to pronounce the word 'shibboleth' with the *sh* sound."

"So the word 'shibboleth' is a shibboleth."

"Yup, basically."

I look into Ayesha's eyes. "I know you're scared. But in my gut I know that Jake's not the enemy." I hope my gut isn't wrong, because it's not just my life I'm risking; it's her life, too.

Ayesha shakes her head. "I don't know, Layla. It's a leap, and a dangerous one."

"I won't take any unnecessary risks," I promise, but even as I say the words, I know they are a lie.

Ayesha gives me a small nod in response, which I take as agreement.

"Have you read any Nietzsche?" I ask.

Ayesha furrows her eyebrows at me and shakes her head. "That's not how I usually spend summer vacation."

"He said something like, all I need is a sheet of paper and something to write with and I can turn the world upside down."

"So you're planning on busting us all out of here with your cruel, cutting words? What is brewing in your brain?"

"Have you ever heard of the White Rose?"

She doesn't answer me. She's looking at Soheil as he approaches the garden. A smile spreads across her face.

"Hey," he says as he draws closer.

"Hey," Ayesha replies.

"Hey," he says *again*.

Then there's silence. Ayesha looks at her shoes and kicks at the dirt a bit. Soheil stuffs his hands into his jeans pockets and shifts his weight from one foot to the other.

"Um, was I also supposed to say 'hey'? Is that the reason for the awkward silence?" I ask.

Ayesha turns to me and widens her eyes in a way that shows she's embarrassed, and also telling me to shut up. I ignore her and move to another rock so Soheil can take a seat on the boulder next to her.

"What were you saying about the White Rose?" Ayesha asks me.

"The White Rose?" Soheil jumps in. "The brother and sister from World War Two who wrote all those pamphlets urging other German college students to resist the Nazis?"

"Yeah," I respond. "I don't remember every detail of their story, but I know they used their words to try to resist the Nazis."

"I'm familiar with their story," Soheil responds. "And it doesn't have a happy ending. They were a group of students, and two of the leaders were Hans and Sophie Scholl. They handed out leaflets denouncing Hitler, totally risking their lives. They even advocated sabotaging the war efforts."

"They sound pretty badass," Ayesha says.

Soheil continues. "Totally brave. But then a janitor at their university turned them in, and they were both executed. Some of the others were, too. By guillotine."

Ayesha raises a hand to her mouth. "That's horrible," she whispers.

"Why were you talking about them anyway?" Soheil asks. "Are you two figuring you're going to agitate? Resist?"

As Soheil talks, I feel bile rising in my throat, but I also begin to remember more of the White Rose story from history class. They were killed because they refused to lie down and do nothing. They didn't stay silent. "During the trial I think Sophie said, 'Somebody, after all, had to make a start.' Didn't she? I think I remember seeing that in my textbook. And she was right. Somebody has to make a start. And it might as well be us."

Ayesha gulps. "But do you want to do leaflets in here?"

"No. I want to write stories that will rile people up on the outside. And I'm going to ask David to get them out there. I know he's afraid. But at some point we have to stop talking and start reminding people of who we are. Americans. Human beings."

"So say we all." Ayesha puts her hand on my forearm. "But I'd like to avoid the capture-and-guillotine part."

"They don't use the guillotine anymore," Soheil says.

Ayesha elbows him. "Not helping. I'm serious."

"You're right. I'm sorry," he responds. "Total crap thing to say or be flip about."

"Guys, look. This whole situation is bullshit. But I know we have to be careful. We can't play around with some half-assed romantic idea that we'll be the next Resistance. We have to think about it, be smart, know who we can trust. But it's like Sophie said: Somebody has to make a start. And it might as well be us." When I say this, I can hear the resolve in my voice, but inside I'm shaking. The confidence is a mask, like some of the lies we tell to make it through the day. "Fake it till you make it" is one of the most American attitudes I can think of.

"Okay, so say, like, you write these stories. How are you going to get them to David—your boyfriend, right? He's on the outside?" Soheil asks. David's name has come up before, but Soheil doesn't know the whole story about how Jake is helping me. When I share it with him, his mouth drops open, and for once he's too stunned to speak.

"So, I'm going to see if maybe I can convince Jake to help me see David again."

"Wait. Wait. I'm sorry. I'm still stuck on the part about David getting snuck in by a guard. An *Exclusion Guard*. One that you're on first-name basis with." Soheil narrows his eyes at me.

"He's not just a guard. I mean he is, but there's more to it—to him."

"Then he should stand up and say something, shouldn't he? Fight back?" Soheil says.

"Maybe he wants to do something but doesn't know where to begin. Or maybe he is helping us, in some way, and we don't know how yet. I trust Layla's gut on this. And it's not like she's telling him all our plans." Ayesha comes to my defense, but I hear her voice falter a little. She wants to believe in me. And I want to be worthy of her trust.

"There is no plan," Soheil says. He's terse, and I can see Ayesha tense up. But she doesn't back down.

"That's the point of this conversation, to make a plan. And anyway, Layla said she was going to write, like, an article and get it to David. That's the seed." Ayesha squares her shoulders to Soheil. "No one is forcing you to be here. But if you're going to be, at least be helpful."

Soheil takes a breath and nods. "I'm here. I'm in. I'm with you. Of course I am." His voice softens as he speaks. "I'm playing devil's advocate, is all. I don't want you to get hurt. Or anyone else, either."

"Same," Ayesha whispers back.

I've only known Ayesha a few weeks, but from the moment we met, I could trust her. It was friendship at first sight. In a lot of ways, it was a new feeling for me—that sense of trust, of loyalty. There was David, of course; he is that and more, and I have friends on the tennis team, and in student government, but no one tight—not recently, anyway. I'm so grateful I have Ayesha. I smile at her and say, "I'm freaked, too. But we won't be stupid. We'll plan. We'll hide in plain sight. We'll protect one another. We'll try our best."

Soheil nods.

Ayesha steps over to me and gives me a hug and squeezes my hand.

"Okay," Soheil says. "You are going to figure out a way to get a message to David—"

"A way that can maybe fire people up on the outside. There are already protestors here, and media. I want to light a match. Be a spark," I say.

Soheil starts pacing around the boulders. "But we also have to find a way to resist inside."

While he's walking, Ayesha opens a small plastic bag and hands each of us a sandwich. She smiles. "I was a Girl Scout. I'm always prepared for my inevitable bouts of hunger."

Soheil and I thank her and take the PB and J she hands us. I notice that Soheil's fingers linger on Ayesha's when he reaches for his sandwich.

Soheil looks at his food. "Fast. We get people to fast. Like, everyone skips dinner. Refuses to eat."

"You have noticed that I get totally hangry, right?" Ayesha says. "But maybe a protest fast—missing the dinner slop at the Mess one day isn't the worst idea ever."

Soheil laughs. "It's Gandhi-esque. It's in your DNA." He points to the two of us.

Ayesha rolls her eyes. "Yes, you're right. All the desis in America have regular meetings about being more Gandhi-like, and we spin our own cotton, too. And all the Arabs here know how to ride camels, right?" Ayesha playfully punches him in the arm, but it was probably a bit harder than Soheil expected, and he winces a little.

"Okay, I hear you. Checking my assumptions."

Ayesha tilts her head. "One upside: Muslims are used to fasting. Who knew Ramadan was preparing us for this?"

I interject, "It's only one meal. Besides, three people won't get much attention. How do we get other people to join in?"

Soheil proposes the threads of a plan. "We start with a core group. I'd like to bring Nadia and Nadeem—the twins on my block—in on it, and some others. Next Friday. The Director is letting us choose seats at dinner to show us his supposed generosity, right? Let's use it. We need a group of us, enough to get attention."

"But how do we know who we can trust? We need to recruit people." Ayesha looks right at Soheil, who smiles back at her.

He responds, "Recruiting is my thing. I recruited, like, half a dozen ballers for the soccer team at school. I'll get people. But we can't all meet here. Three people eating sandwiches doesn't look suspicious, but more than five and the drones will start to sniff out a conspiracy."

Ayesha smiles. "I know! Last week when I was at the Hub library, I suggested a teen vegetable garden to the librarian, and she was into it. She even requisitioned tools and seeds and stuff. So we plant. Get some tools, do some work. Rebel."

Yes, I think. Sow the seeds. Perfect.

CHAPTER 16

Ayesha and I are still buzzing from our conversation with Soheil earlier today. As we walk down the Midway toward the Mess, one of the Director's shiny red drones flies above us, slows down, and follows. We stop talking altogether, too nervous to speak. Then Ayesha mentions the dinner from the night before and goes on to list all the foods she misses from the outside. I turn my chin up to gaze directly at the drone's camera; I wonder if it's sending a live feed into the Director's office. Creepy. Unsettling. I don't like being watched; I refuse to get used to it. We keep walking and talking, building our missed-food wish list: Flaming Hot Cheetos, chocolate cake with real buttercream frosting, In-N-Out Animal Style burgers, Badmaash fried chicken, biryani, *kheema* paratha, samosas, food truck tacos, salmon sushi. And now I'm starving.

But the drone moves on, heading toward the back of the camp, which is weird because everyone else is heading forward, toward the Mess. It's dinner. It's required. The only reason—

We hear yelling and the sound of boots on the ground, and then a dozen guards run past us. I pull Ayesha toward the Mess. Out of the corner of my eye, I see the Director and his private security detail following behind the guards. This can't be good.

"I'm going to go see what's happening," I whisper to Ayesha.

"Are you cracked? We're supposed to be in the Mess."

"I'll only be a few minutes. Besides, something is going on, and I'm sure everyone is going to be distracted."

Ayesha sighs. "Fine, I'm going with you. If only to tell you to hurry up and get back to the Mess, where the major risk is indigestion, as opposed to getting shot out here."

I smile a little. Then, when the guard at the Mess door steps toward the Midway to see what's happening, I grab Ayesha's hand and dart behind one of the admin trailers. We wait, then dash behind some Mercury Homes. We move closer to the direction of the guards and the drones, but keep some distance between us and the Midway so we can't be seen.

Then we hear screams. I stop short. I can't breathe. Goose bumps spring up all over my body. I look at Ayesha. All the blood has left her face. We peek out from behind the Mercury Home. A woman is being dragged down the Midway by the Director's small special force, his personal security guards, as the Director follows calmly, walking with his hands clasped behind his back like he's on a stroll, as if his hands don't have blood on them.

It's Noor.

Oh God. No.

During our first few days here, Noor caught me smiling at her American flag hijab while we were both doing laundry, and she introduced herself. Block 6, she said, rolling her eyes. Arab American. She told me Authority Suits grabbed her from her dorm room for seditious acts. When I asked her if she had done what they claimed, she looked at me with a mysterious smile and said, "Rebellion is as American as apple pie. And so is fascism."

Now she's being hauled down the Midway, pulled by each arm, bleeding from her mouth and her forehead. She's writhing and trying to kick and twist herself out of the grasp of the Director's private security guards. They ignore her screams. Like she's a ghost they can't see or hear.

I can't turn away. I step forward. Ayesha pulls me back behind the Mercury Home, but it doesn't matter. Because no one is in the Mess anymore. Everyone is standing around. Watching.

Out of the corner of my eye, I see two black women run toward Noor—they're young, maybe in their twenties, Block 7 or 8.

No. No. Stop. They'll take you, too, I want to scream, but the words catch in my throat. Neither of the women has a weapon.

The one I've met before, Asmaa, has close-cropped hair and wears a bright-yellow tee with BAD BRAINS splashed across the front in red letters. She lunges for one of the men taking Noor away. An Exclusion Guard immediately steps up, grabs her by the shirt, and elbows her in the face, like she's inconsequential to him. She falls to the ground, cradling her head in both hands, groaning. Two guards yank her up.

Then the action feels like it slows down. There's screaming and dirt getting kicked up and clouds of fine dust filling the air. I hear Ayesha say, "Oh no. It's Bilqis."

In the frenzy, Bilqis—who's wearing a pale-blue hijab—sucker punches one of the guards. Right in the face. Blood spurts out of the guard's nose and mouth. A beatific smile crosses her face, but before she can take another step, two guards are on her. One punches her in the gut, and when she's doubled over, another guard kicks her to the ground and handcuffs her. When they pull her up, the guard she punched stomps up to her and rips off her hijab. Bilqis spits in his face, and he slaps her hard—so hard that her scream could crack the earth. Blood is everywhere, smeared across their faces and clothes. I keel over, sure I'm going to be sick. Ayesha rushes to me.

There is so much screaming. And deep, almost animal-like sounds from the women. People in the crowd yell and curse and cry. Guards hold them back as Noor and Asmaa and Bilqis are taken away. But we don't disperse. Someone from the back of the gathering throws a rock. It hits one of

173

the Director's security team in the arm. There are cheers. But when I glance at the Director, I know this is going to cost us. His splotchy red face looks like it's going to explode. He marches over to one of his security guards, takes his handgun, raises it in the air, and shoots. The shot rings out and reverberates through the mountains. He does it again.

The crowd quiets. Then there are only the echoes of the women's screams.

The Director waits, the gun still raised. He waits longer. It's unbearable hearing the last distant sounds from the women as they're taken who knows where. My God, they are so brave. My heart is in my throat. This is what the Director wants. He wants us to hear the screams. He wants us to know that it could be us screaming.

And then there is absolute silence.

CHAPTER 17

My parents tuck me in. They haven't done this since I don't know when. No one has said a word beyond the absolute minimum since the incident with the three women. The Director let us eat dinner. And we did so without speaking. It was excruciating. No sounds except people chewing, and forks tapping against plastic plates, and parents shushing their babies, who didn't know any better. If fear had a sound, it would be the painful, heavy silence in the Mess tonight.

"Do you want me to stay with you, *beta*?" my mom asks. Her voice is so soft, it's almost heartbreaking.

I smile up at my parents. "No. I'm okay."

"If you ever want to talk, you know, about anything, your mom and I are always here for you. We can always take a walk with you." My dad pats me on the knee. They're trying to be reassuring. But they also probably know that they're failing. It's an impossible task.

I kiss them both on their cheeks, and they step out.

I wait until I hear them shut the door to their room to get out of bed. I step to my tiny desk, turn on the lamp, and take a seat. No way I can sleep tonight. The bloody, stricken faces of those women will not leave my mind. And neither will their bravery. I try not to wonder what is happening to them, what could happen, but I surrender my imagination to its most terrifying conclusion. Honestly, it probably is so much worse in real life.

Since I can't sleep, I open the notebook I brought with me. And I write. I write about life inside Mobius. About Noor. About the brave women who tried to intercede. And the woman with the ponytail at the orientation and the desperate man who was so quiet as they took him away after his partner was disappeared.

And I write about the screams. Those screams will be etched in my memory forever.

I write it all in tiny print as legibly as possible despite my shaky hand while I wipe away tears so they don't soak into the paper. I fold it up into a small square and tuck it under my pillow for now. Before the incident, Jake reluctantly agreed to get the note to David. I'm scared for him. For me. For David. I can't even imagine what the Director will do if he gets wind of this. It would be impossible to talk our way out of it. It's probably treason, like everything else these days. That whole freedom-of-speech thing? That right to petition your government? Yeah, doesn't exist so much inside an internment camp.

I glance at myself in the Mylar mirror. My face is all puffy and red, like I've scrubbed it too hard with exfoliant. I drag myself over to the bed and rest my head on the pillow. My eyes sting. I let them close.

There's clattering in the common area. I bolt up and barely miss hitting my head. I'm never going to get used to having a damn bunk. I swing my legs over the edge of the bed. I feel woozy. I grip the sides of the mattress to steady myself. There are so many times I've woken up confused, wondering whose bed I'm in, whose room. This morning my head feels thick, but I know where I am. I know what I have to do.

I get up, splash water on my face, and change into my favorite jeans and my mom's old *X-Files* tee. All my clothes feel dirty. There's a laundry, but even after the wash, nothing I wear feels clean. It's like the dust in Mobius is woven into the fiber of every article of clothing that touches my skin. Before I head out of my room, I take the note from under the pillow and slip it into my back pocket.

I step into the cramped common space of our trailer. My parents are glued to the media unit, watching the latest announcement. There's no real news, only what the Director wants us to hear. And what he wants us to know today is that everything is back to normal after the "troublemakers" were dealt with. Then he turns back to the goings-on at Mobius.

"Looks like plans for the community garden are under

way," my mom says when she sees me. "There's even a teen garden section." She gives me a hollow smile. She is so pale. We've been in the blazing sun for a few weeks, and yet my mom is a ghost. I take a couple steps and stand next to her. She rubs the space between my shoulder blades—a gesture that always calmed me down when I was little.

I look from my mom to my dad and realize they are not going to bring up yesterday. They're not going to talk about the violence or the bravery.

"Maybe working in the garden will make some people smile. We have to try to get along the best we can," my mom says, her voice uncharacteristically meek. "Be happy we have each other." Her voice falters. "Be happy we're alive."

"Why? Why do we have to sit around and take it like it's all okay? Did you not see what I saw last night? I wish everyone would stop acting like this is all normal. It's not normal." I raise my voice more than I should.

"Layla." My dad's voice is even as ever, cognizant of the camera and of being watched. "Your mother is simply saying that we should do our best to make a community here. Before you know it, we'll be back at home."

I understand why my parents put on a show for the cameras, but I can't stand it anymore. I'm scared they'll start believing what they're saying.

"What if we never get out of here? What if we die in here? People died in American internment camps during World

War Two, and I'd rather die fighting back than going along with everything." I'm so weary of the ever-present gaze. Fury courses through my veins. But I'm being reckless, and that's dangerous for my parents—and for me.

There's a fire raging inside me, and I feel like I could burst into a million tiny embers. I look at my mom's face; her fatigue is painful to witness. I know I'm part of the reason she looks that way. I dig my fingernails into my palms and press until it hurts. I look at the deep red crescents my nails made in my skin.

I sigh and take a shaky breath.

I promised Ayesha that I'd be careful. And that I wouldn't do something stupid and rash. It's a show. I can't forget that.

I bite my lip. "Sorry, Mom and Dad. You're right. I was being stupid. I didn't mean it."

My mom clasps my hands, and my dad's hands rest on top of hers. It strikes me that the look in their eyes—the one I don't remember existing until we got to this place—is a unique kind of fear: You wonder if you'll ever see your kid again when they step out the door. There are layers to fear, and complexities, and being trapped here brings that to light.

I tell my parents I'm meeting Ayesha, but it's a lie, and it's for their own good. I kiss them good-bye, giving them a little wave at the door.

Stepping outside, I nearly trip down the stairs because Jake is standing by my front door and totally startles me.

"Sorry," he says, catching me by the elbow before I fall to the ground. I look up at him. He pulls his hands away immediately. "I've been waiting for you to come out."

We planned to see each other so I could give Jake the note, but I didn't realize he meant that he was going to be stalking my front doorstep. Also, he seems anxious, which is unusual.

I adjust the hem of my T-shirt and straighten my hair. "Awkward" is the first word that comes to mind right now. I look around and reach into my back pocket. Jake puts his palm up, stopping me.

"Come with me. Don't ask questions."

I hesitate, thinking of my conversation with Ayesha and Soheil. Maybe I really have read everything wrong. Why does he seem so nervous? I keep telling Ayesha and Soheil that I trust my gut about Jake. I told David, too. But what if my gut is totally wrong? What if Ayesha was right the first time she warned me about him? I hate doubting myself. A part of me wonders if maybe I *am* foolish for trusting him; I follow Jake anyway. If my instinct is wrong, and he has only been gaining my trust to bust me, then he can drag me away anytime he wants to.

Jake marches me right through the middle of camp. Greeting and saluting the other guards. Nonchalant. Like he has orders to take me somewhere. Maybe he does. We walk past the Hub and head straight for the Mess.

The Mess is only open for dinner. We do our other meals

on our own with whatever rations they give us, which are usually ridiculous. The other day there was a bottle of ketchup in our food box, and on the itemized list it was marked as a vegetable. A vegetable. First of all, tomatoes are fruit, but anyway, ketchup is a condiment with, like, zero nutritional value. But I guess that is not their big concern here.

"Why are we going to the Mess? Are you going to let me steal some extra mayonnaise packets? Mayo counts as, like, what? Eggs?"

Jake gives me the side-eye but doesn't respond to my snark, which I've been trying to suppress, in large part for my parents' peace of mind. But it's impossible to keep all of myself totally hidden, even inside Mobius, where showing too much of yourself can get you hurt, or disappeared.

The lights are off in the Mess. It's echoey and eerie, like it's haunted. Why does he want me in here? Goose bumps rise on my skin. He's quiet. Too quiet.

Jake walks to the back of the kitchen and gestures for me to follow. I do, tentatively, but keep some distance. I'm hyperaware of how far the exits are, and I calculate how fast I'd have to run to get clear of here if I needed to. The kitchen is dark, and Jake opens a closet door.

"Jake. Corporal Reynolds. I don't understand what—" I stumble back a little.

"Layla." David steps out of the darkness.

My mouth drops open. David is wearing a khaki jumpsuit with the Exclusion Authority patch on his short sleeve.

"What the hell?" I look from David to Jake, utterly bewildered.

"I'll leave you two alone. But you don't have a lot of time. The sanitation trucks leave in fifteen minutes. You have five in here." Jake walks into the dining area.

My heart stops for a second. My mind races. "David, what's going on?" I whisper.

David sees me staring at his uniform. "Oh, this? Corporal Reynolds got me this uniform and arranged for me to sneak in here with the garbage-removal service."

"What? How? When did you see him?" My mind floods with questions, and my body pulls me toward David, but I hesitate. Hold back for a second.

"On the outside, by the motel I'm staying in. Listen, I don't have time to explain everything; we only have a couple of minutes. I'm sorry about the other day. About everything. I am so scared for you. I didn't think it through. I never considered what I was *actually* asking—the compromises I suggested you make. I dunno, I guess I was hoping that I could make some kind of proposal to my dad—your freedom in exchange for you and your parents cooperating with the Exclusion Authority. Like I even have any leverage to do that. My dad would never take me seriously. Or help me. Help *us*. I'm sorry. But I meant what I said. If you need me, I'm here for you. Tell me what to do."

For a moment, I'm stunned. At his words. At this impossible

situation. And then I'm in David's arms, and I see myself like I'm outside my body. Drawing closer to him, closing my eyes, raising my lips to his, letting this place melt away. Kissing him feels like the one thing keeping me really and truly alive in this place. It's a reminder of everything that has been taken from us, but it also gives me hope. That feeling lasts only a fleeting second, though, because in the next, I wonder if David can hear my stomach churn. I'm ridiculously overjoyed to see him, but also terrified for both of us. If he gets caught in here, like this, I don't know how much his father can protect him. And my thoughts wander to Jake. I was right: He won't give us up. And that makes me scared for him, too.

When we pull away from kissing, I reach into my back pocket and hand over the post I wrote. Tell him my idea. Tell him about the White Rose. About Sophie Scholl. About what I need him to do. What I know he will do.

Jake clears his throat, loudly. Time. The minutes are long in Mobius, but also there is never enough time.

"He told you, right? There are people talking and protesting, and the Occupy people are here—the rooms in town are all sold out. They're sleeping in cars and tents. They brought the press. There's this reporter at the motel. I talked to her this morning at breakfast. She's super sympathetic. She has Muslim family. She'll get your article out there. I'm sure of it. People will hear your words." Between sentences, David peppers my face with kisses.

"Please be careful. My name isn't on that, but if your name is revealed, they'll come after you. And your parents—"

"My parents would go apeshit. But I don't care. I know they want to protect me, but they need to remember the prejudice they've faced and fought. They need to wake up. I'll be okay." David kisses my forehead. "Trust me." Then he puts a finger to his lips and slips me a small flip phone. He puts his lips to my ear. "It's a burner. Don't tell him. Call or text me when you can."

I nod and slip the phone into my front pocket, happy that this old *X-Files* T-shirt is loose and pulled out of shape so that it stretches down well past my hips and hides the outline of the phone. Then I respond normally. "I do trust you. It's everyone else in this stupid world I don't trust. And things are happening here, too. I mean, they will. We're talking about things happening."

"Layla, please don't give them an excuse to hurt you. This camp is operating outside the law. The attorney general can't even control it."

"I know. I'm on the inside, remember? But I can't sit by and do nothing." Sophie Scholl's words come to mind. "Someone has to make a start."

David pulls me into his arms and his hug feels like I'm enveloped in my beloved *kantha* quilt. "You're amazing."

We stand there for a second. Quiet. And it reminds me of a line from a Walt Whitman poem my dad sometimes whispers to my mom: *There we two, content, happy in being together, speaking little, perhaps not a word.*

"I love you," David whispers, and runs his index finger across the necklace he gave me.

When Jake walks back into the kitchen, David kisses me one more time. His kiss is feather-light, and there is a kind of beautiful and bittersweet magic in it. He picks up two bulging black garbage bags and heads out a side entrance. Watching him walk out of the room crushes me.

Jake pauses, waiting for David to leave before he takes my elbow and directs me back through the main dining hall and outdoors. He's the one I'm most flummoxed by in all of this.

He walks unusually slowly, dragging his feet back to my trailer. He scans the space around us and the sky above us and then comes to an abrupt halt and faces me. "Wait. Please." He pauses. "Writing that story and giving it to David. Jesus. I shouldn't have snuck him in here. I can only protect you so much. I have orders. If you're planning on doing something inside here—some kind of civil disobedience or insubordination—you're going to get caught. There will be consequences, and I don't know how much I can shield you."

Jake's face contorts with worry. Normally he's so composed, barely betraying any emotion. He's taking a risk, too. But that's his choice. I'm making choices for myself.

I narrow my eyes at him and shove my hands into my pockets. "I gave him a note, that's all."

Jake rolls his eyes and tips head to the sky. He takes a deep breath. "The Director is not an idiot. You see the cameras. I told you—there's only so much I can take care of right now. He will see you. And if he catches on to what you two are doing or whatever you're planning to do on the inside, the consequence is going to be far worse than what you've seen. I heard you talking about the White Rose. Those kids were executed. This has to stop now. I'm not going to be a party to this anymore. I'm a fool for letting it go this far. The risks—you have no idea."

My heart stops. So far, the only way I've been able to see David is with Jake's assistance. But maybe I've been stupid to rely on him.

"If we get caught—"

"*When* you get caught." Jake puts his hand on my arm. "Remember that. Not *if. When.*"

"I don't get it. Are you threatening us? If you're going to narc on us, go ahead and tell the Director. It's not like I can do anything to stop you."

"I'm not turning you in. Don't you see that by now? You need protection. Things are escalating in here. It's not only me; I have—" Jake stops. Looks down and shakes his head.

"You have what?"

"Nothing. There are others trying to help, within certain parameters, but we won't be able to save you if the Director orders an extrajudicial transfer and directs his private security detail to seize you in the middle of the night. You don't know what he is capable of. I do. Trust me on this."

"I think we saw a pretty good demonstration of his capabilities."

"People getting tased? Butted with a gun? Dragged away? Punched? That's nothing. That could've happened at a police station. Here, in this camp, once they take you into custody—this land is a designated war zone. Rules don't apply."

"I get it. Our civil liberties have been shredded."

"It's not about violating your constitutional rights. If you're caught and taken to a black-ops site for interrogation, they will do things to you. Things you can't imagine. That woman taken at the orientation? She wasn't sent to black ops. That was getting roughed up a bit. I'm talking torture. You know those guys who go missing? Why do you think they never come back?"

His words slam into my chest. So far, David, Ayesha, Soheil, and I, we've mostly talked and planned and played at being the Mobius Resistance. Now I realize how totally amateur we've been. The stakes are high. The highest. And I'm not sure if any of us are ready to take on the Director and his real-world consequences.

I take a deep breath. "I have to do something. If what you're saying is true, we have to tell people. I don't think people on the outside will tolerate this if they know."

"That's why the Director wants this place airtight. Information does not get out. This camp is the first, another is about to open, and the High Command within the Authority won't stop at two. They want internment to go wide scale."

"High Command?"

"It's all under the auspices of the secretary of war, but it's made up of Homeland Security guys. CIA and FBI, too. You need to understand that the president operates like the Constitution is a blank slate. His party holds the Senate and the House. No one is challenging him. People won't even call him out on his blatant lies."

My shoulders fall. I feel like my entire body is going to melt into the floor. I look into his eyes and whisper, "Help us, Jake."

He takes a tissue out of his pocket and hands it to me. "Let's keep moving. This looks suspicious. I've got to get you back."

As we turn to continue our walk back to Block 2, the Director's very large presence steps in front of us, blotting out the sun. One of the drones follows behind him.

"Director—" Jake struggles to gather himself, then clicks his heels into attention. "Sir."

This is as near as I've ever been to the Director. This close, I see that his jaw juts out, making his swollen purple lips even more prominent.

I turn my head to look at Jake, but his eyes are trained on an object in the distance. I wish I could do that—focus but not focus. But when my adrenaline spikes, like it is now, when my body feels fight and flight in the same instant, everything falls into sharp focus. Almost too sharp. And I hear the grind of a truck's engine starting up, desert floor crunching under heavy wheels. I wonder if that's the truck David's on. I pray it is. I imagine the gate opening and closing and him being safe on the outside.

The Director uses silence. Like after that woman was tased and when he waited for Noor's and Asmaa's and Bilqis's screams to fall away, making sure we all heard. Silence might be a tool, but it doesn't look like one he wields comfortably. He pulls at his collar with his index finger. The sun beats down on us. I watch as sweat beads up on his forehead; he dabs at it with a white handkerchief.

"I see you've ventured on a little field trip, Miss Amin. Not hanging out with your friend on the block? What...watching the soccer players?"

He knows my name. He knows all of us. I've been trying not to draw attention to myself. Maybe I've been careless. The Director might be uncomfortable, but he's not unaware. Every muscle in his body seems ready to pounce like a dog that has been trained to fight.

My chest tightens. Too tight. I pray that this stupid baggy T-shirt conceals the phone in my pocket. The blood rushes to my head, and the world feels like it's tilting. I focus my eyes on a single point in the distance to keep my balance.

I straighten my shoulders and remind myself to breathe. "Uh, yes. Director. Sir. It's just that I—" My mind goes blank. I have no words.

"She lost her necklace in the Mess, sir, and I escorted her there so she could find it." Jake steps in, using the same lie

I gave him; he speaks faster than usual, his consonants not as crisp.

The Director moves in closer. Every cell in my body screams at me to run, but my feet are glued in place. He runs his thick index finger over my infinity necklace. It's the same gesture David made. But vile. My stomach lurches. I turn my face away and close my eyes.

"That looks like a very special necklace," the Director says.

I taste the bile in my throat. "Yes, it is. My boyfriend gave it to me."

The Director smiles. It's revolting. And I realize immediately I've said something I shouldn't have. I made myself less anonymous. I gave him an opening. And I have no doubt he'll use it as ammunition if he needs to.

"A boyfriend? How nice. He's not in here with you? So I don't suppose he's a Muslim, now, is he?"

Shit. Why did I open my mouth? And why did the truth have to come out of it?

"No, sir," I whisper.

"And you are aware that the Exclusion Authority frowns on this type of interreligious mingling?"

I cringe at his words but say nothing. I cross my arms over my stomach and look down at the ground. My breaths feel shallow, feathery. I hear Jake's boot heel grinding into the dirt.

The Director continues, clearly not noticing or not caring how uncomfortable his words make me. No. He wants this— my discomfort, my pain. "So what *is* your boyfriend's religion?"

My eyes start to sting. I blink, willing myself not to cry. But I lose this battle with myself, and a tear falls down my cheek. Lying is not going to work now; it's too easy for him to find out the truth. A quick call to my high school and he'll know David's name, too. "He's Jewish," I say. Saying it out loud feels like a betrayal. America might only be rounding up Muslims right now, and the Director might only be focused on us, but bigots don't generally limit their hate. Islamophobes are likely anti-Semites, too. From the scowl on his face, I'm guessing the Director is one of them.

"Yes, well..." The Director pauses and inches closer to me. I can smell stale coffee on his breath. "Do let me know if you misplace that precious souvenir again. I have eyes everywhere, all the time." He glances at the nearby drone, then turns his eyes back to me.

"Sir," Jake says loudly. Louder than needed for how close we all are.

The Director takes a step back and looks toward Jake. "Corporal?"

"Sir, I'll be taking an additional patrol duty since Johnson was called away. His replacement should be reporting to Mobius within the week, sir."

"Good. I'm sure you have it under control." The Director strokes his chin and nods.

"Sir. Yes, sir."

The Director steps past me, presumably heading to his office in the admin building. Then he stops and turns back.

I suck in my breath and bite my lip. I take a wobbly step backward. Jake places his hand behind my back to steady me.

The drone behind the Director rises up to shoulder level and turns its camera to me. "Remember what I said, Miss Amin. I see everything. I will keep this camp safe. You can rest assured of that," he says, then walks away, threats lingering in the dust of his wake.

CHAPTER 18

Ayesha and I hurry toward the Peace Garden. That's what they're calling it. The Peace Garden. At least fascism doesn't kill irony. Soheil is already at the bare plot, raking the earth, spreading out the soil where seeds will grow. And he has the reinforcements he recruited—fifteen others are here with him, digging in the dirt. The librarian gave us a gardening tutorial the other day. The Director stopped by to wish us all well, but mainly, I think, to make his presence known. To remind us that everything in Mobius exists at his pleasure. Or not. There are tools and seeds and plant food and watering cans that can be filled from a trough. At first I was surprised that they'd even let us have access to metal tools, but as I watch Jake join the two other guards, I realize that the Director's confidence in the Exclusion Authority's gunpower is absolute. He knows we fear him, or at least his "consequences," so he can afford to show a sort of twisted benevolence by letting us have certain freedoms in the camp.

I haven't told Ayesha about what happened with the Director yesterday, not yet. She's going to freak out. Part of me is still freaking out, too. His not-so-subtle threats and warning about having eyes everywhere is not something I can downplay.

Ayesha and I grab small trowels to begin digging little holes in the earth where the seeds will go. Soheil approaches and squats next to us, sweat dripping down his neck. "I see you brought your shadow," he says to me, raising his eyebrow and tilting his head toward Jake.

I look up at Jake. He still has that uneven tan on the back of his neck. When he escorted me to my trailer after that run-in with the Director, he said he'd try to keep a closer eye on me, too. He means to make me feel protected, but nothing about having people—or drones, for that matter—watching me makes me feel safe.

I put my trowel down and stick my fingers into the soil. It feels cool and moist against my skin. They brought in soil for this project because the desert dirt wasn't conducive to growing things. It's an expense, but maybe they think the price of appearing to be benevolent rulers instead of tyrants has a cost benefit—it's cheaper than bullets and burying bodies. The worrisome thing is it makes some of the internees feel that way, too. Like maybe this isn't as bad as it could be.

They're right; it could be much, much worse. And I'm afraid of being the reason it turns ugly. Uglier.

"Listen, guys," I whisper to Soheil and Ayesha. "I think we should put off the fast."

Both Soheil and Ayesha stop digging and look at me. Ayesha squints against the sun as she looks in my eyes.

"What?" Soheil asks in a loud voice. When a couple of heads turn to look at us, he immediately lowers his volume and continues. "Why? I've been recruiting people, as you can see. They're ready. We're ready." His voice is low, but there's an edge to it.

Ayesha rests her hand on his forearm for a second. "Ease up, Soheil. Maybe Layla has a reason." Then she turns her expectant face toward me.

I quickly tell them what happened yesterday—seeing David, almost getting caught, what the Director said. Ayesha wraps an arm around me.

"I'm sorry. Are you okay?" Soheil asks.

"Yeah, Jake was with me."

Soheil raises an eyebrow. "I know you said you trust him—"

"I did. And that hasn't changed." I've doubted, too, but I don't share that with them. I pick up my trowel and start digging again and gesture for Ayesha and Soheil to do the same.

"I trust you," Ayesha says to me, and then turns to Soheil, handing him a seed packet. "You should, too."

Soheil takes a breath and faces me. "I do trust *you*, Layla.

But I don't trust his motives. Watch your back, is all. He could still turn you in at any time. He's a guard. His job is to keep you imprisoned here. Don't forget that."

"I won't. And I'm not forgetting that people could get hurt or disappeared, and that's why I'm worried about doing the fast. Maybe it's too small. We'll all get taken away or tased, and then it will be over. That's a temper tantrum, not a revolution. And we need to organize better and steel ourselves for the days ahead. Whatever we do will be dangerous, and we can't be naïve. Naïveté comes at too high a cost."

"What was that quote from the girl from the White Rose?" Ayesha asks. She takes my hand in hers and squeezes. "'Someone has to make a start'? I'm as scared as anyone else. I'm not a brave person. But I know we need to act before things get worse. This fast—maybe it's small, but it's how we start."

Soheil moves so he's facing both of us but looks directly into Ayesha's eyes. "You're brave," he whispers. She gives him a soft smile. "And you're right, Layla. We do still have to do this. Now more than ever. Don't lose faith. Don't let complacency creep in. We're all scared. Courage isn't the absence of fear. It's doing the right thing in spite of it."

Hearing their words, looking at my friends, I know they're right. It's so hard to act when you also feel terrified all the time. That's what the Director is counting on—terror seeks silence, not screams.

Ayesha nudges Soheil. "Dig, or they'll think you're conspiring. Or worse, flirting."

I grin and look down, feigning interest in my trowel. From the corner of my eye, I notice Soheil smile at Ayesha.

The hum of a drone snares everyone's attention. Before it's on top of us, Soheil quickly murmurs, "Friday. Dinner fast. Everyone here is in. This is happening."

The red metal of the drone glints in the blazing sun; I shield my eyes from the light and stare at the mechanical spy as if it has eyes. I grit my teeth and quash an impulse to throw a trowel at it. Jake catches my eye and gives me an almost imperceptible shake of the head. I'm not sure how he knows what I'm thinking. I mouth an *okay* and get back to work.

We toil away for a couple hours in the heat, sweating and even finding moments to laugh. It's hard work, but I lose myself in the simple rhythm of digging a hole and planting a seed on repeat. As noon approaches, the group begins to break up, seeking shade and food. Ayesha waves to me as she walks toward Soheil's block for lunch. She asked me to join them, but I give them their semblance of privacy.

I dump my tools with the others and then refill my water bottle and take a long gulp. The dirt on my hands turns to mud as condensation appears almost instantly on the plastic. I wipe one hand, then the other, on a small patch of my jeans that's not already dusty.

"My mom loved gardening." Jake's voice comes from behind me. As he approaches me, I refill my bottle.

"Loved? She doesn't any longer?"

"She died when I was twelve." Jake kicks at the earth with the back of his heel. "In summer I always remember her with dirt under her nails and on her jeans. She had a pair she only wore for gardening. I swear the knees were made of mud patches." A melancholy smile spreads across his face.

"I'm sorry," I say.

He shrugs. "It's been a while. My brother was a lot older, already out of the house. And my dad and I, we made out okay." Jake's not looking at me while he talks. He's focusing on the mountains in the distance. It's the same look he had in his eyes when the Director stopped us yesterday. Focused, but not on what's in front of him. I'm also keenly aware that this is the first time he's ever really talked about his life outside of being a guard, and the first time that I've ever really considered that he has one.

"That must've been hard," I say.

"My dad's a military guy, too. Army. Ran the house like clockwork. A rule for everything. I think that's kind of what saved me. The structure. In the military, everyone doing their job, the organization of it, that's what keeps you safe. That's how my dad showed his love, I think. By protecting us. He wasn't big on words or feelings. That was my mom's job. But she wasn't a softy, either." Jake chuckles a little to himself. He doesn't say it, but the pained look in his eyes makes it clear he misses her.

"It's never easy to lose what you love. No matter how much

order you have in your life." My voice cracks a little when I say this, and it surprises me.

Jake finally turns to look at me, wearing that same sad smile, but a part of him is still focusing on something in the distance.

I'm lying on my bed. My parents are still at "work." I'll meet them in the Mess for dinner. Normally I use up my shower minutes at night, right before bed, but my body is coated with the salt from my dried sweat, and a dull ache has settled into my bones, and I want to rinse it all away. I close my eyes for a moment and imagine my deliciously soft bed and the worn *kantha* quilt. That bed, that home, feels like another lifetime. Like I was a different person, and now I have these memories of a life that is not my own.

There's a knock on our door. Ayesha said she'd stop by to give me the most-likely-chaste details about her lunch with Soheil. I whip off my towel turban and let the wet strands of my hair fall down my back and hurry to the door.

Pulling it open, I say, "So how's Soh—"

It's not Ayesha.

It's Jake. "Let me in, quick," he says, then pulls his lips together in a sort of grimace.

I freeze for a moment. Unsure what this means. Why he's here. I feel the dampness of my hair soak through the back of my T-shirt, making me shiver. I look up and down the block.

No one is around. I step aside, allowing him in. Hoping, praying, this is the right decision.

We stand in the common area of my trailer. I dig my hands into my pockets and rock back and forth on my heels, waiting for Jake to say something. Jake steps toward me and smiles a huge fake grin and puts his hand on my shoulder. I flinch. He looks me in the eye and nods at me ever so slightly. He doesn't say a word, but he gestures to my bedroom and begins walking back there. When I don't move, he motions for me to follow. This is a huge leap of faith, and I hope it's not into the abyss.

I suck in my breath and enter my room. Soheil's words of warning float in the air around me: Don't trust anyone. But I *do* trust my instincts; I pray those instincts are right. Jake shuts the door behind us.

"Now what?" I say a little too loudly.

Jake puts a finger to his lips and steps closer to me. "There's no camera in here, but keep your voice down anyway. Sorry to be mysterious, but the bedrooms are the only places the drones and cameras can't get to."

"But they saw you on the camera in the common room coming into my bedroom. Isn't that suspicious?"

"A guard going into a woman's bedroom—let's say it's probably happening, and the Director doesn't care."

"Gross. That's. Just. Wrong. It's a guard and a *prisoner*. A prisoner can't consent. It's—"

"It's coercion. It's rape. I don't know of any guards personally, but there is talk."

"Jake, you can't let it. You have to—"

"I know. And if I see something happening, I will stop it. I swear. Now, listen. What are you planning? Out there at the garden with everyone else?"

"Nothing," I say flatly. Clearly, he knows something, but I'm not sure I should tell him anything. Not even sure it's my right. It involves too many other people.

"I understand why you're suspicious. It's smart. It's survival." Jake makes a quick, precise exhale. And another one. Almost like he's counting them in his head. He pulls off his cap and runs his hands through his short dirty-blond hair, damp with sweat. "Look, the Director—he's talking about bringing more guards in here. He feels the rumblings in the camp, an air of dissent. He's vindictive and petty, but he's not stupid. Remember that young Arab American woman they dragged away—"

My muscles go taut; I clench my hands into fists. "Noor. She has a name."

Jake nods. "Sorry, yes. Noor. You know how she wore an American flag hijab?"

I nod.

"Apparently, it got torn off somewhere in the struggle, and it showed up this morning on the door of the admin building. Ripped, stained with blood. And scrawled across it in black marker was the word 'Resist.'"

A strange kind of elation bubbles inside me. I don't know what happened to Noor or the other women. I'm afraid to even think about it. But Ayesha, Soheil, me—we're not alone. No, it's not joy that's welling inside me. It's hope. "Who? How? His security detail and the guards are everywhere by the admin building and the Hub."

Jake continues. "I know. Should not have been possible. He knows that, too. A part of him fears it could be a guard."

My jaw drops. "Holy shit."

Jake continues. "The Director went ballistic. And it's like he warned you: He wants more eyes, everywhere. He trusts me for now, and—"

"He trusts you? Is that supposed to make me feel better?"

"Yes. It should. Look, it took me a long time to get to this. Too long. It's what I was saying before. I grew up military. Orders were sacrosanct in my house. But I received counter-orders, too. Being in here. Meeting you and the others. I finally understood the real mission, my sworn duty to protect this country from enemies foreign and domestic."

I don't quite get what he's trying to say, and he can read the quizzical look on my face.

"Layla, I'm an Exclusion Guard, but that's not all. I've already said more than I should, put you at risk—"

"What does that mean? And why, why are you going along—" I'm bursting with questions and confusion, and my head feels woozy.

Jake takes a step toward me, closing the distance between

us. "I'm sorry," he says in a gentle, low voice that catches me off guard. "I hate going along with it, but I have to for now. And I'm sorry if anything I've done or may do hurts you. The Director has to trust me; that's why he's having me keep an eagle eye on you. He thinks I have your confidence, and that I'll inform him of anything suspicious. I have to play along for now. It's the only way I can keep you safe." His voice quiets to a whisper, and he gently wraps his fingers around my upper arm. I look down at his hands. Then he quickly pulls them away. I'm startled, but not afraid.

"I'm worried for me, too. For all of us. Most days there isn't a moment I'm not scared, but there's a fire burning all around me, and I can't stand by and do nothing, and you should understand that. And isn't what you're doing putting you in danger?"

"I'm doing my duty, Layla. My sworn duty."

"Well, I'm doing mine, too." My voice is a squeak, and it makes me cringe.

Jake's eyes soften. "I need you to understand. The Director? What he said to you the other day? He won't be trifled with. He will hurt you, and I might not be able to stop him. And I can't—"

Tears well in my eyes. "I know the Director can do things to us without anyone paying attention or caring, but if we don't do something now, if we stay silent, what's next? If we're going to be disappeared anyway, we can't go down without a fight." When I hear the words in my mind, they sound brave, but coming out of my mouth they are weighted down by fear.

Jake rubs his forehead. "I was afraid you were going to say that. Remember, you're not alone. There are dustups on the outside. Protests at the White House. People are talking. The Director is keeping that from you, from everyone, but it's not silent out there. It's loud, and getting louder."

I muster a small smile. "All the more reason for us to rise up on the inside." My voice breaks a little, and a tear trails down my cheek. "I'm terrified," I whisper, and then clear my throat. I feel like I'm confessing something I shouldn't. But I don't know how to act strong, be strong all the time, when I'm mostly scared and alone and lonely. I look up at Jake, into his kind, warm eyes.

He hesitates. Reaches his arms out slightly. Then I hug him. And he wraps his arms around me. And they feel safe. A part of me knows this isn't right, but for this tiny moment I need human comfort, and Jake's arms give me that. I want to draw from his strength to bolster my own as it wavers in fear of what the future holds.

But this also feels wrong. I open my eyes and push back against Jake, almost tripping over my shoes.

He steps back, and a look of dismay crosses his face. "Layla, I'm sorry. I'm so sorry. I don't know what I was thinking."

I shake my head, and words spill from my lips. "It's this place. I feel so alone. I miss David so much. It's like I'm in a crypt and the door is slowly being sealed shut. And I can't hold it open. And no one can hear me screaming."

I look at him and see a guy a few years older than me.

Someone who, in a different world, would be walking across the same college campus, who might help me find my way the first week of freshman year, the handsome senior who's the RA in my dorm. A friend. A confidant. But that world doesn't exist. He's a guard in my internment camp. That's reality. It is my present, and I'm trying desperately to make sure it isn't my future.

"You're not alone, Layla. I'll do everything I can to protect you. The Director believes me. He asked me to report on your activities, so I'll be close by—as much as I possibly can."

I mouth a silent thank-you. "I believe you. And we're planning—"

"Stop. I know I asked, but don't tell me. If I don't know, they can't get it out of me, no matter what."

"Plausible deniability?" I ask. "That sounds so spy movie." I manage a small smile, but I realize what he really means.

If you don't know the truth, they can't torture it out of you.

CHAPTER 19

"Layla, do you want to walk with us toward the Hub?" my mom calls from outside my bedroom door. The burner David gave me clatters to the floor. Shit. "Are you okay?"

"Fine! Dropped my hairbrush. I'll walk over with you guys. Gimme a second," I yell while grabbing the phone and tucking it between my mattress and the wall. I still haven't told Jake about it, and mostly I've been too scared to use it, and I can't have the sound on, ever. I'm trying to save the precious minutes for emergencies. Honestly, though, life in here *is* one giant emergency. Calling feels too risky, but I've texted David and plan to meet him again. Today.

I check my front pocket for the hundredth time this morning. My next article, safely tucked inside. My green-and-purple

Wimbledon shirt hangs over the waist of my jeans. When I walk out of my room, my parents are sitting at the table, finishing their tea. The small table abuts the wall of the trailer and sits beneath a window. This morning, the dust on the window filters the light as it beams in, bathing their daily routine in a kind of soft glow. Every time I step out in the morning and see them, they seem to have aged overnight, like sleep is actually draining life from them instead of recharging their batteries. I suppose that maybe they're not sleeping at all. But right now, in this light, I'm reminded of an old photo in a small oxidized-silver frame that sits on my mom's dresser. It's them, but much younger, before I was born. Sometime when they first met. My mom says a friend took it when they were visiting Paris. They're in a café, sitting at a small, round green table, next to a plate-glass window. Mom's red-lacquered fingernails pop against the cream-colored coffee cup in her hands. My dad's curly hair flops over one of his eyes. And he's looking at her while she looks out the window, soft light falling on her face. Suddenly I realize how beautiful and perfect that photo is. A lump forms in my throat.

I walk over and kiss each of them on the cheek. My mom smiles at me, and my dad takes my hand. "I have something for you," he says, then hands over a paperback, its edges frayed and bent.

"*Persuasion*?" I say.

My dad nods. "The selection in the Hub library is not

extensive, but there are some quality older titles in there. I think you'll really like this story. And don't you think it's time you got back to your regular studies?"

I knit my eyebrows at my dad. My studies. Yes, that is the main thing I'm worried about in here, making sure I can pass the GED. They're running a makeshift school for the younger kids, but as of yet there is no Mobius High giving out diplomas. I am about to say something sarcastic, but I stop myself. "Thanks, Dad. I loved *Pride and Prejudice*. I'm sure I'll love this, too."

"It's about a young woman, Anne Elliot, who is very modern in her own way. It's about characters not merely finding themselves but remaining true to who they are. In some ways, at the time, it was considered quite subversive," my dad says, holding eye contact with me. Then he quickly adds, "Of course, that was a very long time ago, and now you can simply enjoy it, and then I'll have you write an essay on it."

He hesitated to say that word, "subversive." Changed his tune. The cameras, the eyes on us all the time, make us all masters of hiding the truth but force us to find creative ways to communicate with one another, too. More lies we tell to live. "Thanks, Dad. Can't wait to write an essay on it," I say, my tone perhaps a little too chipper.

We head out the door together. My fingers shake. I'm hyperaware of the note in my pocket and the queasy feeling in my stomach because of what I'm concealing now from my parents, from Ayesha, from Jake. It's better for them not to know. Plausible deniability. Isn't that what Jake and I agreed to?

Together with my parents, I walk down the Midway. They smile and offer a salaam to everyone we pass. Everyone returns the greeting in kind. Like our smiles are real. When we're halfway there, I say good-bye to my parents, telling them I want to go back and get my book so I can read in the Hub library.

I turn back and walk toward our block, looking over my shoulder to see them walk into the Hub. Then I cross through the camp to the blocks on the opposite side of the Midway. People are out, heading toward their jobs or taking the little ones to the grandparent day care or school. Some people have laundry bags. Others carry empty boxes that they'll fill up with kitchen staples from the supply area. I don't run; I don't try to hide. I keep my eyes open for the drones and guards. I hear the sanitation trucks enter the gate and see the men in their khaki uniforms fan out around the camp. I don't spy David, but I know he's here. I walk to the side entrance of the Mess. It's usually unguarded and unlocked when the garbage has to be taken out. I glance around cautiously and let myself in.

Palms clammy and heart beating in my ears, I tiptoe to the kitchen. The Mess is mostly dark except for the lights along the perimeter of the room that let off a faint electronic buzz. I take extra care not to touch anything in the kitchen, afraid of the noise, afraid of what could happen.

The pantry door is ajar. A light radiates from inside. I hold my breath and walk cautiously forward. As I place my fingers on the doorframe, a hand reaches out and grabs mine and pulls me.

I fall into David's embrace. He kisses me so softly and deeply that it makes me want to cry. As scared as I am of hiding that burner phone between my mattress and the wall, I'm so thankful that it made this moment in the pantry of the Mess possible. David nuzzles my neck. "I miss you." Then he steps back. "I have to show you something." He reaches into his khaki uniform and pulls his phone out and shows me the screen. A headline screams FASCISM AT MOBIUS: AN INSIDER SPEAKS.

"They put it up as I was getting here," David whispers. "KALA-TV ran the story and read your post on the air. The reporter said to expect it to explode. It probably already has. The whole world is going to know you, or at least your words. Layla, you did it. You're amazing."

David's words muffle in my ears. My eyes fix on the screen. I read the headline again, and it knocks the wind out of me. I scan the words, *my* words. And then I'm there again, in that moment. Hearing it. Noor's screams. The security guys dragging her away. Asmaa and Bilqis, who tried to help her. Their blood staining the dry earth. The Director. The gun. Tears fill my eyes. I whisper, "The whole world will know their names."

David wipes away the tears from my cheeks, then kisses each one. "Yes. Everyone will know their names, thanks to you."

"And you," I say. I run my fingers through David's hair; it's damp from sweat. He's always there for me. Literally, he's here right now, next to me, but in this rare, unrushed moment, I'm aware that there's a tiny space between us, a distance that I don't know how to fill. I'm not sure what it is. Maybe it's because of the fight we had when he first snuck in here to see me. Maybe it's because of the electric fence that seems to separate us even when I'm in his arms. I don't know why exactly, but it feels awful. And I try to push that emotion away because I don't want to feel it. He's taking huge risks to see me, to help me. I want it all to be like it was. I am desperate for a brief moment of Before with David. The minty smell of his soap, the warmth of his arms, how when our fingers intertwine, the brown of my skin and the brown of his are nearly a perfect match. All the familiar sensations of home. I need that feeling so badly right now. But as I grasp for it, I know it's out of reach, even though David is right next to me. I kiss him and then take his hand and pass him another story I've written out in tiny print.

"The hunger strike is tomorrow," I whisper.

"I'm scared for you."

"I am, too. I'm scared for all of us, but Jake is keeping an eye out."

David breaks from our embrace. "I know he's helped us, but are you sure you can trust him? That this isn't all a ruse?"

"I trust him. I know why you feel that way. I can't say more. I mean, I don't even know more. He could've already given me up, like, a hundred times to the Director, but he hasn't. He's on our side."

David shakes his head. "I can't trust someone who has a gun on you, and you shouldn't, either."

I take a deep breath. "He won't hurt anyone, and he definitely won't hurt me. I promise."

David raises an eyebrow. "Is there something else I should know? What are you not saying?" That space I'm imagining between us widens, ever so slightly.

"No. It's not like that. Please, believe me. I love you. Plus, jealousy doesn't suit you." My heart is in a vise. Maybe David feels a little of that distance between us, too.

The door slams, startling both of us.

"Come out now. I know you're in here," Jake's voice bellows through the Mess, and we hear him stomp into the kitchen. I reach for the doorknob, but David touches my hand and shakes his head no.

But it doesn't matter, because Jake pulls open the pantry door. His jaw is clenched. His face is grave and official. Angry. He's every inch the corporal right now. "This was stupid," he whispers, but his voice seethes. "He knows." Then he turns to me. "Do you have another story on you?"

I open my mouth, hesitate.

"There's no time. He's going to be here any minute. You need to give it to me."

I reach into David's pocket and pull out the piece of paper with my handwriting on it. I hand it to Jake, and he quickly tucks it into his boot. David looks at me, his mouth open in shock.

The main door to the Mess bursts open. All the lights are flipped on. The Director marches into the kitchen with two of his private security detail. They aren't military; they aren't Exclusion Guards. They're the two who dragged Noor away. Private security doesn't need to uphold an oath to the Constitution. They are loyal to the Director, and only to him.

"Good work, Corporal Reynolds. Restrain Miss Amin." Spit flies out of the Director's mouth as he speaks. His face reddens to a deep crimson, the veins on his neck taut like wires pulled too tight. All my muscles tense. My breath goes raspy, like there's not enough air to breathe in the room. Every single time I'm frightened in here, I think that I've never been so scared; but always, always, I keep finding there's another level of fear I had no concept of.

Jake is standing in front of us; he turns and looks at me, softening his eyes for the briefest of seconds. He takes me by the arm. I look wildly from the Director to his security detail to Jake and then to David. I jerk myself away from Jake and wrap my arms around David's neck and whisper, "Your phone. Instagram. Now." Jake pulls me back, a look of shock in his eyes.

"It was me. It was all me. David didn't do anything." I say this knowing that none of it matters.

The Director rubs his hands together like he's washing them. "Thank you for that admission, Miss Amin, but I believe there is enough blame to go around. There certainly will be consequences for everyone involved." The Director's face is almost gleeful. It doesn't cause a shiver of fright. I'm long past simple fear. I feel like ants are running all over my skin, like I know I'm in a nightmare and I'm clawing to get the ants off me, but all I'm doing is hurting myself.

I manage a few words. "David's not an internee. He has civil rights. The rule of law exists." Jake, who is still holding on to my elbow, gently tugs at my arm, a warning that I'm digging a deeper hole for myself. But I have to say something. David is only here because of me. Because I asked him to come. Because I needed him. And now he's going to get hurt because I'm a selfish asshole.

"I *am* the law," the Director rages, then motions to his private security detail. One of them grabs me from Jake.

"No!" I scream as the man shoves me against the fridge. It happens so fast. My cheek slams against the hard, cold metal before I can grasp what is going on, and the voices and bodies blur around me. I hear Jake yell something about my being a minor.

David steps out in front of the Director. From the corner of my eye, I see him shaking. "I'm sure the world is interested in how you're the law now and how you're hurting kids in here. Kids." He's holding his camera in front of him, filming. "I'm live streaming on Instagram Live. That's Layla Amin. Californian. American citizen."

I catch David's eye as he steps closer to me and the man who is still holding me against the fridge.

The Director pulls at his collar, his face beet red. He's breathing so loudly through his nostrils that I expect him to exhale fire.

Jake steps forward and moves the security detail away from me, gently pulling me back from the fridge and placing his hand at the small of my back. David keeps filming. Jake speaks in a calm, deliberate voice. "Sorry about that"—Jake pauses slightly and looks at the Director—"accident, Miss Amin. I'm sure the Director would want you to get checked out at the infirmary. The Exclusion Authority has clear regulations on the treatment of minors at Mobius."

The Director clears his throat and takes a step away from us, into the shadow of a large shelf of supplies. "Yes, we want to make sure Miss Amin wasn't hurt because of this little snafu. We are simply trying to ascertain who might be spreading these lies about Mobius." He pulls a tablet from his suit pocket. "Miss Amin, I'm certain you can assure your boyfriend's viewers that these allegations are false."

I square myself to look the Director in the eye. The left side of my face throbs and burns. I ball my hands into fists. "I can do no such thing, Director."

The Director takes a stride toward me, but Jake steps between us and says, "I'm sure Miss Amin can't comment because she doesn't have access to that story, sir."

The Director narrows his eyes. The muscles in his neck bulge so much and he's so red, I'm not sure he's even breathing. I'm not sure *I'm* breathing. "Corporal, please escort our..." He clears his throat. "...our guest off-site and deliver Miss Amin to the infirmary, where I'm certain she'll get excellent care."

David keeps filming as the Director marches out with his security detail.

Once the door slams, David puts his phone down. He was narrating the whole time, I think, but I couldn't hear a thing besides the blood rushing in my ears. I collapse to my knees, crying into my hands.

David drops down next to me and strokes my back. "Layla, are you okay? I'm so sorry. I wish I could've done something."

I raise my eyes to his and see that they're filled with tears. I wipe my face on my sleeve and wince. My cheek is swelling up. "You did, and there's nothing more you could have done," I say, and kiss him on the cheek.

Jake steps to us and helps me up. David stands as well. "I'd say you've done quite enough, David."

I turn to Jake, shocked that he could be so cruel after what almost happened. After what *did* happen. "Jake—" I begin, but he cuts me off.

"Do you have any idea what you've done?" He directs his remarks only to David. "You're on the outside. She's in here. You may think you've gotten away with something, that you were clever. But you get to walk out of here, and she doesn't. And what—giving Layla a burner to keep in her trailer?" Then he turns to me. "Which I will be confiscating, by the way. Security is going to be tighter than ever now. This place will be Fort Knox."

David looks like he was punched in the gut. His eyes trail away from Jake to me. "Devastated" is the only word that comes to mind to describe him. As Jake spoke, I watched David's face and could almost feel the full range of his thoughts—starting with defensive anger and moving on to fear, then sadness, and finally horror. I know, because I felt those things, too.

Jake shakes his head. "We have to get you both out of here. Now."

We walk toward the main gate, Jake between us like a chaperone. David and I can't hold hands, and we definitely can't kiss good-bye. With each step, reality sinks in, that David will never be able to get in here again, even if Jake were willing to help us—which clearly he won't be.

I feel utterly helpless as we stop in front of the gate. David turns to me and mouths, *I love you.* He tries to step closer, but Jake positions himself between us.

David gulps, then offers a hand to Jake. "Please keep her safe," he says, his voice barely a scratch. Jake shakes David's hand and then calls over another guard. He whispers something close to the man's ear. The guard nods.

David and I simply stare at each other. I know he feels like I do: overwhelmed by the truth that we are powerless right now.

The other guard motions to David to follow him. He does, but for the entire distance to the gate, David walks with his head turned back, half smiling at me, like he's willing things to be okay. Jake pulls me away, toward the infirmary, and my heart wants to fight him, but my body can't anymore. Not now. So I give David one last, longing look.

"Will he be okay?" I ask.

Jake sighs. "Yup. Fred will drive him back to town. Make sure he gets to his motel safely. Fred's also going to tell him to spread the hell out of that video. The Director will be furious. It's bad enough David was live streaming, but knowing it will go viral...and after that post you wrote...That's why you were foolish to do this."

"I know."

"You've put yourself in danger. Your friends and parents, too."

"I know."

"And I can't be here all the time to keep an eye—"

"Jake," I say more loudly than I intended. "I know. We totally fucked up. I didn't think through the consequences. I know you could be in danger, too."

Jake's shoulders sink. "Layla," he says softly, "I'm not worried about me. Hell, the Director thinks I got to you first to turn you in. I saved him in there. He'll probably trust me more. But knowing what he could do to you..." Jake touches my elbow.

It might not be the time to ask this question, but what

other time is there? "What are you going to do with the article I wrote?"

"Don't worry. I'll get it out. After that story today, every news station and blog will be champing at the bit for more. You were right. The world needs to know what is happening here. The world needs to learn about the torture at the black-ops sites and the disappearances of citizens."

I put my hand on Jake's arm. His muscles go taut. "Be careful, Jake."

"Don't worry about me. I'm the one with the gun, remember?"

"And what am I supposed to do?"

"Look, there's the Red Cross visit tomorrow. The Director is tense. He wants to put on a good show. He can't afford to look like he's not in control. Command will be breathing down his neck with the information breach in here. So you'll be okay for now. And after that, well…I'll figure something out." Jake grins, but it's a wan smile; there's no heart behind it.

I don't believe his words, and I'm guessing he doesn't believe them, either.

CHAPTER 20

I stand in front of the door to my trailer and press the ice pack against my cheek.

I squeeze my eyes shut. My mind, turning and turning. My center cannot hold anymore. Any minute, gravity will triple and crush me like an empty soda can. When I open my eyes, I want to be on the beach. I want to walk into the ocean until I'm neck-deep in the Pacific, its waves lapping at my shoulders. I want to breathe in the salt air and let the water wash the dust off my body and rinse the fear from my soul. I want to feel the sting of the sea in my eyes and be buoyed by the waves and carried across time to another life. Can that be possible? Can I slash the fabric of space-time and disappear from Mobius? I open my eyes. Apparently, wishing things into existence only works in fantasy. And reality is everywhere around me.

My cheek stings. There is no way I can hide this from my parents. They might not hear about my Instagram fame, not immediately, because even when information does get in from the outside, it takes time; but they'll find out. How do I tell them I risked their lives to kiss my boyfriend? How do I tell them I wrote the post that is probably going viral? This place is already a prison, but when my parents learn what I've done, they won't let me leave the claustrophobic confines of this trailer.

I walk in resolved not to tell them the truth, knowing that for right now, for today, my lying might be best for all of us. As the door clicks shut behind me, an alarm blares across the camp and makes me jump back. Then an announcement echoes through the valley: "Return to your Mercury Homes immediately. Await instructions via your media units." I look out the window and see people rushing back to their trailers. My parents enter ours, out of breath. I look at my mom's disheveled hair and the rattled look in my dad's eyes. Things are going to get worse for my parents because of me.

"We rushed back from the Hub," my dad says, walking to the kitchen sink, where he fills a glass of water for my mom and then one for himself. They both lean against the tiny kitchen counter and take deep gulps. Then they look at my red, swollen cheek.

"My God," my mother says as she crosses to me and gently pulls the ice pack from my cheek to take a look. "What happened, *beta*? Did someone hurt you?"

"No, I'm fine. I tripped on the stairs coming back to get my book and smashed my face against the door. I'm such a—"

The media unit flicks on, and the Director's angry face fills the screen. "Our community has been betrayed. Someone has leaked lies about life here at Mobius, and these deceptions are agitating people on the outside. We will find the culprit; make no mistake. Until then, the entire community will be held accountable."

My jaw clenches. Rage burns inside me. The Director means to scare people into submission. And it will work because, more and more, he wears his hatred on his face, losing the pretense of civility. Good. I'm glad. The mask is gone, and the gloves are off, and I'm going to use my anger to steel my resolve.

The Director continues: "It is up to you, fellow citizens of Mobius, to out this hateful fearmonger who has so willfully disrupted the order in our peaceful community. Keep your eyes open for anything suspicious. If you see something, say something. Your minders are available day and night. Those who cooperate will find the rewards worth their while. As I announced last week, we will be hosting our friends from the Red Cross tomorrow. We will show them the pride we take in the community we've built here at Mobius. We will show them our gardens and recreation areas and clinic and early-childhood classes. We will show them the many benefits of our idyllic camp. They will dine with us in the Mess. And we will all abide the regulations." The Director pauses to smile into the camera. It's not a smile, really. It's more of a snarl. A dare. "Never forget. Unity. Security. Prosperity." I swear, I can see flames in his eyes.

The media unit goes black.

My parents' faces are ashen.

"Who would do something like that?" my mom wonders out loud. "And how? It's completely foolish. They're putting everyone in danger." She rests her head on my dad's shoulder.

"Maybe we don't know the whole story," I say.

My mom raises her head and stares at me, like she's studying my face for the first time. I'm waiting for her to tell me there's no excuse for putting the whole camp at risk. That we should all try to get along in here as well as we can, follow the rules. Since our first moment here, my parents have been painfully cognizant of the camera in the common room of our Mercury Home that captures every second of our lives. There is never a moment of ease, no relaxing. And that gnaws at you.

"You're right, *beta*."

I don't believe I'm hearing this. But I am.

Mom continues. "They have put us in danger, but we're in danger every moment anyway. Progress in this country always carries a component of risk. Every movement has—civil rights, marriage equality, women's rights—"

My dad grabs my mom's hand and squeezes it. He gives her the slightest, almost imperceptible headshake. He glances at the camera, then swivels his head back to my mom. His blood-shot eyes are wide with fear. My mom kisses him on the cheek. In many ways my parents seem so different from each other, but they possess this intimate mode of communication—a gesture, a look, a tone—that I envy. I wonder if I'll ever share that with someone, really find a person who understands me in a way that others don't. I love David so much, but right now there's also the cracked earth between us.

My mom reaches out for me so that she's holding both our hands. She whispers, "We will be okay."

I so much want to believe her. I'm sure she wants to believe herself, too. Maybe she does. Maybe she has more faith than I do. My dad certainly does.

My heart lightens a bit now, here with my parents. Even hearing my mom say those words makes this trailer feel less like solitary confinement. But I'm not willing to endanger their lives. I'll never tell my parents that it was me—that David and I are the disrupters, that Jake is helping, that this is merely the beginning. That a bruised cheek barely even scratches the sur-face of what the Director could do. My parents would try to stop me. It's their job to protect me; I get that. But I have a job to do, too—despite the fear rising from my gut and threaten-ing to explode every cell in my body. So, no, Director, I will not abide.

*   *   *

Dinner in the Mess passes quietly. No one is in much of a mood to talk after the Director's threats this afternoon. The minders greet everyone in their usual too-cheerful-to-be-sincere tones, pretending that everything is normal. Ayesha, Soheil, and I, along with the other gardeners and plotters, nod at one another. The fast is planned for tomorrow, the same day as the Red Cross visit, to be most impactful. To raise the stakes. But with my article out in the world, I've made the risks a lot higher. Is it possible to feel seasick in the desert? Because I do, and it must be written all over my face. When Soheil passes me, he whispers, "Nice work. Dig in. It's about to get real." I nod, try to screw my courage to the sticking place. He means his words to be reassuring, but I don't think any words could possibly sound heartening right now.

People quietly shuffle through the dust back to their Mercury Homes. Even though we are in an open-air camp, we breathe the recycled air of dread and anxiety. Like everyone else, I wonder about tomorrow. Hope. Fear. Anticipation.

The minders assign all of us special jobs for the Red Cross visit. They remind us about the rewards the Director will bestow if the visit runs smoothly. We'll never know what those pathetic rewards will be. Some people will be angry. Some people are willing to settle for crumbs. But the only reward we want is freedom. Though it's not exactly a reward when you're born with freedom and a thief sneaks into your home at night and steals it from you. It's something that's rightfully ours. We want it back.

Every muscle in my body is strained, like a rubber band stretched a millimeter too far.

When I walk through our door, I head straight to the shower. I let the water wash off the dust and the stress and the hurt of the day. I stare at the muddied water as it swirls down the drain. I take my first unencumbered breath. The timer dings. The water stops. Of course it does.

My parents are watching one of the approved TV shows on the media unit and trying to escape into another world. I wish them a good night and step into my room, tucking myself into bed and pulling the covers up to my neck. My body sinks into the mattress, and my eyelids droop shut. My sleep is deep and dreamless, but a nightmare wakes me with a start. I almost bang my head against the bunk but duck in time. I don't remember the dream exactly, but everything inside this place is the stuff of nightmares.

I slide my legs off the bed and step to the small window in my room. The sky is clear and full of stars; the mountains are silhouettes in the moonlight. It is beautiful here. But that's all on the other side of the fence, unreachable—like our freedom. So close. So far. I wonder if I'll ever look at mountains or a starry night sky the same way once we get out of here. *If.* Will their beauty always be marred by memories of Mobius? Will beauty simply cease to exist for me?

I'm scared for tomorrow. The fast—the protest. I look east, past the mountains. I hear Nanni's voice in my head, another prayer she used to whisper over me. A prayer that her own *nanni* shared with her, the one she said over and over during the Partition in India, when she was terrified of the mobs and the horror the British left in their wake. "God, protect me against them, however you may wish."

Protect us.

CHAPTER 21

Boom. Boom. Boom. I wake to loud knocking. A voice bellows through the door, "Get up. They're here."

My heart leaps out of my chest. Those bangs sounded like they came from inside my head. I look around and see the sun screaming through the blinds. My groggy brain realizes where I am.

I bolt out of bed and proceed to bump my head on the frame of the bunk. I'm at a 50 percent rate for smacking my head when I wake up. I rub the unlucky spot on my skull and clear my throat. "Ayesha? Who's here?"

"I'm coming in." Ayesha barges through the door as I stand up, rubbing the sleep from my eyes. She looks annoyingly awake. "Hurry up. Here, put this on." Ayesha hands me my worn gray Wonder Woman T-shirt and a pair of jeans. As

I'm dressing, she continues. "There are people. Press. Protestors. Outside the gate."

"What? I thought you meant the Red Cross."

"Them, too."

I wonder if David is with the protestors. He must've come back. He wouldn't stay away, not from this. I grab the toothbrush that Ayesha has prepped with toothpaste. "How many?" I speak between brushing and spitting.

"I don't know, but let's go."

I pull on a baseball hat, tugging my hair through the loop in the back, and run out with Ayesha. My parents are already at their job assignments for the day, so for now, at least, I don't have to worry about them trying to stop me. We run down the Midway, past the Hub, and then come to an abrupt stop. Outside the fence are a couple hundred protestors. Some hold signs: FREE MOBIUS, NO H8 IN THE STATES, AMERICA ALREADY IS GREAT, AMERICA: ALL ARE WELCOME. Police officers stand in a line separating the protestors from the orange plastic barriers that sprang up outside overnight in front of the electrified fence. In case, I suppose, the protestors miss the giant white signs emblazoned with a DANGER warning. Six white news vans line the dusty road to the camp, and we see reporters prepping to go live with their camera crews. I blink back tears. I don't dare have expectations, but I have hope. I feel dizzy, like when I haven't eaten in a while, and being woozy reminds me that I'm hungry. Then I see David—standing, chanting with the protestors: "No justice, no peace." I see him. Fist in the air, brown hair mussed from the wind. He's wearing the same Wilco shirt I have. And he is beautiful.

"David!" I scream, and run toward the fence. I want him to see me. I want him to know I am okay. I'm ready. A row of Exclusion Guards stands between me and the electrified boundary.

"David!" I call again, jumping up and down to catch a glimpse of him over the shoulders of the guards blocking me, and of the police holding him back. I squint against the sun and peer between the guards to see David grinning madly and waving, sweat gleaming across his brown skin. The police won't let him move closer because they're trying to keep the protestors far from the fence. But we see each other, and I blow him a kiss, and he mouths an *I love you* before being jostled back into the crowd.

A small caravan of cars drives down the road and stops at the Mobius entrance gate so guards can check IDs and inspect the vehicles. As they do, the Director walks out among the crowd that has gathered inside the camp. He has a huge fake smile plastered on his face. I wonder if he's ever fooled anyone with it. I wonder if he can fool himself.

"Okay, everyone. We've got a busy day ahead. Time to disperse. Let's get to work. It's a beautiful morning." He speaks into a bullhorn so he can be heard above the chanting protestors, but otherwise he ignores them. He's not even looking at them. It's like he's looking *through* them, like his brain simply can't compute their existence. The gates open and the Red Cross vehicles are allowed in. The police keep the protestors back.

I strain to get another look at David, but I've lost sight of him.

"Let's go," Jake says, directing me away from the line of his fellow Exclusion Guards. "We need to clear the area."

A lot of us are milling around, and the guards are being unusually nice as they try to nudge everyone to their work assignments or back to their trailers. This is probably the best chance I have to speak to Jake. I scoot up next to him. "How did this happen? Like, when, who, how?"

"Cars were pulling in all night, joining the folks who were already here. Your blog posts went viral in a huge way. And that Instagram Live clip. They were on all the major news stations, and they set social media on fire. There were already people coming together to raise their voices, but your words—you—were a catalyst. Occupy Mobius—that coalition of resistance groups—organized a protest. Their hashtag is trending. They're exploiting a flaw in the executive order. All the land inside the fence is under War Department jurisdiction, but outside that fence, it's California. And the governor here—he's not a fan of the president or his racist politics."

I hear Jake's words; I see the protestors. I smile. Not the usual smile that I muster in here—the hollow, polite smile we all wear that says, Go along. Keep your head down. Pretend.

But a real smile. The kind that makes your body light up from the inside. That makes your cheeks hurt. It's a smile that reminds me I am alive.

The day has been meticulously planned. I watch as the guards shoo internees away and minders usher us to our tasks. The Director does not want to take any chances during the Red Cross visit. And with the press and the protestors here, too, I imagine the burning anger behind the Director's false grin. I hope it makes him spontaneously combust.

The Red Cross team is easy to recognize, with their white T-shirts emblazoned with the large red symbol known the world over. A group of laughing, smiling minders ushers them into the Hub, where their official visit begins. I wonder if all traitors feel so at ease. The Red Cross will be spending the day at Mobius—visiting the clinic, the garden, the playground; watching some kind of star-spangled patriotic revue the early-childhood teachers put together; touring Block 1, where the Mercury Homes have been specially scrubbed and prepped for the visit. Then they will dine with everyone in the Mess. The Director will be with them all day, smiling, glad-handing, and pretending life in the camp is somehow enviable, exceeding humanitarian requirements.

It's all a cosmic joke.

I learned about the Red Cross visit to the "model" Nazi concentration camp Theresienstadt when I visited the Holocaust museum in DC on a trip with my parents. The prisoners there received "special privileges"—they didn't have their heads shaved; they wore regular clothes; they were even "paid" for their forced labor and could use the fake money at a café and thrift stores the Nazis set up in the camp. There were classes and parks for the children. When the Red Cross was there the kids were forced to put on a musical. It was a sick hoax, and the Red Cross bought into the Nazi propaganda. The camp passed the inspection with flying colors. Afterward, many of the prisoners at the camp were eventually sent to Auschwitz or other extermination camps. Most were killed.

If the Red Cross thought Nazi concentration camps were fine, they're going to think this place is a fucking utopia.

I scan the protestors for another glimpse of David, but I can barely see past the fence. Between the line of Exclusion Guards on the inside and the cops in formation on the outside, I can't see a thing. But I hear the protestors: "The people united will never be defeated."

Jake catches up with Ayesha and me to escort us back to our block, but Ayesha and I are not returning to our Mercury Homes. We're meeting up with Soheil, Nadia, and Nadeem at the rock garden. With the Director's attention elsewhere and the drones quiet for the day to make the Red Cross visitors more comfortable, this is a rare moment we need to take advantage of.

"We're good from here, Jake," I say, expecting him to walk back to his post.

"You're meeting the others, right? I'm coming along," he says.

Ayesha looks at him. "How could you know that? We only decided that among ourselves, like, thirty minutes ago."

"I heard Soheil talking about it to one of his friends as the crowd scattered. You're not being cautious enough. Not by a long shot. That won't end well. Trust me."

We look at each other. Ayesha shrugs. "I guess he knows pretty much everything anyway."

When Soheil sees the three of us arriving at the garden, he taps Nadeem on the shoulder and says something to Nadia. They turn to face us.

"It's okay," I say. "He's cool."

Soheil looks at us. "I don't know what you mean. I thought we were going to hang out. I didn't realize we had to do it under armed guard."

Ayesha puts her hand on Soheil's arm. "It's fine. He knows."

Soheil turns and kicks a rock, then watches it sail toward the Midway and roll to a stop, dust rising and settling in its wake. "What are you two thinking? He's the enemy. He's a guard, and don't think for one second he won't shoot us if he is ordered to."

"I wouldn't do that. I won't. Not even if I'm ordered to. You have my word. And I'm not turning you in. I'm here to help you," Jake says.

"And why should we believe that?" Soheil is incredulous. He should be. He's being smart.

"Because he's telling the truth," I say. "He saved David and me. He took another story I wrote and hid it before the Director could find it on us, and he gave it to that blog. He put himself on the line for us. So, yeah, I'm saying we can trust him."

"The Inside Mobius blog posts have gone viral, and the clip of Layla with the Director, too," Jake says. "Every media outlet is covering them, and Anonymous put out a warning to the administration, threatening to dox them all if they don't close the camp down. There's even an Occupy Mobius website that's covering the protest and putting out daily calls to action, and they're starting a podcast on-site—*Voice of Dissent*."

Ayesha hugs me. "You did this," she whispers.

"It wasn't me," I say. "It was all of us."

Ayesha winks at me. "It takes a village to raze a camp." She gets a grin from Soheil.

"Fine," Soheil says. "I'll go along, but I don't like it."

Nadia adds, "But if his ass is on the line, what's to prevent him from turning us all in to save himself?"

"What's to prevent any one of us from doing that?" I ask. "It's not like we're trained to withstand torture."

"I wouldn't give anyone up," Soheil says, "no matter what they do to me."

Nadeem, who is maybe a couple of years older than Soheil and also plays soccer with the little kids on the Midway, puts his hand on Soheil's shoulder and says, "Listen, man. You're my brother, and I believe you mean that. But torture? No.

None of us can hold up to anything serious. Didn't you read about what they did to those guys at Guantanamo?"

"I won't turn you in. Any of you. And I have SERE training," Jake says.

We all look at him. I shrug and raise my palms. "I don't think any of us know what that means," I say.

"Survival, Evasion, Resistance, Escape." Jake speaks in short clips. I can imagine him barking those words in response to an order.

"So that means you won't give in to torture?" Nadia asks, and crosses her arms.

"There's no guarantee. SERE is only training. I'm sure I could sustain some level of duress. Every human being has a breaking point, but you have my word that I will resist."

I look in Jake's eyes and see that he means it. He believes his own words, and I'm glad he does. He has to. But even he can't know the truth of what could happen. What he could endure, what he would confess, if things got bad enough. Human beings are capable of so many wondrous things, but there's no limit to the horrible things we do to one another. I shudder. Honestly, torture is not an idea I want to think about. The word alone makes my stomach queasy, and if I imagine too much, I'm afraid I won't do what needs to be done.

"That's great for you, man," Soheil says. "But you've gone along this whole time. You were on the train that brought us here. You weren't exactly trying to sabotage the tracks." Soheil's voice is tight, strained.

"Soheil, it's not like that—" I say.

"No," Jake interrupts. "He's right. It was exactly like that." Jake looks Soheil in the eye. "I know why you don't trust me. And you're smart to be suspicious. Most of my unit was absorbed into the Exclusion Guard. I followed orders. I did what I was told. Orders are what I know. But for too long I forgot my sworn duty, to America, to Americans. And I am sorry. I have new orders now that countermand the illegal orders that started this camp. I don't answer to the Director, not anymore. But the Director trusts me. We've weaponized whiteness in this country. So why not use mine to your advantage now?"

"Thank you, Corporal Reynolds," Ayesha says.

"You don't need to thank me. I'm not the brave one."

Soheil nods at Jake. "You're right. And I'm not thanking you."

I clear my throat. "I think we know where we all stand. Now, are we ready for tonight?"

"We're ready," Soheil says. "Nadeem, how many people did you last count?"

"Twenty-five," Nadeem says. "They all know what to do. Sit at the first table with empty trays. No food. No water. It's enough people to draw attention."

"What do you think, Jake? What's the Director going to do?" I ask.

"Hard to know. He'll be furious, but the question is whether he will crack down with the Red Cross visitors present. There are two reporters traveling with them, and I doubt the Director will want more bad press. But after they leave, that's when it will get ugly. He'll know who all of you are. He'll know you've been conspiring, and he will not come down easy. As long as the press and the protestors are outside, you'll have some cover, but he's counting on them leaving."

"We can't let them leave," Ayesha says. "But how can we make them stay?"

"Jake, if I write another blog post, can you get it out there? Can you leave the camp with it?" I ask.

Jake nods. "Easy enough."

"Let's do this," I say, trying to sound resolute. "I'll see you guys at the Mess tonight. Meanwhile, keep your heads low."

I leave Ayesha with Soheil, Nadeem, and Nadia and hurry to my Mercury Home with Jake. Once there, we walk straight into my room and shut the door. I pull out a pad of paper and scribble a couple of paragraphs about the fast we're planning for tonight. I write about the Red Cross and the threatening announcement and the meticulous preparation for the visit that is supposed to showcase Mobius as a camp upon which all future camps can be modeled. The writing is rough, but we're running out of time, so it will do.

I hand the note to Jake. "Thank you for this, and for the risks you're taking. Sorry if it puts you in any danger. Is helping us on the inside like this part of your special orders, or whatever?"

"Remember when I told you that when you don't know

the truth, people can't force you to tell it? Best to keep things distant." Jake gives me a wistful smile and tucks the note into his pocket. "I'll get this into the right hands as soon as I can." He opens the door and lets himself out.

I watch him leave, then shut my bedroom door. I go to lie down on my bunk, mind racing.

Everyone is in danger. All the time. The Director demands loyalty from those around him—what would the Director do to Jake if he were to catch him with my note? I've leaned on Jake. I can't imagine going through this without him. And Ayesha and Soheil? Nadia? Nadeem? The others? Once we draw attention to ourselves, there will be nowhere to hide. The Director will know who we are, and hell will rain down.

I nestle my cheek into my pillow and think of David. My body warms at the memory of him. He's outside the fence, out of reach. Will that keep him safe? I might never be able to be in his arms again, but he's here. Close. For now, that's enough.

My feelings bang around in the bell jar of this imprisonment, this camp. I clutch my stomach and close my eyes and wish it all away. Stop the automatic thinking. The spontaneous overflow of worst-case scenarios. There's no time for that, and neither my feelings for David nor my sympathies for Jake are important right now. I need to keep telling our story to the world until everyone listens. I can't afford to be distracted.

The fast is tonight.

People can get hurt.

One of those people could be me.

CHAPTER 22

Since my parents arrived back at the trailer this afternoon from their "jobs," they've been in unsettlingly good spirits. The visit from the Red Cross has buoyed them. I don't want to be the one to burst their bubble. Not yet.

"I talked to one of the aid workers for a few minutes at the clinic," my mom says as she tucks a few stray hairs into her otherwise neat bun. We're sitting on the vinyl sofa in the common area of the trailer while Dad washes the mugs that were in the sink. "She told me folks are thinking of us—they know we're not the enemy of America. Know that we're not an Other, that we're the Us, too."

"That's great, Mom," I say, happy that my mother seems brighter than she has these past few weeks; it's been so hard to see her spirit being stripped away. But I fear her joy will be very short-lived. I imagine the terror my parents will feel when I sit with the others at dinner, refusing to eat, silently protesting in front of the Director and the Red Cross.

"Yes, and I believe the Red Cross staff will be joining our tables this evening. It will be nice to hear some news from the outside," my dad adds as he finishes the dishes and dries his hands.

"I'm going to sit with Ayesha and some of the others, since the Director is letting us choose tables tonight."

"That's wonderful, honey." My mom strokes my hair. "So glad you've been making friends here. It's good to make the best of any situation."

I don't want to make the best of it. And I hate that my parents and I have to put on an act in this trailer—a space that should be private. It's all a reality show, plotted to make the Director happy. But tonight some of us are going off script.

My parents and I walk out of our trailer and join the scores of other internees who are heading for the Mess. When we enter, I see some Red Cross observers chatting with small groups of internees, and others with the Director. Soheil and Nadeem are already seated with Ayesha at the first table. I kiss my parents on the cheeks and join my friends.

Ayesha squeezes my hand under the table when I take the seat next to her. "Ready?"

"Probably not, but we're doing this." I press her hand in return.

In minutes, the tables are full and the Director stomps to

the front of the room in the same dark suit he wore at the orientation. I wonder if his face hurts because the same smile has been plastered on it since this morning. The grin may be fake, but in his eyes there's nothing but confidence and the belief that his cruelty is justified. The Director clears his throat. Then waits. He always waits for absolute silence before he begins. "On behalf of the Mobius community, I want to thank the Red Cross and the journalists who've joined us for a wonderful visit today. They can see what a peaceful, vibrant community we've built here. We embody Unity. Security. Prosperity. Now, enjoy your dinner; you're among friends. The minders will call out tables starting from the back."

We wait patiently for our number to be called. Others file past the food stations, filling their plates and chatting with Red Cross team members who join them at the tables. When a minder calls Table 1 to head to the food line, none of us moves. My mouth is dry as sawdust and tastes like it, too. I rub the back of my neck.

The minder sticks his chicken neck out, staring at us. "Table One," he calls again, louder this time. When none of us moves, he takes long strides over to us, bends his head, and says in an angry whisper, "I called your table; now stand up and get your food." We glance at one another uneasily but stay seated. We don't acknowledge him. I feel twin surges of pride and panic as no one budges.

The minder walks over to the Director, who is speaking with the Red Cross team leader. The Director excuses himself and walks to our table. He's still grinning, but telltale angry red blotches have traveled from his neck to his face. "Table One, take your meals." He speaks slowly and enunciates each word. By now everyone has put down their forks to watch the scene unfold. I'm glad I'm not facing my parents, but even with my back to them, I can imagine the wild panic in their hearts. And I'm sorry, but not sorry enough to stop.

The Director turns his face away for a moment and smirks. It's not the fake smile he's worn all day. I've seen this look before, when he confronted David and me. It's the grin that precedes his rage. He thinks he's in control, but he's not clever and self-aware enough to stop himself from exploding.

He spins around in a fury and slams both of his thick fists down on the table. "I said, get up now!" The table rattles. My brain rattles. His yell rings through the Mess. There are audible gasps. Some people rise from their chairs, and I see two reporters standing by the wall with their phones out, recording.

Soheil speaks loudly and clearly, directing his comments to the reporters. "We're protesting the illegality of Mobius. We're protesting the violation of the civil rights of the Muslim community. We want the world to know that there are internees who have been tortured and disappeared. Here. On American soil. We are being held without cause or trial."

A sheen of sweat appears on the Director's face. His lips curl up over his teeth. I can almost see him struggling, trying to control himself in front of the reporters and the Red Cross, but it's too late. He's lost.

He curls his right hand into a fist and lands a vicious punch across Soheil's face. I hear a crack; blood spurts from Soheil's nose and mouth as he falls to the ground with a thud. There's a single piercing shriek—I have no idea from where—then pandemonium. Ayesha screams. She and I rush to Soheil's side, snatching napkins to wipe away the blood. The reporters leap forward into the crowd that surrounds Soheil, their phone cameras capturing the chaos.

I look up and see that the members of the Red Cross form a cordon between us and the Director, who is raging at them, his face nearly crimson. His own security guards hold him back as he screams at them. The Red Cross team leader, a middle-aged man with deep wrinkles on his forehead, is shouting, trying to be heard above the commotion. All I can hear is "violation of the Geneva Convention" and "prisoners of war."

Dr. Mahar, from the clinic, pushes his way through the crowd. We've gotten Soheil up and seated on the floor, clutching napkins to his nose, trying to stop the stream of blood pouring out. Dr. Mahar bends down to examine him. Ayesha stays at Soheil's side, holding his hand, whispering to him. I stand up to scan the room. The minders work with the guards to get people out of the Mess. I catch sight of my parents, who look at me, disbelief and confusion in their eyes. My mom extends her hand toward me, but she is caught up in the crowd pushing toward the exit.

The Director is now in a corner talking with some of his security guards. The Red Cross team leader is on his phone. The doors burst open and what seems like an entire army of Exclusion Guards marches in, roughly pushing through the crowd. People scream as they are thrown to the ground or shoved out of the way. The members of the Director's security detail trudge up to the two journalists and seize their phones. The reporters object, loudly. One of them yells something about Article 79 and wartime protection for journalists. But it doesn't matter. We all watch helplessly as their phones clatter to the floor. One of the private security guys shatters both with the butt of his rifle.

I was scared before, but as I watch the guards pull apart the wall of Red Cross members in front of us, I'm powerless to move. The team leader protests to the Director, who brushes him off and barks orders to the guards. Dr. Mahar and another man help Soheil up and move toward the team leader, who reaches his arm out toward them as he yells into his phone. A fire alarm goes off and the sprinklers switch on, drenching everyone. The crowd surges forward. I search for my parents, but I can't find them anywhere. My head spins, my stomach lurches; I don't know where to go.

"Come on." Ayesha takes my hand and pulls me out of the crowd; she drags me against the stream of people heading toward the main exit, and we reach a side door. She shoves it open, and Jake takes her by the shoulders.

"You've got to get back to your trailers now! Follow me!" he shouts. Nadeem and some of the others flee toward their blocks. Ayesha and I hurry to keep up, following Jake toward Block 2. He takes a circuitous route around the Hub, away from the mass of Exclusion Guards and internees who are still pouring out of the Mess and toward the Midway. As we pass the Hub, I see the lights blazing outside the camp. Other internees are running, screaming. The protestors are standing up, peering around the police, trying to catch a glimpse of the uproar. Camera crews rush toward the fence and are stopped by police, but they still seem to be filming. The dust kicks up around us, swirling in eddies, and the air trembles with a *thwip thwip thwip* as a helicopter flies overhead. I guess we've succeeding in getting some attention.

Lights from the watchtowers illuminate the camp. People rush toward their Mercury Homes. I stand frozen, watching as a man is pushed to the ground by a guard and then kicked in the stomach and head. I scream, but I'm only one of hundreds of voices that bleed into the madness.

Somewhere in the chaos, I realize I'm not holding Ayesha's hand anymore. Jake's not here, either. I've lost sight of both of them in the dust and swirl of screaming people. I run toward the fence, hoping to catch a glimpse of David. Emergency vehicles race up the road to Mobius, and protestors cover their mouths and noses with bandannas or tuck their faces into their shirts to avoid the billowing clouds of dirt. A police officer yells into a bullhorn, ordering them away from the fence. Some protestors flee to their cars. I run along the inner side of the fence, as close as I can get, calling out David's name, but the sounds of helicopter blades and sirens mute my screams in the blizzard of dust.

I sprint back to Block 2, hoping I'll find my parents already at our trailer. Two other helicopters appear, filling the air with even more dust, so the visibility on the ground drops to a foot or two, if that. My eyes burn, and tears stream down my face and mix with the dust that cakes my cheeks, so when I dab at them, my fingers come away muddy.

Cough. Sputter. Try to breathe.

All around I hear the cries of internees running to their trailers, searching for some air to breathe. People bump into one another, carrying their children, covering their mouths, shielding their eyes.

As I near my block, I see Jake helping my neighbors into their trailers. When he sees me, he runs over and pulls me into my Mercury Home. Slamming the door shut, he steps to the kitchen, grabs a dish towel from the edge of the sink, fills a glass with water, and walks into my room. I follow him and shut the door behind us. He wets the cloth and sweeps it across my eyelids, cheeks, nose, and lips, tenderly removing the dust from my face. He pauses and looks into my eyes, then hands me the towel and the glass of water. "Sip," he instructs.

I take a few tentative sips and then drink the entire glass in a long gulp. It's the first time I'm aware of being thankful for clean, cool water. I hand the empty glass back to him. "Ayesha?" I ask.

"She's fine. Her parents and brother are back with her in their trailer." He moves his hand to cup my cheek, but pulls it away.

I look into his worried eyes. "My parents? Have you seen them? I tried, but I couldn't—the dust."

"I'm sure they'll be okay. Once they get back, you all need to stay put. Do not leave this trailer, hear me? It's a God-awful mess out there. And I'm sure there's going to be a lockdown."

"A lockdown?"

"I'm guessing the movements of the internees are about to get a lot more controlled. No one in or out. The Director is going to have to somehow convince the higher-ups that he wasn't at fault for this shit show and that he is still in control."

I take a deep breath. "Soheil? What do you think will happen to him? Dr. Mahar said the Director broke his nose."

"You should be happy that's all that happened. And he's lucky the Red Cross visitors were here. They'll get him out. The Director stepped way over the line when he hit Soheil. In front of reporters? I mean, the president is going to be apoplectic over this. He's been trying to hide it all, and now he's got journalists whose cameras were smashed and an articulate and charismatic young man who will be on the outside with the Red Cross protecting him, ready to tell his story to hungry press outlets."

"So our plan worked."

"I'd say so." Jake pauses and puts his hand on my shoulder. "Things will be more dangerous than ever for you and your friends now. The Occupy blog posted your story right before the incident at the Mess. Between that and all the coverage tonight's chaos is going to get—you have the world's attention, but the Director is going to zero in on you like a target."

"What about you? They saw you walk in here with me. Will you be okay?" I ask.

"It's havoc out there. I don't know. I have a friend in surveillance, so—"

"A friend?"

"Remember, I said I wasn't the only one here on your side. The only side that matters." Jake gives me a small smile.

"Don't worry about me. I'll be fine. But I have to go back out to find my parents," I say.

We step into the common area.

The trailer door slams open. My parents, like phantoms made of dust, walk in but stop short when they see Jake standing in our kitchen.

I exhale. Deeply. If my parents had seen Jake come out of my room, it might have induced dual heart attacks.

"Ma'am. Sir." Jake nods. "I was seeing to it that Layla got home safe. I told her that it was best for you not to leave your trailer. I'm sure instructions will follow shortly."

My parents look too shocked to speak or move.

"We understand, Corporal Reynolds," I say as I walk past my parents to open the door for him. "We'll make sure to stay inside." When he steps out, I whisper a thank-you. He gives me a sad, obligatory smile and then marches away, disappearing into the yellow, dust-filled air.

"What was he doing here? Are you okay?" my dad asks.

"I'm fine. I stumbled while I was running, and he helped me back."

My mom glances at the camera and chokes back words. The hesitancy in her eyes makes me want to reassure her, but I don't think I can explain in any way that will satisfy my parents.

They walk past me to the sink and begin wiping the dust and grime off their faces.

"What were you kids thinking? Look what you've done." My mom doesn't hold back. "People got hurt. Soheil? It could have ended much, much worse for him. Actions have consequences, and now we're all about to face them, thanks to the stunt you and your friends pulled." Part of me wants to believe she's doing this *for* the camera, putting on a show of anger for them, whoever *they* are. I've begun picturing each camera trained on us as the Eye of Sauron. Perhaps she believes that acting the part of the livid parent will make the consequences less severe for me, show that I was merely being a ridiculous child, that I'm not a threat. But for the Director, even the slightest disobedience endangers his vision of his absolute authority in here. I want her to be proud of me for taking a stand, but if she has any pride at all, it's been consumed by her fear.

"Your mother's right, Layla. That was foolish indeed." As always, my dad keeps his composure. But there's anger in him, too. I can see it in his rigid posture and hear it in the deep, flat tone of his voice.

I open my mouth, but before I can reply, before I can

formulate the right thing to say, my parents turn their backs to me, shuffle into their room, and shut the door.

So they're going with the (mostly) cold shoulder. I would've preferred more yelling from my mom. Or any form of raised voice from my dad, for that matter. The truth: That's what I want. For us to be honest with one another—to be free to hash out our feelings in the open. But there is no open here, only razor wire and electric fences, where all our truths are trapped. I walk into my own room, slamming the door behind me, eyes stinging from dust and bitterness. I strip and throw my clothes into a heap in the corner; tiny particles of dust rise into the air and drift soundlessly back to the ground. Outside beckons—I want to run into the foothills and scream into the canyons. I want my voice to echo and crack the ground beneath my feet.

The shower timer clicks on. I'm guessing it's my mom trying to rinse off her fear and disappointment. I imagine stepping into a warm, sudsy bath and how the water would feel on my skin. The luxury of water seeping into every one of my pores and making me clean again. Dirt-caked fingernails are my constant companions here. Dirty nails and terror. I step to the sink and scrub my hands under the water until they are pink and raw. The door to my parents' room opens and closes a couple more times. When I'm sure they've retired for the night, I tiptoe out and into the shower, but a stream of screaming-cold water greets me. We ran out of hot water.

One more slap in the face. I step out, wrap my shivering body in a towel, and head back into my room. My fingers tremble as I pull on my warmest pj's and add a sweatshirt. After putting my wet hair in a towel turban, I crawl into bed. Every muscle in my body aches, so even this stupidly hard bunk mattress feels welcome.

I wish I could make my parents understand, persuade them to speak up, act out. But they're so angry with me for taking risks. They want to bide their time until one day we are magically released and the president isn't some raging fascist.

That will be never.

I don't want to spend my life in this place. I don't want to die in here. But maybe there are some things worse than death.

CHAPTER 23

The camp-wide siren booms. Six a.m. I roll out of bed and walk into the common room of our trailer. Apparently, my parents either have not slept or have been up for a while, since they are already dressed and drinking tea.

"What's going on?" I ask. My mother simply shrugs. My dad walks to the window and looks out, shaking his head. The media unit blinks on.

The Director's red-rimmed eyes shoot daggers at us through the screen. "After last night's insubordination, we will have new rules at Mobius. You will report for roll call every morning at six thirty a.m., to be marked present by your minders. At seven a.m., you will proceed to your jobs or classes. Those not on duty or in class will be confined to their block. Dinner at the Mess remains promptly at six p.m. A nine p.m. curfew will be strictly enforced. At that time, you are to remain in your Mercury Home until roll call the next morning. Anyone found in violation of these regulations will be dealt with accordingly. Make no mistake: The consequences will be swift and severe. Mobius will also have the pleasure of unscheduled visits from the Red Cross." He spits out the last sentence. He doesn't even try to hide his disgust at the Red Cross observers. They are the only protections standing between us and the violence behind the Director's warnings. It's a thin line, but it's all the hope we have.

The Director continues. "I am sure I don't need to stress the importance of your cooperation in all these matters. Unity. Security. Prosperity." The Director's swollen lips curl back into a menacing smile. "Report for roll call immediately." The media unit flashes off.

My parents and I don't say a word. I'm not even sure what the purpose of speaking would be. Silently, we step out and see other families from our block doing the same, looking around, some bewildered, others clearly angry. I hear my name and see Ayesha waving at me before her mother intercedes and makes her drop her hands to her sides. Ayesha shrugs an apology.

Saleem and Fauzia, our minders—or, as I affectionately refer to them, traitors—motion to the sixteen internee families on Block 2 to form a straight line down the center of the narrow lane that separates the eight Mercury Homes on one side from the eight on the other side. Quietly, asking no questions, we fall into formation, too tired and shell-shocked to do anything but obey. This is exactly what they want, exhaustion and acquiescence.

"You heard the Director," Saleem shouts. "This is every day from now until further notice. Hold out your wrists as Fauzia passes by and scans you in." Fauzia moves down the line with a small scanner the size of a phone. It reads the ultraviolet barcode on the inside of everyone's wrist and marks each internee as present, flashing our camp mug shots for a moment on the scanner's screen. Some grumble as Fauzia walks by. She gives everyone a weak smile and goes back to stand by her husband's side when she's done.

"Do not miss roll call." Saleem's voice is gravelly, like he hasn't slept in days. Good. I hope he gets no sleep for the rest of his life. It's petty as hell, but I don't care. They can take away my freedom, but not my fantastic ability to hold a grudge.

"Do not disobey any of the new directives. Do not go anywhere you are not supposed to go. Do not step out of line. You are being watched. We all are being watched. We do not want our block to land on the Director's list of enemies—" He pauses, then looks directly at me and adds, "Not more than we already are, thanks to the actions of some individuals on this block."

I'm not surprised he's calling me out. There's pretty much no ethical qualm you can have anymore once you've sold out your own people and stood by to watch them get beaten and disappeared. The minder's job is to inform on other Muslims at the camp, and Saleem is making it clear that he will continue his duties, no matter what the Director does to us. A murmur grows in the line. A middle-aged man in a white kurta and gray topi points at me. "She is the one who deserves punishment, not us."

"Pipe down, Adil," my dad yells back at the man. I'm surprised at my dad's quick defense. He usually avoids confrontation. His words make my cracked heart swell a little.

Ayesha joins in. "Yeah—I was there, too." I smile so wide that I feel tears in my eyes. Ayesha is throwing herself into the lion's den with me.

A younger woman with a pale-pink chiffon dupatta wrapped loosely around her braided hair yells, "Adil's right. These foolish kids pulled this stupid act, refusing to eat like they're Gandhi or something. What were you thinking?" She wags a finger at me. "Look what you've done. That kid got what he deserved."

Others nod. Bile rises in my throat. But there's an older woman—she's probably at least eighty—who catches my eye and lifts her hand to her shoulder in a little fist and gives me a nod. When we first got here, she introduced herself as Khadijah auntie. She has a gray bun and lives alone; there's a spark in her eyes. She gives me what I need to bolster my resolve.

"Look at what we've done?" I respond. "Look at what *you've* done. Nothing. You stood by during the election, thinking that none of this would come to pass, that the racism and xenophobia running rampant during the campaign was hot air. And then you stayed silent while your rights were stripped away, and you quietly packed your things and let yourselves be taken prisoner. All of you. All of us. We've offered ourselves up in some kind of twisted Abrahamic sacrifice. But no lamb will be offered instead of us. It's our necks waiting for the ax to fall. We have to be our own miracle—" My mom clamps her hand over my mouth, silencing my speech.

Saleem's eyes bulge out of his head. He walks up to me and shoves an angry finger into my shoulder. "Shut your mouth and watch your step. Don't think I won't report you. And you won't be going to the barracks—the Director, he'll send you out to—"

"Saleem," Fauzia interrupts. "That's enough. We need to give the rest of the instructions." Fauzia coaxes her husband to back away from me while my mother drapes an arm around my shoulders. My dad steps between Saleem and me.

Saleem allows his wife to guide him away, and then he clears his throat and addresses us again. "Each of you will have a new schedule available on your media unit, in your work folder. Report to work when you're required to. If your children are taking early-childhood classes, you can escort them and wait for them in the Hub. Some of you have been assigned new formal tasks in the Mess, the laundry, or the gardens. Instructions are included in your work folder as well." Saleem's angry tone turns to pleading. "Just go along.

Everyone. Please. No more outbursts and demonstrations. Cooperate and it will turn out all right in the end. Remember: Unity. Security. Prosperity. Dismissed."

People shuffle away. I hear my name amid the whispers. Ayesha and her parents walk up to us. Ayesha gives me a tight hug while our parents speak. "I can't believe those horrible people. It's like they didn't even notice I was all rebel with a cause, too." Her face breaks into a grin. Ayesha is gold.

"Any word about Soheil?"

Her face falls, and she blinks rapidly a few times. "The Red Cross took him out of here. Corporal Reynolds told me there's a clinic nearby. Layla, I'm scared. What if they bring him back to Mobius? He'll be number one on the Director's shit list."

I squeeze Ayesha's shoulder. "Maybe he'll be allowed to stay in the clinic until he's fully healed, and then the Red Cross can get him, like, special protection?" I wish I could find more reassuring words, but I can't, because she's probably right. The minute Soheil is back in the camp, there will be a target on his back.

"Do you think it was a mistake? The fast, I mean? What happens now?" Ayesha bites her lower lip.

"I'm not sure," I answer truthfully. "I guess we regroup and—ow." Something smacks me in the back. I turn and see a hardened clod of dirt on the ground.

"What the hell? Are you okay?" Ayesha and I look around. I catch Saleem's eye. The minder is idling on the steps of his trailer, a smug smile on his face. But he's standing in front of me, and the chunk hit me from behind. I pivot all the way around and see an older man with betel-stained teeth standing a few feet away, giving us an icy glare; he spits on the ground. A small patch the color of dried blood blooms at his feet.

CHAPTER 24

Droplets of sweat slither down my neck and into my T-shirt. At the cooling station, I take giant swigs from my water bottle, then wet the bandanna I use to wipe the salt and perspiration off my grimy face. Folding the cloth multiple times lengthwise, I add more water and tie it around my neck, knotting it at the front. Internment chic. I pull my faded Wimbledon baseball cap lower over my eyes and slather my chapped lips with balm. An assignment to work mornings in the garden seemed like a blessing at first, better than laundry or the Mess, but by the time my first three-hour shift was over, I trudged home and collapsed into bed.

At least Ayesha, Nadia, and Nadeem are on the same work detail as me. I thought the Director would separate us, but guards side-eye us whenever we try to speak anything more than passing words to one another. Maybe he figures that this way we're all at the back of the camp, far from the Mobius protestors. Maybe the Director actually hopes we *will* try something else so he can have an excuse to bring the hammer down on us. Whatever his reason, the Director reminds us daily during his announcements that he will not tolerate "unsanctioned congregating" or "untoward fraternizing." And, of course, every time he speaks, he spits the damn camp motto at us: Unity. Security. Prosperity. Like the repetition will make us believe this place isn't a prison.

A few girls on my detail wear hijab, even in this blazing heat. I can't imagine the courage it takes to maintain that part of their Muslim identity in the face of everything. Hijab is an individual choice, but if it had been the choice I made for myself, I have no idea whether I'd have the strength of faith to wear it now.

The camp has been mostly quiet these five days since the Incident, as everyone now refers to the melee in the Mess. But outside the electric fence, an encampment has grown. Protestors have come, hundreds more, setting up a site that looks like a Burning Man village. Jake told me that a leftist billionaire who runs a pro-democracy foundation donated portapotties and thousands of bottles of water and energy bars and tents. The protestors bring media and more scrutiny of the Director and Mobius. When men in dark suits come to take you away under the cover of night, a dread settles into your bones, a fear that you'll be lost forever. Simply knowing the protestors are there assures me that we haven't been forgotten. The future is never certain, but for the first time since we were taken, I know we won't go down without a fight. I know our voices won't be silenced.

I've barely been by the Hub because this garden work assignment puts me about as far from it as I can get, so I've only stolen a few glances at the Occupy encampment. I wasn't able to catch a glimpse of David, but knowing he's there is comforting. Jake's been assigned a fence security detail, so I haven't seen much of him, either, but when he can slip away without suspicion, he gets me updates. So I know that the protests are growing, that there are protestors in front of the White House, too; that Mobius is a nightly topic on the news; that my blog posts have tens of thousands of hits. With Jake's help, I managed to write two more stories about the immediate aftermath of the Incident and of the new, tighter regulations inside the camp. But after Anonymous posted the last story, the Director raged for half an hour on our media units about the leak at Mobius, and he began having all staff and Exclusion Guards patted down before they exit the camp. It's too risky for Jake to leave with a handwritten note. I wonder if I can convince Jake to write his own stories when he's outside.

"We're with you," a soft voice whispers over my shoulder. I turn to see Suraya, one of three black hijabi girls who are also on garden duty. We've exchanged smiles and the occasional word but never really hung out. She's Block 8.

"Uh, thanks."

"I mean it. I know what some of the parents are saying, and they're wrong. What you did, what all of you did, was brave. And we're in, next time. There will be a next time?"

"*We?*" I see a guard eyeballing us. "Help me weed," I say to Suraya, gesturing at her to join me. Suraya kneels in the dirt next to me and begins plucking the shoots of tiny weeds that form around the okra plants. A thin sheen of sweat lines the skin around her American flag hijab. It reminds me of Noor. May God keep her safe. When the guard looks away, I repeat myself but keep my hands busy weeding. "What do you mean, *we?*"

Suraya raises a finger to point toward two other hijabis; I quickly grab her hand, pull it down, and shake my head.

"Right, sorry. I mean Raeshma and Anjum and me," Suraya says. "We're in for the next protest or fast or whatever. There's others, too—the girls from our Quranic study class."

I awkwardly shift my weight from one knee to the other. "Oh, I—I heard that some people were doing that. I haven't really gone to prayers or anything since we've been here."

Suraya laughs. "You don't have to confess to me. Your faith, your *deen*, is between you and God. I won't judge you; you don't judge me. Simple."

I'm amazed she can smile, let alone laugh. This year must have been so much harder for her, someone so visibly Muslim. And black. The Islamophobic micro-aggressions and then real violence were first directed at women who wear hijab—especially black women who wear hijab. There's no way Suraya could've escaped the toxic racism combined with Islamophobia. Since the election launched a wave of women having their scarves ripped off in public, some people in the community actually suggested hijabis shed the scarf, to be less obvious targets. But none of the hijabis I know did. So, of course, Suraya and some of the other hijabi girls are down with joining the protests; they already know what bravery is. Hijab is a choice they made, and in these times, an especially courageous one. I'm embarrassed—no, angry at myself—for not approaching them earlier, wrongly assuming they might be unwilling to stand up to the Director.

I nod. "I think it's pretty clear who the enemy is here, and you're right: We should have each other's backs."

"Some of the parents, they're too scared; but that's not all the adults. I know others will resist. We have to ignore the haters and not worry about what they'll think."

"There're always going to be people who roll over. Look at the minders."

"If you don't stand up for something, you'll fall for anything," Suraya says, smiling with her warm brown eyes. Nanni used to tell me about the parable of the light—an *ayat* in the Quran. She would say that some are touched by God's incandescent light and that it shows on their faces. That's what Suraya's face looks like when she talks.

"Exactly." I smile at her. "By any means necessary."

"By any means necessary to get us the hell out of this prison."

"I'm open to ideas. But I think we need to do something in front of the cameras by the entrance. The police are blocking the protestors from getting too close to the fence, but the cameras can totally zoom in."

"Maybe some kind of silent protest. I mean, we're not supposed to be there, so even gathering would be an act of defiance. But the Director is riding herd over everyone; there are more guards now, too, and they're not slacking."

"We'd need a distraction. Maybe right after dinner. Everyone will be at the Mess. We'll be really close to the main entrance."

"I'm all ears." Suraya pauses for me to explain, but I'm distracted. In the distance, I see Jake's determined stride as he marches toward us. "What is it?" Suraya asks me.

"I'm not sure. Hopefully not trouble, but I have a bad feeling." My eyes follow Jake as he hands a note to one of his fellow guards. The guard gestures at me. I rise, hand Suraya my gardening gloves, and follow Jake without a word. I turn to look back at the garden and see Suraya, Ayesha, and the others looking at me with a mix of confusion and fear on their faces. I shrug and trudge forward.

When we're far enough from the garden, I ask Jake where we're going. "The Director wants to see you," he says. "I'm sorry," he whispers. He looks like he wants to say more, but he doesn't. He doesn't look me in the eye, either. As we walk silently, I glance down and see his hands balled into fists at his sides.

I expected the Director to seek me out after the Incident, but when a few days had passed, I assumed he was no longer interested in me. I was wrong.

"You won't be alone with him. Red Cross observers will be present—they don't have any power, but you're still under eighteen, and that gives you at least a little protection, especially since the Director is wary about more bad press. I'll be right outside the door." Jake's jaw tenses as he speaks. "The Director's security detail will be at his side."

"What does he want with me? What's he going to do?" I'm parched, and my voice cracks.

Jake takes a breath and shakes his head. "Question you. You'll be okay because there will be observers in there, but be careful. Don't say anything rash. Don't give him the upper hand. Don't give him an excuse to target you more than he already has. I know it's not fair to put it all on you, but the Director has no real accountability. I'm sorry I can't be inside with you. I have to go along with orders if I want to keep his trust. He could have me transferred, and I don't want you to be alone in here."

"I understand. You have your orders. You also have his confidence; we can't blow that." I'm trying to sound determined, if only to convince myself that I'll be okay, but I feel like I'm about to face a dragon and I'm without a sword.

Jake pauses and looks into my eyes. "I'm not the only one on your side. You have courage. Hold fast to it. Don't let him bully you."

"I'll do my best."

"I know you will."

When Jake opens the door to the Director's office, I'm greeted by a blast of cold air. It's a freezer in here but a furnace outside. We read Dante's *Inferno* in English class, and I always thought it was odd that the very pit of hell is ice—the absence of all hope and light and love. So, obviously, the Director's office is an icebox. Of course.

He's seated at a desk and motions for me to sit in a chair facing him. He dismisses Jake, who glances at me, the distress clear in his eyes, and steps out. I slump into the chair and take a few deep breaths before straightening and throwing my shoulders back. Two of the Director's security detail are stationed in the corners of the rectangular room, behind the large wooden desk. Two others—a man and a woman dressed in khakis and Red Cross T-shirts—sit, with notebooks in hand, in chairs against the wall. The Director's office is in the administration building—basically, it's a wing of the Hub connected by a narrow, windowless hallway. Admin is a single-level modular prefab building with wide gray paneling and a flat white roof. A large plate-glass window offers the Director a view of the main entrance, where I see the mass of protestors and news trucks. I grin.

"Something funny, Miss Amin?" the Director asks, drawing my attention away from the window.

"No, sir. Not at all."

"Perhaps you're enjoying the show these shiftless millennials and hippie protestors are putting on for the press. It was, after all, the purpose behind the Incident at the Mess, wasn't it? And your little video?"

"No, sir."

"'No, sir'? That's all you have to say for yourself? After your little stunt disrupted the peace in our community here? People were hurt, thanks to your actions."

"*Yes*, sir." The Director's face reddens. If he's trying to keep his cool, he's failing miserably.

"Miss Amin, you're beginning to try my patience. Yes, sir, what?"

"Yes, sir, people were hurt. But that had to do with your actions, not mine. I didn't punch Soheil, sir." The minute the words are out of my mouth, I fear I've made a grave error. A deadly one. I should be filtering my thoughts, but my anger overrides my fear. It might not be smart, but it's my only way forward.

He pounds his fist on top of his desk and stands up. "How dare you? Do you know who I am? What I can do?"

He towers over me, and I shrink into myself a little. I close my eyes for a second. Breathe. Prepare. But that's a joke. There's no way I can prepare myself for what might happen.

"Yes, sir. You're the Director of an internment camp where American citizens have been illegally imprisoned." I hear the scratch of the observers' pens on their notepads; I give them a sideways glance.

"You think these observers will save you?" The Director points at them. "They can't. The Red Cross can monitor and take all the notes they want. They can't interfere with the laws of this nation. And Mobius and all our rules here comply with federal law. Should you get a paper cut, though, I'm sure they will generously offer you a bandage."

The observers shift in their seats. One whispers something I can't hear. I don't look back. I'm too scared to take my eyes off the Director.

He sits in his chair again. He raises a finger in the air and wags it like he's about to make a brilliant observation. "Tell you what. *I* am going to give you the opportunity to save yourself and some of your friends who were involved in your ill-conceived, childish attempt at protesting during dinner. Who organized it? What else are they planning? Who else is involved? If you cooperate, I can make sure that you and your family are taken care of."

"You saw all of us. Everyone was sitting at a table right in front of you. No one else was involved."

"I'm not stupid, girl. I know there were others. What adults were involved? What else are they planning on having you do? Don't protect them; they're using you. If they were brave, they'd put themselves in the line of fire. Instead they're using you as human shields, counting on children to do their dirty work. They are the real enemy here."

"It really was just us. No one is planning anything else, sir. Believe me."

The Director laughs. "Believe you. Yes, indeed. Now, these blog posts: Who is writing those stories? I know *someone* is smuggling them out of here. I thought it was you and your little Jewish boyfriend, but it seems like someone else now. So tell me. Tell me, and I can make life a lot easier for you and your parents here."

"How exactly will you make life easier for us?"

"I heard one of your own people threw dirt on you," he says.

"How did you—" I shut my mouth before I say anything more. Of course he knows. Saleem saw the old man throw that clod at me, and he did nothing but laugh. And obviously he dutifully reported it to Dear Leader. I bite my lower lip and stare at the ground. I don't want to see the Director's smug smile.

He continues. "And I assume you know about the threatening letters your parents received at their work assignments."

I blanch and jerk my head up. No. I didn't know, because my parents didn't tell me. They probably think they're protecting me—don't want me to worry. My chest tightens. I see the Director reading my face. I've given it away.

"No? They decided to keep that from you? Lucky for you,

I have eyes everywhere. Should I give you the details? About what they said they would do to your mother if you didn't stop? What they would do to you? I can make sure your fellow internees know you are under my protection. I have access to certain luxuries here that I can make available to you. Like this pleasant, cool environment you're enjoying right now. I'm sure your parents would appreciate it. You need to help me help you."

I wrap my arms across my stomach. I feel like throwing up. I have no way of knowing if the notes are real. If the threats are real, or if they were planted by the Director to instill fear. In that case, it's working. But I can't let him see that. I can't let him know that. The weaker I seem, the stronger he feels.

"Air-conditioning would be amazing, Director. But I don't have any information for you. I don't know anything about those blog posts. I haven't even seen them. We can't get the internet at Mobius, as you know." I clench my clammy hands into fists to keep them from shaking, but I focus my mind's eye on the Occupy encampment, their shouts and signs and raised fists. I hear Suraya's voice in my head: "We're with you." And something like confidence grows inside me.

The Director looks past me to the two Red Cross observers who are documenting the conversation. "Miss Amin, let me be clear. Those news cameras outside, those protestors? They'll leave soon enough. The observers behind you? That's all they are: observers. Soon it will be just us again. Our little Mobius community. Isn't it better that we're all friends?" The Director bares his teeth in a menacing smile. "Try to keep that in mind, Miss Amin. Corporal Reynolds!" At the sound of the Director barking his name, Jake opens the door. "Corporal, escort Miss Amin back to her Mercury Home. We're done. For now. I would tell you not to go anywhere, Miss Amin. But we both know you'll be close by for a good long time, don't we?"

I stand and turn to the observers and nod. The woman bites her lip, and the man looks away. I might have their sympathy, but sympathy isn't going to set me free.

CHAPTER 25

The next morning, Ayesha and I amble to our garden shift. As we walk, my brain swirls with the information the Director shared with me last night. Why wouldn't my parents tell me about the notes? Are they even real? Did the Director make it all up—some kind of bizarre test to see if I'll say something to them or hide what I know? My thoughts are too muddled. I can't see anything clearly, and when I look up and out past the fence, I only see waves of a mirage displacing the desert plants and the mountains in the distance. Nothing is in its true place.

The heat makes everything slower, steps and thoughts included.

"What was that about yesterday, when Corporal Reynolds

took you away?" Ayesha asks as we drag our feet forward. We saw each other at dinner, like we do every night, but with so many extra guards around, we've all been taking extra care to speak of nothing but benign things any time we're in a group.

"The Director wanted to see if I'd cooperate."

"With what?"

"He wants me to be an informer."

"An informer? He already knows everyone who participated in the 'Incident'"—Ayesha uses air quotes—"and he hasn't hauled us away."

"It's the leaked stories. He thinks I know about them."

"I suppose it tells us he's not a total idiot."

"He wants me to give up the organizers and tell him if anything else is being planned. Apparently, he thinks some adults are using us to forward their radical freedom agenda."

"How insulting. Doesn't he think we can plan anything ourselves?"

I laugh. "I like how you're indignant about him underestimating us. He wants to blame some adult for it because it's easier to send one of them to the black-ops sites, where he can torture them. It's a bigger risk with kids. Plus, I don't think his ego can handle that a bunch of teenagers spat on him, figuratively speaking."

"Please tell me whatever you're planning next involves actually spitting on him. Please. Please."

"How do you know I'm planning anything?"

"I saw you talking to Suraya yesterday."

"She wants to help. Raeshma and Anjum do, too."

"Damn, the hijabi mafia is throwing down. It's getting serious."

"Well, they've dealt with the brunt of the racists *and* Islamophobes, so why wouldn't they?"

"I hadn't thought about it that way," Ayesha says.

"Me either. Which is pretty stupid of me, considering how ballsy someone had to be to wear hijab outside the house after the election. But the whole thing is, we're in this together, regardless of how religious we are. I mean, we are all Muslim enough to be in here, right? We need to do something soon. Like tomorrow. The media isn't going to stay camped outside forever. The last Inside Mobius post was almost two days ago, and you know people's attention span is, like, fifteen seconds these days. It has to be tomorrow after dinner."

"What's it going to be?"

"We're going to march out toward the front gate and stand in a silent protest."

"Well, that sounds boring. Also impossible. Like, how are we all going to get there? The guards won't let us walk that way after dinner; it's straight back to our blocks, remember?" Ayesha stops and puts her hand on my forearm. "Is it wrong that I wish Soheil were here? Not that I want him to be here, but that I want him to be with us. With me. He'd be totally into this, but I'm glad he's safe for now." For the first time I notice that Ayesha's face looks tired. Weary. She really tries to be upbeat, but Mobius is wearing us all down.

"I know what you mean. And I'm sure Soheil wishes he were here, too," I say, and give Ayesha a little hug, then gesture for us to continue walking. "We'll work out the details. I have faith in us," I say as we approach the garden. Ayesha gives me a halfhearted thumbs-up and then walks over to say hi to Nadia, who is already weeding next to Nadeem.

I do have to figure out the details. More people will get hurt, I know. It's inevitable. We have to minimize the risk. Plan it out perfectly. Honestly, though, flying by the seat of my pants would be a step up on the planning scale from where I am now.

I survey the camp, raising my hand to shield my face from the sun. It's been quiet the last few days; even the laughter of the littlest kids sounds hollow. My eyes fall on Jake, who is stationed at the toolshed. I walk up to him and the other guard to get gloves and a small shovel.

"Layla, this is my buddy Specialist Adams. Fred." I've seen him with Jake, and Jake has mentioned Fred, but this is the first guard Jake has introduced me to. "He's a friend. To both of us." Fred raises his fingertips to the brim of his cap, then smiles at me, showing off two rows of perfect white teeth and a dimple in his left cheek.

I nod. "How'd you get this assignment?"

"Fred and I are off duty this shift, so we volunteered to take it from the other two guys who are normally here."

"They think he has a crush on you," Fred says, "so he plays it to his advantage. And they were happy to get an extra shift off."

Jake clears his throat. "Whatever works."

"Right," I say. "By any means necessary. Thanks for switching. I need to talk to the others, and the guards are always listening."

"Okay, the drone circles back in less than ten minutes. Use it, but hurry."

I don't have a lot of time to think, and my body seems to be ahead of my brain. I grab a bunch of gloves and some spades and trowels and gesture for the garden-duty group to join me. Suraya, Ayesha, Nadia, and Nadeem head over, pulling along the others, including a few kids who are new to the group. I'm cautious about trusting anyone new, but I don't have much choice.

We gather in a semicircle next to our garden plot.

I hand the gloves to Suraya and the trowels to Ayesha. "Pass these out to everyone. Real slow." The drones may not be overhead yet, but we're out in the open. We need to act normal. At least as normal as we can.

Jake and Specialist Adams—Fred—stroll toward the water table, out of earshot. "Don't worry," I say to the group. "They'll take their time."

"You trust them?" a kid named Abdul questions.

Suraya silences the questioning. "Abdul, we don't have a lot of time. Layla says it's okay, so it's okay."

"I know Suraya's talked to some of you. The plan is to walk out of the Mess tomorrow and march straight to the area in front of the main entrance, so the protestors and, most important, the media can see us. Then we'll form a line."

"That's all we're going to do? Stand there?" Abdul asks.

"That's going to be hard enough," Ayesha says. "We don't even know if we'll make it there and be able to line up before the guards herd us away."

"We need a distraction—something that will allow us to get out of the Mess without being caught. At least not right away," I explain.

Suraya speaks up. "I was talking to some of the others on my block, and one of them works in the Mess." She pauses and looks at all the sets of eyes on her. "He says he can access the utility box in the storage room and throw a couple of circuit breakers."

"What will that do?" Nadia asks.

"It'll turn off the lights." I grin. "That could be the perfect chance. Our only chance, really. The second the lights go out, exit and head toward the Hub. We can meet by the flagpole and walk the last few steps toward the main entrance together. We probably won't have long before they push us back, but we only need to be there long enough for the press to see us."

"What if we each raise a fist?" Nadia suggests.

"But we're not all black," Abdul says.

Suraya rolls her eyes. "Really? That wasn't obvious at all. The raised-fist salute is about standing up to oppression and racism. It doesn't belong to one race or culture. It belongs to all of us. And it's easy. We stand shoulder to shoulder and raise our right hands in a fist above our heads. That's it. Everybody knows what it is and what it means."

I think about the old woman from our block, Khadijah auntie, who raised her fist to bolster me when some of the others were yelling at me about the fast. I smile. This idea is perfect.

But Abdul jumps in before I can respond. "And what does a hijabi know about standing up to oppression?"

"Are you fucking serious?" Suraya steps closer to Abdul, getting in his face. "Your entire ignorant ass is showing. Maybe educate yourself. I'm not oppressed, and I certainly don't need saving. If anyone needs saving, it's you."

"Seriously," I add. "You sound like one of *them*, Abdul. Do you even know a single damn thing about the history of badass Muslim women?"

"Or Muslimahs today, for that matter," Ayesha says. "Malala got shot in the face by the Taliban, and that still didn't scare her away from fighting for girls' rights. She has more courage in her pinkie than every dude I know."

"Whatever." Abdul kicks the dirt.

"Hey," I snap. "Let me be clear. There's only one enemy here, and he would want us to turn on each other. They want us to be separate factions—that's why they segregated us in the first place. Don't give the Director the satisfaction. You don't want to do this? No one's twisting your arm. But if you join in, you don't bash anyone else. And don't be an asshole. You get me?"

"Yeah," Suraya adds. "United we stand; divided we fall. And all that American patriotic stuff."

I look at the group; most of them nod in agreement. Abdul looks away, chastised.

Jake whistles.

I look in his direction. "The drones are coming. Everyone, get to work. And keep it quiet. Tomorrow, after the lights go out in the Mess."

Suraya walks with me to a corner of the garden and kneels as a drone whirs overhead. "I was talking to Nadia and Nadeem, and we think we can get some others to join us."

"Okay. Be careful. Don't tell anyone you don't trust. And make sure they know the risks. I don't think the Director is going to take this lightly."

"They know. We all know. But there's not much choice, is there?"

"No, I guess there's not."

They can kill us while we sit quietly and do nothing as well.

CHAPTER 26

That night I toss and turn from one end of my pillow to the other, trying to get comfortable, to relax. I kick off the sheets, then pull them back up again. I stare hard at the bunk mattress above me like it's about to reveal life's secrets.

I don't think I've had a single good night's sleep at Mobius. I can't imagine what it was like for the internees at Manzanar. We can't see the former camp from here, but we know it's there. A reminder. A warning. They were in barracks with multiple families. Shanties, really.

But prison is prison, I guess. And being called an enemy of your country, the feeling that you are hated—they probably felt that, too. I wonder if the weight of that ever goes away. Even if we get out of here, will fear become a part of daily life, like breathing? There's not even a real war, not like World

War II. It's all terrorist attacks and retaliation and enemies without borders. There could be no end. I'm afraid we'll rot away and die in here. Erased. Forgotten.

Will I mark my life as only having two parts? Before Mobius and after?

The Mobius morning alarm blasts me awake. I drag myself out of bed and splash water on my face. I change and step out of my room. As usual, my parents are at the little dining table, tea in hand. They mutter their good mornings, not even looking me in the eye.

Since the Incident at the Mess and since they got wind of the Instagram Live video, they've barely spoken to me. They know others blame me for the new regulations. They won't let anyone speak ill of me, but that doesn't mean they approve of what I've done. They asked me to promise that I wouldn't do anything else "foolish." I refused, so the chill in the trailer remains. I get that they're worried and looking out for me, but I can't abide their pleas or assuage their fears. I haven't brought up the threats the Director said they received, but last night when they thought I was asleep, I heard them through my bedroom door. They were talking, trying to decide if they should tell me. They're not going to. They're hiding the threats from me because they want to protect me, but deep down, in their own way, they each believe I'm beyond their protection, and it terrifies them. Maybe concealing the threats gives them a bit of solace, the belief that they are still able to shield me from a few of the horrors of the world. I won't tell them I already know. Let them have that. It's all that is left that I can give them.

Little vortexes of dust spiral around the block as I step down from the trailer with my parents. Others from Block 2 trudge their weary bodies into line for roll call, shading their eyes from the dust and sun. The minders are out, their annoyingly cheery smiles spackled across their faces as if they aren't turncoats, as if their grins make them likable or legitimate. I can barely stand to look at their faces anymore. What they've agreed to. What they've made themselves party to. What they allow to happen to other human beings so that they can have the illusion of power, the barest whiff of control. I think again and again of a story we read last year by Ursula Le Guin about a utopian city whose bliss can only exist because of its one horrifying atrocity. That's who the minders are like—the adults of Omelas, the ones who smile and go about their day and revel in the false illusion of freedom while their souls are withered, desolate things.

But for me, the most chilling aspect here is the automatic feel to it all. The roll call, everyone exposing the underside of their wrist to have their barcode scanned, like we're all fucking produce in a grocery store. The very fact that we all have barcodes now. I rub my finger over the invisible ink. It can only be seen under UV light, but it's there, burned into my skin, branding me forever.

Even the mere knowledge of this mark breeds fear. Enough to make people forget the essence of who they are.

All the more reason not to give in.

Not to give up.

To resist.

When she gets to me, Fauzia drops the pretense of her cold smile. She scowls as she scans my barcode. Good. I prefer her grimace to her syrupy fake smiles anyway. I look back in the line and lift my fingers in a little wave to Ayesha. Ayesha's parents are trying to keep her away from me, afraid of my bad influence, but Ayesha ignores them. Because she is awesome. She pantomimes gardening gestures at me and taps her index finger on an imaginary watch. I smile and nod. Not being alone is everything. Her friendship, a benediction.

I linger outside on my doorstep as my parents head to the Hub a little early for their work assignments. They enjoy the quiet solitude together. I watch them walk away from me, holding hands. A lump forms in my throat. I wish they could understand, be less protective or scared. But for now, I know this growing distance is a kind of barrier I put between us. Not because my parents are the enemy; they're the opposite—the people I love most in the world, and I want to protect them, even in a small way. I hope I'll make it right with them one day. If I can't fix our relationship, it's a sacrifice I'm willing to make, because my lying to them keeps them safer. They've done the same calculus, too.

I remember happier times—movie nights in our old basement, sharing popcorn, and my mother's un-ironic love for eighties movies starring Molly Ringwald. Sometimes David would join us. David. An invisible hand squeezes my chest. I try to bury thoughts of him, of us, deep in my mind, in the part accessible only to dreams. I have to keep my sentimentality in check or I won't be able to go on—I'd be crushed by the weight of memory. I press my palms over my eyes, trying to push back the tears that are about to drown out my vision.

"Are you okay?" I hear Jake's voice and look up. His broad shoulders block out the sun.

"Dust," I reply, blinking.

The block is empty, so I inch over to make room on the metal steps in front of my trailer. Jake wavers. "It's okay," he says. "Everyone is already suspicious of me."

Jake whistles to his friend Fred, who is also on block duty, and puts up five fingers. Then he hesitantly takes a seat next to me. The step is small, and suddenly I'm aware of how close we are. Close enough that I can smell the smoky sweetness of coffee beans on him. "That does not smell like the coffee that's in the Mess. Contraband?"

He chuckles. "I grind my own. It's one of the lessons my dad imparted to me about military life. He was Army to the core. And when I left for basic training he said, 'Always grind your own coffee.'"

"Is that, like, a metaphor?" I ask.

"No, he literally meant grind my own beans. Basic-training coffee sucked."

We share a laugh.

A wisp of a cloud moves by in the sky, allowing the morning

sun to shine brightly on our faces. For a moment it feels good. Warm. But it's not long before the warmth turns to blazing heat. Jake rolls up his sleeves, revealing that compass tattoo I first noticed on his right forearm when we were on the train. It's small. Simple. Two crossed arrows with a black *N* inked between the shafts.

I touch his arm with my index finger, barely making contact. His muscles twitch, so I pull my hand away, but I'm curious, so I ask, "Why the compass?"

Jake rubs his thumb over his tattoo, then turns to look at me with a sad smile that's like a dagger to my heart. "Have you ever been to Castle Lake?"

"By Mount Shasta?" I ask.

Jake nods.

I continue. "My dad sometimes gets a cabin there to write. A couple years ago, my mom and I met up with him while he was on a retreat. For a long weekend. We did a few hikes around there. My dad wrote a poem about it, actually. Well, maybe not that lake specifically, but a glacial lake with still, silvery stars overhead."

"Sounds like a good poem," Jake says and gives me a half smile. "My mom was a big hiker, and when I was eleven, she and I took this hike together, from Castle Lake to Heart Lake. The two of us. She gave me a compass. Made me lead the way, across the outlet creek, eventually getting to a narrow, unsigned trail. It's really a short hike, only two or maybe three miles. Moderate elevation gain. Nothing tough.

But man, was I nervous. There's a saddle where you have to choose your path, and my mom wouldn't tell me which one. She just pointed to my compass."

"A saddle?"

"An elevated spot between two mountain peaks that looks like a saddle," Jake says. "Anyway, I wound our way to Heart Lake—it really is shaped like a heart. And my mom hugged me and told me to trust myself, that I had a good heart. Then she said words I'll never forget: 'A compass doesn't tell you where you are, and it doesn't tell you where you have to go. It can only point you in a direction. It's up to you to always find your true north.' That's the last hike I ever took with her." Jake breathes deeply and looks off toward the mountains.

Without thinking, I reach over and take his hand in mine. I don't care if people can see us. This entire camp is a giant open wound. We shove all our feelings deep down inside ourselves, like we're not even people anymore. We hide it all away from our family, friends, everyone we might possibly love. The only truth we share with each other is the fear in our eyes that we can't hide. I'm so tired of it all. Jake squeezes my hand but then quickly lets it go.

I tilt my head up to look at him with a wistful smile. I sigh. Loudly. "I miss breathing."

"I know," he says. "All the oxygen is sucked out of this place. I wish I could whisk you away to Heart Lake. I've been there a million times since that hike with my mom. In the late afternoons of summer, overlooking Mount Shasta, the sky is orange and gold. It's gorgeous. I could stand there for days. I don't think my eyes would ever tire of that view. The air feels clear up there. You could breathe."

I don't know what to say. There are no words. Maybe some moments are better left unadorned.

We sit there quietly for a minute, looking out, away from each other.

Jake clears his throat. "I sent another post to the Occupy blog. From there, it'll get out everywhere."

"You've become quite the scofflaw."

"It's the least I can do."

"You've got to be careful. They can trace your IP address."

"Don't worry. I'm using an identity-concealing browser. They are, too. They've probably got everything pinging off servers in ten different countries, or some Jason Bourne–type stuff. I'll be fine. Besides, it's nothing compared to the risks you've taken. Will take."

"Me? I feel like a kid getting knocked down by giant waves."

"You're more than that. You're brave. Braver than anyone I've met."

"Well, that bravery—or, as I like to call it, stupidity—is about to be tested tonight."

"I'll be there. The press and the protestors will know, too. I texted David the details about what you're doing tonight, and he'll spread the word to the media and the Occupy crowd.

Word of mouth, not on the web, so the Director can't get a whiff of it before tonight. And don't worry, we're using burners, and we have a kind of code in place. And I'm only using the burner off-site."

"You've been in touch with David?"

"Mostly details about what's going on, and telling him you're okay. He's worried about you. He really loves you, you know? He's a good guy."

I whisper, "I'm lucky."

Jake stares into the mountains. "He's lucky." He's quiet for a moment and then adds, "And I meant it when I said be careful. David is not the only one worried about you."

I open my mouth to respond with some kind of sarcastic remark, but Jake cuts me off before I can utter a word. "Please. You have to take this warning seriously. The Director is gunning for you. The Red Cross has been around, and you're only seventeen—these things have been protecting you, to an extent. But the Red Cross won't be here forever, and he knows your birthday is in a few weeks. I'm afraid he'll haul you off to a black-ops site without provocation. We have to get you out of here before then."

"You think he'll get me a present?" I use sarcasm to deflect the tidal wave of terror that's ripping through my body right now.

"It's not a joke. David is afraid of the same thing. His dad is working on some way to get you out of here before you turn eighteen."

"His dad? He's an asshole. He stood by and watched all this happen and did nothing. Maybe he should have worked his State Department connections before we all got hauled off." I spit out my words like nails. "And I can't leave without my parents, my friends. The Director will go after them—and I can't let that happen. I couldn't live with myself."

"And how do you think the rest of us will feel if something happens to you?"

"I can't think about that right now. I'm sorry. It's literally the only way I can deal with this. I'm not walking out of this place unless everyone walks out with me."

CHAPTER 27

All day I've been thinking about that story Jake shared with me this morning. About finding your true north. About choosing your direction. As I head to dinner with Ayesha, I realize I've chosen mine.

"Do you think it's going to work?" Ayesha asks as we hurry to the Mess.

"That depends on Suraya's friend who works in the kitchen," I respond, my thoughts elsewhere.

"You okay? You seem distracted. I mean, I can understand why. But why?"

I give her a half smile because Ayesha always gets to the heart of it. "I'm worried, I guess. I mean, more than usual. Jake told me that the under-eighteen crowd is protected in a way—at least from being taken off-site. But there's our parents—and also the fact is a lot of us will be eighteen soon. Some are already, and if they get caught, the Director could—"

"Disappear them?" Ayesha completes my sentence.

"Yeah. That."

"Let's hope that doesn't happen."

"Lately I've been thinking hope is kind of a flimsy feeling to hold on to," I confess. It doesn't feel good to say it; it feels like a betrayal, and wrong, and defeatist.

Ayesha squeezes my elbow as we continue walking. "I know what you mean. Hope is basically faith, right? It's intangible. You literally can't grasp it. That's why it's easier to doubt than believe. That's why it's easier to give up than persist. Soheil and I talked about this once—about how the basis of faith is believing in the unseen, the unknowable. About how it actually is important to question, because searching for the answer can strengthen your resolve. But holding on to hope isn't easy. It's work. But necessary. And, well, that's why—"

"Are you about to say 'rebellions are built on hope'?" I wink at Ayesha.

"Dammit. I can't believe I didn't think of that." Ayesha laughs. "But it's true. Hope is all we've got right now. Hope and a ragtag bunch of Muslim teenagers. Look out, world—the Muslims are coming." Ayesha jokingly punches the air with her fist.

"We're already here."

"And we're not going anywhere."

We walk into the Mess nodding at our co-conspirators. Even having a secret feels dangerous. I wonder if this is how the White Rose students felt. Like they were drinking liquid adrenaline through a fire hose. And scared. Scared all the time. For everyone.

Suraya and Raeshma are sitting with some of the other kids from their block. Abdul is with them, but he doesn't acknowledge me at all when I catch his eye. He looks through me like the physical space I occupy is empty. Odd, but a lot of things about him are off. We take our food and eat at a Block 2 table. Tonight it's pizza, a fruit cup, soggy green beans, and milk. This might be the only time in the history of the world that public school lunch lines have been remembered with nostalgia. Not that I miss the food. At all. I mean, gross. But I do miss all the mundane things, like standing in a line and talking to friends and getting a crappy lunch without the heart-stopping terror of looking into the eyes of a man with a gun who is allowed to kill you.

People begin getting up to return trays and get tea or coffee, when the lights go out in the Mess. There's a great clattering of dishes and trays from the kitchen, dropped silverware, people bumping into tables and one another as we're all thrown into darkness. Someone screams, apparently having spilled hot tea. The clamoring spins into chaos. But the lights haven't gone out in just the Mess. When I glance out the windows, I see that the admin offices and the Hub are blacked out, too. I'm not sure what Suraya's friend did exactly, because no backup generator has come on yet. I'm so ecstatic, I'm certain I would kiss him if he were in front of me.

I grab Ayesha's hand and we race toward a side exit. The guards, also in disarray, are too busy trying to sort out the power situation and help people up to notice the twenty or so of us who slip out the door.

Outside it is eerily quiet and dark. The normal hum from the fluorescent lights that illuminate the pathways between buildings is absent. The only working searchlights seem to be at the back of the camp. As they sweep the grounds, I sense them reaching out to me, trying to seize me with their illuminated tentacles, trying to expose my face to the light. But for now I am beyond their grasp. Ayesha and I find the others and hurry to the open yard between the Hub and the entrance gate. We stick close to the walls as we approach, but the frenzy from the blackout compels the guards to rush from their posts to secure the Mess and the Hub. Higher-ups bark orders, and the thunder of hundreds of boots stomping against dry ground reverberates through my body. The darkness and disorder inside the camp lie in sharp contrast to the outside. The Occupy Mobius encampment is bright with car headlights and portable outdoor work lights operated by generators. The protestors line up by the fence, behind the wall of police. They are ready. Waiting. David did his job.

We take our positions as close to the fence as we can. There are thirty-three of us. It's not an army, but it is a resistance. A couple of older aunties and some uncles join the group.

Suraya winks at me when she catches me counting the new recruits. We face the crowd near the fence and raise our fists. Like I've seen in old pictures of the Olympics in 1968, and the NoDAPL protests that have been going on for years, and women in India fighting for justice for rape victims, and the teens—just like me—at the March for Our Lives. It's a simple gesture, and a beautiful one. It calls out through dusty pages of history and echoes from those whose shoulders I stand on—the ones who were hosed down but never retreated, who were beaten but persisted, and the ones whose voices were locked behind walls but whose spirits were never broken. The people united will never be defeated.

For a moment everything is quiet. The world is still.

And through that silence, like the sweetest melody, I hear my name called out. "Layla! Layla! I love you!" David. I can't see him, but he is here. And I laugh. Out loud. And the others laugh. And the Occupy folks raise their fists and start yelling and cheering and clapping. Tears run down my face.

The police outside the fence turn their heads over their shoulders to look at us. We few, causing this ruckus. Other internees who've left the darkness of the Mess see our line and join in. Some nod at me as they step into the formation. Others smile. I scan the line—old, young, black, white, brown. We are all here.

Then I glance beyond the fence at the sea of people. In this place where I thought I was lost, the world has found me. Hope courses through my veins.

Outside, a man with a bullhorn begins chanting, "Set them free! Set them free!" Others join, their voices carrying across the desert and resounding through the valley. Tens, then hundreds. People are streaming out from the Mess now, and guards are running toward us. Someone yells, "Back to your blocks! Now!" But the protestors and the internees drown out the commands.

A shot is fired into the sky; the sound ricochets through the camp. Screaming. A free-for-all. I hear a voice from the outside yell, "They're shooting them!" Then more screams, and the crowd outside surges forward, toward the fence.

The fence.

I'm frozen.

The police outside struggle to push back the protestors. Exclusion Guards race toward the line, and I see another guard rushing to the security booth, yelling, "Cut it off! Cut it off!"

He's screaming about the fence.

The electric fence.

I assumed the electricity for the fence had gone down with the lights. The protestors must have thought the same thing. Shit. They're pushing toward it.

I force myself out of my trancelike state and run toward the fence from the inside. "No! No! Go back!" I scream, but I can barely hear my own voice above all the noise.

When I turn back to look toward the internees, I see guards seizing some, pulling them out of line, shoving others.

Some slip away, but one guard has Ayesha by the arm. I run back in her direction. "Get off! Let go of her!" Then I see Fred, Jake's friend, tell the guard who has Ayesha to report elsewhere. He takes Ayesha by the elbow and leads her away. She's safe. For now.

But another guard pulls off Suraya's headscarf and throws her to the ground. One guard punches one of the uncles who joined us in the line. I stop moving. It doesn't even feel like I'm breathing. I'm outside my body, watching the chaos unfold as if I'm not in the middle of it. I fall to my knees, crying. Huge, heaving sobs. I can't stop. I can't catch my breath. What have I done?

"Layla. Layla."

I look up, searching. "David?"

Jake steps toward me amid a whirling cloud of dust. "Layla, you've got to get out of here." He lifts me to my feet like I'm a rag doll. As he steadies me, all the lights come on. Full force, temporarily blinding everyone.

Jake prods me in the direction of my block. "Now. Go. Now." I nod, still blinking against the artificial brightness. I turn back for a moment to look for David, but he's lost in the crowd.

And that's when I see him, a protestor in the glaring spotlight on the other side of the fence.

Shit.

It's not just a protestor. It's Soheil.

No. No. No.

Of course he's with the protestors. He would never walk away and just leave us here. My screams rip through my body, but he doesn't hear me.

He knows better. He'll stop.

Stop, Soheil. Please.

He pushes past a cop, and for a fleeting second, our eyes meet.

He skirts by the orange plastic barrier, then jumps toward the fence, like he's going to scale it. Like he can bring it all down with the power of his leap. Caught in midair, like a ballet dancer, defying gravity.

Soaring toward eternity.

Like that poem. "Hope is the thing with feathers."

I watch his fingers reaching through the metal.

The action swirls around me in slow motion. My focus blurs.

A hum and a crackle.

A sickening buzz.

A bone-shattering scream.

Then the air is thick with shouts like daggers.

The guards, who were breaking up the protest inside the camp, sprint toward the fence. The hum stops.

Too late.

Soheil falls to the ground. His body jolts and then goes limp.

Some jump to help him; others wrestle with the police.

"Go! Go! Go!" I hear someone yell at the guards, who

are spilling outside the gate to help the police control the Occupy protestors. They are outnumbered and overrun. Chaos, everywhere. People pushing, being shoved, and tripping all around me.

All I see is Soheil and his beautiful, broken body.

Someone jostles me from behind. I run.

I dash for my trailer, tears blurring my vision while the horrible sound and image of Soheil on that fence engraves itself onto my brain and my heart. The swirling dust clings to my wet cheeks. Hundreds of people flood the Midway, rushing to the relative safety of their blocks. I lose myself in the crowd, and my mind swirls. David. My parents. Jake. Ayesha. Poor Ayesha. I can't even remember if she was there, if she saw. I pray everyone is safe even as I know that no one is safe. Not anymore.

Soheil.

God. Why?

And what about everyone else? Maybe the others have made it back to their trailers. It was dark while the guards were breaking up our demonstration; maybe most of the people got home without being recognized. Maybe they'll be okay? A montage of images and sounds plays before my eyes: people getting hit and kicked by guards, hijabs and topis being torn off, and Soheil and that sound and his scream and that briefest of seconds when I saw him, right before. Bile rises in my throat.

I need to go home. I want home. I want to sleep in my bed

and wake up from this nightmare. But there is no home here. And I'm wide awake.

I turn off the Midway toward my block and fall to my knees, grasping my stomach, and vomit in the dirt. I retch again and again, and when my stomach is empty, the dry heaves take over.

"Layla!" my mom calls, and bends down next to me. She pulls my hair off my face and holds it back. She supports me while I try to balance on my knees.

"Mom! Mom! Soheil—" I choke on my words.

Her hazel eyes stare into my dark-brown ones. There is so much kindness and love in her gaze. She takes the hem of her shirt and wipes my face. Then she pulls me to her. "Shh. It's okay, *beta*. I'm here."

"No, Mom. It's not. Nothing will be okay ever again." I pull my face away from her shoulder and look at her. "A protestor was killed. He ran onto the fence. It was...Soheil. The fence was still on, Mom. He—Soheil—he's dead."

Mom blanches. She covers her hand with her mouth as she blinks back tears. Then she cups her hands together and looks into them; I do the same. Then she says, "We belong to Allah and to Him we shall return. May Allah have mercy upon Soheil and grant him the highest place in heaven."

"*Ameen*," I say, my voice and hands trembling.

Mom helps me stand up, and we walk toward the trailer. With each step, I feel like I will shatter, a glass figurine thrown to a tile floor. I suddenly realize that my dad is not with us.

"Dad?" I ask.

"He's okay," my mom says. "He went to look for you by the garden."

My mom helps me up the steps to the trailer. The door is pulled open. Dad is already inside, his face contorted with worry. I don't say a word. I lurch toward the sink, afraid of throwing up again. My mom wets a washcloth and wipes down my face and hands. She helps me to a chair. My dad brings over a glass of water and urges me to take a tiny sip.

My dad looks at my mom, confused. I hear her whisper to him, telling him what happened, what I saw. Then he kneels next to my chair and wraps an arm around me.

He doesn't ask me any questions. Neither does my mom. They sit with me, each holding my hand. Giving me the quiet space they know I need.

I stand up. "I need a rinse," I say. My mom nods. She lets me lean on her as she guides me the few steps to the shower.

I step in and turn on the timer, hoping the water will turn hot. Mostly I want the water to seep into my pores so I can feel clean and free, but I'm not sure if that will ever be possible again. Maybe I'll never leave this place.

I dress and step back into the common room. My parents are waiting for me at the little table with a cup of tea and saltines. I sink into the chair.

"Drink it," my mother says in a voice that reminds me of when I was home sick from grade school. So soft. "Slowly."

I smile weakly. I can tell my parents are restraining themselves from asking me what happened, where I've been. I see the panic and exhaustion on their faces. And also the love. I wrap my fingers around the cup of tea; it warms my hands.

"Thank you," I whisper, my voice raspy as I lift the mug to my lips with shaky hands. My mom drapes her arm around my shoulder as my dad pats my knee.

Soheil's face—his scream—won't leave my mind. I have to find Ayesha. I don't want to tell her. How can I tell her? But I want to be the one who—

The door bursts open.

My dad jumps up from his seat, blocking my view.

Four men from the Director's private security detail enter. "Layla Amin, the Director requests your presence in his office."

CHAPTER 28

Drawn by my mom's screams, people step out of their trailers as I'm escorted down the steps. My parents follow at my heels, and my dad reaches for my arm, but one of the security detail butts him in the chest with the end of his rifle. My dad falls, his head and shoulder slamming against the hard ground. He groans, bringing his hand up to cover his face.

No. No. No.

I try to pull away from the detail, but one of them twists my arm to keep me in place.

"Ali!" my mom cries out, and rushes to my dad and takes his hand in hers. He turns to his side; there's blood on his face. "You're monsters!" my mom screams. "Get your hands off my daughter!"

"Dad! Mom!" I scream as the Director's men drag me

away. My chest tightens. My knees begin to buckle, but one of the men yanks me back up. I strain my neck and see some people trying to help my parents.

Then I see Ayesha. She runs down the block, calling my name. I haven't seen her since we got separated. Does she know about Soheil yet? Has no one told her? My heart thrums in my ears, and my mind moves too fast for me to think straight. All I know is that I don't want anyone else to get hurt. Not because of me.

"Go back!" I shout, fighting tears. "It's okay." Ayesha's father grabs her and pulls her back. She screams and struggles against him. Her dad holds on to her. Good.

Others yell down the block at the men dragging me away. The minders come out of their trailer and try to usher people back to their homes. But the clamoring grows louder as people start yelling at the minders as well. As we turn toward the Midway, a squad of guards rushes past me toward my block.

"What are they going to do?" I ask in a raspy whisper. Everything is a blur around me, and I keep my eyes on the ground so I don't get dizzy.

One of them looks at me but doesn't say a word.

"Where are you taking me?" I continue.

They ignore my questions. I'm invisible.

My body goes limp. One of the Director's henchmen holds me up, half dragging me forward. As we get farther from my block, the din dies down. People watch as the security team pulls me down the Midway. There are some murmurs, but the sound grows quieter the closer I get to the admin building, until all I hear are the scratchy sounds of my shoes scraping lines in the dirt as I'm led forward. The breathing of the security detail is loud in my ears, harsh and open-mouthed. No. That's not their breathing; it's mine. I shake my head, trying to focus, but my mind wanders back to Noor, Asmaa, Bilqis. When the guards hauled them down the Midway, they never came back.

We all know there's a holding cell at Mobius, but I have no idea where it is. The security detail walks me into the admin building through a dimly lit hallway, passing the Director's empty office, and through a door I've never seen. Behind the door is a small windowless foyer, and down the hall are four doors with small rectangular windows about five feet up from the ground. The security detail deliver me to an Exclusion Guard in front of the first door and then turn on their heels and stomp away.

I'm standing in the hall, wiping my forehead with a shaky hand, my knees so wobbly I'm amazed I'm still upright. The guard waits. I notice his angular jaw juts out as he clenches his teeth. It's the only part of his body that moves. His freakish stillness has a kind of mesmerizing quality to it.

The outside door to the building slams. No more echoing footsteps. It seems the security detail has departed.

The guard puts a bottle of water in my hands.

He opens the door to the cell. I walk in. The door closes with a loud thud. There's a single cot to the side. It has a striped mattress with a thin, nearly see-through cotton sheet thrown over it; an Army-green cotton blanket is folded under the single pillow at the head. A small metal sink and toilet stand in the corner. A prison in a prison.

I sit on the bed and grip the water bottle in my hands like it's a life preserver and I'm drowning. But it's only a piece of plastic that can't hold me afloat. I look out the little window in the door and see the back of the guard's head. I walk back to the bed and lie down with my face to the wall and pull my knees up into my chest.

Breathe. I scan the bare walls, not quite knowing where to let my eyes rest. My head pounds, and every muscle in my body feels stretched too far. I walk over to the small sink and run my hands under the water to wash away the ever-present dirt on my fingers, tiny muddy rivulets carrying this place down the drain. I keep the water on until it runs clear. I take some tissue to blow my nose and wipe my face. I shiver. It's hot outside, but in here, I'm freezing.

I walk back to the cot, zombie-like, and fall down onto the pillow.

The logic of sleep pulls at me, but all my edges are too sharp. I feel like my skin is coated with crushed glass, ready to shred me to smithereens if I dare close my eyes and drop my guard. My guard. The guard. The Director's men. Did they go back to my trailer? Does the Director have my parents? Stay strong. Stay strong? Breathe? How? I barely have the strength to sit up. And, God, how I wish I could stop having to remind myself to breathe. I wish I could imagine anything besides the blood on my dad's face. I wish my mom could have one minute of ease and peace, and now I've taken it all away. There is no wishing anymore, though. No imagining and no pretending. The stars have all gone out. Only darkness remains.

The door to my cell clangs open. I have no idea what time it is or if I slept or how long I slept or even if it is day or night. Jake steps through the doorway and rushes to my bedside. "Layla. Are you okay?" His voice is low, with tension in it. A taut wire.

I nod and sit up, trying to rub the weariness from my eyes. My entire body aches. "Jake," I whisper. "What's happening? Are my parents okay?"

He looks into my eyes. "I'm so sorry, Layla. We only have a minute. The Director wants you in his office." He pauses, takes a deep breath, and covers my hand with his. "Listen, I'm so sorry to have to ask, but I need you to go along with this. I can't get you out right now. It's chaos out there. And no one is sure what's going to happen. Be brave. Can you do that?"

My mouth opens. Jake's words are still in my ears, but they don't make any sense. Stay here? Go along? Be brave? I don't know what to say. I nod once. Do I really have any other choice?

"I'm sorry. I have to go," he says, pulling his hand away from mine. He stands up.

Footsteps outside. "I'll take her," a voice says. Jake steps aside so I can see the door. It's Fred.

Jake nods and hurries out. He never told me if my parents are okay.

I stand up from the hard bed. Fred walks over and hands me a banana. "The Director says he wants to see you at six a.m. sharp. I'll give you a couple of minutes to wash up, okay? Layla, I know you're scared. But you're not alone." He smiles at me in a halfhearted way. Everything feels hollow right now. Words. Gestures. Thoughts.

He steps out, and the door slams behind him.

I devour the banana. Apparently, my body is hungry even if I'm not paying attention to it. I wash up and coax myself to pee, silently thanking Fred for standing with his back to the small observation window that looks into my cell.

The door opens again. "We need to go," he says. He leads me down the narrow hall. As we step into admin, the door momentarily hides our faces from the camera in the corner, and he whispers, "Be brave."

The same words Jake said to me. But how am I supposed to be brave when I'm terrified?

He opens the door to the Director's office. The early-morning sun brightens the room. The Director stares out the window. "Thank you, soldier. You can leave now," he says without turning around. Fred hesitates for a split second, then exits.

There is no one else in the room. We are alone. A solitary inquisition.

"Have a seat, Miss Amin." The Director continues to stare out the window, speaking with his back to me.

I sit and wait. And wait. The Director doesn't turn toward me. The room is silent except for his loud breathing and his occasional guttural throat clearing. He taps on the window. The silence feels loaded. I'm pretty certain it is meant to intimidate me—and it's working. I want to scream or cry out, end the silence, but I don't want to give the Director the satisfaction.

I grip the arms of the chair. The sweat from my hands makes them slippery, but I hold on like my life depends on it. I close my eyes, try to breathe through the dread. I inhale and focus on my own breath traveling through my body before exhaling. I feel its resonance in my bones. I mute the Director's breathing and tapping until it disappears.

Inside me, it is still. And through the silence, I hear voices: *You're not alone.* David. Jake. Ayesha. My mom. My dad. *You're not alone. You're not alone. You're not alone.*

I listen. And from the dark quiet that scares me, I discover that love lives in the deepest silence.

The Director is still at the window, pretending to survey the camp. He plans to keep me waiting. To wait me out. But I see his tense shoulders. The veins in his neck bulge. I hear his snorts. He coughs, clears his throat. I can tell he's restraining himself. Waiting for the perfect moment. Trying to find the silence he always demands before he speaks. I'm tired of him getting what he wants, though.

"Are you okay, sir?" I ask. It's no trouble at all to muster mock sincerity.

The Director roars. He spins and slams his fist onto his desk. The entire desk shakes, and the force feels like a gale wind slamming my back into the chair. His red-rimmed, bloodshot eyes brim with fury.

"Shut up. Shut your goddamn mouth." Beads of spit fly from his swollen purple lips; a deep animal-like growl rises from his throat.

I clasp my hands as if this action will hold me together.

He wants so much to believe he is in control that losing his grip only enrages him more. That's when he makes mistakes. It's a risk to draw out his rage, but if he's focused on me right now, he can't focus on anything or anyone else.

The Director skirts around his desk and stands over me. He puts his hands on the chair and bends over me until his face is inches from mine. I recoil from the whiskey on his breath and the sweat dripping from his hairline. I start to gag.

He grabs my jaw between his rough, calloused fingers and squeezes. I twist my neck away, trying to free myself from his grasp, but he only grips harder. The pads of his fingers brand my skin with their force. I try to speak, yell out.

"Shut up," he spits in my face. Then adds, "Does this hurt?"

I don't move. I stop struggling. Don't answer. Don't give him the satisfaction. I may have almost no control, but I still have a choice.

"How about now?" The Director tightens his grip more, and a grin escapes his purple-red lips.

I dig my heels into the floor and wrap my hands around the Director's forearms. I feel like he could tear my skin from my skull. He begins wrenching my face, like's he's trying to pull it off my neck.

"And now?" he bellows so loudly that I feel his voice inside my body. Tears stream down my cheeks. He pulls his hand back, balling it into a fist. I raise my hand to protect my face. His hand hovers in the air, suspended.

The door bangs open. It's Fred. A small mercy. "Sir. Your visitors from High Command are passing through security, sir. They will be here shortly." Fred steps completely into the room. "I can take the internee back to her cell, sir."

The Director lets out a raw, brittle laugh. If there is a devil, this is what he sounds like.

"Lucky again, Miss Amin. Soon I will make that luck run out. Count on it."

Fred takes my hand and gently helps me out of my seat, hurrying me out of the room. He shuts the door behind us.

We walk silently down the small, empty hall back to my holding room. Fred stops at a small closet and grabs a couple of ice packs. He opens the door to the cell and helps me to the cot. Once I'm seated, he breaks the capsules in the ice packs and shakes them, hands them to me. I hold them against each side of my jaw.

"It looks like you're going to have some bruises. I'm sorry. I wish I could've intervened sooner. I—it's so wrong, what's happening here. Jake is right; we need to speed things up. He's trying to."

I look up at Fred. I'm so grateful he's here. "Is Jake back? Where did he go?" I wonder what things he wants to speed up, but my body and mind feel like they might both collapse, and I can barely get any words out.

Fred shakes his head. "He's attending to High Command. He'll be back soon. I know he's worried about you."

I know he has his orders, but I'm sad he hasn't come back. Doesn't he at least want to check on me?

My jaw throbs. My entire body hurts. "If you see him, could you tell him—tell him I—" I have no idea what I want to tell him. Maybe that I feel broken and lost and helpless. "Tell him I tried to stay strong."

Fred nods. "He'll go wild when he finds out what the Director did. Things are getting out of control. That's why High Command is here. With all this media attention, the protestors, they can't afford any more mistakes. The public was fine with all this in the abstract, but it's becoming real for them, and it's starting to make people squirm."

"How long will the Director hold me in the brig? Can I see my parents? Are they okay?"

"I don't know how long he plans on keeping you here. He's forbidden any visitors."

Tears sting my eyes. I'm so tired. I wish I could sleep. I wish so badly that I could see my parents. But I'm still aware enough to realize that both Fred and Jake ignored my questions about my parents. I hope they're okay.

"I'll wrangle you up something to eat." Fred begins walking back to the door.

"Fred? Aren't you scared? I mean, the cameras in here?"

"The IT guy on the security feed right now is with us. Any footage that could cause trouble will meet with a technical glitch. It might not seem like it, but there are a lot of people who are fighting this."

I offer a weak smile. Fred walks out. And I'm alone again.

I clench my fists. I want to punch this stupid wall, but I can barely lift my arm. I fall over onto the cot, my body convulsing in soul-shattering sobs.

CHAPTER 29

They yank me from my sleep before I can cry out. Before I can even remember where I am.

I wipe my eyes with the backs of my hands. This is real. This prison room. These two men from the Director's security team. This pain in my jaw. And the horrible sinking feeling that I am being taken away. Forever.

I yearn for a minute of a gentle, just-stirring stupor, but I can't afford to be groggy. Not here. Not now. My muscles tense. My throat feels raw, like I was breathing through my mouth all night, and my heart whirs like an overwound motor on a toy car.

Neither of the Director's men says anything. One takes my arm and pulls me to standing and cuffs my hands behind my back. I strain against him, against the handcuffs, but he is twice as big as me and has a gun.

"Keep your mouth shut," the other one says. He's taller and has bushy light-brown eyebrows that look like caterpillars. He rips a piece of duct tape from a large roll.

I whip my head away.

"You can make this easy or hard. It makes no difference to me," he says in a dull monotone. My palms sweat. My heart races. I start to gag. I'm panicking. When I panic, my mind starts to go on walkabout, but I need to be here. I have to keep pulling myself back to the present moment.

"I won't scream. You don't need to do that," I say, my voice fading like a wisp of smoke.

"Orders."

I purse my lips as he tapes them shut. The one who hand-cuffed me pushes me forward.

These guys are the Director's private security. Where are the Exclusion Guards? I don't see Fred anywhere. And does Jake even know what's happening? As I step through the door, I see another one of the Director's henchmen waiting in the hallway. He throws a brown cloth bag over my head, tightening it around my neck like a noose. I squirm. I try to push against it, but the more I fight, the less I can breathe. I wonder if this is what suffocating feels like. Was this what it was like for the others? The ones he disappeared?

"Stop fighting it," a throaty, unknown voice whispers in my ear. The third man. "It's only a short walk."

I try to slow down my breathing. And quiet my body. My instinct is to close my eyes, but I force myself to keep them open. It's dark, but not completely. The rough fibers of the fabric allow light from the fluorescent bulbs on the ceiling through. I'm guided down the hallway toward a door to the outside.

No. I can't go outside. If they take me away from the camp, I could be gone forever. No one will find me. No one will know where I am. I drag my feet, but the men pull me forward against my will.

Adrenaline surges through me. I'm suddenly hyperaware of my breathing and the rapid thud of my heartbeat.

Scream.

Run.

Fight.

But there is nowhere to flee. And there is no fight I can win.

The security detail propels me forward. One of them opens the door to the outside. I can taste the dust in the air. I feel the tiny particles swirling about and coating me like a second skin. Even through the bag on my head, the dust fills my nostrils. There is a stillness, a quiet outside. It's the middle of the night. The nights at Mobius have an eeriness about them, a soundless, otherworldly beauty, interrupted only by a chance howl or hoot in the distance.

Occasionally I've snuck out of my room and sat on the steps to my trailer, listening to the night, gazing up at the stars, dreaming. Night is refuge, a kind of mental sanctuary I can access. But being outside right now, under the cloak of darkness, offers the very opposite. My fears hurtle to the front of my mind. A black-ops site—some secret location away from Mobius. Where no one would be able to find me. The security detail said it was a short walk, but it could be a short walk to a van that might be taking me anywhere. And anywhere in handcuffs means those secret sites, hidden away, places where they can erase your existence. Jake warned me, but I didn't believe it was really possible. I thought maybe my age, or the presence of the Red Cross, immunized me against the terrors I knew existed in the camp.

Maybe I thought someone would stop it.

Maybe I thought this couldn't happen here.

In American Lit class once, we discussed America as a metaphor tying it into how the country is represented in books, movies, songs. You know, America is a melting pot. America is a mixed salad. America is a shining city on a hill. America is the country where a skinny kid with a funny name can defeat the odds and become president. But America doesn't seem like any of those things anymore. Maybe it never was.

After walking a couple hundred yards, we stop. I'm pulled through another door—not a car but a building—and ushered into a room that smells like cleaning fluid. Like bleach and synthetic lemon. I hear the screech of a metal chair as it's pulled across the floor. I'm shoved down into it, and it's pushed back, jerking into place. Someone unlocks one side of the handcuffs and drags my still-cuffed right hand to a table in front of me. I hear the other handcuff click onto something metal. I circle my free wrist to rid the phantom weight of the handcuff while one of the security guys pulls the bag off my head.

I blink at the fluorescent lights in the room; a faint buzz emanates from them and reminds me of the lights in my high school library. The room is empty except for the small metal rectangular table in front of me; I'm handcuffed to a metal bar in its center. My blue chair is pulled up close to the table, allowing me to at least rest my handcuffed arm along it; it feels cool against my aching skin. There is one other blue chair in the room, ominously empty. And that chemical bleach smell fills my nostrils. What was spilled in this room that it had to be cleaned with bleach?

No windows.

No cot.

No hope.

One of the men reaches toward my face and rips the duct tape off my mouth. I cry out. I raise my free hand to cover my mouth. The pain brings tears to my eyes. But no one notices, or cares.

The door opens. The security detail files out of the room. Someone else enters. It's him. He's behind me. I can tell from the loud breathing. I try to steel myself, close my eyes and remember Jake's words. Be brave. Be brave. You're not alone.

But an image of the woman tased at the orientation springs to mind. And Noor being dragged away, Bilqis and Asmaa being assaulted, and my dad being butted by the end of a rifle. Blood on the floor in the Mess. Blood mingling with the desert dirt. The electric fence. That terrible scream. Soheil. Soheil. Soheil. My heart thuds against my ribs. I rub my free hand against my jeans, trying stupidly to wipe away the clamminess and fear.

"We meet again. Did you miss me?" The Director's voice seems different than it did…eighteen hours ago? Twenty? I realize I don't know what time it is or even, really, what day. There's a forced, practiced calm in his tone. So cold. And it's terrifying. I bite my lip. Stay calm. I say this over and over in my head, hoping that somehow it will stick.

He slams the door shut; the thud of his soles against the concrete floor shakes my seat as he approaches me from behind. The Director takes his time walking to the other side of the table. He pulls the chair back and takes a seat, tenting his fingers, pointing his chin downward. Smug. It's all very rehearsed. Like this is his stage. And it strikes me that this is exactly that—his show. He's playing the strongman. I guess that's sort of the thing with bullies, though, isn't it? They play a part to mask their own weaknesses.

And that's the small opening. The only one I may have. At their core, bullies are cowards. He is what he always was. He can still hurt me. Kill me, even. But he will never win.

Remember who the enemy is. I've been fighting myself.

My fear. My failures. That's the wrong fight. The fight is in front of me.

"I'll keep it simple," the Director begins. "You cooperate. You protect yourself from further harm."

I stare at him, debating the best way to proceed.

He chuckles. "So that's how it's going to be? Nothing to say? Perhaps you didn't hear me. Cooperate. Save yourself."

"Cooperate with what?"

"Let's say I could use someone like you. For starters, you point out the troublemakers. Tell me who is writing those lying blog posts that are causing such a ruckus. How are they getting the information out? Who is their contact? There's a traitor in my ranks, and I need to know who that is. Now, that's not a very big ask, is it?"

Jake.

I only saw him for a few minutes when they first brought me here. Doubts muddle my thoughts. Does the Director know? Is Jake already in custody—is that why he hasn't shown up? Is the Director playing me, trying to trap me in a lie? A spasm of fright passes through my body and over my face. He sees it.

"So, you do know. Tell me. It's easy. Think of all the people you'll be saving with a few words. Say the names," the Director coaxes. "It doesn't have to be painful." He's softened his voice like he's the good cop now.

"And what's in it for me?" I ball my free hand into a fist and pound my left thigh with it. Keep talking. Stall. Figure a way out of this.

The Director smiles. "I knew you could be reasonable. You'll find it's to your advantage to be friends with me. I believe I mentioned certain perks, shall we say, for you and your family—like unlimited hot water, for instance. Perhaps a visit with that boyfriend of yours. I'm quite a generous man, you know."

"So I name names and—"

"And you calm down the kids you've riled up, get them back to their gardening and flirting. Things settle down. And you tell me if anyone else is agitating to do anything. It's a win-win."

"You want me to tell you if anything else is being planned?"

"I already have someone who will serve that purpose. One of your little friends was all too happy to make a deal and save himself from the consequences of your so-called protest the other night. And those consequences will come down, like a hammer, on all of you. But you have the power to lessen the blow."

Abdul. Of course it was him.

The Director continues. "I want you to be smart. It seems like your little acts of resistance have given some people ideas. Traitorous ideas. I want those ideas to die. I want you to squash those plans so no one else gets hurt. So no one else has to suffer on your account."

My dad. Has the Director hurt someone else? Mom? Ayesha? He wants me to worry. He wants me to ask. I don't. Rage is burning inside me. And fear. But I won't ask.

He looks at me with expectant eyes. He's waiting for an answer. So I'll give him one.

"No," I whisper. The Director rises from his chair. I think he's going to walk away, but he turns back and slaps me hard across the face. My head falls to the side from the force of his hand, and I taste blood in my mouth. My face stings and my cheeks burn. I've been sheltered from violence my whole life, any real violence. There's no way I'm cut out to resist it. How do people do this? How can I do this?

The Director takes a few steps away, keeping his back to me. "Now see what you've made me do? I'm not a violent man. I don't like to treat women—let alone girls—this way, so I'm going to give you another chance."

The salt from my tears mingles with the blood on my lips. I spit on the floor. "Not violent?"

"Yes. You see, I'm a reasonable human being. I've run this place with kindness and compassion. Tried to build a community. And you"—he whips back around toward me—"you've brought nothing but upheaval and violence."

Does he actually believe this? Does he really think he's in the right, like he's some kind of saint, a messiah for the forlorn?

"Remember your friend? The idiot who threw himself at the fence like a goddamn moron? He's dead, and that's on you and your infantile stunts. Or have you forgotten him already? Used him as a pawn for your childish rebellion, did you?" The Director scoffs. "And you think I'm the monster."

My mouth falls open. The blood drains from my body.

"I didn't," I whisper, then swallow my words. I'll never forget Soheil or the buzz of the fence and his scream and his limp body.

"Didn't think about that poor sap, did you? Too busy pretending to be brave and revolutionary. I told you from day one that actions have consequences. Now tell me who is writing the blog posts and sneaking them out."

"I can't. I can't." Tears fall down my face. My cheeks are hot, and my lips pulse with pain.

The Director stomps back to my chair and twists his hand around my ponytail, pulling my head back. "You dumb, stupid bitch." He shoves his face into mine, spit spewing from his lips onto my skin. "Do you have any idea what I can do to you? What I can have *done* to you?"

I can't breathe. The note my parents got. The threats? It was all him. My parents. Ayesha. Her family. Everyone in this place. Like fish caught in a net, struggling against the cords that trap us, trying to squirm free, not realizing we're already dead.

"One more chance, Miss Amin. Understand? You're lucky I'm such a patient man. But my patience has a limit."

I look at the floor and nod.

I hear other people enter the room. "Clean her up. Get her back to the brig," the Director barks, and marches out.

A guard uncuffs me and yanks me to my feet.

I rub my wrists and bring my fingers to my mouth. My face is burning, but the tips of my fingers are cold, and they feel good against my sore lip. I close my eyes and shiver. Goose bumps spring up on my arm.

"I can take her from here." Another person enters the room. It's Fred.

Fred and I watch the other guard leave.

"My God, Layla. Are you okay?"

"No," I whisper.

I wipe the crusted blood from the edge of my lip with the hem of my T-shirt. "I think I bit my cheek."

"I'm so sorry," Fred says, and cups my elbow with his hand. I flinch. "Your lip is going to hurt for a while."

"It'll match the bruises from earlier."

"Let's get you back. I'll find an ice pack and a washcloth for you."

I nod. I take a step but wobble like I'm wearing high heels.

"Lean against me; it's okay." Fred offers his arm.

We walk out into the cool night.

"I thought the Director's security were going to take me to a black-ops site. Or else why the hood?"

"He's trying to scare you."

"He's succeeding."

"No. You're succeeding."

"Me? Soheil died because of what we did. Because of me."

"No. Soheil died because of what the Director did. Because of what the president did. Because of what this country is doing. But it's not going to last. That protest, Soheil dying—it's a bridge too far for the public. And what he's doing to you, and—it's not just Jake and me on your side. A lot of us—this is not what we signed up for. We're National Guard, and we were reassigned without choice."

"Where is Jake?" I don't bother to hide the hurt and desperation in my voice.

Fred shakes his head. "The Director still trusts Jake, and he's trying to use that to his advantage. Following orders. Hang on a little longer. You have allies. He can't take you offsite. Not with all those reporters and protestors right there, beyond the fence. And if an ambulance comes through those gates, it will be bedlam outside. You can feel the undercurrent; we're sitting on a powder keg. It's too dangerous for him to do anything really stupid. He knows that."

"Dangerous for him? Because right now it feels pretty fucking dangerous for me."

"He's being watched. The High Command guys—they're all getting heat from the War Department and the president."

I nod. But I find no solace in Fred's assurances.

It's still night. Dark and quiet are all around, such a contrast to the screaming pain inside me. I close my eyes for a second, allowing Fred to lead me back to the brig and my holding cell and the terrible aloneness that waits for me. Through the silence, I hear my mom's voice, reciting her *dua*. I feel her breath as she blows the prayer over me. I open my eyes and look up into a velvety blanket of bright stars, and it reminds me of a line my dad wrote: *You need only glance to the vastness of the sky and the multitude of the stars to know the infinite depth of our love.*

CHAPTER 30

"Get up." The Director's voice echoes off the walls in my small cell. He kicks the bed when I don't rise immediately. "I said, get up!" he roars.

Slowly I sit up and push my back against the wall, drawing my legs close to my body. I rest my chin on my knees. My jaw still smarts. My swollen cheek aches—it's probably ten different shades of blue and purple right now. My mouth tastes like blood and metal. I eye the door, and then my eyes dart back to the Director's face. There's nowhere to run; I draw my legs closer into me, spinning an imaginary cocoon around my body.

The Director paces from one end of the room to the other—a journey of five steps. Sweat shines on his forehead. He rubs the back of his neck; his face reddens with each step until he's almost crimson. "Thanks to you and your antics, I'm in a bit of a bind now."

I look up but don't speak.

"You see, when your little stunt resulted in the death of that idiot friend of yours, Mr. Saeed, the lying, crooked press—they twisted it to make it seem like it was my fault, like I pushed that fool against the fence, when we all know it was your invisible hand that drove him to his death."

I flinch when he says Soheil's name. How dare he. I want to slap the words from the Director's mouth, but I don't have the strength to do it.

The Director continues, either not noticing the look of disgust on my face or not caring. "So now instead of celebrating the world being rid of one more vermin, the secretary of war is breathing down my neck because the president has him by the balls. Mobius is supposed to be a model. Do you hear me? Do you understand? A model camp. My camp."

I continue to stare silently.

"And now all these damn fake-news people—they've raised you up to be some kind of hero. A freedom fighter, they're calling you." The Director takes a folded piece of paper from his pocket and waves it in my face, then begins to read. "'Miss Amin has given hope to the Muslims of America—indeed, to all democracy-loving Americans. Her brave actions from inside the concentration camp have given the Occupy protestors courage to continue even in the face of the horrific death of Soheil Saeed, who was electrocuted by the live fence surrounding Mobius that the Director failed to shut down during a legal assembly.'

"See how they twist it? How they lie? *Hope*, they say. *Courage.* You've brought nothing but death and chaos. You think your actions have given people hope? They're fools. They don't know what to do with hope. They don't want courage. They don't even want freedom. They think they want it. But hear me, Miss Amin. People want to be told. They are more than happy to do what they're told. Leave them alone with their hope and freedom for five minutes and they'll come running back to order and rules. People want to be happy in their ignorance. Give them aisles full of processed, fatty foods and a hundred channels on TV and put the fear of God in them. Give them an Other to hate, and they will do what they are told. And that's what keeps our nation safe. Strength and security."

My eyes follow the Director's frenetic pacing. I practically see his mind spinning, his thoughts beginning to derail. Silence seems my safest choice.

"But in a way, you've gotten what you want, haven't you—the masses bleating for your freedom. What now? We open the gates and let all you ragheads roam free? Another terrorist will blow something up somewhere, and soon enough, people will be chanting for your heads, again. And you'll be right back here while the president soothes the jangled nerves of the masses who will gladly exchange their freedom for security. It's already done. We know everything. What books you check out. Who you text. Who you sleep with. We know you better than you know yourselves. That's what kept us safe from you lot and your bombs and your creeping Sharia. Since 9/11, the fear of the entire nation allowed us to pass laws that brought us into your homes and your bedrooms and your thoughts.

"What you don't understand, what you're too damn stupid to know, is that when you appease a man's conscience, you can take his freedom and he will thank you for it.

"You think you can win this? You think you can beat me? I could give you your martyrdom. I could burn you at the stake in the middle of the desert with the cameras watching, and in two days you'd be old news. And everything would be exactly as it is now. And your death would mean as much as any other death—sound and fury signifying nothing."

The Director stops in the middle of the room and spins his head around. My silence weighs on him. I see it in his face, his fury rising every time he looks into my eyes.

"And now what? Can't find the inspiration to speak?"

I take a shaky breath. "What do you want me to say?"

"Beg for your life." The Director strides toward my cot, towering over me.

Beg for my life.

Beg.

Accept tyranny.

Bow to a false god.

"No," I whisper.

I know what's coming next. I twist my head away, but I'm too late. He slaps my face, and his clunky gold signet ring splits my lip, and blood pours down my chin. I scream, and it echoes off the walls. I wipe the blood from my face and hear my screams bounce back to my ears.

You're not alone.

Be strong.

Live.

Fight.

The Director grabs my arm and yanks me from the bed, hurling me to the floor. My elbow slams against the hard surface. A scream rips through my body.

The door to my cell opens. Jake walks in, eyes wide. A wave of horror passes over his face when he sees me on the floor. He clears his throat and straightens his shoulders, then turns squarely to the Director and says, "You need to leave now."

"Who the hell do you think you are, talking to me like that?"

"Corporal Jake Reynolds. National Guard of the United States. And you are out of order. I suggest you step aside." He unholsters his weapon and steps between the Director and me.

I am bleeding and sobbing and near hyperventilating, and I have never been so thankful to see another human in my life.

"I can have you court-martialed for this, Corporal. She is a prisoner, and in this facility, I am the law."

"This is still the United States of America, and no one is

above the law. The mistreatment of prisoners is a crime under both international law and the Uniform Code of Military Justice. And you are in gross violation of both." Jake's voice is deep and confident, but I can see a slight tremble in his fingers. When he speaks, he looks past the Director, not right in his face.

The Director smooths his hair and tucks in his shirt and laughs. But his laugh is nervous, with fear in it. He grasps the handle of the door.

Before walking out, he turns to me, eyes on fire, and says, "You're the fucking Angel of Death."

CHAPTER 31

Too stunned and wrecked to move, I sit with my hands folded in my lap. Jake gingerly puts his arm around me and helps me back to the bed. Then he steps away, talking on a radio. I can hear the words, but they sound jumbled to my ears, incoherent. I'm holding an ice pack to my bruised face. I can't stop shivering. I lick my split lip—salt and blood and tears.

Jake walks back over, grabs the blanket, and puts it around my shoulders. "You're in shock," he says gently. "I'm so sorry I didn't come back sooner. I should never have left you."

I look up at him. "Jake," I whisper. But no more words come out. My voice is a dry scratch. I take a sip of water from a bottle that Jake hands me. The coolness of the water feels good against my raw throat.

"He'll pay for what he's done. I swear to you. I will make him pay. It's over for him."

I nod, but it's barely a consolation.

For the second time, the door flies open, and Fred rushes in, stopping short when he sees me. "Layla. Shit." Then he looks at Jake and says, "We should have stopped him."

"I know," he says. "I'll never forgive myself. Fuck orders. I should've kept you safe, Layla." Jake puts his arm around me.

I'm confused, in a maelstrom. The world is spinning and I can't see or understand anything.

Jake holds me. I cling to him. I'm not sure for how long. Minutes or hours. Day or night.

Apparently, Fred left to get a doctor. I didn't even notice he'd gone. He returns with a woman I've never seen. She's dressed in uniform like the other guards, but she's older. Flecks of gray salt the dark brown bob that curves around her heart-shaped face. She carries a leather satchel. She kneels in front of me.

Her voice is soft and gentle. "My name is Dr. Han. I'm a soldier, like Corporal Reynolds, and a medical doctor. I'd like to take a look at your lip and cheek, if that's okay with you."

I nod, and Dr. Han opens her bag and reaches for a pair of latex gloves. She takes out a small light that she asks Jake to hold above my face. Then she lightly sponges away the dried blood. She runs her fingers over the bruise on my cheek and turns my chin toward the light. I wince. It hurts like hell.

"You have some pretty deep bruises. But nothing broken. That lip is going to hurt for a while, but it's already stopped bleeding." She points her pinkie toward my mouth, tracing an outline of my lips in the air. "We can skip stitches. You'll need to keep it clean. For now I want you to go back to your trailer and rest and keep ice on that face and lip to try to bring down the swelling. I'll give you some meds for the pain."

"Okay." I raise my hesitant fingers to my cheekbone.

Dr. Han smiles warmly. "You're a brave young woman. Can you tell me what happened when the Director came into your cell? The more detail you can give me, the better. And I'm going to record what you say, okay?"

"I understand," I say, and tell her everything that happened. How the Director tried to get me to cooperate, the times he hit me, his threats. Jake keeps one hand wrapped around mine. I see his jaw clench when I speak, and his neck go wiry. I'm sure he feels guilty, but honestly, I don't even have the energy for it, or to imagine anything other than this nightmarish reality that is actually my life.

"I think that's all I need." Dr. Han stops her digital voice recorder.

Fred enters the room and holds up a small thumb drive. "I got the recordings," he says to Jake and Dr. Han.

"Recordings?" I ask.

"The cameras," Jake says. "He'll be charged. High Command can't protect him. Won't protect him."

Dr. Han stands up. "Let's get Layla back to her quarters. Specialist Adams, I'm escorting you off-site with that. You're not to say a word to any other Command on-site. For now we're keeping this quiet, until we can get charges pressed. Corporal Reynolds, I'm stationing you outside Layla's unit. This supersedes all other orders. Understood?"

"Yes, ma'am." Jake moves to stand and salute her, but she motions at him to stay by my side.

"At ease." She hands me a white envelope with six blue pills in it. "One pill every twelve hours with food, okay? It will lessen the pain and help you sleep tonight. You tell Corporal Reynolds if you need anything. We are here for you. We should've been here for you sooner. I'm so sorry this happened to you. I'm so sorry for everything that we've become," Dr. Han says before she and Fred leave Jake and me alone in the room.

"I'd like to go back now." I try to stand up, but I'm wobbly.

"Put your arms around my neck." Jake speaks in the softest whisper. Like he's afraid his voice will break me. I do as he suggests. He lifts me into his arms, and I rest my head against his chest and close my eyes. He carries me out of the room and through the back exit of the brig.

It's early—before roll call—but the sun is bright and cresting over the lower peaks of the mountains, casting its rose-tipped glow across the sleeping camp. It seems impossible, doesn't it? That beauty can exist amid all this cruelty. Maybe that's why it has to be here. Maybe the sun has to rise to remind us of what truth is.

My body sinks deeper into Jake's arms. I'm drained, like I've been exsanguinated and all that's left is flesh and the memory of bone. I could sleep for days. But images flash against my closed eyes—the Director's leering red face, a drop of my blood falling to the floor, David's smile, the Mess, the crackle of the fence as Soheil clutches it, Jake. My parents. My parents. I can't imagine what they've been going through.

As we approach my block, I raise my head and look at Jake. "I think I can walk from here." I try for a smile, and he gradually lets me down. "My parents would freak even more if they saw you carrying me in. My mom is probably going to faint when she sees my face, and my dad, he'll—" I head toward my trailer.

"Layla. Stop. Please." I turn around and look at Jake. Whatever he may be about to tell me, I can't hear it. I can't. There can't be one more thing. "Layla, I have to tell you something. I didn't want to tell you earlier, before, in your cell. About the Director and what else he's done. I'm sorry—I'm so sorry—"

"What is it? My parents? Oh my God." I run to my trailer, throw open the door, and rush in. "Mom? Dad?" I walk into the bedrooms. The trailer is empty. I turn back toward the door and to Jake, who came in behind me. I glance at our small kitchen table, where a mug has been knocked to the ground, tea spilled on the chair and floor amid the broken shards. "No. No. No. Please, no." I sink to the floor.

"I'm so sorry, Layla." Jake kneels by my side. "The Director had them seized and taken away."

I double over, clutch my knees, and rest my head against the floor, sobbing, choking. Jake rubs my back. "I didn't know until it had already happened. It was his private security detail. I'm so, so sorry. I couldn't stop it. I wish I could have done something. Anything. But I was too late."

I rise to my knees, then stand, steadying myself against the kitchen counter. "But they're alive? Right? They'll be okay? You can get them out?"

Jake moves closer to me without saying a word.

"Tell me, Jake. Just say it."

"I don't know, Layla. I don't know where they are."

I nod. I rub my forehead. My chest tightens and begins to cave. My breath is ragged. "Okay, okay. Well, I have to figure out where they are and how to get them out and how and if… if I can and when…who…" I move away from the counter. My legs feel weak, and the room spins. My knees buckle.

"Layla." I hear Jake's voice like an echo before everything goes black.

CHAPTER 32

My body jerks from sleep. Adjusting my eyes to the tomblike dark and quiet, I shift around, shivering under the thin blanket. I'm back in my room in our trailer. It's not home, but it's not that holding cell, either. I rub my index finger across my infinity necklace, and the silver cools my skin. My brain feels blank to everything, like a mound of clay, smooth, uninterrupted, and shapeless—without scars or memory. I reach for the fleece dangling off the back of my chair and pull it over my head before curling back into a ball and pulling the blanket up to my ears. In the stillness of the room, I listen. Hoping to hear something, anything, that would mean my parents are back—the whistle of the electric teakettle, the clatter of teacups, the dull rubbery thud of the fridge closing, my dad humming, my mom clinking her spoon as she stirs sugar into her tea. But there is only the sound of my breathing and what I'm sure is the stretching of my heart's sinewy muscle as it reaches its breaking point. The roar of truth reverberates through me. The Director wants to bury me. He wants me to break. And he's succeeding. Because I've never felt more broken. And I'm so tired. And being tired is a luxury that I can't afford.

A knock.

"Layla, are you okay?" Jake's voice filters through the door.

I rub my eyes with my fists and go to open the door to meet Jake's furrowed brow and bloodshot eyes. "Had a nightmare. Where I'm put in a prison camp and the Director assaults me and my parents are taken away and people die. And it's all my fault."

Jake steps toward me and gently wraps his hands around my upper arms. "Nothing is your fault, do you understand? Not one single thing."

I look at the floor and nod. That's what everyone keeps saying. Maybe someday I'll believe it.

"Please hear me. You are not to blame for anything. Not for this camp, for your parents, for Soheil. If anyone is to blame, it's me. So much of this is my fault. Please tell me you get that. You went to battle against a monster. That's courage."

I fold myself into Jake's arms. "Thank you for being here for me."

"Always."

I try not to think about what it means that Jake is the one

comforting me, because I need it right now. I need my mom and dad and David. But Jake is the one who is here. There is a kind of alchemy to it, when one human touches another and makes the aloneness less terrifying.

I walk into the kitchen and take a seat at the little table. Jake's cleaned up the spilled tea. He hands me a glass of water and a banana and sits next to me.

"Ouch." I flinch biting into the banana, the scab on my upper lip painful even against the soft fruit.

"That's probably going to hurt for a while. The bruises, too."

"Great. Never thought I could rock a battle-scarred face, but I guess I have no choice now." I try a halfhearted smile, but that hurts, too. My mind feels thick, and last night's conversation and what Jake just said to me finally make a little sense. "What do you mean, it's your fault?"

Jake looks down at the floor, avoiding eye contact. He sighs and rubs his forehead. "I had orders to let things play out."

"Play out?"

"When the Director took you, I reported it to my superior. I mean, High Command is here. I was told to not interfere. I was ordered to let him interrogate you. They needed incriminating evidence—something unimpeachable—to take down the Director, maybe this whole place."

My mouth drops open. Tears well in my eyes. I've been punched all over again. I was bait for a trap set without my knowledge.

"Layla, I'm so sorry. I was following orders. Trying to see

the big picture. Letting my reason outweigh my feelings. I could have—*should* have—stopped it. I know what I did was unforgivable, but I swear, I'm not going to let the Director or anyone else hurt you ever again."

I hear Jake's words but can't process them through any filter that makes them less painful. Orders. Bringing down Mobius. That's what matters. But how do I go on from this? "Don't make promises you can't keep, Jake," I whisper.

He looks at me. "My word is my bond. He won't touch you again."

I cast my eyes away, not able to sit with this, to talk about it anymore, to face him. Jake was doing what was necessary, but there is this chasm now between us. People make sacrifices to change the world. In the big picture, maybe my being offered as bait will make a difference. But it doesn't take away the horror of being dangled on a hook to catch a big fish. One day, I'll have to deal with it, but I can't now. For now, I have to push the feeling away, lock it in a place so it can't hurt me anymore.

"What time is it anyway?" I change the subject. "I mean, how long have I been asleep?"

Jake looks at his watch. "It's one a.m. You took the painkillers around eight a.m. yesterday."

"What? I've been asleep for, like, a whole day? That can't be right."

"You woke up once, but you fell back asleep. Dr. Han said the painkillers would knock you out, so I guess they did the job."

"I still feel so tired, though."

Jake cups his hand over mine. "You've been through hell. I want—" I pull my hand away.

A knock on the door interrupts him. Jake puts his finger to his lips and motions for me to move to my bedroom. He takes his handgun from the top of the fridge and releases the safety. He walks to the door and stands next to it. "Who is it?"

"It's Fred. I'm alone."

Hearing Fred's voice, I step back into the common area from the threshold of my bedroom. Jake holsters his gun and opens the door for his friend and quickly shuts it behind him.

"What's up?"

"I came to tell you—" Fred glances at me. His jaw drops; clearly, my bruising and swelling look worse than yesterday. "Layla. Are you okay?"

I run my tongue over the scab on my lip. "I'm still here. Thanks."

"I can't believe what that asshole did to you."

"Fred, what did you come here to tell me?" Jake slips into his crisp military voice.

"The shit has hit the fan. Dr. Han circumvented chain of command and took the video straight to the head of the National Guard and the attorney general. Then she leaked it."

"What? No!" I yell. The whole world is going to see it. And I'll have to watch myself get hit over and over. The thought alone makes me sick to my stomach. A tear runs down my face.

"Layla." Fred softens his voice. "I'm so sorry. Your face is blurred out in the video. You're a minor, so they can't share your face or name. But there wasn't any other way. Dr. Han was afraid the AG would bury it, and she wanted to force his hand."

Jake looks at me with a sad half smile and mouths, *I'm sorry.*

I wipe away my tears. Almost every choice has been taken from me in this place; what can I do but add this to the list of indignities? "If it will help us get out of Mobius. If it will help me find my parents—"

"Look, there's a hell of a mess in DC. The secretary of war has been the president's henchman all along, but the president will probably throw him under the bus. The president hates bad ratings, and there's no way to cover this up and make it look good. Not after that protestor died."

"Soheil," I say. "His name was Soheil."

Fred nods at me.

"So what happens now?" I ask. "How soon can we leave Mobius?" I say the words, not really believing anything will change. I'm scared to hope. But I need to get out of here. I need to find my parents.

Fred breathes. "Not this minute, but probably soon. This story is on fire—it's wall-to-wall coverage on every channel and news site. People are in the streets. They'll have to move fast. For now Mobius is on lockdown."

"What about the Director?" I ask quietly.

"He's holed up in his office right now with his security detail."

"Coward," Jake mutters under his breath. "He thinks he's going to shelter in place? That he'll get away with hurting Layla? No goddamn way. I won't let him."

"Ease up, cowboy," Fred says to Jake. "What do you think you're going to do? Storm into his office, guns blazing? His security detail will shoot you in a second."

I look at Jake, my mouth agape. "Don't do that. I can't stand someone else getting hurt."

"She's right, Jake," Fred says. "Don't be an idiot."

Jake stares at his friend, clenching his jaw. "Fine. I'll stay with Layla. Report back with any news. And watch yourself."

Fred nods. "Always do."

Jake walks Fred to the door and pats him on the back as he steps out into the night. Then Jake turns to face me. I walk back into my room without another word and quietly close the door.

CHAPTER 33

In the morning, the trailer is empty. I'm alone.

As I peel off the clothes I've been wearing for the past few days, I'm painfully aware of every bruise on my body, even while I try not to think about the deeper hurts that I can't put words to. The shower only lets out a stream of cool water. I stand in it for the full five-minute allotment. When it clicks off, I'm shivering, but the numbness suits me.

My heartbeat echoes through the room as I get dressed. An only child should be used to the quiet, right? No siblings to fill the silence. For the most part, quiet doesn't bother me. But this quiet has a weight, heavy with the absence of the people who are missing.

Jake left a note for me on the kitchen table:

WENT TO GRAB A CHANGE OF CLOTHES. DON'T
GO ANYWHERE. THE OTHER GUARDS ARE
GETTING BRIEFED AT THE HUB. THE MINDERS
WILL ANNOUNCE LOCKDOWN AT ROLL CALL.

His handwriting is neat, solid, upright. It stands at attention and does its duty. It is exactly Jake.

I sip the tea I made for myself, blowing over the top to cool it and watching as the ripples on the surface move away from me. I touch my bruised cheek and the rough scab on my lip. The painkillers helped, but they can't fix the persistent dull ache in my chest.

No, it's not an ache; it's a hole. I'm not sure if anything will ever fill it. My eyes sting from crying. "How does anyone recover from this?" I say to the empty trailer.

There's a pounding at my door.

"Layla!" Ayesha rushes into the trailer when I open the door. Her hair is twisted into a messy bun, and dark circles paint the skin under her bloodshot eyes. She halts abruptly when she sees my face. "What happened?"

I haven't seen her since the night I was taken. The night Soheil died, when the Director and everyone who created this camp killed him. I wonder if she's slept at all. "Ayesha," I whisper. "I'm so, so sorry."

We hug each other. Neither of us cries. Our pain lies too deep for tears.

"Did you see them seize my parents?" I ask as we sit at the table.

Ayesha nods. "There were, like, a dozen guards. I didn't actually see them take your parents out. After Khadijah auntie told them to go to hell, they forced all of us back into our Mercury Homes. I couldn't do anything."

"If you'd tried, you'd have ended up being hurt, too."

"Do you know what's going on? There was no alarm this morning."

"Jake says they're putting us on lockdown. Apparently, there's some military situation going on, and the government is in chaos—I dunno."

Ayesha nods. "Finally reached the tipping point, huh? Too bad they couldn't have stopped this whole fucking mess before Soheil—" She sucks in her breath and presses her hand to her chest like she's trying to soothe her own heart.

"I know. I know," I say.

Ayesha bites her lip. "Let's hope things get better, not worse."

"Can I make you some tea?" I get up to fill the kettle, but a brash alarm rings across the camp, vibrating through the trailer. We push ourselves out the door.

The wind swirls and dust freckles the air. There are no guards—they're probably all at the Hub. But the minders are out, getting people in line, scanning everyone's barcodes. I can't hide the bruises on my face or the cut on my lip, and I don't want to. I want people to see what the Director did. I expected the stares and whispers. What I didn't expect? Khadijah auntie walking up to me, leaning on her cane, drawing me into a one-armed hug. And then the family in trailer 23, and the two sisters from 27. One by one people offer prayers and kind words for my parents. The minders struggle to get everyone back in order, but after a few fruitless attempts, they stand to the side, waiting, until everyone files back into a row.

I squeeze Ayesha's hand as I join the line behind her and her family. The earth spins around me. Like it could give way, crack, and swallow me whole if I let it. I close my eyes and see my parents cooking dinner in the kitchen. Laughing as they chop onions and caramelize them with garam masala and turmeric and ginger and garlic, trying to replicate my *nanni's kheema*. Their efforts always fell a little short, but not for lack of enthusiasm or love. For a single, illusory moment of bliss, I'm there in that kitchen, *my* kitchen, in *my* home, with my parents. Safe and happy.

Someone roughly grasps my hand. And I'm back here at Mobius. In the present.

"I said, show me your wrist," Saleem fumes.

"Ow! You're hurting me."

"And don't you deserve it?"

"Shut up!" Ayesha yells. "And let go of her. If anyone deserves to be hurt, it's you and your wife. Minders? What a joke. Everyone knows what you are."

"Ayesha, be quiet," her mother chastises, the fear transparent on her face.

"No, Mom. I'm tired of being quiet. All of you should be. Layla's been fighting for us. Literally. Look at her face. And what have any of you done? Nothing but cower in fear."

Before I can say or do anything, Saleem drops my hand and grabs Ayesha's arm, yanking her out of the line and throwing her into the dirt. He raises his hand to hit her with the barcode scanner.

Her mother screams, "No!"

I jump out of line, throwing myself over Ayesha. Fauzia dashes over to stay Saleem's hand.

Saleem snatches his hand away and turns back to us as we rise from the dirt with the help of Ayesha's parents. He points at Ayesha and me. "You're nothing but a bunch of stupid children playing grown-up. You have no idea how much worse things could get for all of us."

"All of us?" I scream. "You threw your own people under the bus. You're as bad as the Director. Worse."

"Shut your fucking trap," Saleem rages. His face is red, and spit flies out of his mouth. He inches toward me.

Khadijah auntie steps up behind him and thwacks him across the back with her cane. He spins around, nostrils flaring, fury in his eyes. "Back off, old woman, or you'll be next."

Saleem's wife clasps his hands and pulls him aside. "Stop— now, Saleem. This isn't right."

"*Besharam.* You should be ashamed," Khadijah auntie continues. Undeterred and apparently with a backbone like steel, she shakes her head at him, contempt in her voice. "You

attack these girls? They are the only ones who have the courage to help us, to stand up to this tyranny. You brutalize your
fellow Muslims, and you take pride in this behavior? You
bring shame on your family and your people."

Saleem shoves his wife to the ground and advances on
Khadijah auntie. I watch the scene unfold in slow motion.
I don't think I've seen anyone as graceful as this eighty-
something-year-old woman, her body straight, her cane at
her side, a spitfire glare on her face. Ayesha and I scurry to
stop Saleem from hurting her. Others step in front of Saleem,
and in the flurry of yells and moving bodies and rising dust,
someone shoves him to the ground.

The minder looks around, his eyes blinking wildly at the
others on the block, now gathered in a semicircle around
him. He scoots backward in the dirt and then stands, dusting
himself off. "You'll regret this. All of you." He takes off running toward the Hub.

We all stand there, looking at one another. Scared. At least
that's how I feel. But also exultant at a tiny, tiny victory.

Khadijah auntie walks up to me and holds my hand and
speaks in a soft, clear voice: "Do you remember your father's
words?"

I shake my head, not sure what words she means.

"It's okay, *beta*." She pats my hand and continues.

> *We shall bear witness*
> *On the Night of Destiny.*

As a hush descends,
And a prayer rises.
There is only the listening, then,
To the beating heart of the earth,
And flashes of thunderous light in the heavens.

It's one of my dad's poems. A lump swells in my throat. "Why are you reciting this to me now?" I whisper.

Khadijah auntie smiles and nods, then squeezes my hand. "Your father is speaking to us. To you. You are the heartbeat. Now make us the lightning."

The people from our block nod, and tears spring to my eyes. I remember my dad reading from his poems to Mom and me. His voice comes back to me now like a bittersweet song.

I was little and saw my mom's eyes glassy with tears, but I didn't quite understand. "Even if you don't know what all the words mean, I hope you can close your eyes and feel the poem pulsing in your blood," my dad said. Mom. Dad. I'll find you. I won't give up.

"Thank you," I whisper to Khadijah auntie, and give her a hug. Then I step back. "It's not a single heartbeat that calls the storm. It's the power of our voices joined together, demanding justice. It's the thunder of our collective feet marching for our freedom."

I turn my gaze to the dozens of eyes on me. Khadijah auntie is right next to me, still holding my hand. "The Director is hiding in his office, surrounded by his private security. I guess the top brass from DC are coming today; that's why we're on lockdown. The press and the Occupy folks are all outside. I think we need to march to the front gate and demand to be released. People on the outside are turning against the Exclusion Laws, especially after Soheil—" My voice cracks. I take a breath. "Especially after Soheil was killed."

"It's a death wish," a voice calls out from the crowd. "That fence could still be live. They could shoot us."

"You can stay if you don't want to join us. Little kids should stay behind, too," Ayesha adds.

"Look, I know it's a risk and you're all scared. I'm scared, too," I continue. "I have no idea where my parents are, and I know that the Director and the Authority could do horrible things to all of us. But I also believe that some of the Exclusion Guards will not stand for any more of this, either. I'm not going to ask anyone to do something they don't want to do. If you don't want to go, I understand, but *this* is our chance. Maybe our only chance to be heard."

"We're with you." A couple steps forward. Then others.

I turn to Ayesha and say, "Can you run to Block Eight and see if you can find Suraya, and grab anyone else who will come along?" Ayesha gives me a huge, reassuring smile.

Her mom reaches out toward her. "Ayesha, wait. No."

Ayesha's dad places a gentle hand on his wife's arm. "*Jaan,* the children are right. I'll go with her. I'll keep her safe." He and Ayesha hurry off in the direction of Block 8.

I squeeze Khadijah auntie's hand and look at her. "Please

stay back and watch the children. I don't want anything to happen to you. You've done enough already."

"*Beta*, I am alone in this world, and I am at peace with God. When my time comes, it will come. Nothing you or I can do will stop that. I am with you."

I want to break down in tears of joy and relief and thanks, but we don't have time for that, so I hug her and whisper a *shukria* in her ear.

"So what should we do?" another voice asks.

I pause for a moment and lick my chapped, scabbed lips. "We need to make some noise."

"But the Director will hear us coming."

"I want the whole world to hear us coming. Everyone, go back to your trailers and grab anything that can make noise. Pots, pans, spoons, whatever. We might not have weapons, but we have our voices. Let's get loud."

There's a smattering of claps and cheers as people rush off to grab their tools of protest. I watch everyone and look up to the sky. I pray. Really pray. "Please, God, keep us under your protection. Please let my parents be okay. Please let this work."

There are so many thoughts and images flooding my brain, but I try to push them aside. Focus. This is a half-assed plan, but in here, we're the Resistance, and that's all I have right now.

When people emerge from their trailers, I thrust my shoulders back, trying to stand up straight. My lungs expand as I gulp in the air around me. I ask everyone staying behind with the kids to separate into groups and take cover in two trailers. People are milling around. I scan the scene: shaking hands, nervous smiles, grim faces, a group kneeling in prayer a few feet away, their hands cupped in front of them. I hear the melodic *"ameens"* and add my own. I wipe my clammy hands on my dusty jeans and clear my throat.

Then I hear them—the muted thump of footsteps in the dirt coming around the corner.

My heart jumps. Guards. I clench my fists and try to steel myself.

But it's not guards with Tasers and guns and hate in their hearts who round the corner. It's not *Them*. It's *Us*. It's Ayesha and Suraya. Nadia and Nadeem. It's girls in hijab and girls with their hair whipping across their faces and girls with shaved heads. It's parents and grandparents. It's young men wearing colorful dashikis and white cotton kurtas and concert T-shirts. It's straight couples and queer couples and friends and strangers and families connected by blood or circumstance. Here we all are. Brown. Black. White. There must be at least fifty people, and it's the most beautiful thing I've ever seen. The groups from the different blocks mingle. Smiling, clasping hands, patting one another on the back. My heart swells.

From many, we are one.

I wish Soheil were here to see this. Maybe, in a way, he is.

Ayesha's and Suraya's smiling faces shine as they approach me.

"So, we hear you want a revolution." Suraya hugs me. "We're here."

"I know," I whisper to her. I straighten up and stand on the step in front of the nearest trailer.

"You might need this." Fauzia passes a small bullhorn to me. "Press that red button when you speak." I don't have time to really be in shock at her gesture, but I'm sure it registers on my face.

I nod at the minder. I hold up the bullhorn, looking at the anxious, bright faces in front of me. I hesitate, then clear my throat. "I haven't really given any pep talks or lead-the-troops-into-battle kind of rousing speeches." My eyes dart to Ayesha and Suraya, who smile and raise their fists to encourage me. I pause for a moment and remember this one smile my mom has that warms her eyes, a smile reserved for me. Especially in middle school, whenever I felt a little lost or discouraged, she was there for me, knowing what I needed without my having to say it.

I keep going. "But I know that America is built on life, liberty, and the pursuit of happiness. All those things have been ripped away from us, and I believe that every American who came before us, who stood up to oppression, who fought to guarantee our right to religious freedom, is looking down on us and telling us to rise up, to speak out, to shout our names to the world. We stand on the shoulders of giants. We *are* Americans. *We* make America great. This is our country. And we're taking it back."

People clap and cheer. My heart pounds as I step down and walk to the front of the block. Ayesha and her father, Suraya, and Khadijah auntie join me in the front line, walking forward, and the others follow. We turn onto the Midway, banging our pots and pans and spoons, drawing attention from some of the other internees who were standing around their blocks. Some merely watch. Others run to join us.

I turn to face the growing crowd. Walking backward, I raise the bullhorn to my lips, remembering all the protestors who came before us. I shout, "The people united will never be defeated!"

A chorus of voices rises up, echoing the words.

CHAPTER 34

As we head toward the front of the Hub, other internees step into the group, and the Occupiers make noise to join our march. Camera operators rush toward the fence, scooting around the orange plastic barriers. Others follow. This time the police don't hold the protestors back. The electricity must be off. Small victories.

We march up to the fence so the Occupiers can see us. Then, together, we turn to face the Hub. People continue banging their pots, shouting to make their voices heard. I raise my fist in the air to quiet them. A phalanx of the Director's security detail stomps out and takes up position in front of the Hub doors.

Dozens of Exclusion Guards rush over, but there's confusion. Some join the line of the Director's private security. But

Jake and maybe six or seven other guards stand by me and the other internees, facing their fellow soldiers. After the dust from all the shuffling settles, a silence comes over the desert. I sense the cameras on me, and feel the desperate hope of everyone who stands with me today. The weight of this moment could crush us all. I wish my parents were here with me, at my side. We have to do this for all our sakes, but in my heart I know I'm doing it for them. My breathing feels shaky, shuddery. Jake takes up position next to me, pressing his arm into mine, bolstering my resolve. I clench my left fist.

I raise the bullhorn to my lips. "We demand that the gates of Mobius be opened," I begin. I pause and shuffle my feet. My stomach quivers. I'm begging myself not to throw up. Out of the corner of my left eye, I see Ayesha, Suraya, and Khadijah auntie. And though I can't see him, I know David's eyes are on me. I clear my throat again. Breathe. "We are Americans."

Cheers from my fellow internees. I repeat. "We are Americans!" This time shouts from the Occupy protestors join ours. "We demand to be released! We demand our freedom!" People shout and bang their pots and raise their fists in the air.

I pause, wait for quiet.

"We know you're hiding in there, Director. We know you're scared of us." I'm goading him. A part of me isn't sure how wise this is, but my memory overflows with the horrifying sound of his voice in my ear, and the stinging slap that busted my lip, and the cruel grimace on his face. I clench my left hand tighter; my nails bite into my skin. My pulse pounds, and I explode, "Come out! Face us, COWARD!"

For a second, everything is still. My call ricochets across the camp and into the canyons.

The door to the Hub flies open.

My parents are shoved out.

Two of the Director's security guys walk out behind them, holding guns to the backs of their heads.

My heart stops. My mouth drops open, but words are beyond me right now.

Gasps and shouts come from the crowd behind me.

My mom's hair is disheveled, her eyes wild with fear. My dad has bruises on his face, and he stands with his shoulders slightly slumped; he's holding his right arm up at a weird angle.

I reach a hand out toward my parents across the distance. My mom reaches back. But we can't bridge this gap.

The Director slithers out from behind them, glaring at me—his suit wrinkled, his face beet-red. "Is this what all the ruckus is about, Miss Amin? Your precious parents? Well, here they are. None the worse for wear. It would be a terrible shame if your actions today caused them any harm. Now, if you break up this little demonstration and beg for my forgiveness, perhaps everyone can walk away from this foolishness alive. Your choice." The Director takes a step back, next to the men who are holding guns to my parents' heads. He bares his teeth like a small, angry animal.

I swallow. I close my eyes and desperately search for the words I need. My insides twist and tighten. He thinks he's won. I won't let him win. I lift my head and gesture toward the fence, toward the Occupy protestors and the media. I pray this works.

"We're not going anywhere," I say into the bullhorn.

"Then their blood will be on your hands," the Director yells at me. He knows just where to stab.

"And then what? You can't kill us all. Are you forgetting the cameras? The world is watching you, Director." The Director takes a step back to eye the press and the hundreds of Occupiers on the other side of the fence. He rubs the back of his neck with his hand. He opens his mouth to speak. But he says nothing. Slowly he steps behind my parents, gesturing the security detail with guns aside.

I hold my breath.

He shoves my parents down the stairs. They trip and fall into the dust. I want to run to them, but Jake holds me back and motions for two of the guards from our side to help them up. I suppose men with guns are better protection than I am. My parents rush over. Mom grabs me and holds me, and Dad wraps one arm around both of us.

"Are you okay?" I croak. I'm trying to stop myself from shaking. I'm willing my knees not to give out. My mom nods and kisses my cheeks, but my dad's arm doesn't look right. Ayesha and Suraya step out and help my parents find a spot behind me; a few people gather around them.

The Director takes it all in as he moves to stand behind his security team. He points a meaty finger at me, and his spite-filled eyes bulge out of his head. "There. You've made your little demonstration. I've given you your precious reunion. Now scurry back into your ratholes, where you all belong, and you won't be responsible for anyone else getting hurt." His words hit me like an anvil. I shift from one foot to the other and swallow. I glance back at my parents. They look so broken, but there's a shimmer of pride in their eyes. Jake cups my elbow to steady me.

I take a deep breath. "We're not leaving until those gates are opened and we can all walk out together," I bark into the bullhorn.

"I suggest you look around," the Director yells, waving his arm over the camp, addressing the internees. "That electric fence? That barbed wire? These men with guns? They're here to keep you inside. To protect America from you. You are enemies of the state to the strongest country in the world. And what? You propose to take over this camp with pots and pans and a little girl leading you? You're fools. Disband. Now." He pauses. "Or there will be consequences. My mercy has limits."

A murmur moves across the crowd like a wave, but no one moves.

Then a silvery voice from the middle of the crowd yells out, "The people united will never be defeated!"

And that's all I need. I yell into the bullhorn, "You're done,

Director. You're over. We will bury you." My mom reaches out and grazes my back with the tips of her fingers.

The Director steps forward, fists clenched, sweat shining on his forehead. His chest moves up and down, and his nostrils flare like he's breathing fire.

The entire camp hushes—the protestors, even the wind. I hear the faint click and zoom of the cameras beyond the fence. My throat is parched, and my heart pounds in my ears. I glance skyward, praying for a storm, a rain to wash away the hate and dust and pain. An epic flood to wipe Mobius off the map and let us start the world anew. I feel so small. And scared.

I allow my eyelids to flutter closed for a flash, a tiny reprieve from the scorching sun. And in that second, I hear David's voice, feel his hand pulling me into some imaginary portal that will take us back in time to the pool house, before the Exclusion Authority came and burned the world down. In this time slip, I'm there with David in the low light of flickering candles and fireflies. Everything is like it used to be, before all this. Maybe if I keep my eyes closed, this version of the world will vanish, and Mobius and the Exclusion Laws will fade into the smoky blur of my nightmares. I think of all the people throughout history who found themselves in a place like this, stepping out from the shadows, raising their voices. Finding their courage, facing their fears so that they could be free. There were so many we lost, the ones who were taken, cut down, for the color of their skin, or the religion they practiced, or the person they loved.

All they wanted was to live.

I open my eyes.

I want to live, too.

I take a deep breath and step out of the line, in front of Jake and the others. The Director squares his shoulders to me, a combatant readying for battle, his neck wiry, his eyes unblinking. He thinks he can cut me down. I'm about to show him that I'm a warrior, too. I drop the bullhorn and talk to the Director in as steady a voice as I can manage. "Step aside. It's over."

The Director's red face stretches into a tight grin; his fists shake at his sides. He looks at me with a rage so palpable it fills the space between us with fire.

"Shoot her," he says. His voice is low, but everyone hears him.

All the motion slows around me. The air is still. And suddenly death feels awfully close. I hear my mom scream, my dad yell something, but the sound is muffled.

The Exclusion Guards and the Director's private security detail don't move. Panic and confusion fill the air.

"Stand down!" Jake roars at them as he steps forward next to me. The Exclusion Guards who joined us earlier follow Jake's lead and step up.

One of the guards who is standing by the Director turns to

him. "I didn't sign up for the National Guard to shoot innocent Americans. I signed up to defend my country."

One by one, the other guards peel off, so all that remains between the Director and the rest of Mobius is his security detail.

The Director bellows at them, "Shoot her, goddamn it! I said, shoot her—that's an order!"

One of his security detail scans the crowd and the guards standing with us, then looks at the Director and slowly shakes his head. "She's a kid, sir."

The Director turns his back to us, his shoulders drawn, hands at his hips.

I don't know if I'm breathing anymore. I can't feel my body.

Jake touches my arm, and I finally draw a breath and speak to the Director's back. "You're alone. You've lost."

The Director spins around, barreling through his remaining security as he draws a handgun from his waistband.

A single shot rings out.

CHAPTER 35

Pop.

Like a firework going off. That's what it sounds like. A firework.

And that is all.

Because in the next instant, time moves like a viscous liquid, dampening all sound. The screams, the stampede of thudding feet against hard dirt, guttural wails, the *thwack* of the Director's body being slammed to the ground by his own security, the barked "GO! GO! GO!" as Exclusion Guards, weapons drawn, rush the Director and his security team.

I try to move and realize I'm down on the ground, dirt in my face. Screams come from every direction. And there is blood. I push myself up and see it on my T-shirt, my arms.

But it's not mine.

I whip around to see my parents. My dad is on the ground, clutching his arm, groaning; my mom hovers over him. I crouch next to them. "Dad! Dad!" I yell.

"He's okay. He's okay—" My mom stops short. She stares past me. All the color drains from her face.

I'm afraid to turn my head and look. Chaos churns all around me. Dust chokes the air. Slowly I pivot my body.

A scream rips through me.

Jake is lying on the ground, clutching his stomach, blood oozing from between his fingers.

"Jake! Oh no. No. No." I kneel next to him, placing my hands over his, pressing down like I've seen in movies. But it's not the movies, and the blood won't stop. It's not stopping. God. There's so much blood. How do I make it stop?

Jake looks up at me and parts his lips. He coughs, sputtering up blood.

Fred races over, and when he sees Jake close up, his face turns gray. He gulps. "Hang on, Jake. An ambulance is on its way." He tears off his shirt and wads it up, pushing it down over the wound. Jake grimaces and gurgles, a deep, awful sound. "Layla, keep the pressure on, you hear?" Fred directs me. "I gotta clear the path for the paramedics to get in here. Talk to him. Keep him awake."

Jake's eyelids start to droop.

"Jake. Jake." My voice catches in my throat. "Jake? Stay awake, okay?"

His heavy eyelids tremble open. His lips part. I can see he's trying to speak. But no words come out. With a jerky motion he moves a hand to his stomach; his fingertips graze mine. A vise squeezes my heart. I press harder against Fred's shirt. It's soaked with blood. I can't stop the blood.

I close my eyes. Tears stream down my dust-stained cheeks. "Jake," I whisper, my voice catching. "Jake, I'm sorry. I'm so sorry. For everything."

Can he hear me? Does he understand? He stepped in front of me. Jake, why did you step in front of me? I know you think you failed me, but this...this shouldn't be your penance, Jake.

"Layla. I...You..." His voice fades.

"Don't talk, Jake. Save your energy. I can hear the ambulance. Keep your eyes open, okay? I'm here. Stay with me. Stay awake." I turn my eyes toward the sky and pray. The rest of the world falls away, until there are only the sounds of my steady inhalation and exhalation in contrast with his rattling, wheezing breath. I sniffle and wipe the back of my hand across my nose. I feel the streak of blood my fingers leave on my cheek.

This can't be how the story ends for Jake. Not here. Not in this terrible place. I want to will this horror away. Bend time and space to give him something better than this. I wish I could give him the magic hour at Castle Lake when he was a boy with his mom. I wish I could give him fresh air to breathe. I wish I could give him a compass to find his way home.

I press down harder against his stomach. His eyelids flutter a little. Don't close your eyes, Jake. Please. Please. I look down. My hands are smaller than his, but it's like he's shrinking, losing his muscle mass. He's trying to wrap his fingers around my hand, but he can't. His skin is so cold; the pads of his fingers are almost blue. His eyes are open but they're glassy, and I don't even know if he can see me anymore.

I can feel his life ebbing away. Please, God. We already lost Soheil and so many others; please don't take Jake, too. Is there something I can do? A covenant to make that will save him? But there is no bargaining with death. When it comes, it gives no quarter and doesn't care about your merits.

I hear my mother's voice and other voices. I glance up and see my parents and people from different blocks kneeling in a semicircle around us. Hands cupped in front of their faces, heads bowed, murmuring a prayer: "Merciful God, forgive him his trespasses. Make wide his grave and light his path. Raise him unto the highest heavens."

"*Ameen*," I whisper. I see Jake's weary eyes close.

I know it's for the last time.

CHAPTER 36

This desert is stained with their blood.

Soheil. Noor. Asmaa. Bilqis. Jake. Others whose names I don't know. I'll learn their names. I'll etch them into my heart. When I step out past the fence with its razor wire, I will make sure the world knows who they were and what they sacrificed. I won't let them be forgotten.

Morning light streams through the window in my trailer bedroom. I pull myself up to sit on the edge of the bottom bunk in this tiny, terrible room. My clothes from last night, the ones marked with Jake's blood, lie bunched in the corner. Before going to bed, I scrubbed my face and hands until they were pink and raw, but his blood still mingles with the dust under my fingernails.

It is surreal. This moment. The one I've wished for, but that came at so high a cost.

I don't remember much after the gates opened yesterday, after they took Jake away, first lifting him like a rag doll onto the gurney and then placing him into the back of that sterile, cold ambulance. It wasn't him, though, was it? Not really. A person is more than a body, more than blood and bone and flesh. More than the sum of their parts. Jake was kind and brave and flawed. A human being, like the rest of us, trying to find his way on this journey where our paths crossed too briefly.

There's a gentle knock at the door. "*Beta*, are you okay? Do you need help?" My mom's voice is so soft, like she's worried that loud words will cut me. The door creaks open. She and my dad enter.

My dad is wearing a makeshift sling tied around his neck—a shirt holding his arm in position, close to his body. My eyes grow wide.

"It's probably only a hairline fracture," my dad says. "I'll be okay."

My mom sits next to me and wraps me in her arms. I don't cry. I'm not sure if I have any tears left. Mostly I feel hollow, like a shell of a person.

"We can go now," my mom says. "We're free to go."

Free? What does that even mean? For now, it will simply have to mean being free to walk out of this camp. That will do.

My parents tell me what I missed in my fog of despair

and sleep. The government ordered the immediate closing of Mobius and the release of all the internees. Dozens more Exclusion Guards arrived last night to help us gather our things and ready us for the return home.

Home.

I can't wrap my mind around the idea of stepping through our front door, sleeping in my own bed. Seeing David.

The Before, my old life, is gone forever. When I walk out of these gates, it will be to a scarred world. The After. Honestly, I don't know how to go on from here. How to truly leave Mobius behind. But I have to. Jake's story ended here. And Soheil's. Mine doesn't, even if I feel like all I'm made of now is dust.

My mom helps me stand up. "Do you want me to help you pack?"

"No," I whisper. I'm not taking anything with me. I want no memory of this place, but I know it is imprinted on my mind forever.

"Oh, I almost forgot." Mom hands me a note. "It's from Ayesha. She knocked while you were sleeping but didn't want to wake you. Her family caught an early transport out, but she said she'd see you soon."

I clutch the note to my chest. Ayesha. She's out. They walked out. I close my eyes, and my heart lifts a little. There's no way I could've endured life in here without her. I'm so relieved that she's safe. That she survived. We barely got to talk about Soheil. My heart aches for her.

"I'll meet you outside. I need a second," I say.

My mom walks into the common area of the trailer and grabs a small bag of her and my dad's things.

My dad kisses me on the top of my head. "We'll be right outside, *beta*." He steps to my mom and takes her free hand in his. They walk out together. The door shuts behind them.

I look around the tiny space that I've occupied with my parents for what feels like forever. I can hear the clatter of their teacups as they sit at the table, trying so hard to have a sense of normalcy here, of home. I hear Ayesha's laugh as we talk in my bedroom. I see Soheil outside my little window playing soccer, motes of dust catching the late-afternoon light. I run my fingers over the invisible barcode on the inside of my wrist. No one else will be able to see it, but I'll know it's there. Always.

One last look around before I walk out into the heat and sun and dust.

Mobius is bustling like an outdoor market. The people who haven't left yet head toward the Hub and the open gate that once shut us in. Some wave at me, and I nod and smile back. "Happy" isn't quite the right word, but I'm content knowing that Nadia and Nadeem, Suraya, and all the others are walking out of here—going home.

There are ghosts at Mobius. I hear their whisperings like dry leaves swirling against hard earth. I feel them in each step on this dry, cracked dirt.

Once, Jake told me about a friend of his who was a

pararescuer with the Air Force. Their motto is That Others May Live. All these things that might happen next, that should happen—repealing the Exclusion Laws, closing the black-ops sites, impeachment—that's what people died for.

So that others may live.

I stand between my parents, gripping their hands. We walk together up the Midway for the last time, holding on to all the parts of ourselves that haven't been taken away. We walk past the Hub and through the open gate, watching, waiting, as others file onto idling buses that will take them to the train station and airports and home.

I see Khadijah auntie walking, resolute, cane in hand. She catches my eye and raises her fist next to her shoulder, giving me a small, kind smile before she boards a bus to whatever life awaits her.

My mom whispers in my ear, "They'll take us to Independence. David will be waiting there for us. For you."

I walk out, unsure of what lies ahead. Of how to recover from this camp that burned itself onto my skin. Blood and dust and razor wire. How will life ever be normal again? I'm not even sure if my body remembers how to take a real breath. If I will ever stop glancing over my shoulder. Ever feel free.

I stare down the desert road.

I might not know exactly where I go from here, but I'll find my direction.

I take a small step forward.

I don't look back.

AUTHOR'S NOTE

When fascism comes to America, it will come draped in the flag.

You don't need to be a student of history to see how nationalism, disguised as patriotism, can take hold of a country, justifying terrible and cruel acts. You only need to turn on the news.

The American government's "zero tolerance" border policy has literally torn more than 2,700 children from their parents' arms as they attempt to cross into America for a better life, many seeking asylum and running from danger. As of July 2019, more than 50,000 migrants are being held in Immigration and Customs Enforcement detainment facilities, with an additional 20,000 individuals being held in Customs and Border Patrol camps. These numbers include more than 11,000 children, who are being held in shocking, squalid conditions—lacking access to soap, toothpaste, or clean water to wash their hands or shower. Babies are being fed from unwashed bottles and often go days without their diapers being changed. By the government's own admission, in a report issued by the Department of Homeland Security inspector general's office in July 2019, there is "dangerous overcrowding" in these camps and detention facilities. These unsanitary conditions have led to outbreaks of lice, flu, chicken pox, and scabies. At least six children have died as a result of being held in these conditions. The United Nations High Commissioner for Human Rights condemned the detention of migrant children, saying that the United States may be violating international law. Yet this administration continues these inhumane policies.

Make no mistake. These are internment camps. This is internment.

Pay attention to the racist demagoguery and scapegoating that aligns with that policy: immigrants and migrants are "animals" who "pour into and infest our country." They are "rapists" and "criminals" who put a strain on our economy. Then turn to our history books to understand the rhetoric of extermination that has been used again and again by authoritarians the world over.

Consider, too, that half of all Latinx characters in popular TV shows are depicted as criminals. Representation matters. Racist stereotypes spread through our culture and politics too easily and give cover for racist politicians, who first dehumanize groups and then enact policies that take away their livelihoods and, often, their lives.

No moment in American history exists in a vacuum. Nationalism and fascism are not new; indeed, they are a part of American soil. This fact gave birth to this novel. The events in *Internment*—though they take place "fifteen minutes" into America's future—are deeply rooted in our history. You are bearing witness to them now, in our present.

In 1924, riding a wave of anti-Asian sentiment, the US government halted almost all immigration from Asia. Within a few years, California, along with several other states, banned marriages between white people and those of Asian descent.

With the onset of World War II, the FBI began the Custodial Detention Index—a list of "enemy aliens," based on demographic data, who might prove a threat to national security, but also included American citizens—second- and third-generation Japanese Americans. This list was later used to facilitate the internment of Japanese Americans.

In 1940, President Franklin D. Roosevelt signed the Alien Registration Act, which compelled Japanese immigrants over the age of fourteen to be registered and fingerprinted, and to take a loyalty oath to our government. Japanese Americans were subject to curfews, their bank accounts often frozen and insurance policies canceled.

On December 7, 1941, the Japanese attacked a US military base at Pearl Harbor, Hawaii. More than 2,400 Americans were killed. The following day, America declared war on Japan.

On February 19, 1942, FDR signed Executive Order 9066, permitting the US secretary of war and military commanders to "prescribe military areas" on American soil that allowed the exclusion of any and all persons. This paved the way for the forced internment of nearly 120,000 Japanese Americans, without trial or cause. The ten "relocation centers" were all in remote, virtually uninhabitable desert areas. Internees lived in horrible, unsanitary conditions that included forced labor.

On December 17, 1944, FDR announced the end of Japanese American internment. But many internees had no home to return to, having lost their livelihoods and property. Each internee was given twenty-five dollars and a train ticket to the place they used to live.

Not one Japanese American was found guilty of treason or acts of sedition during World War II. The 442nd Infantry Regiment of the United States Army, comprised almost solely of second-generation Japanese American soldiers, remains the most decorated unit in American history.

In war propaganda, Japanese Americans were depicted as enemies of America, animalistic, murderous, unable to assimilate to American culture.

And now here we are again. Refugees forced into internment camps. Muslim bans. Border walls. Police brutality. The rights of gun owners being valued more than the lives of our children. Racism. Islamophobia. Ableism. Homophobia. Anti-Semitism. Scapegoating immigrants. The politics of exclusion. The rise of nationalism and white supremacy, unmasked and waving our flag.

I feel a lot of anger.

But I believe in hope. I believe that the things that are wrong with America can be fixed by Americans. I believe that being good is what can make us great. I believe in *you*.

And when I see young people, tens of thousands strong, marching in the street for their lives; when I see my fellow Americans taking to the streets to protest family separation at the border; when I see football players kneeling on sidelines; when I see that beautiful, eloquent image of Iesha Evans quietly taking a stand in Baton Rouge; and when I see a poster of a Muslim woman wearing an American flag hijab held high at a rally, I feel my patriotism stirring. I am compelled to act. And I remember why I believe so much in this nation—of the people, by the people, and for the people.

Fascism isn't going to simply appear in America one day. It's here. But so are we.

There's no room for moral equivalency—certainly not the kind that hears the cries of a toddler being ripped away from her parents and justifies it by quoting the Bible, and definitely not the kind that looks at neo-Nazis and declares that some are "very fine people."

There are sides.

Make a choice.

It's not a simple ask, I know. It takes courage to use your voice. To stand up.

But all around you there are others who will help lift you up, who will take your hand, and who will march—shoulder to shoulder—with you. Speaking your truth and voicing your resistance can happen in quiet ways, too. I hope you find the way that works for you.

America is a nation, yes, but it is also an idea, based on a creed. I hold these truths to be self-evident. That the concept of our nation is neither musty nor static. That it is malleable. That every day we can shape it and stretch it to form a more perfect, inclusive union. America is us. America is ours. It is worth fighting for.

The people united will never be defeated.

Resist.

ACKNOWLEDGMENTS

Publishing *Internment* was an act of courage and resistance. My eternal gratitude to my brilliant editor, Kacen Callender. Their unwavering belief in this story and their keen editorial eye gave this book wings so it could fly. My heartfelt thanks to Alvina Ling, Siena Koncsol, Ruqayyah Daud, and the entire team at Little, Brown Books for Young Readers for championing this story and for their confidence in my ability to tell it. I will remain forever spellbound by Dana Ledl's beautiful cover that so perfectly captures the spirit of Layla's journey.

I am grateful beyond words to all my friends and family— near and far—who read and critiqued early drafts of *Internment*, brainstormed with me about this story idea, engaged in endless discussion about transliteration, and cheered me on every step of the way. My deep appreciation to Hitomi Sasamoto, Lynn Sasamoto, Sangu Mandanna, Eric Smith, Dhonielle Clayton, Joanna Volpe and New Leaf Literary, Kati Gardener, Raeshma Razvi, Daniel Ehrenhaft, Lizzie Cooke,

Gloria Chao, Franny Billingsley, Ronni Davis Selzer, Rachel Strolle, Anna Waggener, Rena Baron, Kat Cho, Claribel Ortega, Amy Adams, Johnette Stubbs, Peter Vrooman, Joe Armstrong, Karim Mostafa, Jihad Shoshara.

To my parents, Hamid and Mazher, and my sisters, Asra and Sara, thank you for your constant support and enthusiasm for my work and for always fighting the good fight.

Lena and Noah, you shine brighter than all the stars: I love you, I believe in you, I am so glad to have this life with you. To Thomas, thank you for your love and unconditional support, and for being a light. You make this life possible. All my love to you.

Finally, my profound gratitude and respect to all the survivors of internment, past and present. In sharing your stories, you remind us of how precious our freedoms are and how much our democracy is worth fighting for. You inspire us to resist. Thank you for your courage.

DISCUSSION QUESTIONS

1. Layla's father's poetry opens the novel, both with its presence in the epigraph and in its citation during the Amins' relocation. How do these two poems speak to the power of the written and spoken word throughout *Internment*?

2. How does Layla's reaction to her family's internment differ from her parents' reactions? Where do you think this divide stems from?

3. Layla remembers her *nanni* telling her that "Praying is important. But you can't simply pray for what you want. You have to act." How do Layla and other characters turn their faith into action?

4. How does life at Mobius attempt to mirror "normal" life? How do the internees attempt to hold on to normalcy,

and how is that different from the "normalcy" the Director tries to create?

5. Ayesha claims Jake used the phrase "Insha'Allah" as "a shibboleth....A word you can use to distinguish who's on your side and who isn't" (page 163). How do characters indicate their allegiances throughout the book? Are words or actions a stronger indicator of someone's true purpose?

6. How do the minders treat the other internees? What motivates the minders' actions?

7. Layla observes of Suraya: "This year must have been so much harder for her, someone so visibly Muslim. And black" (page 263). What role does the intersection between race and faith play in the treatment of the internees? How does this intersection, and other differences in experience and culture, factor into the privilege afforded different characters?

8. The Director tells Layla that "people want to be happy in their ignorance....Give them an Other to hate, and they will do what they are told" (page 328). How does this belief manifest in the Exclusion Laws? How does it relate to the way the internees treat one another?

9. What role does the media play at Mobius? What differences exist in how information spreads through traditional media channels versus how it spreads through social media? How do different characters attempt to utilize media and the spread of public information to their advantage?

10. In her author's note, Samira Ahmed cites specific events from America's past and present that inform the plot of *Internment*. How specifically are these events reflected in the novel? What other historic or current examples of authoritarianism do you see echoes of in Layla's story?

RESOURCES

If you want to learn more about the illegal incarceration of Japanese Americans, these are just a few of the many books and websites you can go to. Of the ten internment camps in the United States, Manzanar War Relocation Center is one of two that remain—a designated national historic site in California under the auspices of the National Park Service.

Books

Farewell to Manzanar, by Jeanne Wakatsuki Houston and James D. Houston (New York: Houghton Mifflin, 1973). A memoir that follows seven-year-old Jeanne Wakatsuki and her family's journey as they are forced into the Manzanar internment camp.

Impounded: Dorothea Lange and the Censored Images of Japanese American Internment, edited by Linda Gordon, Gary Y. Okihiro (New York: W.W. Norton, 2006). A collection of images taken by photographer Dorothea Lange, originally censored by the US Army.

Looking Like the Enemy: My Story of Imprisonment in Japanese American Internment Camps, by Mary Matsuda Gruenewald (Troutdale, OR: NewSage Press, 2005).

Only What We Could Carry: The Japanese American Internment Experience, edited by Lawson Fusao Inada (Berkeley: Heyday Books, 2000). An anthology of poetry, prose, documents, drawings, and photographs.

Websites

Asia Society. "Japanese American Internment: Asian Americans and U.S.-Asia Relations." https://asiasociety.org/education/japanese-american-internment.

Franklin D. Roosevelt Presidential Library and Museum. "War! Japanese American Internment." http://www.fdr libraryvirtualtour.org/page07-15.asp.

Japanese American Citizens League. "Power of Words Handbook." https://jacl.org/education/power-of-words.

Japanese American National Museum. www.janm.org.

Library of Congress. "Ansel Adams's Photographs of Japanese-American Internment at Manzanar." http://www.loc.gov/pictures/search/?st=grid&co=manz.

Manzanar National Historic Site. "One Camp, Ten Thousand Lives; One Camp, Ten Thousand Stories." https://www.nps.gov/manz/index.htm.

Erielle Bakkum Photography

Samira Ahmed is the *New York Times* bestselling author of *Love, Hate & Other Filters*. She was born in Bombay, India, and has lived in New York, Chicago, and Kauai, where she spent a year searching for the perfect mango. Find her online at samiraahmed.com and on Twitter and Instagram @sam_aye_ahm.